A Life in a Box Studios Trade Paperback Original

www.lifeinaboxstudios.com

ISBN: 978-0-9915873-0-8

TALES FROM THE AGES

VOLUME ONE

**A COLLECTION OF SHORT STORIES FROM
THE MANA CRYPT UNIVERSE**

**CREATED AND WRITTEN BY:
JUSTIN CALVIN**

To my family,
and to the adventurer in us all.

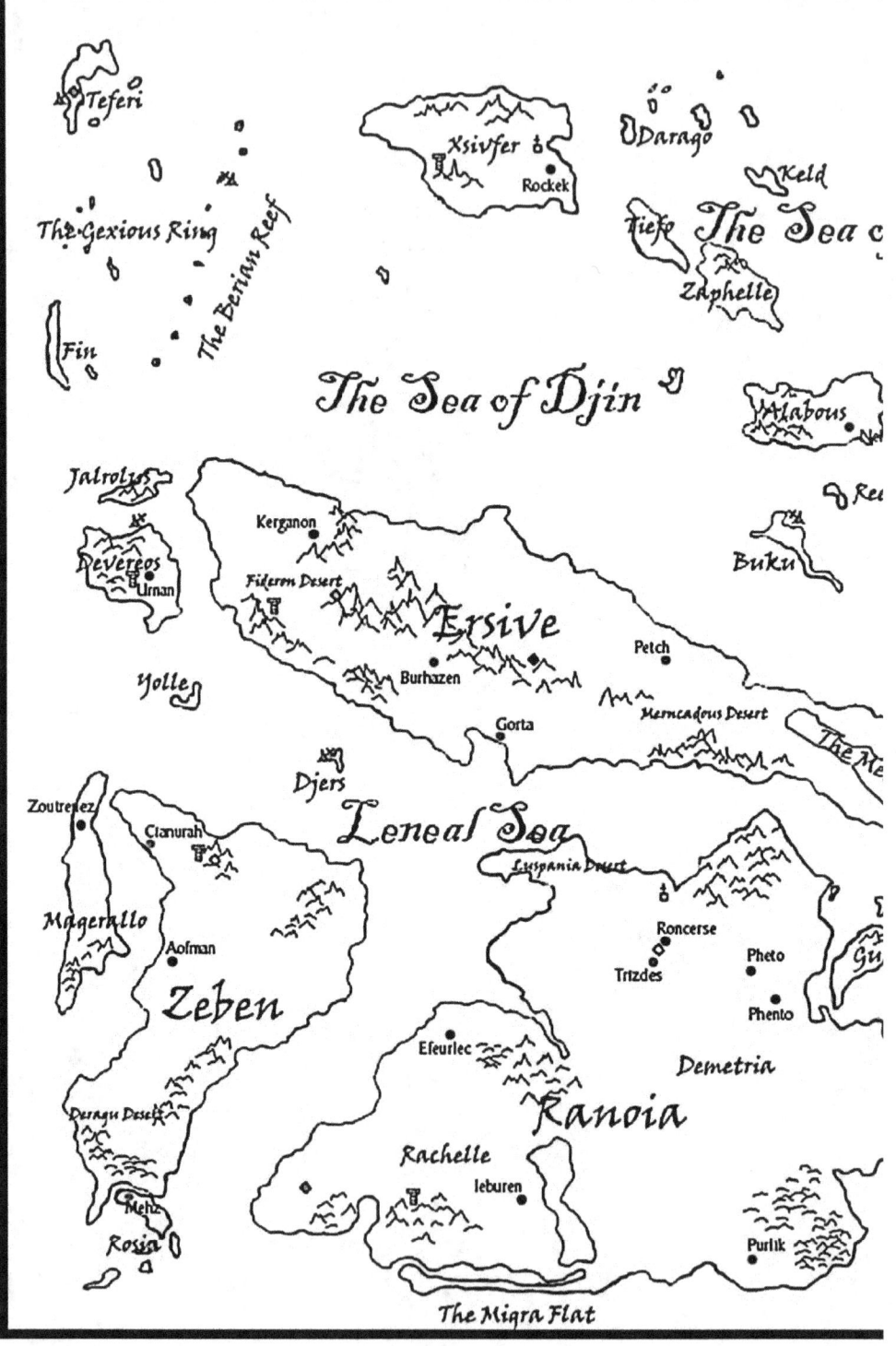

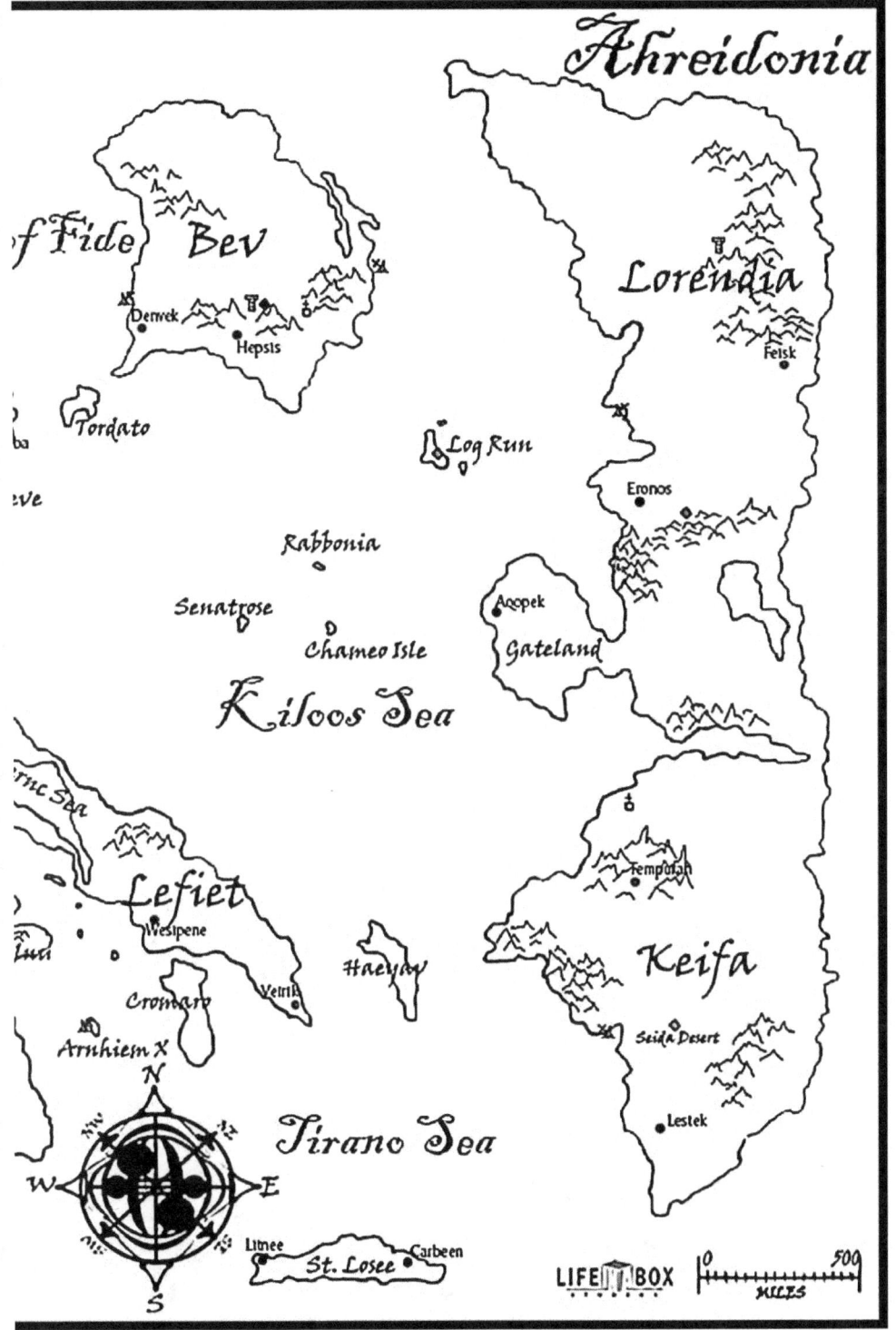

CONTENTS

TALES

INTRODUCTION

Creating any kind of world (whether fictional or not) is usually one of the hardest things for any writer to get right -let alone write about. During the creation process of this series, I struggled with so many ideas, concepts, laws, and feelings, for what should be right, rather than what my gut told me. At the end of the metaphorical day, I found that if you allow your world to describe itself to you, rather than you describe it to your characters, than you'll be pleasantly surprised by the results. All together, I'd say it took me a good seven years to finally get to finishing and publishing this short story collection, and as proud and exhausted as I am, I realize that I still have at least three more short story collections, one novella, and five novels to go. It might seem a daunting task, but I truly believe that if you have fun doing it, than little things such as 'time' and 'work' have little influence. If I could simply write all day for the rest of my life, I'd probably just smile and ask for a pen and paper.

In my youth, I was always drawn to fantastical and science fiction elements. The ideas and stories that seemed to interest me the most were the ones based in completely different worlds. Ones where characters, places, and beauty were far our rivaling our own and seemed to create a sense of wonderment and dream-like nature that captivated and held my interest all through school really. Why were these concepts so thrilling? I often asked. I think the real question comes down to whether or not a person feels the need to escape or find a better alternative lifestyle much more gratifying than their present one. And again, this was true for me as well. Awestruck by the idea that a warrior could find himself walking down a city street, and all of a sudden find himself pulled into an adventure leading to monsters, treasure, and escapades. A youthful individual working on a farm who one day discovers he had magical abilities and must now save a nation. This relates very strongly to the principles of the "Hero's Journey", and why this core concept has reached the minds and flavored some of the best entertainers today with rich and interesting stories.

The "Hero's Journey", told famously and coined by famous author and mythologist, Joseph Campbell, became the foundation and starting point of my series and many of its tales and legends. Who were these characters? What kind of challenges are they going through? What will they learn or carry with them? Mana Crypt was based upon those ideas. Starting with a basic planet it grew and expanded so much, that I could barely contain it. Characters, events, artifacts, and history, all began spewing forth -sometimes uncontrollably. This is why I like to write. It gives those a freedom and ability to craft a living, breathing world. And, if I get anything out of it, it's the satisfaction that no matter what, it'll always be there. Sometimes it may even surprise you.

The idea for short stories actually came about when I discovered how hard writing an actual novel would be. The core mechanic of a novel is to hook the reader through one larger story, and at the time, I felt I wasn't ready to undertake such a task and have it done the way I wanted it to be. This is partly where the short stories began. While detailing the world and its vast overwhelming characteristics, I got the idea that perhaps developing shorter tales involving snipets and small windows into the timeline, would allow readers and myself to gain a broader and much richer history and idea of what the Mana Crypt Series actually is. From there, the stories just took off. Currently, I have twenty eight of them planned with many more to follow if desired. Now, I know that sometimes writing short stores can be just as hard if not harder to write than a novel, and this is very true. But, if you have fun doing it, those small details won't bother you.

The following are a series of short stories (or tales, as I keep referring them as) that all take place on Ahreidonia. A world held together by a mana core and crafted by ancient beings, it is now home to the likes of Humans, Elves, Orcs, Goblins, Druids, Dwarves, Merfolk, Genomorphs, and many more. Spanning across just a fraction of the rich and detailed history; these tales are held together by magic, legends, battles, and betrayal. Knights wishing to retire, a creature escaping his old life hunting for a new one, two children tossed about the high seas; their destinies uncertain, a tournament of the undead, a child fueled by rage and power, two kings attempting to assassinate each other, a man born under a rare star following a man with even greater powers than his own, a troupe of goblins trying to return home, and lastly a highly dangerous man tempted by wealth and becoming a slave to a cities corruption.

My hope is that these tales will give you an insight into the lore and challenges Ahreidonia goes through. The dangerous creatures, heroic deeds, epic sized wars, civilizations wiped out, power hungry warlocks, ancient devices, godly abilities, buried secrets, and various other tales are being written every day, and I look forward to sharing them all. This book is but a sample of some of the first, and certainly not the last.

Enjoy!

TIMELINE
OF
AHREIDONIAN HISTORY

FIRST ERA
(¥0-5000)

SECOND ERA
(¥5000-5527)

THIRD ERA
(¥5527-9027+)

THE DAWN
(¥0-4700)
-DAHJO'S BLADE-

THE GREAT WAR
(¥4700-5000)
-THE TALE OF OLD BERSOOL-
- DARK HORIZON-

- -

THE AGE OF DRAGONS
(¥5000-5400)
-THE KINGS WAR-

THE FORTHCOMING
(¥5400-5412)
-OEDEPES-
-KNIGHTS & FISH-
-TRADE WINDS-

THE AGE OF REBIRTH
(¥5412-5512)
-STORM OF SAVUUR-

THE AVATAR WARS
(¥5512-5527)

- -

THE NEW AGE
(¥5527-8527)
-GOBLIN TALES-

THE AGE OF JUDGMENT
(¥8527-9027+)

¥ = YEAR

A BRIEF HISTORY OF AHREIDONIA

I'm a firm believer that some things are better left as secrets (even if they include factual info). Over the course of Ahreidonia's rich and expansive history, often times the characters are left in the dark on matters such as; their origins, family, abilities, past, future, and many others to name a few. The reason I bring this up, is because I wish to inform you –the reader- to as much background information and history that's to be expected in order to gain a broader understanding of the Mana Crypt Universe, as well as, to allow you the ability to grow and learn just as the characters do during their own struggles and tales. That is why the following is a brief, very brief, history of Ahreidonia for the history buff in us all.

At the planet's center, lies a core made of raw mana. Thought to be the work of Gods, many took this as absolute. Over the years, as the creatures and inhabitants expanded and evolved, the world slowly took on more magical and dangerous elements. A multitude of races such as; Elves, Humans, Dwarves, Orcs, Goblins, Merfolk, and Druids are but a few to emerge and expand across its vibrant and wonderous landscape. Due to irregular events, large underground fractures (or veins) erupted from the core to the surface, allowing the raw mana to pour outwards in overwhelming amounts. These are what came to be known as "Mana Veins". As the raw mana travelled towards the surface, it became diluted, transforming the colorless and overwhelming power into one of five types of mana colors. The fissures were exhausting so much mana that the planet itself started to become unstable. Thus, the people were forced to create a seal overtop the five largest veins, in order to halt further destruction. This allowed the mana to settle and be reabsorbed into the core; thus completing the cycle. These seals came to be known as "Mana Crypts". Over the years, civilizations came and went, cities and towns prospered and dried up, and tales of heroes, weapons, and beasts were shared and written.

Ahreidonia is a magnificient and dangerous world decorated in a multitude of creatures, land formations, climates, magic, and the unknown. The planet's future is still unwritten, and as to what may follow, only a select few would ever know the answer.

* This is only a fraction of the history found within the universe. For more info, lore, and secrets to all things Mana Crypt, please visit...

www.mana-crypt.com

KNIGHTS & FISH

MISSION 27
TORRIGON

The hot sun was searing my pale green forehead causing my scalp to itch and turn a light cherry red. We have been sitting outside under the blazing heat for what seemed like the entire day, and it didn't help that I was the only one stupid enough to not bring a helmet or head wrap. Lying down amongst the tall geris grass we were stuck waiting. I tried to wrap some of the dried grass around my sensitive scalp, praying its thin stalks would grant me some cover from the increasing heat. Meanwhile, I looked up at the floating clouds high above, staring at them trying to forget about the sun, the time, or the damn waiting. The sky was clear. I watched as a single small puffy cloud passed overhead, and I wished my life could float away with it.

"Damn bugs!" Lein blurted, slapping her pale white neck loudly. Swatting a few more times she continued, "Of all the places to have to wait, why do we have to sit in a field right next to a stinking bog?"

I looked towards her direction, than back up at the peaceful cerulean sky. "Do you really want me to answer that?" I inquired, unsure of why she asked when she clearly knew the answer.

Laughing a little mostly to herself, Lein struck one final loud time, her cheek turning as red as my scalp, "That wasn't a question Heurts, you didn't need to respond."

A bird call suddenly echoed across the field, startling me from a light nap. I rolled over, flattening the weeds and grass with my hands, watching Lein arouse as well. I felt at peace as I gazed at her light brown hair gently falling across the fair complexion of her face and eyes. She sat up, brushed her hair back and quickly performed her own bird call. Just north of our position near the edge of the forest, our captain appeared from behind some tall thick birch trees.

"Grab your things Heurts, it's time to leave," she spoke, rustling through the tall grass, disappearing from out of view.

Already packed and ready, I signaled for Crehak who was on the other side of the field. The orc waved his giant hand overhead then together we headed towards the much cooler and shadier forest; a relief that we graciously accepted.

The birch trees stood tall and lean, but were well covered in fresh foliage and other large bushes and trees, creating much needed cover from the mid-day sun. Once deep enough inside and safely from view, our captain began to brief us on the situation.

"Well the situation seems a little grim." He looked down at the ground, pacing back and forth. His arms tucked behind him, while his face and chin stared downward. Sighing softly he started again, "Torrigon seems to have gone from being attacked once a week, to now being attacked and pillaged nearly every day."

"Any idea who they are, or what they want?" Lein broke in.

The captain peered over at her, "Ordstril reported that they are bandits and thieves. I don't think they are that organized, but from the looks of things it seems they have taken the town hostage, claiming all of their resources for themselves."

"What kind of numbers are we looking at captain?" I grumbled curiously.

"For the last time," the captain sighed, "don't call me captain. I have told you guys to just call me Artrov." He looked over his shoulder, as if he had heard something then continued to talk as he turned back around. "As for numbers, I think it's a small group of around twelve to sixteen. Once Darnhor arrives we will have an exact amount."

"As long as we get a chance to take them down I'm game," blurted Crehak from behind us. He flexed his arms, pretending to be prideful, if for a moment.

The captain nodded, "Don't worry you'll all have your share in good time."

As the sun went down, the air grew colder, giving us a more brisk feeling as the wind rattled the leaves and branches. The forest came to life with each small gust, causing nearby animals to chime in as well. Suddenly the animals around us fell silent as a shadowy figure jumped down from the trees with a soft thud.

"Sorry to keep you waiting captain," the intruder spoke.

"It's Artrov, but please continue with the report, Darnhor," requested our captain.

The short, dark-tanned human, padded off his lean shoulders and tight pants, shaking off some dirt before he exclaimed, "I have successfully infiltrated Torrigon and the bandits' camp. I have counted fourteen men and one woman, which when we're closer, I can show you where they reside."

"There will be time for that later," the captain responded, "Tell me what they want with the town."

"Right, sorry I'll continue," Darnhor stuttered. "The gang seems to be rather small. They only want the usual things like crests and loot. I don't know why they continue to attack the town, but we should not delay any longer. The people there seem to be very weak from the fighting and lack constant threats. The gangs' leader swore to kill some of them tomorrow."

Looking satisfied with the report the captain finished, "Alright, thank you Darnhor." Turning back towards the rest of us he promised, "Get some sleep tonight everyone, for tomorrow we take back Torrigon and return home before noon."

My sleep was worse compared to many of the previous nights. Lately I have been having dreams that didn't make much sense and by the time I managed to wrestle myself awake I couldn't care less about them. So, when I finally awoke this morning, I almost wished I had a real dream; one with thought and purpose. It was almost like I relied on their vivid and sensual properties, even though I hated them. It wasn't until they were gone, did I truly want them back.

Looking back now, I often kept a journal regarding such instances. Things such as mountains, hills, and rivers flooded each page and kept me wanting more. Once the fights were over, and the realization kicked in, I was left with nothing but an empty shell. Sure I drank, ate, slept, and killed like any real person, but the dreams offered an escape.

I hate nights.

After a quick meal of half stale bread, pigmy fruit, and dried orran bark, our team was just about near the edge of the forest where the small village of Torrigon was nestled a mile or two out. Our captain broke us up into three teams for a simultaneous attack. The tactic has worked before on other small gangs and this seemed no different.

My team consisted of Ordstril and myself, positioned on the northwestern side of the village. I had never worked with Ordstril alone before, mainly because he acted as our spy and usually worked alone, so it was good to finally get to know him a little better. The two other teams were situated on the southern and eastern sides respectively. We were to remain quiet and out of sight until our captain gave us the signal, until then we just had to wait.

I hate waiting.

I watched Ordstril rub an axe with his stubby fingers. He carefully examined its thick blade, fondled the tip, and even kissed the hilt once or twice. Trying not to stare, I picked up my own sword and wondered why I did not feel the same kind of emotion and respect like Ordstril. It was true that I was not a dwarf, a fact my mother often jested about when I was but a kid, but a knight should still care for his weapon. Like an extension of his arms and spirit, it should be well cared for and respected. Even after all the missions and training I had undergone I could not even feel anything as I stared at my own ugly reflection in the metal surface.

"If yer wonderin' why you don't care for your blades as I do, it's because you don't believe in them," grumbled Ordstril, clipping his axe back into its holster, securing it next to its twin with a final nudge.

"I believe in my blade," responding, sheathing my long sword. "I rely on it to kill my enemies and protect the innocent."

"No you don't," Ordstril humbly emitted. "You only think you do. Words can't even compare to the blessings and skill that my axes were given." Scratching his rustled light brown hair he asked, "Listen Heurtsvor, have you ever heard of Hodren?"

I could see the dwarf's eyes begin to glisten as he stared. I thought

4

a moment, believing I had heard the name before, but I answered truthfully, "No, I haven't."

Smirking beneath his thick wavy beard, he nodded with acceptance, "Aye, I figured as much. Hodren is a famous dwarven god. It is said that he helps craft dwarven weapons as they are being forged. This gives them a sort of blessing, as you would call it." He adjusted himself, while he continued, "Together with skill, I believe this is what truly makes a man who he is. By taking care of my axes and praying I am honoring Hodren for everything that he has done. You will see. Even if you mock me now, the reason I am alive today is because of him."

As Ordstril finished, I wished we had more time to discuss calmer things, but a loud bird call erupted from the south, meaning our conversation must come to an end. Rising from the ground, I grinned, "Now is the time to put those words into action."

Leaping over a small vegetable cart, I unsheathed my long sword, bringing it down onto the back of an unaware bandit. The blade jutted downward, carving through muscle, tendons, severing tissue and bone, causing the man to collapse immediately to the ground. To my right I could see Ordstril, already ten yards ahead of me bursting through a window and into a small nearby house.

Up ahead a few more bandits rushed out from homes, unsheathing swords and clubs. Confusingly they packed into the road looking around to see what all the commotion was. Just as one man was beginning to shout something, an arrow pierced deep into his neck. The man gurgled before seizing up, watching blood gush uncontrollably from his throat.

Peering through the hustle of people I spotted Lein on the far side of the village, arrows drawn and bow already extended. A few yards to her left, Darnhor was throwing his own deadly projectiles towards some confused bandits, striking them with knives before they could even draw their weapons.

As for Crehak and the captain I had no idea where they were. It didn't matter anyways, soon a handful of bandits were charging at me with a blood like rage in their eyes.

5

Sidestepping just as a crossbow bolt whizzed by my head, I continued to twist my body around, blocking a slash aimed at my head. Standing a foot or so over them and being much heavier, I could still maneuver, outpace, and predict them all. Following another slow attack aimed at my sides, I quickly returned with an assault of my own. A few quick stabs into his stomach and chest were all that was needed. The man clenched his opened stomach, waddling away a few feet before dropping.

A man with a facial tattoo and an appetite for savagery lurched at me with a couple of arched daggers. Trying to roll behind me attack my legs, I easily predicting his pattern. Performing a diagonal slash upwards, I forced him to sidestep right into my second blade. Grabbing hold of the hilt with both hands, the man screamed as I continued to drive my blade into his side, up into his collarbone. His eyes rolled back in pain and shock. Kicking his limp body over, and freeing my blade, I scouted around for anymore fools.

As quickly as the battle had begun, the end was already here. Once the attackers were dealt with, the rest of the bandits surrendered. We began to round them up in the center of town. The captain had asked Darnhor and Ordstril to seek out any stragglers or hiders and eliminate them. Lein was already scouting the surrounding forests and fields for any more bandits who might have run away from the town, her eyes piercing and bow drawn as she surveyed the lands ready to shoot on sight.

Four men were all that was left. The villagers stood around in a large circle trapping the shaking men inside along with the captain and the rest of us. Staring at the circle of civilians I could see just how oppressed and harassed they were. Children were hiding behind parents, as the elderly deep in mourning of those who had previously fallen.

Our captain peered into the eyes of one bandit who had decided he was confident enough to begin shouting insults at him. A feint shimmer followed. The man's head rolled along the dirt, as his body tipped slowly over. Our captain sheathed his long sword after wiping it clean and walked over to yet another bandit.

"What happened to your friend was unnecessary." Cautioning he continued, "However, what lies ahead for you might be far worse." He slowly walked over to another man who covered his face with his hands while curling up into a ball. "The King of Keifa despises anyone who dares pillage and rob one of his towns, no matter how small or unprotected." The man shivered as the captain bent down closer, his shadow blanketing over the man. "You will be escorted to an outpost south of here. There you will await orders on when you will be sentenced. As royal knights to the King we hold certain privileges over the law, so unless you want to join your friend here I suggest you keep your mouths shut and accept your fate." Our captain turned around then walked out of the circle. On his way out, he whispered something in Crehak's ear, patting him on the shoulder as he disappeared past the crowd.

That night, our group stayed in Torrigon. Half of our team was given rooms in the local inn, while the other three slept inside a farmer's house across the street. The hospitality of the villagers was heartwarming. Many children thanked us personally, while the elders and some farmers made sure we had everything we wanted to eat. Our captain made it clear that we shouldn't accept any resources from the people, us being knights of the king, but our stomachs seemed to disagree.

Once again I had a restless sleep. Even after the butchering of today, seeing the faces of lawless men slaughtered before me, I was unaffected. For as many of these missions as I had been involved with, I was growing very tired of this life. My body, mind, and spirit were beginning to take a toll, and I tried really hard to picture something that could boost my morale. Only one image appeared before I fell asleep. It was an image of me as a small child with my father. We were in a very small fishing boat, laughing together. The image blurred and distorted until only blackness was left, leaving me all alone, uneasy and ill-tempered.

MISSION 31
BLACK SOOT

His name was Ferilos; a middle-aged plump noble from Tempurah who we are now privileged to escort to the southern Keifa mountains. Not one of us has ever seen or heard of the man before today, and I'm sure he could care even less about us. What little information we knew, we had all heard from our captain a few days prior to the mission. Apparently, Artrov has been around the nobles in Tempurah long enough for us to coerce him into revealing more.

"Oh yeah, give him a pinch of diluted yak milk and he'll fall over in less time than it takes a woman to..." he stopped, biting his tongue once Lein shoved her fist into his side. "Anyway, there is one other thing." he moaned rubbing his sore spot.

"Alright, last one," the captain grinned.

"Good, good," spouted Artrov. "Apparently, like most city nobles, they despise royal knights."

The captain and I shared a quick glance. "Well, that's already a given." he chuckled.

"So, may we also presume he hates the king as well?" Lein asked, still slightly perturbed over the previous remark.

"If you already know these things, why bother sending me?" Artrov commented, looking slightly confused.

Ferilos distrusted us so much that he brought along five servants to act as personal bodyguards and assistants for all his daily needs. The noble mostly kept hidden inside his iron and wood carriage. The only time he could be seen was when he poked his head out the side window where he'd crane his pudgy neck towards the sun, before murmuring something to himself before hiding once more.

After a few days of rough travel and very little sleep we had arrived at the base of the Hurou Mountains. The slopes were craggy and grey, littered with loose rocks, boulders, and other debris. As I looked upwards the clouds seemed to wrap around the highest cliffs, fog gently flowing along the ledges and steep crevices. To the far west lie the bright borders of the Seida Desert. Where the mountains and desert overlapped a graveyard of dead trees and thicket grew, creating a warning to all those whom attempt to enter. Lucky for us, we were to guide Ferilos along the eastern side a few miles along a different path, where he was to meet secretly with another noble from Lestek. That was all the information given.

By the time we had traversed along the base of the first mountain, nightfall had arrived.

"My lord," our captain hollered from the front. "We'll continue on in the morning." The noble grumbled something, not even his servants could make out. Then we didn't see or hear him the rest of the night.

Climbing down off my horse I unbuckled my gear and began to set up my post. While unraveling a worn wool blanket I noticed Lein slowly trotting her way towards my direction. Her head held high as she grasped her bow in one hand, while clasping a large goat leg in the other. "There you are Heurts." She shouted happily, plopping herself down in the dirt next to me. She laid her bow against a small rock in order to free a hand so she could take a large bite out of the meaty leg. "If you're hungry I killed a mountain goat with Crehak not too long ago." She mentioned, before greedily taking another large mouthful then licking her lips clean of the juices. "There's still half or so left, but you better hurry, I think Ordstril has a bottomless stomach." She laughed to herself, while taking another bite.

By the time the moon had risen in the clear night sky, I found myself awake, not in the mood to sleep. Sitting with my back against a large flat rock, I found myself slowly staring around the camp wondering what everyone was thinking. Lein was a few feet from where I sat; her face hidden within blankets and her slender frame curled up into a ball. A couple yards from her was the carriage where Ferilos snored quietly, while his five servants were forced to sleep on the cold ground. We offered them a few extra blankets, which they gladly accepted. Crehak and Ordstril were next to each other on a rocky slope staring at the carriage as if in contest, trying not to blink. As for the captain and Darnhor I had no idea where they were. Either they were farther than I could see, or they were in a place they did not want to be seen.

Feeling my eyes become increasingly tired, I soon felt my body also wanting to shut down. The air was crisp and cool, while the breeze from the mountain gently blew down from the precipices, pulling some fog along for the ride. That was the last thing I could remember before the image of my father and I fishing against the quiet backdrop of my hometown forced its way into my mind.

The image lasted much longer this time, allowing me to admire and reminisce over simpler times. The lake was calm and crystal blue. A cloudless sky reflecting off the mirror like surface, until the occasional small ripple from our boat or fishing lines stirred the calm. The line grew taught as a fish got snagged. My father and I held the pole tightly. His hands gently fitting over mine as the pole bent ever so slightly. I watched the line swirl in circles then twitching back and forth. I heard my father saying something in my ear, but I couldn't quite make it out.

It was morning. The dream - if you would call it one - disappeared immediately, followed by the sounds of a horse galloping, shaking the ground nearby.

"Heurtsvor, kindly wake Ferilos and his men. Inform them we are leaving in a few minutes," asked Artrov as he grasped the reins of his steed guiding his horse to turn around, not even looking back to make sure I was indeed awake.

Sitting up after stretching my back and neck I noticed the glare of the sun casting a silhouette around the figure of our captain. Covered my eyes with my hand I nodded in obedience. After collecting and securing my things to my horse I walked casually over to the large carriage where Ferilos still slept. Some of his servants had begun to awaken when they heard me walking along the gravel. The rest soon would wake up when I rattled the carriage with both hands, causing its wooden frame to rattle back and forth. "Ferilos, wake up we're leaving. No time for breakfast either." I shouted while continuing to rock the carriage.

Walking back to my horse, I caught a glimpse of the noble's chubby head poking out from the side window. His beady eyes blinked and shifted trying to avoid the sun's blinding rays as he opened his mouth to yawn. I managed to catch a slight hint of aggravation glaring from his beady eyes, before he once again vanished back into the shade.

This morning the captain seemed very anxious to get to the meeting place as fast as possible. Leading the caravan personally; he took the front point, steering the course for those of us following behind.

Up ahead, we had to enter a small ravine nestled between two mountains that seemed to have grown too close to each other, and were now fighting over the space like children. Many large rock formations covered both sides, forcing the path to bend and wind like a serpent. A few more yards in and we'd have to ditch the carriage for it was far too large. The servants looked exasperated when they figured out they wouldn't have to drive or lift the carriage anymore.

The captain gave a nod over to Ordstril who steered his horse next to the side of the carriage. With a few raps on the side door, the half dwarf shouted inwards, "Excuse me Lord Ferilos, but I'm afraid you will have to walk from here."

A few noises came from inside before Ferilos responded in a slow grumble manner. "It figures. Oh well, I wasn't expecting much from you knights. My legs are getting cramped anyways."

The carriage began to rock as the balance of weight shifted around the cabin. Slowly the door handle turned and Ordstril had barely gotten his horse out of the way, before the door flew open, slamming against the carriage body.

The first object to appear was a small foot, the likes of which was attached to a similarly small boot. After which, a strangely shaped cane glided its way out from the inside. Clasping the shaft was a small stubby hand and a round hairy human closely behind. Ferilos, a man four and a half feet tall, was dressed in royal blue garbs with white and red trim and buttons down the sides. With a face lined in a short curly beard and dark curly hair on his head, he almost looked like a rich dwarf. His cane - which was almost as big as he was - seemed to be made of silver and had three strange crystals embedded into the top of it forming a triad of gems. "Alright," he grumbled, the rest of us still staring, "Let's get moving."

A few hundred yards in we were soon forced to ditch the horses as well. The sides of the two mountains felt like they were pressing down on us from all sides. Above were giant boulders on loose cliffs, while below were dead trees, unstable gravel, and even more rocks. We were now in a tight single line with Ferilos in the middle. Watching the man try to climb over rocks and through small openings helped keep our spirits high. During the ordeal he was yelling and shouting at his men every half-minute. He pulled on hair, swatted backs, braked every minute or two for pebbles in his shoes, and even cursed the gods themselves.

A half hour later and Ferilos was covered in sweat. He was breathing heavily and was no longer walking, which caused everyone behind him to stop and complain. "I believe the place is just up ahead, past that corner." He pointed with one of his stubby fingers. Even performing this simple gesture seemed hard for him as he strained to lift his flabby arm a couple of inches off the rock he was using to maintain his corpulent body. Turning his thick head around he gasped "I insist you wait here. This is a private meeting after all."

Through a red soaking wet face, he still managed to show a large grin as he waddled up ahead. His servants followed silently behind him, quietly squeezing past the captain and Darnhor who stood at the front. Ferilos was soon out of sight, when our captain hollered over to Crehak and everyone else behind him. "As much as I hate to side with the lord, we must wait here." He grabbed Darnhor on the shoulder, whispered something into his ear, and turned to head towards us as Darnhor climbed over the ridge behind him. "The meeting might go on for awhile. I suggest you all get comfortable." He managed to speak before disappearing behind a ridge.

Suddenly, a large explosion erupted from the path ahead. Turning around I noticed the as the air fall silent yet again. Another smaller explosion bellowed from the same direction. The captain immediately appeared again shouting, "The noble. Quick, everyone follow me!"

12

Running past skeletal branches and around jagged corners, I followed closely behind Ordstril. The small half-dwarf ran and leaped nimbly around jagged rocks and prickly branches, while I slowed down trying my best to avoid them with my larger frame. Looking back over at Crehak I noticed he used a different method that involved his sword slicing anything in his way.

By the time we had reached the clearing, I bear witnessed to a horrible disaster. Four of the servants were slain on the ground, and Lord Ferilos was nowhere to be seen. "Spread out!" yelled the captain whom was already climbing down the rough path sword in hand.

Drawing my claymore I carefully treaded around the far right wall. I made my way over to one servant who I could now see was suffering from severe burns and probably internal bleeding. His charred flesh and clothes were black and flaking. Scanning the area, I saw Lein who was examining two other bodies. "Ferilos!" the captain shouted around the clearing. "If you can hear me, say something!"

Just then, some rocks shifted, tumbling away near the far side. "I'm...here" a rough voice let out.

Artrov pointed for Crehak who was nearby to assist the man. The large orc tossed the heavy stones aside, creating a large enough hole for a flabby arm to poke through. "It's Ferilos!" Crehak hollered, turning his head.

"Great!" our captain responded. "Carefully help him out and find out what happened."

Pulling the large man out from the pile of rocks, Crehak was about to lay the man down when a knife flew across the area impaling him deep into his right leg.

Crehak knelt down, yanking the thing out. Rearing up he drew his large double-sided axe yelling, "Ambush!"

A few more knives shot forth into the clearing, aiming straight for our team. The captain easily dodged the few that were sent towards him, while the rest of us dove or shielded ourselves, deflecting the others. When the knives stopped, roars of men began to echo from over the mounds. Without warning a horde of savage looking men

13

began to appear over the cliff sides and rocks.

"Heurtsvor, assist Crehak with protecting Ferilos!" yelled Artrov drawing his sword. "Ordstril you're with me, and Lein you know what to do!"

By the time I had met with Crehak, he had already slain four men. Looking towards my right, I swung my sword down upon one man's wooden shield, splintering it into fragments and severing his arm in the process. The man screamed as I thrust my sword into his chest then kicked him aside. Crehak was busy carving people into pieces as I blocked and parried a few other attacks, while still trying to keep an eye on the defenseless Ferilos. Currently he was huddled into a corner between some boulders. His head shaking, his hair a mess, and he was mouthing some form of gibberish.

Lein was down to her last few arrows as she finished off a man attempting to crawl away, spiking him in the head with her last one. She then tossed her bow aside before unsheathing her twin knives into another man's gut. His stomach and insides spilled out, as she prepared for another man charging with an axe.

As their numbers were dwindling, I had heard a feint sound right before a large explosion struck a few yards from us. The blast tossed dirt and rock fragments everywhere, temporarily blinding my vision. When the dust cleared, I saw a strangely dressed man in dark robes crouching on top of a small ridge. His hands glowed with swirling red mana as he seemed to be preparing a spell. Cutting down another man, I could now see that the mage was focusing on Lein. However, the captain was already dashing full speed in his direction from the side. Before the man could let release whatever it was he was conjuring, our captain leaped and slashed towards his side, forcing the mage to divert from Lein and focus on dodging the assault.

Focusing on the captain's battle, I had forgotten all about Ferilos. By the time I tracked him down again, I could see an even larger number of men climbing down from rocks and over steep ridges above us.

"Another ambush!" I cried out, clasping my sword.

The captain saw this as well and responded, "Everyone fall back. Take Ferilos back to the carriage!"

Lein was the first to reach the small passageway. Ordstril followed closely behind her, stabbing at a few fallen men with his axes, making sure they were dead. I signaled for Crehak to follow, though he insisted he would wait for the captain. Deciding to leave anyway, I gently tossed Ferilos onto my shoulder, before huffing it to the small ravine. I could hear the yells and trampling of feet from our pursuers. They were close behind us now. Running at full speed the carriage was almost in now in sight.

"Alright my lord," I smiled, while gently lowering Ferilos back to his feet. "In you go!"

"They're right behind us!" he rattled.

"Then lock the door," I jested, before turning around and realizing that the war sounding men was growing quieter. The hollers and screams that had echoed throughout the mountains seemed to have vanished as quickly as the winds. It was as if they had all disappeared. Checking on the status of my team I could see everyone else was just as confused as I was. Darnhor appeared over a cliff to our left. He climbed down and met us in the path.

"Where were you?" I barked, "And where's our captain?"

Before he could answer there was another huge explosion, blasting the cliff side and shooting rocks and debris high into the air. I was knocked down, covering my face, as dirt and stone rained down from the sky. Rolling over I could now see that the carriage had been blown up. Its remaining fragments engulfed in red hot flames. Debris continued to rain down around us. We could do nothing but stare.

The captain and Crehak finally emerged from around the corner. Witnessing the devastation that happened mere moments ago our captain said, "Please tell me no one was in that when it blew?" Crehak gazed around counting the heads of who was here.

We watched our captain run over to the carriage inspecting the damage.

"Captain," I exclaimed. "Ferilos."

The captain peered over towards my direction. His eyes racing back and forth as the realization soon set in. "How did this happen?" he asked. Picking myself up, I explained, "I had told Ferilos to lock himself in the carriage to protect him from the invading men who were right behind us."

"I see. Then I fear we have failed." The captain turned around with his back to me and signaled for Crehak to get the horses. "Our next step after we inform Tempurah of this tragic news is to find out who is responsible for this ambush and deal with them immediately."

Lein approached, sheathing her knives. I turned around hoping for some kind of guidance from her. She nodded then put her hand on my shoulder, "You did what you thought was best Heurts. If it were me I probably would have done the same." For some reason though, I believe she wouldn't have. I made the decision, not her.

There were no peaceful dreams of fishing for many nights. What replaced them were the scenes and images of an innocent noble being burned to death, screaming my name. Lein's face appeared in the stones and rocky cliffs. She was mouthing, "I'm sorry."

Mission 32
Black Soot II

The next day we took an early start as we headed back towards the eastern side of the Hurou Mountains. Our captain made it very clear that we must inform the king and the nobles of Tempurah about Ferilos' death. After salvaging what we could of the destroyed carriage, we led our horses back through the tight foreboding crevice and out into the warm sun of the craggy grey mountainside.

Our captain insisted we take it easy for a few days, encouraging us not to think about life and death for a while, says it clouds the brain. Sometimes we all share drinks at the local bar. Everybody but Darnhor would be passed out. Our captain, as red faced as he was, smiled, paid the tab then kindly waited a few days before giving us our next mission. Whatever was going through his mind this day, I knew we wouldn't be laughing and drinking for quite some time.

Slowed my horse down, I fell to the back of our group where Ordstril was looking out towards the southern horizon. Casting a similar stare I tried to picture what it would be like to not have to serve as a royal knight. I also wondered what Ordstril was thinking about as he gazed aimlessly with a small smile showing through his coarse beard. Perhaps he had someone waiting for him back home. Through these years, I was always too modest to pry.

In fact, none of us ever talked about our homes or families. The captain insisted those discussions would only bring up emotions that would later hinder our skills in battle. On a few occasions I believed Lein wanted to tell us all something about her family, but one look from our captain made her swallow hard and hide her tears.

"Who do you think that mage was?" asked Ordstril looking at me curiously.

Cocking my head I was unaware he was talking to me until I felt his gaze piercing the back of my head. "What?" I spoke, blinking a few times to free myself from the short daze.

Pressing his lips together he looked back ahead. "Oh, I was just wondering to myself why there was a mage alongside those barbarians we fought."

"Maybe they hired him," I responded, not expecting an answer in return.

"That's true," The dwarf nodded. "Or, someone else did." Inquiring further, I turned to face him, "A bunch of mountain folk hiring a mage."

His eyes squinted, whilst he smiled and then put his finger to his lip. "It's just a guess here, but perhaps someone else did the hiring. Would make more sense would it not?"

It was clear he had given this much thought. I hesitated, thinking about rushing back to the front again, but I humored him by responding. "Have you shared this with the captain?"

"You share that you've taken a piss with him too?" he chuckled. I rolled my eyes, this time grabbing the reins and preparing to shove off. "No," he finished. "I assume he already knows this."

As the sun rose to its peak, we broke out into the surrounding wasteland. High above the sky became increasingly clearer, losing much of the grey and cloudy atmosphere which the mountains cast. The only visible shade for miles was a large naked tree near some tall patchy grass. The old shriveled branches poked high into the sky, spreading like tendrils or lightning. The bark was dark grey and the absence of any leaves would make one think that it had been cursed. As we approached closer, preparing to rest, the horses began to whine and shake in fright. Our captain took to the front immediately. Together with Crehak they coerced the horses closer to the mighty tree one step at a time, careful as to not spook them further.

As a light breeze swept by, it also brought along a stench of pure rottenness. The smell singed my nose hairs, almost causing Ordstril and me to gag. We looked up ahead at our captain, knelt down, along with Darnhor, in the brown grass near the base of the dead tree. The rest of us walked closer, the stench growing ever more pungent. Flies buzzed around whatever lie ahead. Together we all froze a moment before talking.

"This worm is on his last breaths of life," clamored Crehak.

"Perhaps he can give us some info over the recent attack," broke in Lein, covering her whole face with her hands.

Before us lay a man, half mangled, and with his legs shredded by what resembled huge slashes. Flies were covering his mid section and left arm. Blood stained the ground and grass where he lay. Our captain made a notion to Darnhor, before walking away from the scene and back to his horse.

Kneeling down beside the man, Darnhor unsheathed a small dagger from his waist and gently poked it into the man's cheek. "Wake up." The man's eyes shifted beneath his eyelids. He began to stir, forcing one of his less crusty eyes open to see the sharp point of a knife, centimeters from his eye.

"Go...ahead...and kill me." The man slowly exasperated as his chest heaved with each word. I was shocked that he was still alive. Watching now in silence, we gave the two of them some room.

Darnhor shifted his blade away from his face, then down to one of the man's wounds on his leg. "Tell me what you know about the attack."

The blade gently scrapped along the dark red wound. The man screamed as the tip pierced deeper into his leg, clearing the way for flesh blood to trickle down.

"I...don't know. All I...can tell you...is where we were going next." The man almost blanked out from the pain. His eyes rolled to the top of his head. Sweat forming on his brow. His head and chest began shaking uncontrollably. Darnhor put his blade away and leaned in closer.

His mouth just inches from the dying man's ear. "Where?" he whispered softly.

"Resak...we are supposed to go to Resak." The man cried out these last few words before his wounds finally caught up with him and he became as stiff as the bark he laid against.

Darnhor stood back up, turning his head to face the captain who was fixing the reins on his horse. The rest of us walked away from the dead body. Preparing for whatever our captain was about to say.

He leapt up onto his horse, speaking out for everyone to hear. "Alright then, I guess we are going to Resak."

It was nearly half into the night when the thick grey smoke rose up over the tree canopies, gathering together into a large luminous cloud. We had raced all day on horseback till we escaped the wastes, making our way towards the town of Resak. The horses were now running full gallop as the town rose over the horizon line. The once quiet farming town was now burning in a giant wave of fire and ash.

Embers flew skyward, lighting up the dark smoke filled night, before raining down as ash and soot into the eyes and lungs of the innocent people cowering and screaming below. Approaching fast, we began to pass wagons that were toppled and corpses strewn about. Shattered remains of houses littered the dusty ground, as random fires sizzled and blazed. Dogs were barking and many of the fields were already black and crisp.

Immediately our captain turned, he had a look in his eyes that made each of us hang onto his every word. "Find those responsible for this at once. I want none left alive."

"Sir," I asked coughing a little from the thick smoke as it blew past. "What about the civilians? We should try to help them first."

The captain steered his horse around and nodded for Crehak to follow him as he shouted, "It is too late for these people. If you want to stop this from happening again I suggest you catch those men, they couldn't have gotten far."

With those last words, the captain, Crehak, Ordstril, and even Darnhor were following behind, leaving just Lein and me.

"I'm sorry Heurts," she spoke, placing her gentle hand upon my shoulder. Our horses shook as ash began to cover their manes and hair. The smoke was beginning to irritate all of our senses. I looked back at her with a saddened face, trying hard to cover up the fact that I had second thoughts over our captain's decision. Not once had I ever disobeyed or even questioned my orders. Back in training, I was one of the few orcs that were allowed to become a royal knight. If it weren't for Artrov speaking on my behalf, I might never have gotten a chance to become something I was proud of. But today I was hesitant.

Lein grabbed the reins of my horse tugging on them gently to guide us along. I could see that she was holding back her own emotions. Blaming the smoke in the air or ash in her lungs she looked the other way; she would have slapped me if I ever brought it up again.

The night was almost over, just as the last bits of fire smoldered down and disappeared. Dawn was arriving soon. The town was completely reduced to ash and charred wood. Out of the small population of farmers that had once lived in pure happiness, only a quarter or so of them survived to see their paradise destroyed.

We found no signs of those responsible for the fire. While our captain was off running some errands, the rest of us stayed in town, assisting with repairs and treating the wounded. Families became homeless, children were hungry, and many relatives were in mourning. The few fields and gardens that were untouched by the flames would not be enough to feed everyone till next season. Everyone in the village knew what would have to happen, yet no one wanted to admit it.

After gathering the townsfolk the entire town was abandoned. Half of us led some people back towards Torrigon, while the captain, Darnhor, and I, guided the rest of the people towards Tempurah; the capital city of Keifa.

The road was long and harsh. For the families that had nothing left, this was their last hope. I watched as the children slept in carts full of hay, while many of elders tirelessly traveled in silence. Gently guiding my horse to the front of the line, I felt an urge to discuss some past actions with our captain.

"Can I help you?" he asked, continued to gaze straight at the road ahead.

Hesitating on what I would say I murmured, "Do you really think by taking these people to Tempurah, that you will be freeing them from their woes?"

"No," he responded in a softer tone than usual. "But it is all I can offer them. Tempurah is a great place to start life anew."

Speaking a little louder I continued, "You could have prevented this."

The captain halted his horse. Some people behind also stopped, "Do remember the time you were in training Heurtsvor?"

"Yes, of course," I replied.

"Then do you also remember when I spoke to the king on your behalf because I knew you would be a grand addition to our team and our cause. I knew that you were no ordinary orc; one who was not wild and mindless, but who had a heart with a sense of purpose and devotion."

Pausing to catch his breath, the captain turned around, signaling those behind to keep going. He then looked in my eyes. "I believed that you were a man who would trust in me and my actions; that you would not hesitate to follow my lead, knowing that whatever I asked, you would always remain true to my heart and that of our king."

Grabbing my arm and steering his horse closer he said, "Heurtsvor, I would gladly call you my friend, if it only meant that you would not question our duties as royal knights for the crown. I know you have wanted this position all your life, and I beg of you not to jeopardize what you have worked so hard and so long to accomplish."

Grasped his arm in return and looking in his eyes with the same devotion that he showed me I replied, "My mind, body, and spirit will always belong to this team and to you. I am sorry to have ever questioned your rank and guidance."

With a final shake of hands we let go and continued our march; the captain in lead and me following right beside.

MISSION 35
REGENCY CALL

The air around the castle was crisp and clean; not at all like most castles that I have had the displeasure to visit. Since the castle rested near the Tempurah Mountains, the air was always crisp with water the purest I have ever tasted.

I gulped down a tall glass full as I waited patiently with my team in the guest dining hall of Kerganon Castle. The room was very large and open, and there were many decorations, banners, and flags outlining vast amounts of windows and doors. In the middle laid a grand red-oak table, with chairs twice the size of any normal man.

Prepared upon its surface were decorative flowers, bread, nuts, and fresh fruit. An hour seemed to pass, and I found myself itching to get up and stab something. Scanning the area for anything remotely exciting I then noticed Lein, slouched down in her chair playing with her long black hair while humming softly. A few guards with long black pikes were standing guard near the main entrance door along with Darnhor who was watching them on the other side. Crehak was busy finishing off the rest of the sweet bread, and Ordstril was taking a light nap in one of the large chairs. His body sat slumped, his hair and beard masking a low snoring sound.

While waiting I decided to try and visualize the fishing dream that I have been having. I imagined the warm sun casting its rays down upon the vast shimmering lake. I tried to also picture the look upon my father's face as he witnessed me catch and reel in my first fish. All I could remember was his long black hair and sea green skin with light black patches spread over his arms and head. From the face of my father I imagined that I brought him nothing but joy.

Just as the fish was pulled out of the water, the daydream ended and I awoke with the sound of two large wooden doors opening. Sitting upright and straightening my coat, I watched as our captain walked briskly into the room followed closely by two men I have never seen before.

The first man to sit down was a fairly youthful looking elf. He had short blonde hair and green eyes. These matched his green and gold overcoat which he took off to reveal an all black outfit with royal emblems shimmering from the light.

The other man was much older and rounder than the elf, and by the look of his royal garbs and seals he seemed to possess a much higher rank. The older man had slick black hair, with a matching long mustache. Both the men had embroidered swords, and both the men waited for our captain to talk first.

"Alright guys, I need you all to pay attention and come over here!" The captain broke in, making sure even the sleeping half dwarf could hear. His voice echoed throughout the dining room, stirring even the guards who were startled by the yell. As the rest of us took seats closer to the center, the two royal men exchanged glances.

"These two men here will be hearing each of your descriptions on the recent attacks that have been happening." We all looked curiously at one another than back towards the captain as he continued. "I have already told them and the king of everything that has happened, but they insisted on hearing your sides and opinions as well."

Ordstril made a small notion like he wished to talk, but the strange older man stopped him by speaking first, "I believe we should introduce ourselves before we begin."

"Yes, I believe you're right. I'm sorry I forgot to mention that," said the captain.

"My name," the older man announced, "is Grenwall. I am the senior admiral to the king, as well as one of his nobles from Tempurah."

Waving his hand towards his elven companion, the elf responded in kind. "I am Iraph, the second in command of the king's personal royal guard.

We each paid our respects, and then the captain continued the discussion. "These two already know of the attacks and information that I have provided them. As far as we can tell the attack on Torrigon and the burning of Resak are not related."

Ordstril raised his hand and signaled to talk. "I believe that would be a correct assessment."

"Thank you Ordstril," he replied. "What we don't know is who the fire starters were and what they plan to do next. Iraph here has had his men question the people of Resak, and not one of them could give us an exact description."

"I'm sorry to interrupt Artrov, but may I intervene?" spoke Grenwall passively.

"Yes, of course," waved our captain.

Grenwall double checked with Iraph before speaking, "The best thing we can do for now is to scan the surrounding areas, and check in with all the towns and villages in Keifa making sure there will be no more attacks."

"I agree as well," motioned Iraph. "The king has asked for you Artrov, to take your team and head towards the Seida Desert. There you will patrol the surrounding borders and even penetrate the desert in case we are dealing with nomads."

"Is there anything else?" inquired our captain.

Iraph scanned the dining room including all of us before he smirked to himself, "Lein, you look like you have something to add."

We all turned around, wondering what she could want to possibly ask. Even Darnhor who was way in the back of the room leaning against the shadowy walls raised an eyebrow.

Lein folded her skinny arms, smiled in my direction, then spoke up, "I think I know who these men might be, or at least what they are after."

Grenwall and the captain lifted their heads with a quizzical expression. Iraph responded, "Oh and you believe your keen senses have come to this decision before any of my personal trackers or elite men have?"

"Yes." She almost smirked in retaliation, "During our stay here, one resident of Resak told me that a few men came to the village the night before with a cart full of ruby ore. The woman claimed that the men were trying to sell it to some of the merchants before storming off after a heated argument."

"Ah, this is news then," Iraph quietly commented. "Then it is good you are travelling to the Seida Desert like we asked. Once there track down the ore caverns and eliminate the men responsible."

Ordstril and I looked at Lein like she deserved a far greater reward. However, her face was lit up and I could tell that she thought she had already done enough.

"We would still like to discuss each incident with your men Artrov, so please wait outside till we are done," requested Grenwall.

"Of course, I wouldn't have it any other way," nodding as he took his leave. We watched him head back through the mighty wooden doors, slamming them shut as he disappeared.

That night we all slept in separate rooms. The castle floors became ice cold, and the windows were left open enough to only tease us with the full moon shining brightly outside. I could tell that we all still had much to talk about, but I didn't want to disturb anyone from their peaceful sleep. I realized that tomorrow we would have plenty of time to discuss these new findings.

Apparently Lein thought she couldn't wait until morning, as I awoke to find her standing over me in bed. Startled, I accidently bumping heads with her, causing us both to lie back down. She took a seat in a small chair by the window, as I lay in bed propped up with some pillows. She seemed to have a lot on her mind, as her hands never remained still. Looked around the room her eyes never focused in one place for more than a second.

"You know something Heurts?" she let out, her hands wrapped

tightly around herself, then in her lap, and then back around herself again.

"What?" I asked.

She gazed at me from the shadows, all I could see was her bright eyes and glimmering hair. "Do you ever wish that you never joined the royal knights?"

I looked at her awkwardly. I could see that she thought I was making fun of her, but I really wanted to answer her truthfully. "Not until recently."

"I have, all the time," she whispered enthusiastically. "Even while we were training, I have had second thoughts about what I was getting myself into."

Propping myself up higher, I eagerly wanted to know more. I just didn't want to prod her into feeling uncomfortable. This was the most she has ever opened up to anyone before and for some reason I was feeling more like her friend. "Please, go on." I insisted.

"All the fighting, bloodshed, and travelling, has really only made things worse. I know I don't show it as much, because I hide it deep inside, but it's true." She paused a moment to run her hands through her thick long hair. "My family is all but gone now." She looked as if she was going to cry. I took a moment to let her rub the tears away, but she insisted she go on. "This is my family now Heurts. This small group, along with Artrov, is all I have left. So you see I belong here now. I have tried my best to deal with these emotions. I know some of our ways are not always the best, but they are what must be done."

I felt my insides cramp up as she spoke each word. I closed my eyes to try and forget what she had said. I tried to imagine the warm sun, blue lake, and face of my father. However, none could be mustered. When I opened my eyes, all I saw was Lein's sad white orchid face, staring at me from the cold dark corner of the room.

I watched as she got up, walked over to me, and kissed me gently on my forehead while whispering, "You do what you think is right. Just follow your heart and you will be fine. Don't worry about me, I'll be alright." With those final words I watched as she left the room, leaving me all alone. The moonlight shined down into the dark room, stretching its light along the floor and up to my face. When I fell asleep, I dreamt of my father and me fishing on the lake; the visions of which eased my mind, making me forget the sadness in Lein's consolation. The captain was right. I know now why he wished us to remain closed hearted.

Mission 39
Unknown

The air around the Seida Desert was unlike anything I had ever experienced before. It was most certainly not like the pure clean air I had the pleasure of enjoying whilst I was in Kerganon Castle. Salt and sand found its way into my clothes, my hair, and my face. There was no escaping the small particles that stung all of our unprotected areas as each gust of wind nearly forced us to our knees. There was no escaping the sun either. What little shade we had, came from a few small boulders and dead trees that littered the borders circled the borders. That was miles away now.

The night before, we had arrived at a small caravan that travelled around the northern boundaries. Made up of maybe thirty people; all of them heavily garbed, wrapped, dirty, and spoke with a heavy accent. The group was a mix of all races, and so we had no trouble blending in while as we loaded up on supplies and information.

Ordstril and Darnhor were in charge of gathering what they knew about any hostile gangs in the area, while Lein was sent to get some supplies. Crehak and I were told to watch over the horses as our captain met up with some old friend from long ago.

Even though we both were on the outskirts of the caravan we still observed the constant stares. It probably wasn't everyday that the people here have had a chance to see two large orcs in iron and steel armor, sitting out in the heat staring back at them. A few curious children walked up to us, trying to sell us dried fruit and cactus flowers. Crehak ignored them completely, as I gently extended my hand offering to buy one or two.

Lein saw the children run by her as she carried two large baskets of goods back to the horses. I could tell she was much happier today than the previous nights, so I didn't bother her with petty small talk.

Loading up the horses with fresh canteens, fruit, bread, and cloth, she smiled and looked over at the two of us. The sun's rays cascaded down from the sky, highlighting her best features like her shiny hair, skin, and eyes. Wanting not to get caught staring I turned away looking back towards the caravan. "I hope this trip doesn't take too long." She joked.

"It will be fine," broke in Crehak. "We know where they live. It will all be over soon."

Hearing him say those words so casually made me hesitant on what we were still trying to accomplish. I know the captain made it clear that what we were doing, what the royal knights stood for, was what I was trying to become all my life. Was this really what I wanted though? If I am supposed to feel so proud and good, then why do I feel so confused and lost? Why do I have dreams of happier times some days, and nightmares of the dead other nights?

Darnhor arrived first, followed by Ordstril who was carrying something in a small crate. The two of them looked exhausted as Ordstril plopped the wooden box down hard next to himself before sitting on top of it.

"Where were you two all day?" Lein politely inquired.

Ordstril took a long deep exhale allowing Darnhor to speak for him. "Just wait till the captain gets here than you will know."

Lein mumbled under her breath something I wished I could have heard, before she left and took a seat nearby.

It was a half hour later when the captain finally arrived. Walking with a bounce in his step he seemed overly satisfied and rejuvenated. None of us dared ask him how it went, for we knew our place, but Darnhor looked a little puzzled when he came back empty handed.

"Alright guys," the captain began, "Lein, do you have the supplies?"

Lein stood up and brushed the dirt off her pants before talking. "Yep, everything is all set. Though I think we only have enough supplies for a few days at most. That's all the money you..."

"It will be enough." The captain interrupted. "We won't need more than two days max to do what we need to do."

Getting up to stretch, I saw that Ordstril was now standing on the crate he had carried over. A look in his eyes was dark, and he began to blurt out rashly, "And what is it that we came here to do exactly?"

The captain lifted his head, "I'm sorry did you have something to say?"

Ordstril began to wave his arms about, raising his voice for all to hear. "I was just curious as to what our true goals are here."

"You know what we are here for Ordstril, but if it pleases you, than tell me what reason you think it might be," he responded ever so humbly.

"Alright then," Ordstril nodded. "While Darnhor and I were asking the folks here about gangs in the area, I came across an older gentleman who was selling a small amount of ruby ore."

Crehak raised a few brows than got up and walked behind the captain quietly. I took notice of this, and almost going to stop Ordstril myself, I halted curious as to what he was getting at

"Asking the man," the half-dwarf began again, "I came to hear that he got the ore from a few knights from up north who in turn gave it to a few desert people." Ordstril kicked over the crate, revealing a bunch of ruby ore that scattered everywhere. The dark red ore glistened from the sun as the jagged pieces toppled and rested in the dirt. I turned my gaze from the ore to our captain who didn't seem at all faltered. In fact he was smiling.

"Now tell me what we are really doing here, captain!" the small half-dwarf folded his arms, staring down both the captain and Crehak who towered behind them.

"Alright then," the captain shrugged. "There's no reason to hide it from an intelligent knight such as you. Plus..." he paused, turning around to look at everyone else. "You all deserve a right to know too I suppose."

Now I was even more confused. I couldn't believe that what Ordstril was talking about would hold some truth to it and the fact that he was even questioning our captain made even less sense. If I were him, I probably would have just ignored what I had learned and never brought it up to anyone, let alone calling him out on it. Despite his size, Ordstril was much braver than me. Whatever happens now, I am glad that not all of us still hide our emotions.

The captain took his overcoat off, handing it to Crehak to hold onto while he paced a moment. I watched as he stared up into the sky and then back down at his dirty black boots. He kicked a large ore on the ground, then stepped n it, burying it into the sand. He still had a smile upon his face, though now he seemed a little less humble than before.

"Twelve or so years ago," he started, "before the Black Steel Knights were created, the kingdom was in a state of emergency. The Kings people were beginning to hate him and they distrusted him almost to the point of dethronement. The king was on the brink of insanity before a few of his most trusted advisers came up with the only option to prevent total rebellion. Do you know what that option was, Heurtsvor?"

He looked at me with the most petrifying stare I had ever seen. I felt very small and worried over what he might say next. However, I was too stunned to talk, so he spoke in my stead. "Fear," The captain barked. "Fear is what the great providence of Keifa needed in order to protect itself. The king issued a secret force to hire local thugs and gangs to begin ravaging and attacking various towns said to be harboring disloyal citizens."

My jaw dropped at the mention of the king hiring anyone with a murderous intent. All feelings of trust and loyalty were now gone. I began to feel unwanted and used. I glanced at Lein who I thought would have a hard time dealing with this as well. She seemed at ease. Her face was motionless standing like stone, looking as if somehow she already knew and understood everything he had said.

The captain continued, "The knights found the ore caverns and used the ore as an untraceable currency to help reclaim this kingdom. Once the villages had enough, they turned to the king to protect them.

The king hired a select few to see that they would be safe, and in return he gained their unruly, obedient, and unparallel devotion." The captain folded his arms and stood still for a moment before speaking again, this time more quietly and depressed. "It was a foul and horribly action to take, I know. But, it had to be done. It had to be performed in order to save the kingdom, as well as, our humanity." He then returned his attention back to the half-dwarf. "Don't look at me like that Ordstril; I'm glad you found out."

The half-dwarf sat quietly, his back resting on the toppled crate. His small rough hands rubbing the ore back and forth in his palms while he spoke, "There should have been a better way."

"I'm sorry my friend, but this was all we were left with," the captain responded. "Do you have anything to add Lein?"

She stood motionless. I could tell she probably had a million things to say, but none of which that she had the nerves to muster. The only thing to come out was, "What about Ferilos? Was that an accident or your doing as well?"

Looking down at his boots once more, the captain quietly said, "He was conspiring against the king. He was a rebel and it was a necessary action, I'm sorry. And what about you Heurtsvor, I would like to hear from everyone whether or not you will still perform your loyal duties to the crown." the captain demanded, looking over at me, as I felt even more ashamed at what I had been a part of.

Time stood still while my brain was in full throttle. Images and words raced through my head as I tried to piece together what was real anymore. It seemed like my entire life was a lie, and I just couldn't take it anymore. I felt like Lein and Ordstril had spoken enough, and now was the time I use my courage to stand up for what I believe in, even if it meant my life.

"No!" I blurted, standing up as tall and straight as I could. "At one point in my life I thought that this group meant everything to me. I thought that you meant everything to me. However, now I understand that this was all a lie!"

The captain shifted his eyes a few times, caught off guard at what was coming from my mouth. Crehak became slightly angry and I could see that he feared I might jeopardize our group if I continued.

So, I did anyway.

"I don't care about the crown or the kingdom. I am tired and exhausted from all the killing. It haunts my once peaceful dreams, and even though my mind is telling me to stay, my heart knows that this is not what I truly want. I am leaving now, and I hope you all find what's best in your own heart."

With those final words I turned around, leaping onto my horse. I didn't even look behind to see Lein's face one last time. No one followed me as I left. No one chased me, and no one even said goodbye. That was the way I wanted it. I knew that this was what was best for me and only I could make this decision for myself. I had hoped that by the time I reached the outer boundaries of the desert that I would see the faces of anyone else from our group that had decided to quite also. Scattered dead trees slowed my speed. I slowed to a steady gallop, before turning around, hoping for the best.

No one was there.

What I wouldn't do to see Lein or Ordstril's face again. To hear them laugh or speak of simpler times. All that was over now, and I wasn't going to look back ever again.

FINAL MISSION
FISH

I no longer had dreams or nightmares. The once bloody faces of the dead were now gone from my mind. The quiet serene lake was also no longer needed nor wanted. I had the real thing now, and every day I got to experience it just as I did when I was a small child with my father.

The place was called Gorta. I discovered this small piece of heaven while travelling away from the providence of Keifa. I managed to get an old fishing boat that took me over to the providence of Ersive, where I travelled down the coast. Eventually, I stumbled upon a small fishing village where I am now.

Selling my old weapons and after managing to work a season as a fisherman's apprentice, I finally saved up enough money to purchase a small boat house with only one small boat tied in its docks. A few weeks later, I patched it up, setting sail for the first time. The lake was not as blue as my previous dreams were, but the fish were just as big and plentiful. It took me some hours to even catch one, but during that time I felt truly at peace. There were no more wars or fighting, and all I had to worry about was how to cook the fish when I got back in evening.

Days soon turned into weeks, which turned to seasons, and then those in turn changed to years. I have not heard anything or anyone from my past kinghood days. Staring at the door, I caught myself wishing someone I knew would drop by.

The entire town was made up of orcs all friendly and kind to me. I remember one time; a little girl fell out of a tree nearby. She must have but a small child, but she picked herself back up, dusted off, and then continued to play. Not one tear ran down her face. She reminded me of Lein. I picture the two of them next to each other playing and catching dragonflies. Ah, how I missed those days when we used to talk to each other. A friendly chat as we hiked up a steep mountain, a casual joke, as we rested near a brook.

The next day I awoke like every other day before it. I performed my daily rituals, and when it came time to head outside I noticed a small paper wedged in my front door. Setting down my fishing gear I took the letter and opened it up. It was written on some old yellow parchment, and there was a small signature on the bottom.

The letter was addressed to me. It read;

To Heurts,
I'm sorry I couldn't meet with you personally. My feelings and

past might get the better of me, and I would never be able to leave. I want to thank you. Through the years we have worked together, you became the closest thing to a friend I've ever had. When you left, I had wanted to stop you. I wanted to grab hold and prevent you from leaving. However, if I'd done so, it would've caused you even more pain. Letting you go was the best thing for me. Because of you, I was able to leave the knights as well. I attempted to track you down, but gave up when I feared you might not want to see any of us again. Finally, I had enough courage to write this letter. I am glad you were able to find peace. You deserve it the most. Now, I must do so as well.

- Lein

Folding the letter in thirds, I pocketed it in my front shirt before picking my gear up and heading down to the docks.

As I sat in my boat, rocking back and forth, I focused my eyes out onto the water where I could slowly see the image of my father, holding me in his arms. I smiled softly, looking up at the warm sun and clear blue sky. The heat warmed my body and face, as I gently padded my pocket.

"I am glad she finally found her true self."

THE TALE OF

OLD BERSOOL

PROLOGUE
-1-

Dancing shapes swayed and disappeared amongst a miraculous landscape. A plethora of colors rose and fell like the ocean tides as a vortex of fluorescent images popped and blazed, like a festival of lights above a lake at midnight. There I stood; suspended in the center of it all. Face forward, eyes fixated among the cascading wonderment which was the spectacle before me. A surge of bliss pumping through my body, and at the same time I felt a soft sadness creep over me. Escaping outwards from my heart, the happiness faded and I began to wonder.

Where were the people, the cities, and the danger? Could a world such as this truly exist?

Leaning forward I stretched out my arms, basking in the warmth of the sky, pretending to see far into the distance.

What was waiting behind that magnificent spectrum of clouds and mist? Was there a town past the gentle swaying waters or further past the fields of endlessness?

Behind the peaceful violet mountains, over the twisting labyrinth foothills and the calm azure streams, I was perplexed. Through all the beauty and serenity this place offered, being at the center of it all I felt as if I belonged someplace else. In the shadows of the mountains, possibly hidden away in the small cracks and crevices this place was hiding, there had to be a place where I could call home.

I never received an answer.

A small tremble sprouted deep within me. This world was cracking open from below. Like massive tree roots it grew outward, with me still at its center. The colors faded to soft grays, the beauty and wonderment became swallowed up by the fissures. The landscape became butchered by the seismic activity, twisting and crumbling into dust. All the while, I stood motionless; confused as to whether or not I cared that this was happening.

Awaking, I found myself dizzy-eyed and motion sick. Ahead was an iron door, and to the sides, rock and stone. I'd wish for more dreams, if they didn't all end the same, awaking to this damp, dark prison. This was my home, suspended in mid-air by several large bands of chains and heavy rusted shackles; my own weight constantly putting a strain on my back and arms. My head and neck pounding from the exhaustion, sweat, and hunger.

The sickness was finally subdued. I was greeted with the same depressive sights I've had the misfortune of gazing upon since for as long as I could remember. Flickering torches lined the dark hallway outside my cell. Enormous stonework forged the foundation of my cage; a thickness far beyond any physical measure. Peering to my side I noticed a small slit in the wall. Almost every day I'd peer through that opening with the hopes that I'd see something or someone. Instead I was honored with mysterious groans and shrieks almost nightly, providing a constant and haunting choir.

I let my body go limp. The exertion to look around was too much. After some more time had passed, my chains grew limp enough for my body to collapse to the ground. Prickly straw padded my gigantic frame, as I heaved with exhaustion, folding over myself the best I could. With my head low against the cold stone floor, I heard footsteps inching their way down the hall. They moved from place to place, halting only a minute or two, before continuing a few steps further. Eventually, they were loud and close enough where I could sense them just beyond my door.

At last, substance had arrived.

The footsteps stopped. A platter slid under the door, skidding along the grungy surface of my prison. Some of the white slop splashed onto the cold worn stones. Pinching the crude metal plate between my claws, I guzzled down the mess within seconds. I even licked the floor clean to make sure I had consumed it all. It was a sad sight, but when the body is desperate, you'll find that the mind will do desperate things too.

Ignoring the sleepless days and the pitch black scenery for a moment, there were some days when I was visited by others. These were what I called "the luckier" days. The days when my chains were drawn so tight that my muscles ached and my tendons were on the verge of snapping. My body hung vulnerably and exposed, eyes focused forward, waiting for the door to open. There upon, a woman would sometimes come in. Her hair long and golden, just like the fields in my dreams. She had a slender frame, soft skin, and face matching the purity of the moon. Looking into my eyes, she studied them as she wrote some things or had others behind her do it for her, speaking in a tongue I was barely able to understand. I can recall a few times when she studied my body; measuring it with prickly metal and wooden tools, listing things as she conversed with her associates. Laying her smooth hands upon my thick bumpy hide, I began feeling an intensity and warmth similar to those felt in my dreams. As she ran her smooth hands around my sore joints, muscles, and whatever else she could feel for, the sensation of those peaceful times came back to me. The times I was dreaming, trying to forget.

She wasn't the only one I became entranced over. Another, much shorter man visited me many times in the earlier years. With white hair all over his face and arms he came and talked to me many times. Speaking in many tongues, he often arrived with many taller beings behind him. They stayed around for hours. He mostly smiled and nodded, then whispered to the people behind him, all while taking notes or laughing. The man was kind to me though, much kinder than the golden woman or the mysterious food-bringer. I could sense it somehow; in his eyes, in his tone. I understood that he was interested in me, but never why or who he was. I'd hear many words being spoken, and through the years his visits grew fewer and less frequent. That's when the other women began coming. That's when I had begun to have the dreams. Those were days long past now.

I am not ashamed of who I am. Nor am I scared of what I might become. I consumed the slop because I believe it is necessary.

Necessary for me continue on.

Necessary for me to return to my dreams.

PROLOGUE
-2-

I awoke in a dizzy haze. Lying in a heap among the floor I found my chains loose and draping over me. There was a black cloud around my cell. It burned my eyes and irritated my nose. Coughing and gasping for cleaner air I could feel that my life was in danger. I called out for help, but there was no answer. Instead, I gathered up the chains around my arms and pulled as hard as I could; trying to break the links in the walls. Gasping, I moved my head to avoid the putrid black air whilst gathering the chains around my claws for another attempt. I could feel the strength in my shoulders weakening as I held my breath. Gathering the chains at the base of the floor, I wrapped them several times, this time higher for greater support. I then pulled until I couldn't take the strain any longer...*snap!* The cross links broke. I heard the sound of freedom as the metal rings scattered among the stone floor.

Rubbing my sore arms, I scampered to the door. Using the force of my body, I began slamming against it as hard as I could. The hinges buckled. Soon, I was able to slowly pry it open. Upon doing so, a sudden bright flare lit up my face, searing my hand that held the door. A burning sensation flared up, but that was negligible compared to the hot light that was erupting everywhere else. The hall was decorated in mysterious and mesmerizing flames. No longer was it a silent, dark prison. All at once, it became a dream-like menace. It was a place full of heat and colors like the sun, like the torches, only with an uncontrollable lust for spreading their light and wanton destruction to all things. Fearing more of those burning and blinding sensations, I had decided to avoid touching or getting close to the bright, dancing flares. Instead, I gathered up what strength I could, and began shambling down the hall.

Marching slowly, I arrived at the first intersection. The thick black air was everywhere. Laying my hands upon the walls I could feel the warmth and heat as if they were roasting from the inside. Peering around the corner I saw a few bodies very similar to the ones who came into my cell. Their bodies were scattered among rubble, many crushed beneath giant rocks. Walking past the flattened beings, I came across one with hair the color of the very flames that were consuming them. Was this the golden haired woman who came to visit me? Some type of bright red liquid was coming from her mouth, head, and arms. Her skin was still soft and pink, but her eyes no longer looked lifeless. Instead, they were cold and dim, as if the part of her that reminded me of my dreams had left. I continued forward, soon coming across even more bodies. Their flesh smeared, burnt, broken, and mangled among the debris and erupting hot flames. One body along the wall was fully enveloped in the light. A sizzling dark pile was all that remained of the once soft skinned being; its face frozen with a look of sheer terror.

Creeping along the debris, I heard a feint voice much like the people who spoke the common tongue. Making my way to a large part of a wall which had toppled over, I saw a young man pinned beneath some stones. He was moaning, laying face up, eyes closed. His skin was still pale like the others, but he had small streams of the crimson liquid flowing out from his body. Leaning in closer, I studied his features; his ridged nose, his short brown hair, and his round face. The man yelled out as I leaned in farther, my hand supporting myself on the rock. It was then I had noticed that the same rock I was leaning on was also on top of his legs. The young man opened his eyes; a look of pure madness was upon his face. I could hear feint noises like he was trying to speak, but no words came out. My ears picked up another sound. I began to hear the thumping of something rapid in his chest. A constant beating or thumping was growing louder. The man gasped again, this time I removed my claws from the rock and he winced in relief. The internal thumping continued.

I thought maybe he wanted help from the rocks. So, grabbing hold of his upper half, I used my large claws to get a firm grip onto his shoulders. The red water squirted from the place where I held him. The man screamed, this time much louder than before. Pulling on his arms once more, I saw more of the red water flowing onto my claws. Yanking one final time, I felt my claws crushing something in his body. Upon hearing several more cracks I noticed the man opened his mouth and collapsed. His eyes were open, but his body refused to move. I tried to rouse him again, tapping and pulling on his body to free him, but more of his flesh came apart like loose paper, the red liquid now making large puddles on the floor. Slightly dazed, I walked away from the man and continued onward. I was trying to comprehend what had happened, but decided it was best to focus on escaping this place, before the walls and rocks fell on me as well.

The temperature was rising the further I walked. I couldn't risk stopping anymore, but my mind pestered me to take advantage of my newly acquired freedom. With this kind of opportunity to escape, also seem to rouse a suppressed feeling of curiosity. Along the way, I found myself stopping briefly in front of other doorways and cells very much like my own though containing no one within. I had stopped in front of one large glass window, where I could hear some noise unlike anything I'd heard before. The door was damaged, but offered enough room for me to peer inside without having to open it further. At first, I saw nothing, but then something moved along the back wall. Trapped like I was, I felt a hint of fear from this creature. Pacing back and forth along the wall, it seemed to have a much skinnier frame than mine. Peering closer through the gap, I noticed it had a body and texture much different than any others I've seen. Its skin was smooth and greenish in color. It's face baring four-eyes. I spoke through the door, trying to get its attention. The creature suddenly froze. Crouching low it lifted its head in my direction. Standing perfectly still, I watched. The creature leaped. A single claw jabbed through the small door hole. Quickly stepping back to avoid the attack, I almost tripped over myself. The creature's body hit the door hard, but it held firm. The claw scratched and dug into the metal as a high-pitched screeching noise came from within. I felt the same feeling as when the burning flames hit my arm. Only this time it was coming from my ears. I left immediately, escaping the attack and calls.

Finding myself in front of a much larger door, I stopped and watched as some dark figures within were wrestling around on the ground, throwing their arms at each other. Some of the people inside the shadowy room fell to the ground. Suddenly, a very tall, muscular creature leapt from the ground. Growling and heaving it noticing me. Quickly it ran up to the cell bars. When the light from the flames lit up its face I was able to see short white hair covering its entire body. Some spots of skin were pink on its face and stomach. The creature stood firm, its two long pointed ears focused ahead, while its deep emerald eyes never blinked. I was also motionless. The red liquid was splattered over its face and claws, dripping down its chin as it continued to breathe heavily. The creature stretched its mouth open to almost double that of its face. Large white fangs lined the inside of its mouth. Averting my head slightly, I watched as it followed my own motions, its emerald eyes shifting as I took a step back. I felt like it was studying me, just like the golden woman or short man had previously done. Eventually, the creature shifted its attention behind and ran off. It's figure disappearing into the blackness.

Leaving, I soon arrived at a dead end where I heard a large booming sound. Turning to see what it was, I noticed a huge ball of light coming from the way I'd just come. Running down the next passageway I came to, I soon stopped in front of another wall. Another blast of immeasurable sound and light exploded in front of me.

Crawling on my back, I opened my eyes. At first, I had thought that I was wrapped up in the flames and would end up motionless and charred like all the others, but my body was slowly being warmed by a different sort of light, and I could breathe fresh air again. As some time passed my eyes cleared up and I was able to bear witness to what I had been dreaming of for nearly all my life.

Brightness and shapes stretched for miles similar to those in my dreams. Soft white clouds decorated the sky above. Greens and browns blanketed the ground beneath my sore feet. And in front of me sprawled tall objects both green and yellow, spreading their small prickly arms skyward, as if attempting to reach the sun. The beauty I once beheld only in my dreams, were indeed a real place. Shackled no longer, I breathed in a sigh of relief. Turning around I watched as the structure behind me soon became swallowed up in several more blasts. Large flames and smoke enveloped what was once my old home. Wanting nothing more to do with the place, I immediately fled; my destination unknown. Promising to myself I would never return.

CHAPTER
-1-

King Tiolt extended a gesture of good faith towards the only other man he'd consider his equal. Sir Almrich, prince of the riverlands, and skillful tactician. The two stood in silence, measuring each other's skills.

But, what's this!

A group of Shadow Pact thugs – a ragged group of merciless men, sellswords, and cutthroats- emerging from the thicket and overlooking tree tops; each of them without honor, justice, or pride. They came barreling out from the dark corners of the forest, axes, knives, and arrows all aimed with sinister intentions.

"Sir Almrich!" King Tiolt shouted, drawing his silver sword. "I had taken you for an honorable man, not a coward who hires worms to do his bidding."

The knight sneered, crooking his lips, "Why fight honorably only to die? When I can just as easily dispatch you with a few copper coins?" Tiolt parried his first assailant, a scruffy dark haired man, barely older than himself. Circling around the trunk, he blocked again, and then stabbed for the man's open chest, his silver sword tasting its first victim. Sir Almrich slowly backed away, his white steed snorting and growing anxious as the fighting grew louder and closer.

King Tiolt, easily slew another two men, both fell to the ground as he walked over their corpses, continuing his sword dance. Carefully and methodically he was inching his way towards knight, his own glimmering sword in hand, eyes fixated towards his advancing rival.

Aiming his bloody covered sword down upon the knight, close enough for him to smell the blood of his fallen goons. This agitated him fuelling his temper. Sir Almrich lifted his rapier high. The sword was embroidered with four cranes meeting at the center of the pummel. He spat at the king, "You believe you fight for honor!"

Tiolt stood quietly.

Sir Almrich continued, "My own daughter slain by rebels!"

"Rebels, whom you fed with false promises," he responded.

Sir Almrich now as furious as ever shouted, "If you would've accepted the deal you could've had everything! So, I ask you..." he paused as his sword wobbled in his shaking hands. "What do you fight for?"

King Tiolt took one last look behind him at the bloody sight of those who'd fallen; his sword still pointing at Sir Almrich's throat. The king lifted his sword high into the air, "I fight for..."

"Tiolt!" The call came from the overgrown path behind him. Recognizing the voice he lowered the branch held tightly in his hands, moaning in the process.

Looking up from the riverbank, his cousin, Lara, came out from the bramble, adjusting her wrinkled cream blouse, and picking the leaves and small twigs from her shiny long brown hair.

"You know, I hate it when you follow me," grumbled Tiolt.

Lara carefully slid down the bank. Small pebbles and slick grass preventing her soft padded shoes from gaining any sort of friction. Inching down the slope; careful as to not letting her skirt get muddy, she called, "What are you doing down here? You know father doesn't like it when you play near the river."

Tiolt jabbed the worn stick into the mud, prodding at clay and stones as his cousin continued her decent until she was standing in front of him. "Nothing" he answered.

"Well come on then," she stressed, extending a hand, "I came to get you for dinner."

"It's still light out," Tiolt whined. "I'm gonna go up the bank a little more."

"No you won't." demanded Lara, "mother will take it out on both of us if you dawdle too long." Tiolt started walking away, his long stick in hand, carefully skimming the bank for whatever looked remotely interesting.

Growing angry, she bit her lip and hiked up her skirt after him. "Wait for me then!" she barked, trying her best to hold up the brown folds, while running along the uneven bank after her foolish cousin.

43

punched him in the arm.

"It's just a stupid river," she blurted.

Tiolt stopped, eyeing a large half-buried stone in the bank. Washing it off, he then preceded to hand it to his cousin. The warm rock was clean, grey, and seemed to have been broken from a much larger stone at one point. Lara looked confused as she eyed the misshapen stone in her tiny hand. "Uncle told me that this place used to be a large quarry," Tiolt said, continuing to walk slowly forward. "As the city grew, the quarry vanished and this river was all that was left. That stone, and many just like it, were here long before any of us were. Long before the river, the city, and even before our ancestors." Lara was about to toss the rock aside, but Tiolt spotted her, yanking it back. "Even if we don't remember what went on back then, this rock does. We must return it to its birth place." He gently let the rock slip from his hands and tumble down the cliff until it splashed into the calm waters below.

"It's just a stupid rock," she insisted.

Tiolt continued walking. "Yes it is."

Lara skipped farther up ahead, towards the open field. Purple lilacs and wildflowers swayed in the open air. Slowing down his pace, he then continued over some steep hills, where a large patch of condensed trees, bushes, and thicket formed a blanket beneath the cliff. Tiolt approached the ledge carefully. His mind set on the horizon and dancing waters below.

Suddenly, the dirt shifted from under his foot. He could feel the ground giving way. Without warning he slipped off the edge, hands desperately clasping for anything. Grass, rocks, a branch, nothing could hold his weight. Tumbling down the slope, loose rocks, mud, and sand blew up in his face, arms, and backside. Protecting his face as he flipped, he closed his eyes as he continued to roll and slide down the hill, till eventually he collided into the deep thicket. Opening his eyes and re-orienting himself, he began to feel sore and ripe with bruises. He had a few cuts and scrapes on his arms and could feel his whole back and buttocks throbbing with pain.

The grass and weeds were tall and disorienting. His head was throbbing so much that he had to crawl, trying to escape the brushy, snagging maze-like brush. With hands sore, he finally managed to pull himself to his knees. Calling out for his cousin he found his voice also carried no strength.

Continuing forward, he started to see water. He then noticed the far bank on the other side. It was a little far, but barely visible as the setting sun came down overhead. Wading into the muck, he came closer to the edge of the bank, the water felt cool and refreshing on his sore legs and muscles. His hands squished through soft mud and sand. Hearing a soft splash ahead, he kept quiet, gazing out toward the far bank again. Something stirred in the distant waters.

A dark hulk gently rose from beneath the water. It's frame larger than himself, maybe larger than a small horse. It seemed to be heading out onto the bank. Two large arms swayed and shifted as it pulled its body out from the water. Tiolt kept quiet. Unsure of what he was witnessing was actually real or something he was imagining.

Watching without noise, he continued to watch the creature making his way towards a large cistern entrance. His uncle mentioned the city cistern system exiting near the river and surrounding pastures, but as usual he paid them no mind. And now the creature, or whatever it was, was climbing into one. It's large dark frame highlighted just briefly by the setting sun, before being covered in the shadows of the hills and disappearing into the sewer.

Tiolt gulped; his eyes and mind still unsure of what he'd just seen.

Lara called his name from on top the hillside. Again and again, he could hear her calls getting closer, but was still unable to respond. His emotions began to overwhelm him. The sudden urge to follow this creature, get closer to it, raced through his head.

Pulling himself up higher, he waded through the river, his head low trying to avoid being spotted by his cousin. This was his chance to get away for awhile. The river bank came closer into view. The imposing entrance was gently trickling out water. He looked back to see if his cousin was behind him. She was not. Crawling closer, he grabbed hold of the stone pipe. The dark chilling tunnel seemed to call out to him, until he managed enough courage to stand up and stare back into the void.

Taking one last look back he climbed up into the entrance.

CHAPTER
-2-

The cistern reeked of the foulest things Tiolt could imagine. As much as he could muster, he pressed his nose and mouth tight. The light grew darker, soon he was fumbling his way through the twisting pipes and sludge filled water. The creature was not far from him. He could feel it, sense it. The sounds of the hulking beast echoed along the cylindrical passageways; a feint light up ahead steered him towards an uncertain future. Curiosity was not the only emotion he was fighting. His very mind -his once best friend and most treasured possession- was beginning to turn on him. Feeling a sudden chill, he looked back, shadowy figures danced and stretched eerily along the walls. Ahead he saw eyes or faces where there previously had not. His heart raced, clang desperately to the edges, his back firmly against the sides of the sewer, trying to keep a cool head. His hands and legs trembled as he concentrated ahead. Careful not to step into anything or touch the slime or many rats that passed by, he wadded deeper into thick pools of muck.

A light grew larger ahead. He hesitated, frozen in fear. The creature's shadow was also in front of him, cascading along the tunnel walls. All of a sudden the silhouette dashed forward. Tiolt quickly moved ahead, praying he could catch up to it, or forever be lost forever in the sewers.

The light ahead grew in size and warmth as he approached. He could now hear the sound of rushing water. Turning another corner he stopped again, this time in front of a large open room. It was a grand chamber of pipes and various waterfalls all pouring down into one large, ominous hole. A large pit was at the center of the chamber, gushing water was pouring around him.

There was no sign of the creature. Looking around, he saw many other passageways. The creature could have led him into a trap. Swallowing hard, he began to inch his way around the slippery water pipes looking for the best course to proceed.

Knowing the creature to be large, he spotted the biggest entrance, determined that it was the best option.

Crawling up the side of another pipe, the warm water began to soak his pants, legs, and arms. The brown and black water –though cleaner than most of what he walked through- still stank of rotting food and all manner of dead things.

About halfway along, he was now completely soaked. Turning around was now not an option. Looking behind he peered down into the large gaping hole. The waterfalls around him disappeared into the blackness, and where it went, or how far, he didn't know. Reaching for the next thing to hold onto he began to feel his arms growing tired. His foot slipped on the rim. Catching himself with his free hand, his heart raced. His knees scrapped along the hard stone. He bit his lip to hold back the pain. Wounds from his earlier tumble down the cliff were beginning to flare up again. Desperately trying to ignore it, he scampered up until he found his footing. Suddenly, he slipped again. The gushing water became too strong. He could feel the water pushing against his sore body. The darkness below was hungry, it called out to him. He tried to ignore the chilling sounds, but kept feeling his strength fade.

"Ahhhhhh!"

Tiolt fell.

With a jolt, something caught his arm.

A sharp pain jutted along his shoulder all the way to his wrist. Crying out in pain, he felt his eyes getting tired and head throbbing. He began to spot blood trickle down his arm, absorbing into his shirt. Looking up, he noticed a large brown and green claw clamping down on his arm. His body was weak, his head still splattered by the falling water.

At once, his body was beginning to be pulled out from the waterfall. With his strength depleted, his eyes too heavy to see anymore, and the pain unbearable, he collapsed.

A red flickering hue greeted him as he slowly awoke. Finding himself dry, and growing increasingly warmer, he noticed several candles were placed next to him. His body still felt incredibly sore, but at least he was beginning to feel safe.

Supporting his back, he began to scour his surroundings. The room was well lit, wide, clean, and littered with books, metal tools, melted wax, various pots and piles of bone, fish bones to be more exact. Slowly his imagination began to piece the scenes together. He wasn't as much scared, as he was surprised that something could make its home down here.

Just then a door swung open from his left, and a hulking figure was standing in the doorway. Wanting to scream, he bit his lip again. He tried to focus with his eyes, but failed due to a lack of strength. The creature shuffled its way in, closing the door with one large claw. It stepped closer before taking a seat near a small chair and fur carpet. The candles in the room were now presenting the creature in full light.

"What are you?" Tiolt stared, his eyes and body frozen.

The creature was large, maybe twice the height of his uncle. Its body was dark brown and green colored, resembling that of a large shell of a crab or lobster. Its massive legs were as thick as tree trunks. Two large arms with enormous claws and pinchers dangled at its sides. It had a flat face, a small flat nose, and two tiny pitch black eyes, almost making it look half-human and half-crustacean. Finally, it had bumps or small warts all over its body, along with two short antennae gently moving independently on its head.

Tiolt cowered as the creature shuffled closer to him. His massive body seemingly growing larger the closer it got. It's small black eyes unblinkingly, its chest slowly heaving as it gazed at the small boy now two feet in front of him.

The creature extended a large pincher towards Tiolt.

"Ahhhh, keep away from me!"

The creature stopped. It backed away, almost like it understood, then remained motionless as Tiolt opened his eyes, finally noticing his arm was bandaged. Examining it, he touched the wrapped shoulder where he remembered being pierced. The blood was still there, but his sleeve and skin was wrapped with bandages along with some large leaves and a strange white substance. His body still felt sore, but his arm didn't hurt quite as much. He shifted his eyes back to that of the crab-like creature.

"Did you," he began softly, "that is, dress my wound?"

The creature remained still.

"Thank you," Tiolt managed to stutter.

"Ir mor," the beast replied, startling Tiolt.

Reclaiming his wits, Tiolt repeated, "Thank you", rubbing and pointing to his bandaged arm.

The creature shifted, "Ir mor." Its voice was low, resounding across the entire room.

Tiolt leaned himself up higher, his back cracked, but he was beginning to feel greater comfort now. Wanting to keep still, he asked, "What are you?"

"Who you?" it asked in return.

Now, further shocked that it could speak the common tongue, he placed a hand upon his chest speaking slowly, "I am Tiolt. I live across the river, near Tarrinfield, do you know where that is?"

The creature stirred. Its eyes unblinking as it arched its back seemingly to stretch. "Here home." It spoke. "Bersool"

"This place is Bersool, or your name is Bersool?" Tiolt asked.

Raising a claw to its chest it tapped, "Name Bersool."

Tiolt smiled at the mimicking behavior. Imagining what his cousin might do, if he they met. Then he remembered his cousin. "She must be looking for me." He clamored. "If she tells my uncle I'll never be allowed outside again!"

Tiolt struggled to lift his shaking body up, it seemingly resisting all of his commands to budge, perhaps wishing to remain where it was, in the warm relaxing room. Causing some throbbing pain in his spine, he finally got to his feet. The creature also rose up, its massive height now huge and foreboding. Ignoring the beast he began to head towards the door. The creature grabbed his arm, Tiolt yelped as his skin was pinched in its massive grip. "Stop that!" he yelled, "It hurts!"

The creature let go, tucking its head in shame. "No hurt." it spoke.

He rubbed his arm adding, "You need to watch those claws of yours."

Shuffling to the door, the creature avoided eye contact.

Tiolt once again looked around the room, "Do you know the way out? Remember, back to the river?" he tried motioning with his arms.

The creature lifted its arms again, but this time towards the door. "Bersool, leave."

This time, the creature grabbed at him again.

Closing his eyes, he prepared for the worst, but soon felt his body rise up in the air. The creature was lifting him up, high onto his shoulders, the ceiling almost scrapping his head. Tiolt had to keep his head low as they ducked beneath the door frame and out into a large shaft.

"Don't drop me now," Tiolt demanded, "And whatever you do, watch where you put those claws."

They began to march through several lengths of pipe. The tunnels were hot and damp like before, but this time he wasn't treading through the stench and stagnant waters. Tiolt felt safe riding atop this Bersool creature. What was it, where did it come from? He didn't care if he ever got an answer.

Tiolt almost fell asleep, when the creature stopped without warning, jostling him. "What is it?" he asked, looking down.

The creature began walking again, hunching further as the walls grew tighter and more claustrophobic. "Someone calls for you," he said.

"A call for me?" asked Tiolt, mostly to himself.

Suddenly, he too could hear a feint call. It sounded like...Lara.

The calls of his cousin began to echo down the tunnels, growing closer and louder the more they pressed on. So, she was still looking for me, he thought. "Bersool, would you like to meet my cousin?" he politely addressed his new friend.

The creature kept walking; its pace slow and steady. "Cousin?" it spoke.

Tiolt replied shaking his head, "Never mind, I'm sure she would love to meet you. Just let me talk to her first."

The end of the tunnel came without much warning. The orange light from the setting sun greeted them. Bersool gently let Tiolt slide off his back once they were safely outside. The cool water was a refreshing change of pace against the stifled, foulness which flowed from inside the cistern. Tiolt breathed the fresh air again, as Bersool lowered his body, remaining motionless, his attention focused on something near the bank.

Tiolt turned, also curious as to what the creature was staring at.

Lara.

Terror was in her eyes, and she screamed.

Turning around, she ran back up the bank as fast as her legs could go. Tiolt laughed, looking back at Bersool. "Well, I'm sure she'll warm up to you in time."

As he began to run after her he shouted back, "I'll meet you back here tomorrow!"

The creature stood silent in the waters. His eyes steady, as he watched the young boy disappear over the hillside.

"I don't care what you call him," his cousin fumed, "He's a monster! You want me to be eaten don't you?"

Tiolt pulled her along the trail down near the soft river bed. Though she was severely hesitant last night, she sort of warmed up to the idea that such as creature might actually be friendly.

"Here's where I first saw him," Tiolt pointed out. A smile lit up his face, while a mark of cleverness also arouse.

"Yeah," Lara commented, and right over there is where I had the honor of meeting him too."

Tiolt began to tug her down closer to the water laughing, "Yeh you about pissed yourself real good. Come on then," he pressed, "I told him, we'd be back today."

"You mean that beast actually listened to what you have to say?" she asked humorously, fidgeting as they both entered the shallow water's edge.

They continued to tread through the river calm and carefully. Stepping on large rocks to avoid the muddier parts, they eventually arrived at the cistern entrance.

Lara rested on a nearby rock up the side of the bank, watching her cousin peer into the large pipe. He tucked his head in closer, hollering for his the beast. His voice echoed, vibrating off the walls, causing the water to ripple.

"Maybe we both made the whole thing up?" she said growing agitated, while looking towards the soft white clouds in the bright afternoon sky.

"You gonna pretend you didn't see him then, are you?" replied Tiolt, facing her with his hands crossed. "I'm sure he's around. I'll check farther down the river, maybe there's another entrance."

Lara rolled her eyes, before taking notice at some bubbles beginning to rise out from middle of the river. "Tiolt," she said nervously.

Her cousin also took notice. He shuffled away from the entrance and up the bank closer to his cousin. The bubbles continued to grow larger, and now heading their way. The two children's hearts began to race. Each of them huddling closer, watching the bubbles creep closer as well.

The bubbles stopped before the bank, and suddenly the back of a creature rose up out of the water. An eruption of water splashed along with it. The creature lifted its head as it began to approach. Lara clung to her cousin in fear, he mouth open as he body trembled. Tiolt held her tight, a small amount of fear also rising as the creature's menacing frame walked up the bank.

Its hulking green and grey mass shifted and swayed, until it stopped a mere foot or so in front of them. Water was dripping down its body, soaking the sand and dirt before them. The creature stood in silence, its antennae twitching as its dark eyes observed the world around it.

Tiolt was the first to speak. "Bersool, it's me, Tiolt. Remember?"

The crab beast narrowed its eyes, slowly kneeling down to get a better view of the tiny shaking humans.

"This is my cousin, Lara. You know, the girl who pissed herself yesterday." Lara nudged her cousin hard in the side with her elbow.

"Lara," the creature resonated.

Tiolt continued, loosening his grip on his cousin, "We've come back. Just like I promised, remember?"

Bersool stood back up, and then began to head towards the

tunnel entrance. Tiolt followed the beast, hollering, "As much as I would love to see your home again," he checked back with his cousin. "My cousin would like to take a walk outside. We can talk, get to know each other." His still frightened cousin nodded in silence.

Turning to face them both, Bersool was silent. Eventually, he walked back over to them, his enormous feet leaving large indents into the dirt and mud.

"Here," Tiolt extended his hand, "Let's head this way."

They walked along the windswept grass, passing by a few scattered trees and loose rocks decorating the country landscape. Tiolt remained in front, leading the way ahead with stick in hand, while Lara followed closely by Bersool, remaining half obscured by Bersool's giant shadow.

"Where do you come from?" she blurted out, while looking almost straight up.

Taking such large and slow strides, she was almost jogging to keep up with the giant as they walked. Bersool, noticing her poor attempts to catch up, slowed his own pace before responding, "Where do you come from?"

Lara placed her hand to her chin, "My mom."

Bersool blinked for seemingly the first time. Mimicking her gesture he said, "My father."

Lara looked a little confused, but continued her barrage of questions. "How did you get so big?"

"How did you get so small?" he responded.

Giggling she skipped along, "I may be small now, but I'm constantly growing. Mom says I eat more than my father sometimes."

Tiolt stopped up ahead to pick up some small rocks he found. Bersool and Lara watched as he tossed a few down the slope and out towards the calm water.

A scarlet and blue butterfly landed on Bersool's shoulder, only lingering a moment before fluttering off. Lara gazed at the insect, as did Bersool. Sharing a brief moment of joy, Lara prodded, "Do you live out here. All by yourself, I mean?"

"Bersool enjoy alone," he answered.

"I was alone once too," she said. "Tiolt came to live with us, and now I mostly play with him." She watched as her cousin was running up to catch them. "He's not so bad," she giggled once more.

The three of them continued until the sun was growing closer to the treetops. They had walked back and forth along the bank watching fish, insects, birds, and other wildlife. Bersool never seemed to grow tired, but Lara was beginning to complain about her feet, while Tiolt was growing anxious to eat something.

Being reminded of home, they both walked with their new friend back to the cistern entrance where they first met.

"Bersool," Tiolt started, "Would you like to come back with us. Maybe meet my aunt and uncle. They're really nice people..."

Bersool waved his claw, shaking his head slowly. "Ter a'ros," he said.

"Did he just speak dwarven?" Lara asked, her eyes lighting.

"Kind of," Tiolt tried to remember, "Ir Amor"

"Ir mor," mimicked Bersool.

"Yes, that means you're most kind, or you're welcome, in Dwarven." His cousin flaunted. Remember the dwarven books that Old Greykiin showed us last spring?"

"Who remembers that?" joked Tiolt.

"I do," she replied. She now looked at Bersool smiling, "You can speak Dwarven?"

Bersool stood in silence.

"Hmm," she said, "Now we have to show him to mom and dad."

"I don't think he wants to go." Tiolt shook.

Bersool looked at them both, and then said, "Bersool stay here. In time, Bersool meet others."

"What are you talking about?" pleaded Lara.

Tiolt grabbed her arm, "Perhaps, we shouldn't rush this."

His cousin frowned at him, and then pouted.

"What I mean is," he quickly interjected, "If we showed Bersool to them now, they'd scream like we did."

Again his cousin pouted.

"Look, we'll slowly bring up the idea over the next few days, and then when they've adjusted well enough, they can meet, deal?"

"Fine," she nodded

"Good," he said.

After saying their goodbyes, Tiolt gathered his belongings then grabbed hold of his cousin's hand as they started to ford the river back to the other side. Waving from the far they watched as Bersool mimicked their gesture before climbing into the cistern and disappearing from sight.

"And to think that gentle beast is afraid of people," Lara spoke. "He knows Dwarven, is kind, and he's super huge. I mean, did you see those claws?"

Tiolt held her tightly, as they moved across the rapid water. "He is fascinating," he added. "But I'm still worried."

"Whatever for?" responded Lara. "We are friends with a gigantic crab beast who lives alone -albeit in a rather smelly place- can speak, and didn't eat you when you first met him."

Arriving on the bank Tiolt concluded, "That's precisely why we should be a little careful."

CHAPTER
-3-

Smearing the sweat from his brow, Tiolt began noting the dampness and humidity the day was becoming. Lara, looking equally hot and sundered, had her hair cross braided back and tied in a knot. Today she was wearing short slacks folded up from the bottom baring her skin to the extremities of nature. Both of them eager to complain, but while Bersool carried forward, showing no signs of tiredness or fatigue.

Soon, their new friend guided them along a shadier path, one that was covered in large trees, ferns, and vines. Tall oaks and skinny birch trees provided a roof to guard them along the fallen nut and dried leaf trail.Arriving before a long slender wooden bridge, Tiolt and Lara paused, looking down the sides. It overlooked a small creek that was filled with tall grass and rocks, the creek probably long since dried up. Tiolt started to take the lead, when he noticed Bersool had stepped back. Together they heard the sound of horses drawing near. Lara grabbed Bersool's claw and began to lead him farther back amongst some bushes and low hanging branches; her cousin leaping down next to them.

Keeping low and quiet, they watched the bridge ahead. Soon, a pair of light brown horses trotted into view. Behind them appeared a traditional wagon, followed by two smaller carts and six men carrying sacks and barrels over their heads.

The horses pulled the wagon up to the bridge before slowing down as the front rider turned his head back to the men whom followed. Tiolt and his cousin watched nervously. Worried Bersool might make a noise; they both looked at him only to realize that he had the same patient stare he always had.

The carts and wagon slowed as it approached the wooden bridge. The man atop the wagon tugged at the reins, guiding and controlling the horses, which began neighing and seemed frightened.

"Easy now, easy," The wagon master exclaimed pulling the reins.

"Slow it down some!" a man behind yelled to the front.

"I don't think the bridge is what they're scared of," replied the driver.

As the caravan approached the other side, Bersool lifted his head. Tiolt took notice and tried to keep him from moving so much, pulling on his rough shell and arm. Lara meanwhile, also was looking worried. "Is it too late to turn around?" Tiolt whispered, "They might head left if we are lucky."

His cousin didn't reply. Her mind was too busy with undecided thoughts and visions of terrible outcomes if they were caught or how their giant friend might react.

Suddenly, Bersool lifted a claw causing the surrounding branches shake and rattle. Quickly Tiolt grabbed the arm, his feeble strength fighting desperately to get him to stop moving. "Dang it Bersool," he whispered, continuing to struggle against the overwhelming strength.

Lara and Tiolt, who fought to control their friend's movement, failed to notice the caravan taking the right most path, which was the same path they were hiding in close by.

"Look sir," one of the men called. "Up ahead in the bushes."

"Len, grab your spear. Might be our dinner," spoke the driver, pulling the reins, halting the horses.

The man named Len grabbed a spear from a nearby cart, then began heading in their direction, followed by a few other men close behind.

As they approached, it became evident to Tiolt that they had two options. Either they should run for it, and maybe the men wouldn't give chase or, they could just give up and hope for the best. Tiolt didn't have time to decide. Bersool was already standing up heading out from the cover and right into the path of the advancing men.

"Everyone get back!" Len shouted.

The giant creature now stood fully erect; his monstrous height and size matching that of a huge pillar or statue. He slowly took a few steps towards the frozen men, still clasping their weapons and watching as the creature's antennae spread out taking in the air. Tiolt and Lara could only remain motionless, crouched together, each one biting their lip and clenching their hands.

"Bersool," his voice erupted, slowly brought one claw to his chest.

The man in front pointed his spear fearing for his life. "What in the Nine Divine are you?" he stuttered, courage fading fast as his spear shook nervously in his hands. All of the men behind him were just as frightened.

Bersool once again tapped his chest, "Bersool," he repeated, taking a step forward. The man stumbled, trying to retreat. Gathering courage, the man pointed his spear at Bersool's chest.

"Get back! Stay back!" the man shouted.

Bersool took another half-step forward, his claws reaching out for the shaking human.

The man's eyes filled with fear. His arms and entire body were now vibrating uncontrollably, as a look of dread began to spread to even the men behind him.

Suddenly, and without warning, the man jutted his spear forward into Bersool's chest. The tip bounced off his rock hard skin. Bersool stood motionless.

Lara leapt out from the bushes. "Stop it!" she screamed, "He means you no harm."

The man heard her voice but couldn't see past the giant crab-like creature hovering over him. The wagon master, seeing the small girl, as well as Tiolt, whom now gave up his hiding place in order to come out, gave a holler. "Children, run for you lives!"

Tiolt and his cousin exchanged glances of confusion. "You have it wrong!" Tiolt called out. "He's gentle!"

His shout was unheard amongst the neighing horses, and the shouts from the fearful men behind. "Men," the driver shouted. "Protect those kids and kill that beast!"

"No!" shouted Lara attempting to run to Bersool's side. A man stepped forward, grabbing Lara's arm, trying to pull her over to him. Noticing the man, Tiolt raced ahead, attempting to intervene.

The man clasping the spear thrust towards the creature's stomach again. Each time the point bounced or ricocheted off the beasts' hard shell. Bersool ignored the man, instead focusing on Lara as she was wrestling with the stranger.

"Dar'en nii Lara!" yelled Bersool, his gigantic arms flinging up in a rage. The spear man got shoved aside, his claws pushing him effortlessly. Within a few bounds, Bersool was now standing on top of the man whom held onto Lara.

Within the next moment, his claws hammered down upon him, crushing the unaware man. Lara was let free, rescued by Tiolt as they both fell to the ground. Slightly dazed, she looked at her assailant who was now a bloody mess of broken bones and meat. Bersool looked at them. His face sincere, his eyes kind, and soon tears ran down her face.

Suddenly a man began slicing at Bersool's legs. The blade nicked and skidded off his hide. It wasn't until another man joined in cursing, that Bersool started to take notice. Attempting to grab the attackers, he waved and lunged with his pincers, however they were quick, able to out maneuver every attack. Surprised by the monsters tenacity, one man was caught off guard. Pinching the man around his torso, an entire claw lifted him into the air. The man screamed as his blood started pouring down to the ground as Bersool continued to hold onto him, attempting to grab the other man. Then, with a single motion, the man was flung hard into a large tree trunk.

The carriage driver became enraged, determined to bring down this creature who was slaughtering his men. He'd given up trying to save the children. Looking slightly confused, he noticed they were hiding behind the beast, as it continued to focus on the last man.

Bersool kicked the man tripping him up, before bringing his claws down onto his body. The pincers easily impaled the man's ribs, neck, and chest. He twitched, coughed up blood, and then collapsed.

"Run!" Tiolt shouted. "Bersool, Run!"

He seemed confused, his face and eyes innocent as the midnight sky. Lara could not muster a single word, while tears slowly rolled down her face. The only thing she could was, was clasp desperately to her cousin. Relaxing his stance, Bersool leapt into the foliage behind them.

Tiolt cradled his cousins' head against his chest. "Those men will want revenge." He whispered into her ear.

The driver, hollered to the last of his men, "That cursed beast slaughtered three of my best men. The king must be informed!"

Turning his wagon around, the entire caravan sped away back along the bridge and road.

"There's going to a hunt," Tiolt spoke softly.

"Are they going to kill him?" his tearful cousin replied.

"They'd have to find him first," he responded. "Come on," he began to lift his cousin up from the dirt. "You're parents will be worried."

Lara nodded, rubbing her eyes clean and sniffling as they walked back along the shady path.

"I'm scared for him," she said.

"I know," he added, "I am too."

CHAPTER
-4-

"Right over this way," claimed the curd trader. His muddy boots and faded blue robes snagged on low hanging branches, roots, and almost tripping moving through the brush.

He was leading a group of men down to the river. Pointing across the water he continued to ramble, "Seven feet he was, no, eight or nine at least." His hands waving about as he wadded up the bank. "Huge claws, monstrous ones. Poor old Thom; snipped him in half he did."

The trader stopped when he reached the other side. Along the bank the leader of the group hunched over, scanning and panning the soil and gentle flow of the muddy river water. Another man approached him quietly from behind, staying back enough so as to give him space. Now resting his weight on a large boulder, the leader continued to watch the trader as he pointed things out.

"Right here!" his hands now highlighting the large cistern entrance. "We tracked him here." The frail man stuck his head inward, his spine shivering as he quickly pulled it right back out and headed back. "Couldn't of gone too far, I'd reckon."

The leader, resembling a hunter wasn't paying him any attention. Instead he began scouring the area, walking with his second in command.

"Thank you Keerwit," The hunter at last spoke, "You can go home now."

The caravan man stumbled closer, splashing through the water and fumbling about. "But, what about the creature." he asked. "You guys going to smoke him out? Maybe set a large trap or something? I'd reckon..."

The hunter interrupted him, "Keerwit what is it that you do?"

Tripping over his own tongue he said, "I...uh...transport shipments of goat cheese and wine, why do you ask?"

"And what is it I do?" the hunter kept going.

The man looked a bit confused. "You uh, hunt things."

"I hunt things," the hunter nodded.

Taking a break to speak with his other men, the hunter continued to ignore the trader and his ramblings. "Thank you Keerwit, you may go home now," said the hunter.

His second in command pulled the trader away and guided him back up the path. The hunter approached the wide entrance to the sewer. Laying his hands against the cold material, he traced and studied the edges.

Tiolt and Lara raced towards the cistern entrance. It was late in the evening and visibility was starting to deteriorate. The bright purple and orange hues of the sky greeted them as they ran through the thick forest and out onto the hills near the river. Arriving at the bank the two halted, almost knocking Lara into the river below. Torch lights were moving up and along the opposite coast. Tiolt put a hand to his forehead. "Those must be the hunters." He said quietly. "Let's wait till they enter, then we'll follow along behind."

Helping each other down the bank, Lara whispered, "We must help Bersool."

"What do you think we're doing?" responded Tiolt. "You think I like going back in that retched shit filled cistern?"

Approaching some bushes near the water's edge, they watched across the river as the men were beginning to head into the tunnel. After a few moments, their torches had all but disappeared inside. Checking around, Tiolt then led his cousin carefully across the river. High above the moon was half-hidden from view.

Entering the tunnel once more, Tiolt was still unprepared for the dark and alien-like atmosphere. His hands nervously guided him along the walls as he helped support his cousin through the maze of slime and sewage. A few times Lara felt the urge to scream, her cousin holding her mouth shut. They crept along making sure to stay far enough behind the feint lights from the hunters up ahead. Every once in awhile some voices echoed. Some were too soft to understand, while others were merely fragments of a sentence or casual conversation.

As the children approached a fork in the tunnel, they were forced to once again hunker down and wait for the hunter's lights to continue past. Hanging together, they waited nervously. Suddenly, they could feel a soft breathing coming behind them. Tiolt craned his neck to get a better view. Bersool was crouched behind them. One claw extended outward, gently tapping Lara on the shoulder. Tiolt braced tried his best to brace her for what was surely to come. Tears filled her eyes, as she wobbled over to him, clasping him in a warm embrace. Bersool's eyes blinked as he lowered his head.

"Bersool!" said Tiolt quietly. "Those hunters..."

Lara interrupted, "Bersool you need to run. Go somewhere safe." Her arms still clung to the bumpy shell that was his chest.

"Safe here," Bersool said, tapping his free claw against the smooth walls of the sewer.

"No." Tiolt shook. "Follow us, maybe we can smuggle you back to our home."

His cousin was still crying as she peered deep into her friends' eyes. "Please," she spoke.

Bersool focused on the dark tunnel ahead. Tiolt also now heard something, but he couldn't quiet tell what it was.

Tugging on the children, Bersool quietly led them down a different passageway. Together they quietly shuffled along the smaller pipes, his large shell and rough body fitting just barely fitting. The two children struggled to keep up, slipping on moss and slime, soaking their pants and shoes with the filth that littered and flowed along the bottom.

Eventually, they arrived at the same large pit that Tiolt encountered Bersool. The gushing water now roared overhead, drowning out their movements. The children stopped, watching as their friend began looking around nervously.

Tiolt grabbed his cousin's hand, guiding her carefully along a rail.

A man stepped forth from the shadows on the far side. Extending a torch out he said, "Now the trap is complete."

The man whistled, calling another three more men who approached from the other tunnels, blocking the other passages, each one grinning with torch in hand.

"Come to me children," the hunter said. "That beast is dangerous."

"He's not dangerous!" shouted Tiolt.

"Oh," the hunter responded, "He's killed and injured at least three people. Are you willing to risk your own life?"

Tiolt held his cousin's hand tighter, the flowing water rushing beneath their feet. Bersool shifted his body around, studying the men whom had them surrounded. Some had swords drawn, other had rope, knives, and an assortment of bags and gear. The tall slender hunter in the front was only carrying a single torch. Dressed in a worn shirt, pants, and belt, he calmly expressed, "What do you plan to do with him?"

"He's our friend," shouted Lara in retaliation.

The hunter smiled, "That he is. But, I am afraid even friends must answer for their sins."

Suddenly, a large gush of water came flowing from the tunnel behind them, a hunter stepped aside, as the water poured down upon Lara's back. Tiolt tried to pull her over to him, but her feet slipped from under her, and she was pulled free of his grasp. Screaming, she slipped down catching the ledge with one hand as the water continued to poor over her. At once, Bersool lowered his claw close to her.

"Lara!" her cousin yelled.

The hunter nodded to the man on his right. While preoccupied, a hunter jutted a long slender knife into the hinge of Bersool's underside, where his shell-like body was softer and much weaker. The blade pierced easily, causing Bersool to flip around, smacking the man away with his other claw. With a force like several large hammers, he knocked the man to the floor, shattering his leg, ribs, and thigh.

"Bersool!" Tiolt yelled, watching helplessly as Lara was losing her grip. Bersool, once more bent down attempting to save her. She reached for the claw, bounced her body around, and forced her eyes shut. Meanwhile, Tiolt kept calling her.

Suddenly, Bersool let out another bellow. Another hunter had fired several arrows into the unprotected places along Bersool's side.

"Stop it!" Tiolt yelled towards the leader. "He's trying to save her!"

The man remained still, his nerves unhindered by the events happening below. "And I'm trying to protect hundreds." He replied, though the gushing water muffled much of it.

This time, Bersool managed to grab hold of another hunter, the man screamed, as his claws tightened around the man's neck instantly severed his arteries. Bersool tossed the limp man over the rail, flinging him down into the watery depths below.

During the event, Bersool accidently bumped into Tiolt. The water carried him forward, knocking his head against the wall. Blood began to mix in with the water, as Bersool watched it trickle down Tiolt's forehead. He watched for a moment, before dashing towards a tunnel, pushing aside another hunter.

"Bersool!" Tiolt shouted, his hands clasping the back of his head. He began to feel dizzy, as he tried to focus on the direction his friend escaped to. The leader handed his torch to another man before he started to climb down to the lower platform. Another hunter wrapped a blanket around Tiolt as his vision faded and then passed out from exhaustion. The last thing he saw was the leader kneeling over the falls, bringing up his cousin in his arms. The tears from her eyes kept pouring, while she coughed up water. Unknowingly, she hugged her savior tightly around the neck.

CHAPTER
-5-

Lara found herself awakening in a warm and inviting setting. Lying beneath warm blankets she realized she was inside of a large tent. A table, some chairs, crates, and candles helped prevent a feeling of homesickness, and allowed her to be less afraid. Her eyes were still adjusting as she stretched her aching body from the night before. Ears still waterlogged, she combed her fingers through her tangled hair, pulling gently and tugging as straight as she could.

Her cousin came rushing in, wearing a white loose shirt and brown trousers. His embrace helped relieve stress until she started to worry over where they were and what would follow.

"Thank the nine you are safe," Tiolt spoke.

She nodded, reserving her strength, reassuring him no harm had come to her.

"We need to get out of here and find Bersool."

"Where are we?" Lara asked, looking around the beige tent.

"You are in our camp." A shadow moved from the opening."We're about seven miles from the cistern where the girl was saved, and about five from Dershire, where I believe you both are from."

Lara quickly hid behind her cousin, praying he hadn't noticed. The man stepped closer inside, revealing h tall and slender frame. He looked no older than his uncle, and had short dark brown hair slicked back, a brown over shirt and loose black pants.

"I want to go home," she cried; unable to hide any longer, wishing to be home again.

The hunter pulled over a chair, "We all want to go home." he said. After pouring two glasses of water and handing them to the children he continued, "Would you believe I miss my home as well?"

Tiolt rejected the offer for the both of them, "Just let us go."

The hunter sat up, adjusted his belt and shirt tucked into his pants, "By now you probably can assume I've been sent to hunt the creature. And you'd be correct in guessing so." The children remained still, as Tiolt spied around the room for an escape plan. The hunter took a sip from his own glass, before announcing, "I am a hunter, that's true, but, I'm also a father. I know that you both are tired, scared, and really want to go home. I'm even willing to take you home myself, once this matter is taken care of."

"You mean Bersool is taken care of?" Tiolt interjected.

"Is that the beast's name?" the hunter asked. "Is that *his* name, or is that the name you both came up with?"

"It's not his fault," piped in Lara.

The hunter bent over looking her square in the face. "Not his fault that he murdered a few men?"

Lara fell silent again. She let her thoughts wander; reminiscing of better, playful times they spent together. "He's our friend." shouted Tiolt.

The leader approached cautiously, "As you can see, your friends are safe." He called.

Tiolt heard his cousin cry as he turned toward the tent, watching as a man was pulling her out from the tent, securing her arms. Her face was red, but her eyes lit up in joy and fear as she saw her friend standing across the clearing, smiling as they were reunited.

"I mean you no harm." The leader hollered. "I heard about what you did to Thom and some of the other traders. I've come on behalf of the king to bring you in for the crimes you've committed."

Bersool kept silent; his eyes steady and ever watchful. Lara was shaking as she was led over to Tiolt where they both held hands and nervously watched.

"Can you understand me?" asked the leader.

"Ai," called Bersool. "Tyr no faarden hast vur kopen"

"Ah, dwarvish," said the hunter. "Hie kopen teiv Brannin, ust reskrieg braifel hur knoft."

The children looked in wonder, Lara whispering into her cousin's ear. "I told you it was dwarvish."

"Bersool, you need to leave now!" shouted Tiolt.

The hunter and Bersool kept talking. "Allow me to speak in the human tongue so your friends behind me can follow," spoke the hunter.

The beast nodded.

"Thank you," The hunter smiled. "You and I both know that this is the best option. These children still have a future. Dreams, choices, many other freedoms life offers. I promised them no harm, and as evidence I have already saved them when you yourself have chosen to abandon them."

Bersool glanced at the children. His friends were tired, crying, and fearful. Tiolt looked up, his eyes met Bersool's, and they both seemed to share a deeper understanding of one another. Tiolt nodded in understanding.

"Friends," Bersool spoke as clearly as ever.

He then walked forward, his massive hands low and at his sides. The hunter stepped back, leading Bersool into the center of the clearing. Tiolt and Lara were also led back by a hunter. Tiolt watched as hunters came out from the trees and surrounding thicket with ropes in hand. Bersool got to the center just as ropes flew over his body. Creating a makeshift net, they enveloped and ensnared the giant crab beast. Lara cried into Tiolt's chest. He was also holding back his own tears.

As the men gathered closer, Bersool knelt down crying once more, "Friends!"

Just as promised, the hunter personally escorted Tiolt and Lara back to their farmhouse on horseback. It was a bumpy and tearful ride, but the children comforted each other with memories and remembrances. The hunter occasionally glanced at the children trying to come up with something to say, though knowing that no matter what he tried to comfort them with, they would forever hate and despise him; a small price to pay for what needed to be done.

The evening soon arrived along with cool breezes. The dirt trail and light forest trees opened up to the farmlands and acres of vast acres of crop. "Our house is that second one in the distance," pointed Tiolt.

The hunter silently acknowledged, clasping the reins, and guiding the children home.

Lara's father opened the door, welcoming the children into his burly arms. Lara's mother had already prepared a vegetable stew and corn loaf, greeting them once they entered.

"I'm very sorry for any trouble, but these two were assisting me with some fence work near Gaoton Point." said the hunter, shaking hands.

"Ah," Tiolt's uncle replied. "So that's where the little sprouts were. I'm glad you kept them busy though," he chuckled, welcoming the hunter into the hall. "It's hard enough to get them to do any work around this place. This is my wife, Genneht."

"Please to me you, ah," sticking out her hand, waiting for a reply.

The hunter gave a courtesy, "Brannin, miss. Simply, Brannin."

"Please, come in and have a bite," she gestured. "The dinner table is already set."

Brannin was not one to refuse an offer and while the children were mostly depressed, trying to forget they ever knew this man, they kept quiet.

Lara's mother passed them each a bowl and slice of warm bread, "What's the matter, you act like you somebody died?" she joked.

Lara was deafly silent, while Tiolt spoke for her, "We just had a long day."

"Brannin," his uncle broke in, trying to lighten the mood. "You a handyman?"

"Yes, in a way," he replied smiling, "How did you know?"

"Oh, I know most everyone around here, but never seen you before. So, I thought you'd have to have come from elsewhere as a hired hand."

"I've done some work in the city."

"Well, I'm just glad these rascals didn't give you too much trouble." He rubbed the top of Tiolt's head. "Their mother spoils them, but I figure, as long as they come home with their hands dirty, that's good enough for me."

"You said they helped with fence work, Brannin?" said Genneht offering a third helping.

"Yes," the hunter replied. "If it wasn't for these two, I'd never be able to get my work done. I owe them."

"Pah," the uncle waved it off. "Consider this warm meal an even trade."

"Thank you," the hunter said while looking around the table. "For your hospitality and your assistance."

After the meal, the hunter said his goodbyes, and then jumped back onto his horse. The children retired early, both just wanting the day to be over with.

Late in the night, Lara snuck into her cousin's room. Whispering once inside, "Tiolt, we have to help Bersool."

Tiolt mumbled, trying to pretend he was sleeping. Lara, spotting the faker, jumped on his bed and body, "Come on, we just have to help him. He need us."

"I miss him too, but what do you want us to do? Tiolt rolled over. "Sneak out at night. Make our way to the city, trying to find him before it is too late?"

Lara's eyes lit up.

"Oh great, why did I say that?"

Lara and Tiolt got dressed and headed for the front door. They snuck past their parents whom were relaxing by the fire and conversing about crops, weather, or some other boring adult thing.

Once outside, the two stuck close, heading west towards the city. Their mind was set on getting there no matter what. Their friend was waiting for them, and they owed their lives to him and everything he has done for them.

CHAPTER
-6-

A heavy presence filled the air. I could feel the heat from the sun high above; my ears ringing from the sheer noise. I sat motionless as voices from high above began to stir. The crowd died down. A young woman cried out, followed by a few men whom shared in her displeasure of my existence. Something hit the platform nearby. Then another piece of something hit my chest. I hardly felt the impact, but I still felt the sadness and fear from the thrower.

The crowd fell silent once more.

The deep voice of a man spoke loud and directly. "I, King Atrinon, the first of my name, bring before you the responsible party for at least four victims and probably more uncounted for."

The crowd booed and let loose a barrage of debris and curses.

Falling silent again at the behest of some guards, the king continued. "This...monster will ultimately be charged and sentenced to death following a few statements from those who witnessed his atrocities."

Another voice rose up, a man it seemed, only less deep and not as old. "Please bring forth the trader, Keerwit."

"There's the beast!" shouted the curd trader, walking up the steps and onto the wooden platform high above the crowd. "I'd recognize that hideousness anywhere."

"Keerwit, can you please verify that this creature was the one responsible for destroying your property, murdering your partners, and upsetting the peace?" asked the court marshal.

"That beast," he spat while pointing, "had almost ruined my business. I nearly lost my own life during the incident."

"Keerwit would you," the court marshal tried to speak.

"That beast should be hanged or set a blaze for what he'd done."

The marshal asked again before being cut off. "Keerwit,"

"Five barrels of my freshest curd was destroyed faster than a goblin can shit."

"Guards will you please escort Keerwit away," called the agitated marshal.

As he was being escorted, Keerwit continued his babbling, "Hang him I say! Hang him!"

The court marshal waited until the laughter of the crowd settled before announcing, "Please bring forth the hunter."

Bersool could smell the man even before he could hear his voice; the man who ultimately captured him; the one who placed both his friends in danger, and saved their lives as well.

Standing relaxed in the center, the hunter looked out at the crowd and not once towards the tied beast below.

"Is it true," the marshal began, "that your group was hired by our king to capture this creature and bring him to justice?"

He shifted his eyes, unfolding his arms before noticing both Tiolt and Lara standing on a small platform at the very edge of the plaza.

Averting his eyes, he spoke loudly, "I was hired by the king to investigate recent attacks and claims by several people in the area. Whether or not it was this creature, we still did not yet know at that point."

The marshal continued, "And was it also true that you tracked down the beast responsible and that this is the beast in front of us?"

The hunter found himself staring at the beast below while trying to respond to the question. He could sense fear and disdain coming from the creature, but noticed it was still focusing out toward the children in the distance, the very ones he sacrificed his life for.

The marshal spoke even louder, "Is it true that this beast even murdered two of your own men?"

"My men are fully aware of the dangers and responsibilities of my kind of work. I do not hire..."

"A simple yes or no will suffice," interrupted the marshal.

The hunter again studied the beast. He was bound in many layers of thick rope and chains. His body heaving, his eyes blindfolded. He then turned towards the court marshal, then the crowd, then up to the bright mid-day sky. "I have been hunting creatures since before I could lift a sword, and throughout those years I have never come across any whom could feel remorse for their actions."

"This creature you see before you is no more a beast then anyone of us." A few gasps from the crowd surprised even the king from his light nap atop his chair.

"This beast..." the marshal tried to speak before being cut off by the hunter.

"Will be the last hunt I ever take on." The hunter then ran down the stairs ignoring guards and disappeared into the crowd.

Tiolt and Lara, watching the spectacle continued to look on. They cried on and off as the crowd booed and continued to toss objects and obscenities at their friend. Lara felt a hand on her shoulder and when she turned around she saw the hunter
standing behind the two them.

Tiolt attempted to punch him hard in the gut. He made no attempt to avoid it. Lara looked at him somberly, "Please save him."

"I'm sorry," he lowered his head.

The three of them watched silently as the proceedings ended and Bersool was taken backstage. After some time, the crowd eventually dispersed, leaving the three of them alone. Tiolt comforted his cousin one last time, as they prepared to leave.

The hunter offered them a ride back home. And together they took what seemed like the longest ride they ever would take.

* * *

It was the final days of the month of the Pale Moon, and Lara met up with her cousin down by the river front. She came to offer him some water and spy on whatever it was he was working on this these past few weeks.

"Tiolt!" she hollered making her way to the abandoned docks.

"Lara!" he surprised her from behind. His complexion much darker, with plenty of dirt and wood shavings latched onto his thick brown locks. "Come quickly I have something to show you."

He dragged her along, almost spilling the water she had brought. The two made their way to the edge of the river where a tarp was covering something.

"Here it is," Tiolt said anxiously. Giving a heave and lifting the tarp aside.

She took a moment to let it sink in. "A boat. Your big secret is a boat?"

"Not just any boat," he smiled. "I'm going to take sail this boat when I'm a little older."

"Where will you go?" his cousin laughed.

Tiolt pointed down the river toward the direction of the nearest ocean. "You don't expect me to stay around forever?"

His cousin starting to tear up, catching herself when she remembered a promise she had made to a friend. "What will you do?" she asked, offering Tiolt some water.

"I'm not sure," he chuckled. "Don't worry though; I'll come visit you all."

"Will you let me come with you when I'm older too?" she asked.

"Of course," he laughed. "I'm gonna need someone to do the dishes and clean up after me.

Lara splashed the remaining water in his face. The two of them took a seat on the docks, laughing.

The sun was beginning to set, casting orange and red hues along the sky and water. The peacefulness in the air, soon led them to begin reminiscing about their friend they had met last season. As the day grew darker, they both packed up and before they left, Lara and Tiolt noticed something moving in water some distance away. A shadowy form of something large stood for a moment before vanishing beneath the surface. The two of them shared a smile, and then departed for home.

.

TRADE WINDS

PROLOGUE

-ASHORE-

There is no such thing as justice.

My father once told me that the sea held no favorites. It wasn't judgmental, nor did it care whom it swallowed beneath its waves. If I could remember my father now, I'm sure he would have taken me in his arms and carried me away from this desolate place.

I awoke with sand stinging my eyes, salting my mouth, and falling out from my scraggly black hair as I combed through it. I felt a sudden sharp pain and after inspecting it, I found there to be a large gash on my head and dried blood crusted over my face. After washing off with stinging salt water, I took a moment to take in my surroundings.

The beach I washed up on was littered with broken wood, smashed barrels, and torn cloth scattered and sticking out of the sand up and down the coastline. I gave a yell as best I could, but no one seemed to be around. My voice was cracked and sore, yet I continued to try a few more times. No one answered. I assumed the worst when a few bloated corpses of men I didn't recognize washed ashore further up the coast. Their faces were cut and bellies slashed open when I flipped them over; the smell of decaying flesh and salty brine burned my nose. Turning away resisting the urge to gag, I desperately tried to remember anything. Even a bleak fracture or trace of something would have calmed my nerves perhaps making me feel less alone.

I walked what seemed like a mile or so down the debris filled coast. The wreckage piles slowly dwindled, ending with a large section of a ship, half buried in sand and being slammed against the rising waves. Looking ahead, I squinted into the setting sun. Before me rose a small figure climbing out of the damaged haul, standing and facing my direction. The sun was very hot, shining directly in front creating a silhouette outline of his small skinny body. As I slowly approached the figure, I could tell that it was studying me. Once the glare diminished, I was now shocked when I saw that it was just a boy. His short blonde hair was ragged and tangled, and his face was scratched, but he seemed to be in alright shape. For such a small kid I was surprised that he wasn't crying or showing any sign of trauma or despair. Again I wanted to remember, but the fear of being alone made me stick my hand out and grab hold of the child's tiny arm.

"Hello, my name is Ardus," I spoke.

ONE

-THE CRIMSON DRAGON-

Dark waves of bloody water splashed over the gunwale and rained down onto the slippery deck. One suicidal man tried to swing across to our ship, not knowing we had four of our men with steel tipped arrows aimed right at him. He was quickly pelted with arrows, falling instantly from the rope and disappearing into the turbulent sea.

After their ship had sunk, and the last survivor of their crew had been slain, our salvage team began to haul everything from their ship, carrying the salvage over the gangplank and into the vault for Zeetrok to divvy up later. I was able to witness the whole fight from a small port window in the captains' quarters where I was told to stay put until we had safely won. I stayed glued to the window like a barnacle, fogging the panes with my hot breath, until my father knocked secretly on the door signaling to me that it was safe. Racing to the heavy iron slab, I unbolted each lock, and then leaped back to the window right as the door was pushed open with a loud clang.

"Well, did you enjoy the fight Ardus?" asked my father from the entry.

"Actually it was rather boring," I responded, nose still pressed to the glass.

"I guess you're right, we have been in tougher situations," he chuckled, "Zeetrok's splittin' the loot now. If you hurry he might let you choose first."

Before my father even finished, I had already squeezed past him, running down the hall, and out into the living quarters where the salvage team was still carrying loot into the vault. I tried to peer into the doorway as best I could, while the salvagers carried armfuls of heavy chests and wine barrels through the tiny doorframe. When the men finally moved out of the way, my eyes widened at the site of all the treasure, weapons, crests, and rare oddities that were stacked as high as the ceiling. After the last man dropped off one final stack of crates, I saw Zeetrok waving at me with his large grey hand inviting me in.

"Come in, come in, boy. Did ya father send you here, huh?" his rough voice barked.

As I walked forward into the stowage I noticed him sitting at his desk, fingering through papers while I responded, "Yeah, he said you might let me choose something first. You know, before the crew takes it all and I'm stuck with nothing again."

Twirling as small knife in his large orc hands he continued, "Ah, ya know that's not true. Alright then, since yer almost six years now, I guess it would almost be cruel of me to not let you have a gift."

"Really, thanks Zeetrok, thank you very much!" I shouted, looking incredibly surprised.

"Oh, it's no trouble at all. See that chest over there?" He pointed over towards the back area of the vault, laughing; a place even I have never noticed until now. "You can choose any object ya want. Free of charge."

I looked over towards the iron chest he was pointing at with his knife. It was silver trimmed and shoved into a dark corner, as if to stay hidden from prying eyes. I walked slowly over, inching my way through dusty crates, makeshift boxes, and barrels of all shapes and sizes. When

I finally reached the chest, I gently placed my small hands under the lid, taking in a breath. Then, very quietly I began lifting it up and over, almost like I didn't want anyone other than me to hear.

"Hurry up now lad. The cap'n will be here soon, and you probably don't want to let him see ya in his private chest," he chuckled as he pretended not to be spying.

I lowering my voice, speaking out of the corner of my mouth, "Sorry Zee, I'll try to hurry."

As my eyes peered down into the chest, it seemed like I was witnessing my richest dreams. There were so many objects, oddities, and strange gold and gem filled things that I have never, and could never, have imagined. However, for some strange reason, whether it was a gleam of light, or just my gut, I found myself being lured to an object resembling a short rod or flute. I picked it up in my hands, gazing at it from all directions. The object was cold to the touch and it had five holes drilled into along its body. The flute seemed to be made out of gold, but not quite as heavy. And when I held it tighter, the more I came to realize that this flute might actually be something more.

Tucking it inside my pocket, I quickly closed the lid of the chest, and then ran out the door before Zeetrok could even say another word.

-THE GRAY TILLA-

The slow rocking of the boat against the waves created a harmonious rhythm that made traveling on *The Tilla* a most unique experience. The Arien family knew that, the moment they purchased the small trade ship from a port on the coast of Zeben. When Serdas and his friend Hyleer decided on a life of trading and selling goods, they knew they would get much farther in life than regular fishermen ever could. And the more money it brought in for their families didn't hurt much either.

"Careful along the sides, you don't want to end up like your father's last shipment." exclaimed Serdas grabbing the rails along the starboard side.

"What's that supposed to mean?" yelled Hyleer in retaliation, climbing out onto the sun deck.

The two goblin deck handlers looked at each other quizzically. The shorter one, Dod, hollered, "Me know, me know! Double check hold lines and secure cross nets and rigging, me know okay!"

Hyleer walked over to where Serdas was standing, looking out towards the fading coast.

Serdas quietly watched the wave's crash far in the distance against the craggy beach. Hyleer, never one to interrupt a man from his peace, felt he had to say something to comfort his long time friend.

"You know, we will see it again," spoke Hyleer in his usual coarse voice.

Serdas continued to stare out at the coastline; a small sliver of land was all that was still visible. "One more trip my good friend, and I'll leave this tiresome business to you." he smiled. "Then my family and I can live in our own house, away from all the fishing and trading."

"Bah," his friend rolled his eyes. "You've been saying that every time we set sail."

The sea was calm and sunny. They watched a few coastal grey birds fly over head, before circling and heading back towards the coast.

"It's different when you have a family," Serdas added.

"Aye," replied Hyleer puffing up his chest. "And I don't suppose after spending nearly all my life, or my son's life, constitutes as family either?"

"You know what I mean," he laughed.

"Sometimes you speak too much with your head, and not enough with your heart," his friend concluded. "Fine, tis' a deal then," Hyleer chuckled in agreement, slapping him on the back. "We'll take this last shipment to Rosia, and then you can finally settle down."

Turning to Hyleer and looking him in his dark blue eyes Serdas replied, "Tis a deal indeed."

The next day, *The Gray Tilla* was still riding the crosswinds, following along the western coast of Zeben. Small trade ships and other boats learned to maintain site of land at all times, in case they run into trouble. Serdas and Hyleer have heard their share of pirate and sea gangs that have attacked in the open waters, destroying many of their friends' and fellow traders' lives. This is also why Hyleer decided to hire two goblin mercenaries, Dod and Weersker a few months prior, to work as bodyguards in case of any trouble. And, on the off chance there wasn't any, they worked as mediocre handymen and fumbling deck handlers.

"Hey Dod, have Weersker say something," yelled Tyris sitting on a deck platform.

Weersker paid no attention to the remark made by the only son of their employer, Hyleer. However, Dod, who was carrying crates next to him, called back, "Ya know he ain't gonna talk master Tyris. He only talks to me. He not trust you humans for long time now."

Hyleer opened the topside door hearing the commotion, "Ty, stop buggin' them and come eat your morning meal."

"Fine," Tyris sighed, running over to join his father. "You guys are boring anyway."

For a crew of eight, *The Tilla* actually has quite a lot of room down in the haul and cabins. Below deck, each family or group has their own quarters. There was a small galley and saloon down one hall. And at the other end was the stowage. And right above that; the captain's quarters. At the main table, the Arien family ate their breakfast alongside Hyleer, his son, and their other family friend, Soaban. The two goblins liked to eat in solitude so they were hardly ever seen at the table.

"Serdas, can you please check on Johen, I think I hear him crying," Jesni insisted calmly.

"Alright, I'm sure he just wants some food," responded Serdas, getting up from the table and kissing his wife lightly on the cheek.

When Serdas came back in the galley holding Johen in his arms, Hyleer began again. "So, what I'm tryin' to say is, we should've sold the scrap metal for a much higher price, or at least sold it to a higher bidder."

Serdas handed his son to his wife, so he could finish his meal of salted pork and rice. After finishing chewing he added, "Actually, we would have lost seven silvers to them either way."

Laughing under his breath, and trying not to let others hear him, Soaban broke in, "Well what's done is done. The important thing now is the shipment we have, as well as, our heading." He excused himself from the table, cleaning his plate in the wash bin. "And I agree with Serdas. We would have lost seven crests anyway."

Noticing his son chuckling quietly, Hyleer immediately smacked him across the back of his head. "See Tyris, pretty soon this will all be yours someday. So, you better pay attention to how the business works." Looking over towards Serdas he asked, "What about Johen? You gonna teach him a thing or two, and have him grow up like his old man?"

"Well that would be up to his mother," Serdas said jokingly. "But really I think the ways of a trader or sailor is not the life a young boy should be looking forward too. That's another reason why I'm eager to finally stop all this."

Hyleer taking a huge bite of bread and drinking down some mead spat, "Bah, you're no fun".

Serdas looked over towards his sleepy eyed son. He gently held his tiny soft hand in his rough one, while smiling at his wife. "I want my son to have a peaceful life, even if it meant the cost of my own happiness."

TWO

-THE CRIMSON DRAGON-

Everyone was afraid of the captain. Heck, even my father, the great Spearhead Faseru, as the crew called him, would avoid lasting eye contact.

While scrubbing the quarterdeck, I remembered a previous time in which I slipped. Looking up, I saw the captain stop in front of me. I thought my heart was going to explode out from my chest, as I found myself accidently staring up at him, as if expecting him to offer a hand.

My father, whom had seen the blank look in my ace, ran over, pulling me quickly off the floor. "I'm sorry captain," he blurted apologetically. "My son knows better, he will never do it again."

Captain Bajres continued on past, never addressing the matter. He was a tall; though not nearly as tall as my father, and was wearing a large captain's hat, long red and blue coat, and his hair slick back into a knot.

"You idiot, what have I told you about embarrassing yourself, and me, in front of the captain?" My father spat, looking down upon me with his dark green squinting eyes.

Refusing to look him in the face, I kept my head down pleading, "It was an accident. The deck was slippery. The soap..."

"Alright it doesn't matter," he spouted waving it off. "Just finish your chores then go straight to the galley to help Bolidos and the rest of the crew." Leaning on the floor, I watched as he ran to catch up to the captain who was standing near the rails studying the horizon.

After our evening meal, I had to help wash the plates, tables, and floors. Out of all my daily tasks, I hated working in the galley the most. Even though I liked hanging around Bolidos and listening to his stories, it did not make up for the fact that I still had to clean all the filth, spilt liquor, grime, scrapings, and stench.

I was about half way done scrubbing the floorboards, when the warning bells rang in from outside, echoing throughout the ships haul. Not soon after did I begin to hear the crew running around the lower decks. The ruckus was so loud I almost couldn't hear Zeetrok through the door, yelling for Bolidos and me to head topside.

When my short legs managed to finally climb out on to the deck I could see nearly all of the crew standing in a huge crowd on the port side. Looking around, I saw my father and the captain talking near the center mast of the ship. I began to make my way over, yelling out a few times for my father to see me, however the crew was too noisy and the captain was whispering in my father's ear, making them fall on deaf ears.

Walking over, my father abruptly turned to the crowd shouting, "Attention everyone! By now you're probably aware that we are approaching a small vessel due east of us!" The crew began to quiet down, forming a large circle around where the captain and my father stood. "Once we've learned more about the situation, we'll inform you. Stand by for further orders!"

The news of a potential assault greatly boosted the crew's morale, sending many of them into a frenzy of shouts, cutlery, and fists. I tried my hardest to pry through the crowd, slowly inching my way past hulking towers of muscle, grime, and savagery. Almost backing out for fear of being trampled by the raging crew, I decided against it when I could see my father almost within arm's reach.

By now the moon was high in the night sky, and the crew was thirsty for blood. Before things could get worse, the captain held up his hand, calming them at once, "We are pirates, first and foremost," he started. "We ride *The Crimson Dragon*. Wait just a little bit longer and I guarantee you will be satisfied."

The crew gave a final roar before retiring to their previous posts and duties. After the mob disbanded, I saw my father give a final nod to the captain as he too retired to his private stateroom. Running over to my father I was anxious in what he had to say. I knew that he would tell me what was happening. All I wanted to hear was what the captain and he had talked about.

"Tell me everything father," I blurted out as he picked me up in his large muscular arms.

He then gave me a long hug, before carrying me inside. "I want you to lock yourself in the captains' chambers when I tell you to okay?" he explained.

"What?" growing sourly, I asked.

"You heard me," he replied. "And that's an order."

-The Gray Tilla-

Hyleer and Soaban were busy tying the morning catch to the drying rack, when Jesni climbed topside, carrying Johen in her arms. The warm presence of the sun awoke the child from his deep peaceful slumber. The sea breeze was calm, and the gentle sway of the boat cast a sense of peace over the crew.

"I see ya let little Johen there enjoy the salty warm air of the ocean like we do," Hyleer spoke humbly, chopping the head off a blue-scaled trout. The head toppled to the floor, where he then kicked it into the water unsympathetically. Soaban glanced at him, as if silently scorning his constant pesters. Hyleer laughed a little under his breath before he finished slicing another trout and continued to work.

Jesni returned the favor by laughing, "His father likes to deprive him of such treasures. Though I protest, no one should have to grow up without ever seeing the beautiful ocean or gorgeous sunsets." She then kissed her son's tiny forehead, gently disturbing him from a nap.

Not soon into midday, did the two goblins, Dod and Weersker, crawl out from their bunks.

"You think master let me use twisting dragon or dark fury better?" asked Dod.

Weersker shook his head, leading the two out on deck with tool belts in hand.

"Oh, I know." Dod spoke up, "We show him hawkbitter. Remember when we…"

"Uhg," Tyler moaned from the nearby step. "Aren't you two late for…I don't know…catching flies or something?"

Dod attempted to lash out, but Weersker held onto his shoulder reaffirming his friend just who the fat-lipped brat's father was.

"Bah," Dod shoved it off. They both ignored the remark and made their way to the rear of the ship. "That boy really swamps my pits," he added.

Weersker nodded again, handing his friend a belt.

"Alright," smiled Jesni climbing out from below deck, guiding her son up the last step and out into the refreshing air. "There's your friend Tyris."

She carefully walked little Johen over to Tyris, who was still sitting on the deck, playing with a small braided rope. "Do I have too?" he moaned, clasping the child's hand as his mother waved her goodbyes.

"Thank you again," she said. "I just need a small break. The men are below checking inventory if you need anything."

"Yeh, yeh," he waved back, as she disappeared back below.

"Alright," Tyris began, still holding his tiny hand. "What shall we do today?" He then paused before bending down to pick up a small wooden sword nearby. Holding it above his head, Tyris yelled out, "Prepare pirate scum. You face the blade of a true defender of the seas!"

Johen giggled, looking at the tip of the makeshift sword as it hovered a hair length from his tiny nose.

"You dare mock me!" shouted Tyris even louder. Glancing back at the child, Tyris couldn't help but lose character. He began to laugh and giggle as much as Johen was doing already. "You stupid baby, you probably don't even know what a pirate is."

Just then, Tyris could hear his Jesni's voice echoing down into the haul where they were playing, letting them know it was time for dinner. He tucked the sword into his trousers and picked up Johen cradling him with both arms trying not to drop him.

Back in the kitchen, everyone was already at the two tables eating. After Tyris and Johen were seated, Soaban placed a trout fillet on each of their plates. Tyris immediately started to devour his portion, while Jesni carefully cut pieces of it for her son.

Passing a plate down to Hyleer, Serdas began, "I heard you lost a bet with Dod."

The goblin's face lit up as he almost jumped out from his seat, "He did, he did."

"Well," his friend murmured, adjusting himself, while grabbing for more ale. "It was more of a one sided deal." Everyone around the table rolled their eyes.

Hyleer continued to placate his own façade. "I was plastered at the time."

"What?" asked Jesni, finding herself getting involved.

"Oh, now I really want to know," added Soaban.

Hyleer grumbled, trying to mask his overwhelming embarrassment. "No, it was stupid." he moaned. "The little green..."

"Watch it," Serdas broke in. "You did hire them, but I think even coins won't protect you from a goblin's pride."

His friend paused, trying to see if he could change the subject. However, after the table remained fixated on some proper excuse, he admitted, "That bastard took advantage of the poor state I was in."

The table broke into laughter.

Soaban leaned over motioning with his hand, "Dod, just tell me how much he lost?"

"Well..." the goblin sneered. Giving quick glances towards his payer and the chance he had to make a greater lasting impression.

"You son of a bitch," glared Hyleer.

Without warning, a loud slam was heard above. Everyone paused upon hearing the sound. Serdas suddenly stood up, as if he knew what was going to come next. Weersker ran down into the galley before anyone noticed. His small legs flew over a counter where he then ran over to Serdas, whispering something into his ear. Not a moment after he finished, Serdas signaled for Hyleer, Soaban, and Dod, to come with him above deck. Jesni and the two children were left confused as the men abruptly left.

After a few minutes had passed, Serdas came back down the stairs clasping his wife's hands, speaking calmly, "Jesni, I need you to take Johen and Tyris down to my cabin and lock yourselves in. Bolt the door or create a barricade if you have to, just make sure you stay in there and don't let anyone in but me."

"I love you Serdas," shouted Jesni, as she disappeared down into the dark haul, with Tyris close behind.

"I love you all too, very much," replied Serdas right before he lost sight of her, running back up the stairs and out into the cold, full moon night.

THREE

-THE CRIMSON DRAGON-

I could see *The Crimson Dragon's* large white sails flapping in the wind as if rebelling against the turbulent gusts. Staring upwards at the crow's nest I noticed Asdref -who was a friend of mine as much as my father- yell some commands down to the relay team posted on the prow.

"It's a trade ship alright," he called. "Tell the captain it's probably a small crew of no more than ten or so. Also, tell him we should be on them in a few more hours."

One tall lanky man I didn't know ran from the prow down into the quarterdeck to inform Captain Bajres.

My curiosity got the best of me, so I hurried behind the skinny man, following in his shadow. Not caring if he saw me or not, I ran past him, hiding behind my father who sat in the saloon where every high ranking crewman was packed in. I looked around the small room trying to see or hear why everyone was just standing around, whispering quietly. Moments had passed, and I was still unsure what was going on. Finally, I turned to my father's coat, tugging on it until he paid attention to me.

When he at last looked down I immediately began, "Father why is everyone huddled in this room waiting? Is it because Captain Bajres isn't here yet?"

He gave a small smile that was barely even noticeable. However, when he bent down to one knee, and grabbed hold of my scrawny shoulders he stressed, "All of the top crewmen were told to wait in here for the captain to arrive. Since I'm the first mate it's my duty to be here. Besides, he'll be here real soon, and then you might even get to see us fight again."

My dark eyes lit up like two bright torches. Ever since my mother died and I was brought aboard this ship, I have grown to love watching our crew fight and sink ships. I admired the way ours was so much better than everyone else's. The whispers and rumblings between crew members began to fade away, and the only voice I focused on now, was that of our captain, who just now entered the room.

"Alright my friends," he beckoned. "After reviewing all possible actions and conditions from which we will soon be entering, I have just decided that the small trade ship ahead of us shall become our next victim. My scouts inform me that it is a fairly stocked ship and with a crew of no more than ten, it would be a disgrace not to pillage it." The captain paused, allowing the room to fill with roars and cries of battle hungry men. Raising his hands, the room simmered to a silence.

"We shall reach their tiny ship within the hour," he continued. "So you all should be at your posts and ready before that time. I want no one, you understand no one, to try anything that might damage their ship or sink it until I give the order." The captain waited, his eyes scanning the saloon and all the men who would follow him to his grave. My father and I sat in a chair to his right, a grin permanently plastered on my father's face.

"That is all."

With that, the captain left the room as quickly as he had entered it. When the door slammed shut, the room rose back into a cheer and everyone started yelling for booze, broads, and blood. Grabbing my hand, my father led me through the crowds of people, trying to make his way to the door on the other side of the saloon. Before we could get there, a man yanked on my father's shirt. It was Bolidos.

Putting a frying pan up to his chest and pointing it at him with his other hand he exclaimed, "So Spearhead, ya gonna lock the kid up again?"

My father almost chuckled, "I was going to, but seeing as there probably won't even be a fight, I guess I can leave him with you in the galley."

Bolidos squinted, gazing down at me standing by his side. "Well I'll probably go out on deck and have a look see for my self. So, I guess the boy can come too. Who knows it might even be good for him."

As he spoke, Bolidos rubbed his greasy hand through my hair and patted me on the head. My father nodded, and we both began to head out the door when Bolidos bellowed, "How 'bout it boy, you wanna see your old man beat up some weak merchants?"

-THE GRAY TILLA-

"We better run full sail!" barked Hyleer from the aft. "Raise the high sail, and prepare for the worst!"

Dod and Weersker were already manning the bowsprit and securing the lanyards and rigging, when Serdas came onto the deck.

Running over to his friend, he started, "Is the ship still heading our way?"

"Has it ever stopped?" Hyleer jested. He then noticed his friend wasn't amused and straightened his jerkin, while coughing. "Yes, it is."

"I guess now's your chance to prove me wrong about hiring those two," Serdas indicated, pointing towards the goblins.

Hyleer smiled, "Well, they can't be any worse at being handymen, that's for sure."

The two shared a laugh, and then Hyleer signaled for Dod to come over after Serdas disappeared back below deck.

Grabbing the goblins tiny shoulder he preached, "I know the two of you were only hired as extra help, and I know you guys can fight, but it seems the time has come for you two to show us why we hired you. Not many people hire goblins these days, let alone for sailing, but Serdas is depending on you guys to protect this ship and our families. Now can I count on you?"

"Master," squeaked Dod, placing his boney hand back on Hyleer's, "Unlike most goblins, Weersker and I have had more experience and training in what we do. Just wait and see." After winking and running back towards his companion, Hyleer went back to work, keeping an eye on the mysterious ship that was stalking them.

They sailed another mile, dreading their predictions on who they were. It became clear that it was indeed a pirate vessel, and a fairly large one. The luminous dark red flag and similar sails only made *The*

Gray Tilla crew ever more fearful of the inevitable.

Serdas already made preparations to make sure his wife and child were safely hidden if there was ever an attack. Jesni, Johen, and Tyris were locked in his own private cabin, behind a few bookshelves, and further hidden by a secret hatch leading to a pantry. The cramped, dark space was a small price Jesni would go through if it only meant she could protect her only son and nephew for when the inevitable would strike.

Out on deck, Dod was throwing small knives towards his companion standing on the other end of the ship. Weersker then threw the daggers back, after catching them effortlessly. The cycle continued as Hyleer, Soaban, and Serdas walked by conversing with each other on a plan of action.

"We could always make a run for the coast," explained Soaban.

"Or, we could try to outrun them." Hyleer replied, knowing full well that this idea would never work.

Serdas scolded, "Hyleer now is most certainly not the time for jokes. Their ship is running double our max speed, and with wind gusts increasing, they will be on us in a matter of minutes." Looking over to Soaban he continued. "No use heading towards the coast; where would we go? They would have us cornered and vastly outnumbered against the craggy shore."

Serdas stopped pacing, and then looked outwards towards the approaching threat. The ship was dark, large, and only a mile behind them. Hyleer approached his long time friend, with Soaban stepping up on his other side. Agreeing together, they awaited for his decision.

"We coast around the ship," Serdas realized. His friends paused, wondering if he'd gone mad.

"*The Villa* will be pulled around the wake and we can maneuver easily past them. Then all we have to do is fight the men who try to board our ship as we circle around. If we can manage to this for a few hours we can reach Rosia and dock there."

Soaban added, "Rosia is a much better place to fight on land."

"Yeh," Hyleer spat, "But the ship will be ruined once we dock. That is, assuming they don't damage the hull or burn it up."

"When has that ever stopped us?" Soaban asked.

"Uhg, it's a moronic plan," spoke Hyleer.

"But it's the best chance we got," replied Serdas. "Soaban," his friend glanced to him. "Rosia, or risk a frontal assault?"

Soaban pondered scratching his stubble, "Rosia does sound like a safer answer."

"Very well," Serdas ended. "We have a plan."

Hyleer shrugged, "Aye, then we have a plan."

FOUR

-THE CRIMSON DRAGON-

The towering ship cut through the ocean, bobbing and slamming against the erupting waves. Our crew was running around the deck, mast, and rigging. For all of their battles on the sea, and all of the times they had fought similar ships, they were completely caught off guard by the tactics this one was using.

I was on the promenade, watching from the bulwark with Bolidos next to me. He hadn't said a word since my father left to go below deck. I desperately wished to go with him, but the fear of him scolding me, placing me in our quarters, was too much. It was nicer out here anyway. I could see the small skiff riding around The Crimson Dragon, like a pest or minor annoyance. I stood laughing, imaging the looks on their faces when their pathetic ship was destroyed before their eyes.

Hearing the deck door shut, I looked down along with Bolidos, to see who arrived topside. It was my father. He seemed to be garbed in his battle outfit. Wearing a leather hide, black pants, chain vest, and iron pauldron, he came prepared. Securing his two sabers at each side, I noticed he also brought along three of his best spears strapped to his back. Hunching over the rails, sticking my head lower to try and hear over the crashing waves, I smiled, waiting for him to make an announcement.

"All of you, maintain positions around the rails and outer nets," my father, the great Spearhead Faseru, broadcast. "Prepare arrows and spears. If you have grappling hooks use them while their ship circles. These are your orders. Make your captain proud." After his short speech, my father walked back below deck, followed by another slam from the huge iron door.

"Let's see what happens next, heh," whispered Bolidos, grabbing me back from the rails.

"I would think it wouldn't even have taken this long," I said jokingly. "Though I sometimes wish the fights would last longer, I really enjoy them."

Bolidos tilted his eyes and then back towards the ocean. "By the looks of it you might just get your wish," he hinted.

The small skiff was easily maneuvering around The Dragon's large haul. Some of our more eager crew cut ropes off trying to swing over as their ship was passing. The few men that tried it, where instantly met with arrows and knives from some of their crew on deck. Peering closer, I could see that they were a pair of goblins. I couldn't make out anything more than their small stature, and lanky greenish skin.

"Bolidos," I tugged on him, "Are those really goblins down there?"

Letting a smile shine through his stone-like expression, he affirmed, "You don't see many a goblin out on the sea anymore. Sailors and merchants can't trust'em. That's why there are none on our ship. The captain wouldn't let'em."

"They seem very skilled," I said, leaning on one arm.

"Aye," he agreed. "But, given enough time, anyone can be skilled at throwing knives and shooting a bow."

For a small ship with such a small crew, they sure were putting up a fight. After their ship had made four circles around our ship, the captain came out to check on the progress. As soon as he made his way to the center mast the entire crew fell quiet. Joined at his side, were my father, Zeetrok, and three other ranked men I had never really talked to. Bolidos grabbed my hand, pulling me over to the rails, where we would have a better view of them talking.

After Captain Bajres lifted his hand up he began to shout so all could hear, "This ship seems to be prolonging the inevitable. Or, perhaps I need to find another crew who is capable of bringing down a tiny vessel."

My father whispered something into the captain's ear.

After a brief pause he continued. "There is a storm approaching from the south. We shall wait till then. The storm will make it impossible for their small ship to keep running around, and we shall take them down in one stroke." The captain's voice rang louder with each word. "We shall slaughter the whole lot, while their precious ship sinks. No one disrespects *The Crimson Dragon* and lives!"

The crew erupted with roars and cheers alike. The captain headed inside, while my father and Zeetrok remained on deck patrolling and barking out orders. "Use the grapples and hook the ship to one side," my father hollered. "If even this proves to be too difficult for you, then Zeetrok and I shall be happy to deal with your incompetence!"

-The Gray Tilla-

The arrow stuck deep, penetrating into the savage pirates head. As the man began to fall off his rope, Weersker had already shot and struck another man through the neck. Dod was perched on ropes above the jib. He was calmly judging distances and deciding which man was a more dangerous threat. As one crazed pirate tried to jump aboard, Dod met him with a single knife in the forehead. The two goblins barely showed any emotion; as if they have done this many times before.

As The Gray Tilla maneuvered and crashed around the enemy ship, Hyleer and Soaban were constantly looking out on deck and reporting back to Serdas, who was at the helm.

"Serdas," Hyleer shouted peering through the main doorway.

"Are you tryin' to kill us?!"

"This old ship ain't what she used to be," his friend responded. "The waves are picking up, and I can't avoid ramming their ship as we circle around anymore."

Hyleer glanced back outside, and then back towards Serdas who was clasping the wheel with all his might. "I'll try to help the goblins. They're doing a very good job on their own, but if we keep getting closer to the ship, they're going to have even more company."

"Thanks Hyleer," Serdas yelled. "Soaban, if you want you can help outside, but please check on my family first."

Soaban made a single nod, then ran out the back door, "Don't worry, I'm on it." By the time Soaban had opened the pantry door that revealed Jesni and the two kids, Johan and Tyris were already fast asleep, tucked in Jesni's arms. Soaban wasn't willing to stay long, but he did want to make absolutely sure they were all fine. This crew was the closest thing he had to a family, and he felt as much responsible for their protection as Serdas himself.

Noticing Jesni look up at him from the shadows he whispered, "I'm sorry Jesni, Serdas sent me to make sure you all were alright."

"Thank you Soaban. We are doing just fine; cramped, but fine," she softly smiled back.

Looking down at the two boys Soaban continued, "I can't believe they fell asleep. The ship has been rocking and slamming nonstop, for quite awhile."

"They looked like they would never get any sleep, yet after a few minutes into the battle, they passed out," replied Jesni. "You better head back now. Serdas and the others will need you. Don't worry about us."

Soaban returned a small smile of encouragement then began to shut the door. "Don't worry; I'm sure it will all be over soon."

Back outside, Hyleer had joined Weersker portside. Dod was still throwing knives and killing helpless pirates who had believed they could just jump across to their ship with no consequences. When Soaban stepped on deck, Hyleer gave a wave, shouting for him to come over. Weersker slowly crooked and arrow, gently adjusting for height and distance. Letting loose, the arrow had shot like a bolt of lightning past two pirates, to meet a man who was behind them, ready to throw a grappling hook at their ship.

"See, now that's what I call skill," laughed Hyleer, leaning over the rails, as the man disappeared into the turbulent sea. You ready for a fight then?!" he yelled. "Serdas says the weather is picking up!"

Soaban replied in a humble tone, "Whatever."

"Aye," Hyleer's eyes lit up. "It makes my blood boil with anticipation!"

FIVE

-THE CRIMSON DRAGON-

Piercing rain fell from the pitch black clouds high above. The crew's of both ships were becoming a mess of blood and steel on the decks and sea below. Waves were becoming increasingly larger with each minute, by now *The Crimson Dragon* was being lifted and tossed well above the height of its hull and mizzen. Fearless the crew was, but when faced with the elements and god's not even the captain could remain calm.

As the storm fury grew, Bolidos took me inside the quarterdeck. Ignoring their soaking clothes, we ran over to the nearest porthole, gazing out as the two boats fought each other and the storm.

The tiny skiff was now being protected by just four men who were sprawled out topside, while there were just forty of so of our own crew. A few vengeful pirates tried to swarm the ship in one quick sweep; however two of them were immediately eliminated by an arrow and a knife. As for the other two, they made it to the deck, but were instantly slashed and cut down before they could even defend themselves. After awhile, many had become scared and reluctant to

99

jump or swing down to the small ship swirling around the water. Even the ones that looked like they were ready to jump were seen with arrows and knives sticking out of them as their bodies tumbled over the rails before they could blink. When Spearhead Faseru gave the signal to launch the grapples and begin to snare the trade ship in position, the crew's spirits lifted and the yelling and shouts of war rose into the cold night air again.

Around the other side of our ship, six or so men were waiting in the shadows for the small skiff to bounce and sail around to their side. The men sneered and tightened their holds on the large grappling hooks each one held tight in their white knuckled hands. Each hand-picked and trained by Zeetrok, they were masters at what they do.

When the skiff rose up from a massive wave, the boat became eye level with the men in waiting. This was the moment. Two pirates at the end of the line were stricken with arrows and knives as soon as they stood up out of the shadows, collapsing to the deck with puddles of blood beneath their now lifeless bodies. The other men paid no attention to their fallen brethren, their minds were already full of rage as they let loose their hooks and impaled the side of the boat. When the wave and ship began to sink back down, the chains grew taught and the hooks penetrated deeper in the fragile haul. The men fastened the chains to the side rails as another group of men began to shimmy down the lines ready to board the vessel that has been so elusive.

The tall man standing near a goblin immediately met some of the invading pirates. He was skinny and covered in the shadows of our ship. Wearing a long coat and black bandana, he ran up the chains and slashed at the men's hands and faces forcing them to release their grip and fall into the sea. He did this until no more men wanted to climb down that line. As for the other groups, the goblin pair was already piercing their chests, necks, and skulls with arrows. Arteries were punctured, necks bled, and men screamed. It wasn't until they both ran out of arrows and knives that the men regained their composure and continued their assault. A group of pirates who managed to climb down to the bow, found themselves being attacked mercilessly by a large man wielding twin cutlasses. The man's face was masked by a dark thick beard and the last thing they saw was his furious blood filled eyes.

The crew was dwindling fast. Officers were frightened and pointing fingers. Spearhead had never seen a ship like this before. He had never fought so long and hard for such a trivial catch. He began to grow curious as to how strong they really were. So much so, that he decided to check it out for himself.

-THE GRAY TILLA-

Hyleer had sliced a pirate's back down the spine, finishing the man off and kicking his opened body into the sea to join his brethren, when he heard a huge roar unlike anything he had ever heard. He looked up towards the mast of *The Tilla*, along with the goblins. Out from the pouring rain and searing wind, a large shadowy figure stood poised, ready to leap.

"We need to restock!" yelled Dod to Hyleer. The goblins quickly darted from their posts, heading below deck. Hyleer didn't nod, nor did he even look in their direction. His eyes and total concentration were focused on the looming figure on the enemy's ship. At that instant, the mysterious pirate drew a long spear from his back and threw it towards him. Just as he did, he also leapt from the ship while pulling the other two spears out from behind him. Hyleer barely side stepped the first spear, as its head and shaft buried deep into *The Tilla's* walls. Tossing the second one, Hyleer dove to the ground barely dodging it. The spear hit the boards hard, forcing its way deep into the planks. Hyleer knew he had no time to avoid the third; however Soaban, watching the fight, had thrown a crate towards him at the last moment. Grabbing the crate, Hyleer used it to protect his body from the last spear. When he opened his eyes after impact and lifted the crate away, he noticed the spear drove itself through the crate just enough to pierce his left shoulder half way through.

With no time to recover, the pirate landed on the deck and immediately closed in on Hyleer with two sabers pointed at his neck. The man looked worse than any of the other pirates that died before

101

him. The raging man was taller than even he was, and more muscular. Hyleer, barely pulled one of his giant knives in front of his neck, just before the man had slashed, blocking it. The two of them began a vicious fight of steel and wits.

As the rain poured down, the winds started to pick up even more. Hyleer followed the man up a chain and onto the pirate's deck, Soaban was nowhere to be found, and just as Dod and Weersker came back from below deck, the worst thing began to form a few hundred yards in front of them.

The wind began shattering glass and pulled rails and boards from both decks. Many men tried desperately to hang onto ropes and rails. The two goblins remained outside, securing themselves to the boom by their waists and feet. As the two ships sailed closer to the giant tornado, their hulls were beginning to crack. Suddenly *The Gray Tilla* lifted up, out of the water. Wood splintered and mutilated many of the rest of the pirates still out on deck. Dod and Weersker were being blown around in the air like they weighed nothing, while below deck, people fared no better.

As the ships neared the eye of the storm, the battle was over. The hooks and grapples broke free and *The Tilla's* cabins were ripped clean away. The sails of *The Crimson Dragon* were torn loose strangling and netting many men as it flew around the cyclone. As *The Gray Tilla* was pulled, it collided into the promenade of the pirate ship; smashing both cabins together, scattering wood and men to the winds.

Bolidos got pinned against the door, wood pierced through his body and into the hall on the other side. The fragile cabin broke apart into many segments. Berth and shelves flew in one direction, while a secret pantry was revealed and its contents thrown around in the other. Bodies, wood, cloth, and hope smashed in an instant.

When the sky cleared and the waves calmed back down, nothing was left.

EPILOGUE

-ASHORE-

The boy didn't respond back.

I called again and again, telling him what I could remember. Perhaps we came from the same place. I even started to think that maybe we knew each other. It didn't matter anyways, the innocence in his face and eyes made me feel warm and welcomed. Even though he hadn't said a word to me, I felt closer to him than I ever had with anyone else.

I brushed his clothes off, and helped him wash his face clean. After which I grabbed his hand and began to take him into the thick brush off the beach. He was reluctant to go at first, but I soon grew tired of his whining and carried him on my back. The child fell fast asleep, and soon I began to feel drowsy myself. Slowing my pace I set him down in the thick grass while I looked around for a place to sleep.

Out in the distance I could see a feint light shining towards the direction of the water. Waking the boy up, I grabbed his hand to lead him back towards the beach. I didn't care if it was someone I knew or not. I didn't care if they were going to kill me or this small child. By the time we both stepped out of the tall grass and back onto the sandy shore, the mysterious light had now stopped in front of us, waiting near the water's edge.

The light came from a lantern that was hooked to a small frame of cabin of a boat. There was an odd man who stepped off the boat, disturbing the water and making his way onto land. He had a large backpack and his boat was filled with decorations and weird oddities.

As he walked towards us, I felt frozen in place. My voice was gone, my legs stone, and the boy next to me rubbed his tired eyes and yawned.

The man bent down in front of us, kneeling into the sand, while removing his large bag. The only words that came from his mouth were perhaps the best words that I have ever heard before.

"Don't worry," the man smiled. "I saw what happened."

For some reason I had forgotten all about the wreckage and how I ended up on the beach. My mind had been reset. My emotions took hold, and I reverted back to a time where what I needed most was being with a family.

The man continued, "Don't worry you two you'll never have to be alone again. I can take you to a peaceful place to stay with me. I'll be your new father, master, and friend."

DARK HORIZON

DARK HORIZON

Stepping inward, away from the cool damp air that surrounded the castle exterior, I began to feel my body warming to the glow of torches and candles welcoming me into the long grey foyer ahead. The room opened up into an even grander living space. Lining the edges and walls stood elongated tables of grey and dark red oak with magnificent, highly elaborate engravings along their sides. Covering the tall windows hung fanciful curtains of auburn, bright green, and amber. Mounted above the shady alcoves were decorated plates and along the floor were vases large enough to fit a full grown orc or two. And at the far-end was a massive black marble table with light shimmering on its surface from the candelabras high above. Its corners and edges trimmed with silver metals and royal emblems. Hovering over the surface of the table stood my king. He communing with five other advisors all huddled over him; clinging to his sides like leeches feeding from a corpse. I had made my way past the last towering archway, its stonework far more impressive than any of the homes and keeps I've visited before. Shifting shadows in the rafters danced with the matching torch lights, when the guard to my right, wearing a silver plated chest piece and royal robes signaled my entrance.

The king looked towards me, his visage slightly masked by the shadows and his own facial hair. He kindly nodded. I could make out his short dark-grey beard and curly thick black hair. He was wearing a deep blue regalia and underneath a gold-hemmed white tunic. His advisors also glanced over, but by the time I had walked over to the table they had each stepped back, giving the king and I some much deserved space. Almost immediately they took to whispers and small talk; making the new space seem more beneficial to them.

"My king, I am sorry for the delay," I began, speaking almost too earnestly.

He waived me over to his side, hand extended; his fingers bearing several rings. All gem filled, all golden. I properly bowed, while greeting him in the traditional Bevarian manner.

"I understand you have been keeping busy with preventative measures over the Ranoian power struggles?" I politely inquired.

"Yes," he started, "My cousin in Trizdes has been keeping in touch with me almost daily." His words well enunciated; his voice always solid and clear. "I hear many things from the south. We were lucky in that it seems to be a mere local struggle. I feared it might spread, but you never know." He passed some papers over to an advisor behind him. "I assume you are already familiar with Lord Yerilov, Zeydiin, and Krigren?"

I turned around noting that he had already invited some of the other nobles from Hepsis. I must've missed them coming in. It was always like them to hide in the shadows. No doubt they had plenty of time to spread rumors over my already tardiness, but I suppose some things never change.

"Yes," I concurred, returning to him. "We are all familiar with the situation, and I am anxious to assist in whichever way we can."

"I had hoped as much." he reassured. "Bev is now entering the revival stages from that dreadful plague. Most of my towns and cities have begun to recoup their losses and civilians are beginning to come back." He signed softly, as he continued. "The same cannot be said of Hepsis. I know you've had problems in the past that no amount of force or law could repair, but we desperately need something to prevent an uprising from the locals."

Pulling out a handful of papers I had prepared, I suggested, "My king, I have detailed our current condition and have a list of plans presented here and here." I pointed.

He flipped through them almost too fast to assume he was even skimming over them. After passing them to his advisors, he focused on me again, "Urgency is a priority here. We need something now and something that will cater to both sides." His advisors behind him nodded and continued to listen quietly. Their stares and whispers a constant distraction. "What do you think about solidifying a governor-like position chosen from a representative of the people?"

I could feel their eyes probing me, judging my current state and future intentions and offerings, but what do I know about the day-to-day lifestyles of royal advisors whom no nothing of the outside world. I pondered for a moment, unable to speak my true thoughts.

"A high position such as a governor would not last long without some form of public protection," spoke Zeydiin coming out from the shadows behind us.

"Excuse me, my king," I spoke up, glaring at Zeydiin for a moment. "Even with public protection, he wouldn't last long."

Lord Krigren also commented, stepping closer to the center table, "Hepsis is in a constant struggle with the denizens and fear from who might try to take charge. In fact, we've had serious offers from several outside parties these last few months." His voice was snake-like; putting great emphasis on *outside parties*.

"And I'm sure you graciously hesitated when you thought about our council?" I interrupted.

Krigren voice rose, "Believe me, you wouldn't be around if I didn't!"

The king waved a courtesy for the commotion to simmer before continuing, "Am I safe to assume that among money, fear is what also keeps your denizens in check?"

"My king," I spoke up once more, clearing my throat, "Although we'd hate to admit it, fear is something that Hepsis requires on a daily basis."

"Very well," he nodded. "Since fear is exactly what we need, Lord Dyok. Over the next few days I want you and the other nobles to come up with an event or some method of deciding how you will fill this false position. I shall grant the city a respectable amount of guardsmen and before the day's end, we shall have secured someone, who through some demonstrated force, shall be feared and who'll still serve allegiance to me."

"A festival of sorts might help to build awareness." Lord Yerilov spoke from the corner of the room.

"Yes," the king agreed, "Announce to all of Bev of this event and make sure it is one best suited for less bloodshed and more of

107

something your city is famous for."

Grabbing my shoulder he concluded, "The last thing we need is more bloodshed. Promise them wealth, promise them power, but above all, promise them an event unlike any other."

I could hear the faint agreement from his advisors behind us. Looking toward my own fellow nobles, they too all smiled and nodded.

HEPSIS

It was a city built on misery, crime, and bereavement.

Like a hideous mole or scab it grew and festered, damaging and ruining all those that came near. The original foundation has long been gone; sunk beneath the swamp it was built upon. After many years of blood and sweat, the city was finally realized as a place of darkness, a place of ill-intent, a place only the most wretched can survive.

Expanding nearly seventeen miles across, the great black city of Hepsis stood on the southern region of Bev. Slave traders, wealthy nobles, vengeful guilds, and power-hungry witches all enjoyed their share of ruling, none of which lasted very long.

After a plague nearly destroyed all of Bev, the king stepped in. Hoping to subdue and control the madness he ordered the city to be managed by a governor who would be feared, yet obedient and loyal to the throne. Eventually, the city began to change. It went from being the black, murderous, eye sore of Bev, to a foul, dirty city, whom just happened to house many beggars, failed magicians, and thieves.

Stank and mildew spewed out from the large, nearly seventeen feet high, eastern gateway of the city. The other entrances fared no better. South, West, and North all had various smells of rotting fish, diseased animals, or stale bread with a mix of vomit and foul magic.

The eastern sector was home to the beggars, the lost, and the misfortune. Beggars Alley was another term for the wobbly stone street, dark alleys, and overturned makeshift houses and shacks. Picarious himself seemed to have abandoned it. Next to Beggars Alley was the Abandoned District. It was a refuge for wild mages, whom practiced dark arts and alchemists whom desired to be alone. Many of the homes were blackened and brittle from past fires, explosives, murder, and mishaps. Even the royal army feared entering the place, as many haunting and spectral forces seemed to howl and feast on the nightmares of its inhabitants.

On the northern side of Hepsis was the marketplace. Rows upon rows of stands, shelters, booths, shacks, and complexes so tall they stood above the walls. Anything and everything could be found here. Chances are if the market doesn't sell it, it doesn't exist.

The western edges of Hepsis were where the city guard, noble, and business quarters laid. Guard posts were placed every mile or so around the walls, while the luckier ones were stationed inside noble houses. And across there were the guilds, the plaza, the arena, and the general housing districts.

Throughout the ages, through wars, famine, disease, and distraught, through bloodshed, backstabs, power struggles, and thievery, and through shadows, trickery, corruption, and annihilation, this city has stood the test of time; outlasting them all. Most believe the city had a will of its own. It takes what it wants and will always have the last laugh. Justice has abandoned it; even the gods have abandoned it, but somehow it prevails.

Pre-Event

The door swaggered open, revealing the lofty scent of bread, seasoned ale, and orc musk. For mid-afternoon the place surprisingly had a large amount of patrons.

"Teinbal!" a familiar voice shouted.

Walking over to some tables on the right, his friend stood up greeting him.

"You still owe me ten tins," spoke Mirdorf. It was evident his friend had started the drinking early. A half-drank golden ale was perspiring on the table.

They both sat down, as a bar maid from across the room looked up.

"Forget about the tins for a second," Teinbal started. "Get a load of this!" He yanked out a folded paper from an inside pocket, unfolding it out on the coarse wooden table.

"And?" questioned Mirdorf.

The bar maid came over, swishing her silky blonde hair, that outlined her sturdy frame and slightly round face. "Brashire Ale," he said quickly, "whatever you got." He pointed, "It's gonna be huge. There've been talks of the prize money all around town."

Mirdorf took a gulp of his drink. Some residue dripped down the sides of the glass and a few landed on his faded tan shirt. "How much?" he asked in response.

"A lot"

"What's this say down at the bottom?" his friend pointed while he kept his other hand seemingly glued to his glass.

The bar maid came over. Teinbal ignored her flaunting gestures, while she placed the tall brown ale in front of him. His friend kept eyeing her backside every chance he got. She didn't notice, or maybe paid it no mind.

"It's just mentioning that it's open to everyone."

"Everyone?" he repeated.

"Yes."

"You know what that means right?" he said, shifting his eyes. "With those kinds of promises, we're gonna have every cutthroat, dark arts, backstabbing, psycho, baby killing, wannabe coming here."

"You still know that guy from the Bleeding Den?" Teinbal whispered slightly under his breath. His hand resting up to his mouth, as if he thought the other patrons found their talk worthy of eves dropping.

Mirdorf rolled his eyes, finally putting down his glass, if only because it was now empty. "He's not gonna help us."

"Ask him."

"I'm not gonna ask him," he shook his head.

Teinbal began pleading, a few patrons half drunk from the tables around them glanced in their direction. Finally, his friend lowered his voice, "I already owe him over one hundred tins. You think he's gonna keep letting me owe him?"

"How about," Teinbal divulged, "we get that guy. You know the one with the scar down his left side of his face."

Mirdorf motioned for the bar maid. She came and he placed another order. Again, he was distracted for a moment before replying, "We'll need another loan."

"I know where we can get one, his friend smiled.

"Oh really, you gonna go sleeping around or are you gonna swipe it from those drunks over there?" he made a motion with his head to the guys at the front of the bar. Most of which were in fact assed out drunk.

Some commotion arose from a man sitting at one of the back side tables. The bar maid headed over. She began sweet talking him; placing her hand on his shoulder and neck. Mirdorf glared and then smiled.

A pair of greenbacks suddenly came in. Their raggedy clothes and off-putting odor made many patrons, including them, raise heads and watch as they each took a stool at the bar.

"You see what kind of filth this event is gonna be bringing," Mirdorf retorted, his head lowering.

"With any luck, it'll only assist in lowering their population," added Teinbal.

Laughing, they both took a drink then continued.

"When's this thing gonna start anyway?" asked Mirdorf.

His friend grabbed the paper and looked at it one last time before folding it back up and putting it away. "In one week."

"One week!" blurted Mirdorf. "Geez, talk about fast."

"It was announced over a month ago," spoke Teinbal. "Where were you?"

"Oh you know where I was," Mirdorf replied; both laughing

111

again.

Suddenly at the bar someone shouted, "You're gonna wish you were taller bog-pisser, else you wouldn't have bumped into my cousin!"

The two of them looked over and watched as a pair of dwarves began squabbling with the greenbacks.

"Maybe if your cousin was less hairy," claimed a goblin, "I'd feel more inclined to mistake him for a proper gentleman."

The bar maid approached cautiously, as the tavern owner came out from the back room.

Suddenly, one dwarf grabbed the goblins head and slammed it down onto the counter. Blood gushed from his nose as the other goblin jumped and clung to the attacking dwarfs face.

The two collided into a passed out patron, then started wrestling on the ground.

Teinbal and Mirdorf turned back around, trying to ignore the fight while securing their drinks.

All of a sudden more people starting getting into the action. Bottles were shattering, the owner was grabbing people by the collar, even the bar maid slapped a man twice.

Mirdorf was still checking her out as she grappled with a rather hairy large man.

"You still liking this idea of a province wide tournament?" asked Mirdorf his eyes still focused elsewhere.

Teinbal got up, "This place has been through worse. Only this time they are inviting the mayhem to their doorstep."

As Teinbal turned to leave, a drunken patron punched him right in the face.

Mirdorf took another gulp.

*　　*　　*

"No!" he shouted, "You got to use your right hand. The left is for creating the flow and control."

"But I'm left handed. Why can't I just reverse it?"

"Do you want hands anymore?" yelled the first necromancer. "Because that is what'll happen."

"Ugh," shrugged the second necromancer. "Where do I put the Zel'ahk again?"

Slapping him in the face, the first necromancer responded, "Around your neck, stupid!"

A mile or two outside Hepsis a couple necromancers were busy practicing under the heat of a mid-day sun.

Just then, another figure in all black robes approached from the west. He was riding a beast of sorts. It wasn't until he got closer, that the other two necromancers saw that it was an undead horse. Its bones were showing through holes and gapes in its flesh which was barely hanging on, making it look like draping garments. The man atop was sitting on a worn saddle carrying a single large pack behind him. The rider approached, stopping before the two.

His features were covered in a dusty black material, but they could tell he was tall, lean, and perhaps even boney himself.

"Is that a Zel'ahk?" the rider asked, his voice not at all befitting his demeanor. It was soft and casual, with a hint of curiousness.

The two necromancers, much smaller than the one now before them, watched as the rider dismounted before replying, "Maybe," the first necromancer said cautiously.

The rider approached, almost as if a long lost friend. The other two were at first taken back, "Are you supposed to where it around your neck?" asked the second necromancer taking a step towards the mysterious black rider, his face hidden from view by his hood.

The first necromancer sighed.

"That depends," postulated the rider.

"Depends on what?" blurted the first with a resenting tone, stepping out from behind his friend.

"Well," the rider asked, "Are you using it for enhanced concentration or disabling a minor spell?"

"It can do that?" lit up the second; almost pretending they certainly were long lost friends.

"I thought everybody knew that?" the rider exclaimed.

"Alright, alright," chimed the first necromancer. "Who are you anyway?"

The rider extended his arm, "My name is Lyronaech the Great."

The second necromancer greeted him, almost too enthusiastically. "Pleased to meet you." he said. "My name is Freilith, and this is Zarlom."

"The pleasure is all mine," uttered the rider. "My enemies call my Lyron, on account that it's easier to pronounce."

The first necromancer grumbled something under his faceless robes.

"Are you headed towards Hepsis by chance, Lyron?" asked Freilith.

"Yes, I am headed that way," he noted.

Freilith grabbed hold of his companion, "We're also heading to Hepsis."

Zarlom removed his fellow necromancers hand from his shoulders.

"There's supposed to be a grand tournament." said Lyron.

Freilith added, "Unlike any seen in Bev before."

Zarlom looked skyward. The hot sun was at its zenith, causing him now to second guess wearing these particularly dark robes today.

"Where are you two from, if I may ask?" questioned Lyron.

"Well," started Freilith.

"We're not from anywhere," interrupted Zarlom.

His friend tried again to blurt, "We both are from…"

"What I mean to say," Zarlom cut in again, nudging his cohort in the ribs. "We are from many places." He chuckled, "Always travelling we are."

The rider nodded silently.

Just then the three of them heard a distant sound. Looking to the west they watched as another group of riders came galloping over the far ridge. Steel armor clanked along with the horse's steady speed. Their garbs and regalia seemed to suggest they are soldiers or perhaps hired guards. One of which was holding a small dark blue banner; the insignia too small to make out from the distance.

"I wonder who they might be." said Freilith to no one in particular.

Lyron began taking a few steps towards them. Zarlom taking notice that he began chanting something under his breath.

"What are you doing?" he asked.

Ignoring him, the rider concentrated on his chant, while gazing at the riders whom were probably fifty yards away, moving at a steady speed.

All of a sudden, a collection of dark missiles shot forth from his boney hands. They began chasing the riders, as the two other necromancers watched in silence.

Like dark trailing clouds, the missiles caught up to the men attempting to pierce each one in the back. They penetrated their armor, almost ignoring any protection or speed they seemed to have. The men collapsed to the sandy ground. Dust kicked up as their horses became frightened galloping away with fear in their eyes.

Lyron turned back towards Freilith and Zarlom whom were astonished.

"So, have you heard about the winning prize?" asked Lyron casually.

*　　*　　*

"Guards, guards!" shouted the vase merchant. "Wait till I slice off your hands!" he continued shouting. The merchant began chasing a child down the grimy cobblestone street. "How are you gonna steal when you got no hands!?"

They both disappeared.

Another man, sitting alone at his trinket stand said, "The market district was buzzing with activity today. In fact, business has been steadily picking up everywhere for the past few weeks. It would seem this tournament is actually doing some good."

He looked around expecting someone to reply back, but everyone seemed preoccupied with other stalls, wine tasting, fresh foods, and pretty girls.

The trinket merchant was positioned in the far back row, aisle thirty-four, right across the way from the Iron Praur, a horseshoe maker, and Greedy Mead's, a notable terrible bar, not even worthy of the wretched to sleep near.

Yet, despite all of this, even he was making some money.

"You like gold earrings?" motioning at two passing young women. One whispered something in her friend's ear. Giggling they both ventured over and began perusing his wares.

"Yes, yes," said the merchant. "I've got gold, silver, brass, and even," laughingly he pulled out a pair of sapphire earrings from a drawer below, "these beautiful ones."

The women showed some interest, but ultimately left empty handed.

"Bah!" the merchant exclaimed, putting everything back.

"Seems to me Phalin, you should've gotten into the knife business," snickered Jurra, the heavy-set merchant such as himself, whom happened to own the stall next to him. His stand was larger, more decorated, and he even hired girls part-time to lure in more customers during busier times. Though he would never admit it, he was occasionally jealous.

"You and your knives," spat Phalin back at his neighbor.

"Yes," his rival continued to mock, "knives which have given me a wonderful home, a beautiful wife, and so much gold to bath in."

"Bah!" he shouted again.

It was still early afternoon. Crowds of surveyors all came and went. Humans, Orcs, Goblins, Dwarves, and some even Phalin weren't sure who they were. Serra, the bakery girl stopped by and offered them both lunch. She was always such a lovely girl; kind, fragile, and motherly. Too bad she was married to a twit named Theodor, a bread maker with more moles on his face than in his mothers' garden.

A promising customer arrived, looking at the trinkets he had laid out front. The man fingered a beautiful ruby gold circlet. He admired its brilliant symmetrical golden frame, decorated with inlaid rubies and a large ruby star in the center. Moving to the pearl ones behind, his face and eyes lit up even brighter.

"I got those from a merfolk off the coast of Reeve last year," the merchant smiled. He could tell the man was very interested. "Since you seem to have an eye for great craftsmanship, how about I give you a deal on them?"

"Do you have this design in maybe a longer version?" said the man pointing at the pearl earrings. They were an extravagant set of blue pearls with a swirl pattern of silver and tiny gold engravings. "I think she prefers longer ones," he added.

"Let me just check and I'll get back to you," replied the merchant. "Give me just one moment." He smiled, and then began contemplating what kind of deal he should give the man upon his return. Turning around, he ducked behind his counter and began to unlock his chests and drawers, perusing his own inventory. He almost felt like humming, but caught himself, remembering that the last time he did, it didn't end well.

Discovering a pair of longer pearl earrings, he shouted, "Spectacular!" and began to lock up. Turning back around he presented them gleefully, "I believe these will suit her very..." He opened his eyes and stopped. Suddenly the man was gone. Or, at least he was no longer standing in front of his stand.

Phalin turned and looked. "Jurra!" he hollered. The knife merchant was busy showing his own wares to the man, whom he must've lured over while his back was turned.

Jurra smiled sinisterly back at his neighbor, who right now was growing red.

Phalin put the earrings down, folding his arms.

After the man left, Phalin shouted, "What does a nice man like that need a knife for? He was looking to get a pair of beautiful pearl earrings."

Jurra was busy flashing his money purposefully, "Perhaps he feared her wrath."

"Bah!" spat Phalin.

The afternoon had now passed.

Iron clad warriors, robbed mages, black garbed necromancers, races and people of all sizes and colors walked the streets. The tournament was about to commence in two days and the city hasn't been this busy since the king himself visited all those years ago.

Phalin watched as Jurra was busy selling some cheap silver knives to a young boy, before he spotted an elderly man making his way over to his stand. He was hobbling on what looked like a cane made from white oak. He wore a white cloth shirt tucked into brown trousers and small matted shoes. His beard was long and straight and he was bald as a newborn.

"Hello, my dear sir," the merchant began, pouring his heart into his opening line. "I have a wide selection of earrings, necklaces, bracelets, and rings, all at special discounted event prices.

The old man mumbled something. While rubbing his chi, he bent over to peruse the offerings.

Phalin gave the man some room, resisting the urge to pester the man with small talk.

"Mind if I see that ring there," the elder pointed; his long boney fingers pointing to the dragon bone ring lying in front of the glass.

"Ah, that is a good eye sir," Phalin gleamed. "That is an extremely rare and beautiful ring I got while visiting Alabous many years ago." He handed the man the ring to look at while continuing, "I might even be able to give you a deal; you having a great eye for craftsmanship and all." The old man fondled the ring in his boney cold hands. A twin dragon spiral was engraved along the sides forming into one at the center and clasping a black orb.

The man held the ring up to the sky, as if he was looking for something only the sun could reveal. Afterwards, he nodded. "Do you know Lord Krigren?" the man asked.

"Oh, yes." His eyes lit up, "Who doesn't know Lord Krigren?"

"Well," the old man stated. "I am one of Lord Krigren's vassals, and I'm sure our Lord would be most gracious if you sold him this ring."

The merchant was speechless. "Lord…Krigren." He managed to sputter. "It would be my honor."

"Excellent!" said the old man. "Would say, 32 silver be sufficient?"

Phalin almost collapsed. He had to take a step back and breathe slowly.

After reclaiming some composure he replied, "Let me check my safe box. It'll be just a moment."

The merchant could barely contain his excitement. A deal this good was what he dreamed about. He quickly began unlocking his safe, scouring through his earnings. After a quick count, he locked the safe back up and turned around ready to graciously accept the money.

The old man was gone.

"What the..." the merchant said out loud. "Jurra!"

He looked over at his neighbors stall.

There was the slimy snake of a seller. He had the old man foaming over his own dragon bone offering.

Phalin couldn't contain himself any longer.

He stormed over to the stall.

The old man intercepted him, showing Phalin his newest purchase, a slender dragon bone knife. "Lord Krigren will be so pleased." The elder grimaced as he hobbled speedily away.

"Ahhhhhhh!" yelled Phalin, now furious, retreating back to his stand.

"I can't believe it!" he shouted.

Without warning, Jurra made his own shout while Phalin's back was turned. A few crashes also broke out from the nearby stall, causing Phalin to finally turn around and see.

A group of three masked men ran off carrying several boxes and crates of Jurra's wares. Phalin stood on his toes to get a better view. He leaned over, now watching as blood was now flowing from around the stand, soaking into the pavement and dusty soil.

Phalin was silent. The thieves were nowhere to be seen. It was like nobody even noticed except him. And nobody seemed to care.

After a minute or two, he found himself smiling. Almost laughing inside over what had just transpired.

But soon, a terrible sinking feeling began to creep over him.

He sank back into his stand, slowly realizing that maybe this tournament wasn't such a great idea after all.

Opening Ceremony

A beckoning triumph erupted.

The sounds of long horns herald the tremendous applause.

Twice, three times they bellowed, as the remaining seats filled. The wealthy packed in tightly in the stands, while the homeless shuffled under loose floorboards beneath them. The entire city had been slowly gathering in numbers, food, and money, all building up to this day.

The horns stopped. A red cloaked man came out from the arena gates. His arms stretched to the crowds of people, the crowd cheered and hollered with anticipation. The man lifted his hood, revealing a young face covered in tattoos of bones and swirls. The crowd was in full uproar. The bone man taunted them driving their excitement until the king himself appeared from atop an outdoor throne, high above the arena overlooking the crowd. Bystanders standing in the filthy streets below looked skyward. The platform rose nearly fifty feet higher than the stands themselves, and was built on top of a building a week prior. Lofty chairs, service, and the best view were all assembled for this event.

The bone man signaled the crowd to gaze upwards towards their king.

Alas, he made his entrance.

Approaching the balcony he took a moment to clear his voice. "To the people of Hepsis, the people of Bev, I personally dedicate this grand event of a lifetime to be yours." He paused again, taking another moment as the crowd bellowed and jeered as he spoke. Many denizens were still shuffling in. Filling whichever gaps and small openings were left around the arena. Fathers, sons, mothers, and daughters of all races attended. "We have all suffered, Bev has suffered, and for that we shall wash away the past and bring a new future today!" he exclaimed to the heavens.

Behind him sat the top six nobles of Hepsis and their families. From the northwest sector, Braedor and his wife Lilycia were sitting to the king's right, their four children behind them. Dyok, the appointed Event Headmaster was sitting patiently on his other side along with Yorvich and his wife Mercia, and their two children. Behind them were Yerilov and Lord Krigren, the two nobles from the south, along with their wives Jurlicia and Marigreen respectively. Along the back was the noble from the western side of Hepsis, Odibur, his wife Urlin, and their five children. And lastly was Zeydiin -noble from the east- who leaned against the back wall. All of them watching and listening as their king spoke to his people below.

"Lord Dyok this event has really come together over the last few weeks," spoke Jurlicia. "I congratulate you."

"Thank you, Lady Jurlicia," commented Dyok, "It was a heavy burden, but I did it for the good of our province."

"And what good it did," broke in Yerilov. "We saw a rise of nearly 300% in both wealth and mass. I'd say with any luck this event shall help wipe the city streets clean from many past mistakes and bring in a brighter future for us all."

"Indeed," agreed Dyok. "Though, we still must be careful."

"Careful?" continued Yerilov. "We've got over two hundred guards in this sector alone. And just outside those doors we have another fifty," Yerilov laughed.

Dyok contemplated, "It's not the people I'm worried about, nor this event." he paused; It's what'll come after."

The king waited until the crowd calmed, "For the next three days, you shall bear witness to the greatest contest of strength, power, and cunning the likes of which have never been seen. I present to you the Dark Arts Tournament!"

"My dearest Urlin," whispered Lord Yorvich. The middle-aged red head gained an interest. "I fear ever for your skin and delicate frame daily, what with how much your husband brings home. I shall invite you to one of my homes for you are far closer to death than he'd

121

have you believe."

Urlin giggled and blushed. Her wide girth jostled and shook the very chair she sat upon, as her husband Odibur fumed and glared at his neighbor from across the row. He spotted Lord Yorvich glancing down her cleavage then winking in his general direction, as he continued, "I insist you share a feast with me and my wife after these events are over." Urlin smiled. Her husband attempted to grab at Yorvich's throat, but she kindly intercepted them.

"Now, now" she spoke delicately, "My husband and I would love to attend."

Yorvich smiled and politely turned back to his own wife, whom mostly ignored their flirtatious conversation and was in fact staring at Lord Braedor's eldest son, Martaer.

"Have me down for seven crests on Lord Zeydiin's leading man," motioned Yerilov to Lord Krigren. The two switched seats and were now conversing over future bets.

"You really would bet against me?" replied Krigren.

Yerilov grabbed a small purse from his wife, before passing it along to Krigren. "Add that to the bet as well." he added.

"I am astonished," Marigreen interjected. "To think you'd accept such an outrageous bet against your own house.

"My dearest," Krigren spoke, "If Lord Yerilov wishes to throw away some pocket change then who am I to refuse?"

The king suddenly announced, "Official Kehgan!"

"Yes, my liege!" spoke the cloaked bone man from down below.

"Let the opening ceremony commence!" shouted the king.

Kehgan the bone lord signaled the gate keepers. Suddenly the massive front gate creaked and budged. It began to lift upwards, and soon a single file of contestants came through and lined up inside the center of the arena. The crowd grew into in unstoppable barrage of clamor and applause. Royal guardsmen also flooded in, lining up along the outer perimeter of the arena walls. Wearing full armor and bright red regalia they maintained and held order against the chaos that was unleashed inside. With so many power hungry and dark art wielders all in one place, the king and Dyok were taking special precautions.

"Sir," Dyok motioned for the king behind him.

He stepped away from the balcony and gave his ear. "Yes?"

Dyok was already near his side and lowered his voice. "There is no stopping this now. Whatever happens…"

"Whatever happens shall be for the good of Hepsis." The king interrupted him. He then returned to the balcony and raised his hands once more.

Down below the contestants were eyeing each other up. A golden staffed mage, a black onyx knight, a necromantic imp, a man with blackened skin and yellow eyes, a woman as tall as two men, a skeleton, a being wrapped in light purple fog, a screeching creature with sharp claws and red tongue. They all gathered together.

The bone man took a stand atop an even higher stand and hollered, "I will now quickly go over the rules so we can get this event started! Any breaking of these rules, non-sanctioned killings, cheating, or otherwise lawlessness will result in your banishment or the more likely event, your death. Firstly, this spectacle is a one-on-one contest only. This means no parties, gangs, double teams, or other magic misuse for multiple fighters. Second, All matches are final. Once matchups are declared, the fighters participating cannot change and their can only be one winner. Third, only magical, necromantic, or mana assisted fights may take place in the arena. This means the acting participator must be undead and cannot be assisted by an outside member. And lastly, our king is the ultimate decider of all things. You will obey his word, and obey his mercifulness. He is our king and our event savior."

"Five-to-one says the king gets targeted sometime within the first three matches." whispered Yorvich.

Hearing this, Dyok turned around, "You are insatiable" he spat. "He is standing right there."

"I'll take you up on that," added Braedor.

"I can't believe what I am hearing," expressed Dyok.

"As will I," spoke Zeydiin from the back.

Blood Sport

"Rip off his arms!" Grotan yelled to his minion; a nearly nine foot tall skeletal creature. Created from a variety of animals, it had the legs of an elephant, the arms of a gorilla, and the skull of a lion. A construct of bone and decay it hobbled, moaning towards the crowd.

"What are you doing!?" Murchev screamed, waving his arms at his own combatant; a much smaller undead warrior with blades hidden under his arms, and foul green ooze dripping from several large protruding fangs. It hissed and clawed at the air, like an ill-tempered and savage beast.

Their masters exchanged glances from opposite corners of the arena. Tension was amassing in the stands, and even the guards felt uneasy. Upwards the sun was buried beneath a clouded sky.

The giant charged in first. The animal macabre was too slow for the faster hissing warrior. It's slow, heavy attacks kept missing, pulverizing the dirt with tremendous thuds. After each successful dodge, the smaller undead creature was able to lunge in, swiping and flailing at the unprotected underbelly. Fragments of bone, cloth, and green ooze decorated the arena grounds.

Meanwhile, across the wide arena grounds, standing atop a platform gazed the Match Official. Studying with great enthusiasm as the creatures below fought furiously without remorse or emotions. Fueled by the rage and lust from their masters, they shuffled about the arena with a single thought in their nonexistent minds. Win, at all costs.

It was still early in the day; Dyok, Braedor, and Lord Krigren, as well as some other respected and wealthy denizens of Hepsis were under the pagoda, towering above the arena. An assortment of fruit, nuts, bread, and wine were being constantly brought in and placed on fanciful auburn and mahogany tables. The children and guards could be seen sneaking a mouthful or two while their fathers, mothers, and masters were entertained by the commotion and spectacle below. It

was breezy. The stench and vile emanating from the lower classes didn'
t quite reach their height, so through most of the day it was a pleasant,
yet loud experience.

"Quite an assortment today, would you say?" spoke Braedor; his
hands grabbing for his glass of red wine. He fumbled for a moment
unable to find it, not realizing till a steward had picked the cup from
the ground that it had been out of reach.

"I believe there was an assortment of folk who hail from Ersive or
even farther, if you'd believe it?" spoke Krigren.

"They all came together?" laughed Braedor, almost spilling his
newly poured glass which the steward kindly refilled.

"It would seem, Krigren added. "Say, Dyok." He leaned over,
attempting to rouse the attention of his fellow noble whom was busy
leaning over the rails admiring the view and spectacle below.

"Dyok!" Krigren called a little louder.

A half dazed Dyok turned to face him. "Yes?"

"Do you think any of the southerners even stand a chance?"

Dyok's attention now became undivided, "What makes you so
concerned about the southerners all of a sudden?"

"Just humoring myself is all," Krigren spoke. He nudged Braedor
in the side, "We nobles grow so bored, even during exciting events
such as these."

Braedor put his glass down and called over a servant. It was the
same steward as before, but he failed to notice. "Fetch me some nuts,"
he griped.

The animal giant lunged. Another loud thud echoed across the
field. His over extensions gave the wild small warrior his chance.
Dashing forward he savagely clawed and dug into his foes entire lower
half. The mighty elephant leg bones were starting to splint and crack
from the repeated onslaught. A sudden cracking noise rose out. The
creature's enormous weight was suddenly too much for the chipped
and splintering legs. The mighty creature bellowed as he started to
bend crashed to all fours. The animal giant went out of control,
desperately trying to grab at its assailant with both arms and jaws. His
master jeered on from the sidelines, "Kill him! Kill him!"

His face was frozen. His creature was losing and he knew it.

The clawed minion scampered up the animal giants back; claws scraping along and chipping away at the spinal column and ribs. The giant flung his shoulders to the side, growling and attempting to trip the small creature over. All of a sudden, the clawing foe lost balance, toppling to the ground finally caught in the large, gorilla hands of the huge skeletal beast.

Chomping down ferociously onto its bone fingers and wrist, the small creature became desperate.

It was all over.

The giant squeezed tightly, shattering its small frame and almost all of its bones. The remainder of the creature was then torn apart and flung all over the arena.

"YES!" yelled the giants lord from the sidelines.

"Congratulations!" yelled the arena headmaster almost immediately.

The noise from the crowd rose to an all time high.

"Well, I got to be leaving," hinted Braedor; two of his own servants assisted him up and out of his chair. "Husband do this, husband do that." he chuckled; his legs still a little wobbly.

"I guess, we both lost," spoke Krigren graciously.

Braedor turned around, his glass still in his hands. "Let's just say it was even." he laughed.

"Dyok!" Krigren called once more.

"I'm still here." His friend responded from the corner.

"What do you think?"

"About what?" added Dyok.

"About the win," Krigren blurted. "Braedor seemed to suggest that the larger the warrior, the better his chances."

Dyok smiled, though the day was still young he felt tired; a sudden exhaustion rising, "And what do you think?"

"I think he got lucky," said Lord Krigren as he too got up and headed for the door with his own guards following closely behind.

＊　　＊　　＊

The iron clad knight stood like a wall. With broad sword held at his chest, pointing skyward, he awaited command. Across the opposite side crawled his competition; a heap of flesh, bones, muscles, and sinew vaguely resembling a large tiger. With little to no facial features in which to speak of, it made no noise as it crawled along the ground, both of them awaiting the signal.

High above, the Arena Official sat in his chair. He glanced towards the crowd as if measuring the excitement. His heart raced. Hands clasping the rails, he leaned over finally beckoning below, "BEGIN!"

The knight was the first to move. Dark blue waves forming a chain of energy coursing through its body as it took each step, maintaining a reasonable distance and stance. The fleshy tiger soon began encircling the knight, approaching the middle like a beast getting ready to pounce. Each one constantly being fed mana by their master's from the sidelines. Black, blue, and red magic began wrapping around their arms, flowing towards their undead abominations. Tension was in the air as the crowd watched from the distance.

The city watch was ever busy. There wasn't a moment when they weren't arresting vagrants, chasing pilfers, or creating a presence to help simmer the dozens of small brawls erupting all over the city. During each match there was always at least thirty guards positioned around the arena walls and perimeter. Three royal mages were always stationed near the higher perches, and surrounding the noble entrances, keeps, and box seats, were another twenty guards, two mages, and several elite royal guardsmen.

The flesh tiger suddenly leaped, seizing a guardsman in its jaws, crunching down on steel and flesh alike. The unaware guard screamed in agony as his innards splashed out and onto the floor from the tiger's mouth. Immediately the alarms were sounded. Some guardsmen tried to assist their fellow man as the tiger rampaged around the arena walls, pouncing and attempting to gather more men in its mighty jaws. Meanwhile, some elite royal guards poured in from the nearby gate, surrounding the necromancer whom controlled it. The necromancer pleaded, his cries falling on death ears. The guards pierced him swiftly with swords and spears alike. A few guards also began encircling the other combatant. Standing still with arms high, the other necromancer halted his minion. As the last dying breath left the necromancer, so too did his flesh tiger, collapsing into an indiscernible heap.

The crowd was still.

The nobles high above watched with the same shock and awe.

Almost all of the regular nobles were in attendance, except for a few wives, some children, and Lord Zeydiin, who often came and went without anyone really noticing.

"Quick, barricade the first three doors and call forth a mage, yelled Dyok to his standing commander. The seasoned guard nodded, quickly hollering for a few of his men to follow as they ran outside, locking the door behind them.

"Quite a brutal death," mentioned Jurlicia, a cloth brought up to her mouth.

What did you expect!" added in Lord Krigren, "That's what you get for breaking tournament rules, let alone attacking the city guard."

"Now this was more like it," Braedor chuckled. "Truly a spectacle to be excited for!" his wife offered him another glass of wine and some roasted pork morsels seasoned with basil.

Dyok was frozen. He was stuck in this room with people whom he hated. These kinds of attacks were to be expected, but nothing could prepare him for what he felt. He took the blame for the lives lost. He would cower in a corner if only to avoid the shame on himself and his king for choosing him as event advisor.

The commotion was quickly subdued. Already the bodies of several mangled guards, as well as, the necromancer were being carried away. A cleanup crew quickly dispatched the pile of flesh which was once a ferocious man-eating tiger, and a few minutes later, the door behind them unlocked.

"My lord," the commander began. "I've been asked to gather all Event Officials and yourself to the committee room for an immediate ruling regarding the match."

Dyok snapped out of his coma, "Very well."

He then followed the guard out and back down the stairs. His face buried deep into his shirt, shielding himself from his fellow nobles.

"After talking with the other officials, as well as, the king," the leading Arena Headmaster began. "We have decided to call this match...null-in-void"

About half of the crowd booed and hissed, while the other was still in shock over what had transpired earlier. The Headmaster attempted to calm them down, continuing with the announcement, "Since Zarix and his minion did not actually participate. And before his challenger decided to end his life, we are granting him another match, which will be decided upon at a later date."

The crowd erupted, with many calling for blood, while others shouting injustice. Whichever the case, it was decided.

"I guess, this counts as five losses for you," Braedor jokingly said to Yorvich.

"This one shouldn't count!" Lord Yorvich replied. "There was no way, any of us could've known..."

"Ah," broke in Krigren. "But isn't that what makes the game that much more fun?"

Yorvich pulled out a hidden pouch. Handing some coins over to one of his servants he grumbled, "You won't be keeping that money for long."

"Wasn't the king supposed to be an attendance this evening?" Odibur asked out loud.

Krigren piped in, "Last I heard, he was overseeing a meeting with several nobles from Denvek."

"Those coastal fishermen are just jealous," added Yorvich.

Krigren continued, "Apparently they also want to hold a large event to help rebuild their city."

"Bah!" Braedor spat. "What's to rebuild? They got fish. Isn't that all they need?" he laughed.

His wife chiming in, "Now husband, I'm sure they're just stricken with jealousy as Lord Krigren suggests."

"Whichever the reasons, he should be here." said Odibur. "With the utmost respect to Dyok, the king's presence will help qualm many of these breakouts."

"Or increase them." added Zeydiin from the rear. Everyone turned around.

* * *

Gragorith the Mountain they called him.

He was a large man from the broken cliffs of Keifa. During his time, he was a ferocious pirate, burly barbarian, savage warlord, and unstoppable beast; and he was now here in the arena. Nearly 400 years after his death. Resurrected and with two extra arms stitched to his sides. He was a hulking abomination of muscle, power, and rage.

"Rraaaoorrrrrr!"

Barreling down, unsheathing four double bladed axes, one in each of his four arms. He charged forward, leaping high into the air before coming down hard atop his foe. A combination of spikes and shields collided with sparks and savagery in the middle of the arena. Hailing from one of the southern islands, his combatant was built from an orc skeleton with dragon teeth and steel melded into his bones. He was called Backbreaker; tough as the Wintering Wastes and slayer of war chiefs.

Gragorith came down again and again with an unrelenting assault. His anger seemed to rise with each strike as his steel clanged against his opponents' hard defense. Their masters from the edges of the field were also heavily focused; each one channeling extra strength and mana to try and give some sort of momentary boost or increase of strength.

Backbreaker knelt down absorbing an axe into his right shoulder. The blade was wedged heavily into his spikes and plating.

Pushing it away, he then dodged another attack aimed at his skull, as he grabbed hold of the one that was stuck, and yanked it out from his frame, before tossing it aside. Rearing up, he charged back into the fray. Gragorith met him again. Backbreaker pulled out his own weapon. A large club with several spikes protruding from it. The crud weapon was heavy and slow, but as it collided with each axe it easily pushed them aside, forcing its way down upon Gragorith's head, arms, and sides. Pieces of bone began to chip away as each fighter pounded with all their might, slowly breaking into each other's body and soul.

＊　＊　＊

Mid-day lunch had just finished. The nobles and other high-class citizens sat in perches and box seats, watching, judging, and laughing at the stage below. It was a grand fight. Even their children were becoming enthralled and acting out several past matches. With wooden swords and shields they battered and swore to cut throats and sever heads.

The lords, Krigren, Braedor, Odibur, and Zeydiin, were watching from the front, as a few other wealthy members and family were situated towards the rear of the vestibule.

"You both can't place bets on the Mountain!" shouted Odibur. "That would break even my own spending for today."

"Your loss then, my friend," Lord Krigren added.

Braedor pointed down toward the arena, his laughter and excitement bellowing out, "That's it! That's it!"

His second son, Haerold, climbed onto his lap. "Father, I want that man to crush the other one!"

"Oh, he will, my son," Braedor huffed, securing his chubby son over his better knee. "He will."

Krigren called, "Zeydiin, want to lose some money too?" He spotted his fellow noble hanging out near the far rails, back against the wall.

"Zeydiin!" Braedor also clamored.

The lord sighed, and then excused himself past the others, until he now stood over them.

"How about it?" asked Braedor. "I'll even spot you the first ten."

Lord Zeydiin bent down, "If you two are both done playing, I believe the final games will be held tomorrow."

Krigren looked quizzically at his friend whom let go of his son, who ran back and joined the other children in merriment.

"Here's a little taste of what's to come," Zeydiin also added.

A small dart impaled the hand of Backbreaker's master. The necromancer winced; closing his eyes then soon began to breathe heavily. His minion also suffered from this sudden drop in spirit and strength. Gragorith seized this opportunity. Dropping his own axes, he grabbed hold of the massive club with all four hands, ripping it from his assailants grasp. He then pounded the weapon down onto his stunned foe, shattering the skull and head entirely. The creature fell to his knees, and yet Gragorith kept the assault going. The beating was unrelenting. Bones cracked, shattered, and exploded. Gragorith the Mountain pounded that weapon into him until almost all of his bones were smashed or grounded into the dirt. Finally satisfied, and his bloodlust ending, Gragorith tossed the club aside and raised his fists triumphantly into the air.

The crowd exploded. The necromancer ran towards his creation in the center as the Event Headmaster was also smiling and applauding from his high perch.

The other necromancer soon collapsed from exhaustion. His hand clenching at his now seized heart. Cursing the lands, he finally stopped moving.

"Hey!" Odibur jumped out of his chair. His face growing redder as his servants all came to his aid. "What's the big idea?!" he shouted.

By now Krigren and Braedor also rose. They looked around the room for Zeydiin, but he was nowhere to be seen.

"How dare he spit in our faces like that!" yelled Braedor.

"Easy now," Lord Krigren whispered.

The guards around the room were all watching them. The wives grabbed for their children as Odibur clambered over towards them, "I call for a refund!"

"Sure," Krigren motioned for his banker to hand over the money from his bet. Odibur seized the sack. As he left he blurted, "To think what you both would do for a few coins."

Braedor took a deep breath then reassured his men to be at ease.

Krigren also took his seat, both looking at each other. "I suppose we should attend these finals that Lord Zeydiin brought to our attention."

"As much as I hate the bastard, I agree," said Braedor.

"Make no mention of this to the Dyok or the king," Krigren followed up.

Braedor added, "What do I look like?"

LIVE OR DIE

With a silent nod, the guard opened the door. Lord Yorvich and Lord Krigren entered rather small room. Almost like a single person storage den, it was lined with a simple large stone formation with a few random torches and an even smaller table situated in the middle. Not to their surprise, Braedor was already there. Sitting in a large leather chair that didn't appear to belong in the room, smiling. Next to him sat Lord Zeydiin, the only eastern noble. The only one who willingly ventured into Beggars Alley. They halted their conversation. After a quick Bevarian courtesy, they sat. The few guards were dismissed.

"Lord Zeydiin why must you insist on bringing these two into our private affairs?" begged Braedor.

Krigren and Yorvich scowled at him, whilst Zeydiin prepared some wine in the other two glasses.Handing them to the new arrivals, he said, "Come now Braedor, we mustn't keep secrets from our fellow nobles."

Braedor chuckled and nodded, "Aye, you say that now. But to be honest that one there." pointing to Yorvich whom had just finished a sip, "is more likely to rat us out if it'll fill his pockets."

Yorvich stood up defiantly, "I'll have you know..."

Zeydiin cut him off, motioning for his feuding friends to take a seat. After they settled back down he continued, "Since this meeting will hopefully benefit all of us, I trust Lord Yorvich will do his part."

Yorvich sighed, gave Braedor another quick glance, and then clasped his hands.

133

"If I may ask?" spoke Krigren. "Why isn't Lord Odibur or Dyok, or any of the other nobles here?"

Zeydiin took a sip then rested his glass on the small table. "No, this is something that must stay between only a select few. And besides, as a Hepsis matter, I see no reason to let the other cities benefit from our work."

"Alright," said Braedor. "Let's just get on with it then."

Zeydiin sighed. Clasping his own hands he started, "This tournament, as fantastic as it is, will soon be over." The nobles all nodded. "We will soon have a winner, and that winner shall be granted power and wealth along with his new title, correct." The nobles nodded again. "Now, we can't have just anybody given this kind of power can we? We need to help decide who it shall be."

Yorvich broke in, "I didn't think you'd..."

"Come now," Braedor interrupted him laughing, "This is Hepsis after all. You'd really think we'd just let this happen without our say in the matter?"

Zeydiin hushed his fellow noble, sensing he was growing quite loud.

Krigren spoke up, "You act like this was all your idea. Not a moment ago you were just as surprised..."

"It doesn't matter," said Zeydiin, cutting him off. "It's all laid out."

"And are we just going to assume it's in our benefit as well, without so much as notifying us beforehand?" Krigren added.

"It was already too late," Zeydiin commented. "What would you have had me do?"

The lords all looked around, watching the flames from the torches, as the shadows and flames bounced off the thick walls. The nobles quietly shifted in their seats under the claustrophobic setting, taking silent sips from their glasses.

Zeydiin pointed towards the door, "At this moment, right outside, is going to be the start of a new era. A peaceful one, I might add. And if you'd think me, let alone the king, would stand for an untrustworthy uncontrollable outcome when we have so much influence then I suggest you leave this city immediately. Each of you already has high stakes here. You make that decision."

Lord Zeydiin topped off his glass.

The other nobles were silent.

❋　❋　❋

Sand flung skyward. The massive hammer came down multiple times with little effort. The audience was overflowing with noise and cheers. The stands were over max capacity as a continuous stream of people began pouring in from all over. Fights were beginning to break out all over the city. The guards were all on high alert. As a precaution, Lord Dyok called for double the normal protection and presence of city and royal guards. Any and all that were available were stationed around the city, arena, or next to the officials.

The dust settled. Suddenly, the shadows of two combatants became visible; their frames massive in size. Bone, flesh, and mana helped stitch them together. Their hooded master's controlled them from the sidelines, feeding them life and power.

Like a raging animal they dived towards one another; weapons clashing, the crowd feeding from each moment. All were in attendance; all were unable to look away.

High above, the king was staring with an utmost desire. He was about to bear witness to a lifetime event. With an almost maniacal face, he beckoned for more, as those behind him also jeered and craved an even more brutal fight.

"What's the real reason you omitted Lord Odibur or even Dyok?" questioned Krigren.

Braedor laughed, "Dyok is too committed."

"It's true," said Yorvich, sitting to his right. "The man has too much honor and pride. He'd never agree to these decisions."

Zeydiin also added, "As for Lord Odibur, my sources tell me he's already in support of the other fighter."

135

"That bastard!" Braedor shouted.

"I guess that's to be expected," noted Yorvich relaxing back into his seat.

"Whatever the case," spoke Zeydiin, "Have we come to an a greement?"

"Aye" said Braedor, almost too quickly.

"I see little choice," Krigren added.

"Oh there's always choice," said Zeydiin. "As I've said before, you can leave. However, ignoring this situation is another sign for abandoning your duties to this city. I figured you of all people would understand that much."

Krigren pondered a moment, his thoughts drifting as he stared down at his half drunk glass. Swishing the red wine around, Yorvich spoke next, "I assume everything's in order?'"

"That would be correct." replied Zeydiin.

"Well," said Yorvich, "If you'll excuse me, I'd like to see how this fight ends."

"Yes," added Braedor. "The wife will never let me hear the end, if I don't make at least some appearance."

"That'll be wise for all of us," said Zeydiin. "The king might ask questions if we failed to at least present ourselves during this final event."

"Are you coming Krigren?" asked Yorvich, halting in the doorway.

Lord Krigren sat his glass down. "I'll be right there."

❉   ❉   ❉

"Ah, husband," said Lilycia as she welcomed her husband with a kiss on the cheek.

Braedor smiled as him and Yorvich took their seats in the high platform. "I'm ever sorry for missing the beginning," he pardoned, "Did I miss much?"

His wife offered him a drink, which he gladly accepted, "No, it's still going on. This is truly the greatest spectacle I've ever seen."

Marigreen also commented, "Yes, truly a memorable event." Looking at Braedor she added, "Was my husband with you?"

Braedor turned to face her, "No, but he should be arriving. I do remember bumping into one of his servants; the clumsy fool."

His own wife cradling her hands around his wide shoulders offering him some grapes and smiling as the warriors below were lost in more dust.

The two warriors seemed to be caught in a deadlock, neither one falling back or gaining an upper hand. As the two were exchanging blows, a crack soon appeared from beneath the stage. A few feet away from the warriors another appeared. The crowd, too busy watching the fight, failed to spot them. One warrior got kicked back stumbling right onto one of the cracks. All of a sudden his foot sank into the dirt. He was held in place, struggling to break free, the ground almost seemed to have swallowed his right leg all the way up to his knee.

Almost in anticipation, the other warrior yelled, lifting his mighty hammer before smashing it down upon his rival. The hammer collided with the trapped foe's spiked helmet, denting it, before knocking it away. The other warrior attempted to block with one hand while trying to free his leg with the other. Meanwhile his rival was pounding on him from all sides.

Eventually, the warrior broke out and rolled along the ground, nearly avoiding a fatal vertical blow, which missed and caused more dirt to pick up.

Angrily, the other warrior adjusted himself before charging towards his enemy.

Right before they would collide, another strange occurrence happened. A sudden gust of wind hit the once beaten warrior, taking him by surprise. When looking at his rival he noticed he wasn't moving. His hammer dropped to the ground. All strength and vigor seemingly left his body. The warrior approached cautiously. Suddenly, he froze. The top half of his body slid away. Taking this opportunity, the warrior performed a flurry of slashes with his swords chipping away and mauling the remainder of his foe. Broken pieces of bone flew off, as the crowd, now at an all time high, cheered with massive applause.

"He did it!" yelled the Event Headmaster from the high platform.

"Congratulations!"

Lords Braedor, Yorvich, and Krigren all looked over hoping to spot Zeydiin, but after realizing that he wasn't there, they turned back around cheering along with the rest of them.

CHAMPION

"Here's to Horvich!"

"Here, here!" shouted the crowd.

Everyone raised their glasses.

Official Kehgan announced, "Master of the undead and winner of the first annual dark arts tournament!"

The room was filled with noise as every man, woman, and child, held up their glasses.

It was a grand feast; held in the master event hall with seating for nearly three hundred. Twelve nobles and their families were using the place for their own private gathering. City guards were lined outside and among the entranceways. And along and walls and inside were another twenty royal guards.

"Master Horvich," Braedor began.

The tournament champion was engorging himself on the roasted lamb in front of him. "I believe it's Governor now," he managed to mumble.

"Ah yes," spoke Braedor, clearing his throat from the glazed chicken he'd just finished chewing. "Governor Horvich, later tonight we'll need to discuss…"

"Can't it wait?" Horvich grumbled.

"Well," Braedor looking a tad confused. "I suppose."

"Good," Horvich finished. He had taken another large bite before greedily moving onto the poached duck.

"I suppose we should wrap up some pieces, you know, for our king." Braedor laughed. "'Tis' really a shame he couldn't see this to the end." He gulped down some red ale before adding, "Oh, well.

Zeydiin spoke up, "Yes, we'll have you deliver it to him personally."

"Here, here!" yelled a few others from around the table.

The children were mostly quiet, as the wives were growing louder than even their half-drunk husbands.

Through all the noise in the room, Yorvich hollered for Lord Krigren whom sat three seats down. "Lord Krigren!"

He looked up, and after clearing his throat waited.

"No regrets then," Yorvich held up his glass.

Krigren in turn, raised his.

The discussions and dining went well into the night. During that time, three guard changes took place, and with many of the children sent to bed with the wives, the nobles were now free from most noise and could start to get down to business.

"Dyok!" spoke Odibur.

He looked across the table, "Yes?"

"We really should all congratulate you with putting on this grand spectacle."

Yorvich, whom sat closest to his left added, "Even I must say..."

BANG!

A large thud erupted from the front doors.

The sound of glass breaking also came from the top windows.

BANG! BANG!

The guards stationed at the front moved in closer to inspect, weapons unsheathing.

WHHHOOOOOSHHHH!

The doors flung open; followed by a blast of cold air. Two guards now lay collapsed among the debris. Half of the nobles stood up, while the other half were looking around confused.

139

Without warning, six men dressed in dark black and wearing masks jumped down from the ceilings. Daggers went soaring through the air, puncturing guards in their necks and faces; three, four, seven, all dead simultaneously.

"GUARDS!" cried Braedor.

"Protect us!" screamed Yorvich at the top of his lungs.

Pouring from the outer hall entered another ten or twelve assailants wielding swords, spears, and even deadly magic. Any guards remaining were being slaughtered like sheep in front of them. There was hardly any resistance.

Lord Dyok and the others stood motionless. In front of them laid what was left of the city's best guards.

The dark assassins crept closer to the front table, while a few of them fanned out, checking the other walls and surrounding the rear exits.

"Mercy!" pitched Yorvich, "Mercy!"

"What is it that you want?" asked Krigren calmly.

As the men approached closer, Odibur tried to duck out of sight, but was seized violently and thrown back into his seat.

It was at this time that Dyok regained some of his composure enough to look around taking in their situation. He then remembered that their champion, Horvich was seated next to them.

A few other nobles must also have realized this fact. Almost consecutively they were all staring wide eyed at their champion who was dead. He was face down in a pool of his own blood; a sharp, black dagger protruding from his neck. Dyok craned his neck and observed his eyes. They were white, and had rolled back into his head. A terrible twisting grimace of agony was all that remained.

Krigren spoke out, "If what you seek is power, then by all means, we are the ones who can grant you it."

A tall man, presumably their leader, approached. He advanced upon Lord Krigren, spear steady, pointing it at his throat.

Soon, every noble in the room was being pressed upon by sharp blades and dark set eyes.

"You really think all we want is power?" the masked man asked,

140

his voice rough, almost purposefully grainy.

Krigren gulped, "Money?" he managed to sputter.

The man turned shouting, "Who here believes they can grant us what the city itself cannot?"

The room fell silent.

The nobles all contemplated. A few were starting to point fingers, and Dyok himself was reluctant to speak up. He nervously bit his lip, thinking about his title as Event Overseer, putting his life in jeopardy. He shivered at the thought of his fellow nobles using him as a scapegoat; although, it hardly seemed that surprising.

"Listen," Zeydiin began.

Suddenly the leader nodded, and the man that was guarding him pierced his throat. The head of the spear erupted out the back of his neck. Blood sprayed outwards like an eruption. The table and food became soaked as his body fell limp. The man then yanked his spear free and allowed Lord Zeydiin's body to collapse to the ground. The rest of the nobles fell silent, motionless.

"Obviously," Dyok finally mustered, knowing full well that it was up to him now. He looked over at the champion's body, "He wasn't strong enough to lead our city."

The leader pressed his blade up to his neck. Dyok could feel the cold steel. It had already been coated with the blood of a few guardsmen. He could smell the stench of his slain protectors. He turned to face the leader. Wanting to spit in the man's face, he could only hold back his true feelings and ask, "As the rules of this tournament, we must have the next strongest. That is the idea, right?"

The man appeared gratified and backed off a little, "That man was an embarrassment to this city," he dictated.

The remaining nobles were flabbergasted. A few even gave a sigh of relief, with thoughts of maybe they'd be able to escape with their lives.

Suddenly, a few men slashed the neck and pierced the body of another Noble. The rest watched, unable to move or even scream as the noble Braedor was no more.

The murders took a step back, wiped the blood off their weapons. "Fear, is not enough." Their leader demanded.

Dyok watched the man come up to his face again; his blade hesitating a mere inch from his own neck. "I expect no more complications," he whispered.

"We'll make the announcement first thing tomorrow," Dyok commented.

* * *

Later that night, Dyok was alone in his chambers. His bedroom door was open, allowing him to occasionally stare as his wife cradling his newborn in the adjacent room. He stared long and hard as fear and imagery of the future haunted him.

This was his city, but sometimes he felt like the city allowed him to stay here. Like a creature of free will, it decided who lived and who died. Was there really a future for this city?

Was it even a future he himself had a hand in? He looked toward his wife again. The small cries of his daughter permeated his heart and kept him warm even as the night grew colder.

He hated this city.

* * *

"My king," Dyok started, walking into the meeting room once again. The guards herald his arrival, and after waiving them off, he ventured closer to where his king was seated.

"Ah, Dyok," the king graciously invited him closer. "Welcome, welcome." After the traditional Bevarian greeting, they each took a seat.

"My king, I must…" Dyok tried to speak.

"Now, now," the king interrupted him. "I'll have none of that."

"But," he added before being cut off.

"We are entering an age of prosperity now," the king began. "The past is behind us."

"My king," Dyok broke in, "That's the problem."

The king raised a brow, but mostly ignored the noble's protest. "You said it yourself. Fear and power will help drive Hepsis into rebuilding itself. Even if that means destroying it, I'll do what I have to do to protect my reign."

"My king, I'm sorry." Dyok's head lowered.

The king relaxed, taking a breath. Himself, feeling a little overwhelmed. "Dyok, there is a reason why I granted you the title of Event Overseer."

"Why is that, if I may ask?" responded Dyok.

"Because," the king added, "those other fools would gladly watch Hepsis burn to the ground if they could but gain a few coins out of it."

Dyok folded his hands and pondered again the future his city was headed towards. Once images of his wife and child came up he quickly washed them away and looked back up.

"That's right," said the king. "I knew you'd be able to make the best decision that would keep the city and my reign a top priority."

"Against my honor," broke in Dyok.

"What's honor anymore?" blurted the king. "You get your name on a plaque or are memorialized in stone, visited by shadows. No, you of all people know how the city works. Trust me, you did a fantastic job." The king stood up and grabbed his shoulder. "You are being granted ownership of Lerinstad Keep, as well as, sole Event Overseer until otherwise seen unfit."

Dyok was quiet. Eventually he stood, thanking his liege before leaving the room.

During his trip home, he continued to ponder on all the recent events that had led up to this. He understood it now. He could no longer fight it. This was a place he belonged.

"Why is that, if I may ask?" responded Dyok.

"Because," the king added, "those other fools would gladly watch Hepsis burn to the ground if they could but gain a few coins out of it."

Dyok folded his hands and pondered again the future his city was headed towards. Once images of his wife and child came up he quickly washed them away and looked back up.

"That's right," said the king. "I knew you'd be able to make the best decision that would keep the city and my reign a top priority."

"Against my honor," broke in Dyok.

"What's honor anymore?" blurted the king. "You get your name on a plaque or are memorialized in stone, visited by shadows. No, you of all people know how the city works. Trust me, you did a fantastic job." The king stood up and grabbed his shoulder. "You are being granted ownership of Lerinstad Keep, as well as, sole Event Overseer until otherwise seen unfit."

Dyok was quiet. Eventually he stood, thanking his liege before leaving the room.

During his trip home, he continued to ponder on all the recent events that had led up to this. He understood it now. He could no longer fight it. This was a place he belonged.

STORM OF SAVUUR

-ONE-
FAMILY

My father told me it wasn't anybody's fault. He said she was very sick and sometimes these things just happen. Whether it was good people or bad, we simply cannot change fate.

I was four at the time. Feeling alone and desperate, I clung to my older sister for support and motherly love. We held a very deep bond from then on. I looked up to her with admiration, knowing she held great courage in the face of death. My father on the other hand, began to lead a much darker life. It seemed like every day he'd bet his savings, drink his health, and curse the gods away.

Every morning before the bright golden sun rose, my father would leave our little wooden shack, heading into town to seeking or begging for whichever small jobs he could get. My sister and I never knew why he left so early in the morning, or why he never said goodbye, but we knew whatever he was doing was probably in the best interest for our family; something he reminded us about regularly.

Late in the afternoon our father would slowly make his way home. He usually brought a basket of food, a loaf of bread, or pocket full of crests.

As my sister and I greedily stuffed our faces and filled our empty stomachs, our father sat tired and sleepy in his favorite old ash chair, never speaking a word.

This pattern soon became a ritual, which soon became the norm and our way of life. Being at such a small age, my sister and I never asked questions or understood what was going on. At the time we didn'

145

t care as long as we were together and our bellies were full.

- Three Years Later -

This went on for many years. During this time I hardly ever saw my father, and each day I also found myself spending less time with my sister.

One day my father spoke to her alone for a while. Together they went into the kitchen, while I sat unnervingly still in our bedroom, patiently waiting for her to return.

When she eventually came back into our room, her face seemed not as bright as it was when she left. She didn't even say a word as she quietly unfolded her bed sheets then climbed into bed, going to sleep early.

Creeping over to her silently and nudging her arm to hold, I asked what was wrong.

"I won't be able to play with you much after today," she spoke quietly; her head and eyes never moving. Small insects chirped and hummed near the solitary bedroom window.

Laughing a little assuming she was kidding I responded, "What are you talking about? We will always have time to play."

This time she turned her head around, her long golden hair sliding around the pillow as she gazed at me with dark brown eyes. "Father is making me come with him tomorrow. I don't know the details, but he said I will need to work from now on in order to help provide for us."

Clasping her hand tightly, I cringed at the thought of what this meant. I feared that she would drift away like our father has done, and I would soon lose her as well. Shaking my head at the mere thought, I leaned in closer.

"Listen Shio," she whispered. "All this means is that we might be apart for a few hours every day. If this is what it takes so I can help our family, then I gladly accept it. Don't look at me like that."

Some tears began to run down my cheek and onto our hands. I

tried to wipe them away before she saw, but a part of me wanted her to know what I was truly feeling.

"Father told me that very soon we will be moving to a new town. Isn't that great? Just imagine we will be leaving this old house and maybe into a really nice one."

My face brightened a little as I spoke up, "Maybe one with large windows and a fireplace?"

"Sure." She smiled, now looking into my bright green eyes, running her fingers through my blond medium-length hair. "Just hold on a little longer, and you will see. I'm doing this for us Shio, and I'm doing this for mother."

- ONE YEAR LATER -

Our new place was many miles away from our old quiet home in the city. The scenery was different, the sky was different, and even the air felt odd and unwelcoming. Before we left, my father had purchased a small ox cart which we over-packed with as many things as we could fit. Everything that couldn't, my sister and I had to carry on our backs, while our father steered the ox and guided us along the bumpy roads of northern Demetria.

The house -or shack as it seems to resemble more closely- was nothing at all what I had pictured or dreamt weeks prior. It only had one floor, the roof was peeling in several spots, and even from some distance away I could see that it was older than all of us. Turning to my sister I could see that she wasn't fond of the new place either. Our father on the other hand, lit up with joy, insisting we hurry and unpack before dawn.

After the unpacking was finished, my sister and I decided to head outside and explore our new playground. I could sense that she knew we only could play this evening, for tomorrow she would be gone just like our father, and I would be alone. With a loud consecutive laugh, we hurried outside, slamming the door behind us.

Standing on the front porch; with Taela running ahead, I saw a few acres of tall bright-green grass to my right. At the point where the grass ended, way on the other side, were patches of trees and shaggy shrubs outlining a border for a land we could call our own. On the other side of the house laid the winding dirt road and some much shorter brown grass and dried mud. There were a few other small houses scattered up and down the road to either side, but they were few and far between. This new landscape was much different than the town we had moved from.

My sister quickly ran along the side of the road, skipping about and waving her hand for me to come join in. I pretended not to pay attention, but after some persistence I ran off the porch and joined her hand.

Strolling along the twisting path, my sister and I pointed out various houses and neighbors along our trip.

We soon found ourselves stopping in front of a large red brick house, with big apple trees scattered in the front lawn. The house seemed a lot more inviting and warmly than ours did, and my sister dared me to grab an apple from the nearest tree. Staring disappointingly, I then peered around, observing the house for any activity. Gulping hard, I hesitated, till suddenly, she patted my shoulder gently and ran to pluck the apple herself.

On our way home, the air grew brisker, and the sun was now resting on top of the creamy orange and red horizon with a sliver of yellow haze along the few visible clouds. I could feel myself growing sleepy, convincing Taela to carry me on her shoulders.

From this new vantage point I opened my eyes wider at the beauty of our new home. It was true this was most certainly not a city or even a town, but for some reason the quiet farmlands and lush country side seemed not as harsh and different as I had first made them out to be.

A few stars were beginning to come out from behind their daylight mask and the insects seemed to emerge from the trees all at once, creating a soothing melody that caused me to fall asleep immediately.

The next day, the morning was perhaps the worst I have ever had awakened to. No one could be heard, no breakfasts to smell, and no sister to rush in and pounce on the bed. Despite the wonderful evening I had yesterday, this morning was turning into a nightmare.

After many long minutes of lying in my bed, hiding under the sheets, my stomach finally forced my body to get out of bed and find some food. Walking along the hallway and into the kitchen made the wooden beams creak beneath my feet. It seemed overly loud and disruptive, and it startled me to step as fast as I could into the kitchen.

Peering into cupboards and storage barrels, I found no trace of food. An apple core was discovered on one table, but sadly nothing else. I hungered for even a crumb or keel of bread, something a mouse might have even left, but for an old and decrepit house, there was none.

Coming to the conclusion that I would just have to wait until someone came home, I shuffled over to the living room chair and sat down. With nothing else to do, I took the time to daydream about Taela and what she might be doing at this moment.

I saw visions of her in a merchants' store, greeting the customers and handling any curious questions they might have. Another vision placed her in the employment of a handyman, painting and fixing up an old woman's rickety porch.

Any place I dreamt her to be, she was always smiling. I could not picture her any other way. Changing to my father, I tried the same thing. Only this time, his face was grim, dark, and brooding. I could not picture him happy. Why were they so different? What could've happened to him? By this point, my father was all I could think about.

Awakening to a loud thud, I jumped up from the rocking chair to see Taela placing some small sacks down in the kitchen. Immediately I ran to her, leaping onto her back, wrapping her up like a snake with my arms. She laughed and tugged at me to get off, but I could not muster my emotions to let go. When I finally did, she turned around I could see from her expression that she had missed me even more.

Our father had just entered through the doorway. Pausing, we watched as he went straight to his room without ever saying a word.

"How about you help me with the food?" Taela asked, pulling a large melon from one sack.

"As long as I can eat while I work," I laughed back.

Maybe this change was for the good.

-TWO-
DISTANCE

- TWO YEARS LATER -

Relaxing near the warm sizzling fire made my head feel clear and at peace. Any troubles or sadness I may have had during the lonely afternoons were happily baked out of my brain and never brought up again.

The fire danced and flickered, enveloping the logs like a blanket. The occasional ember or spark shot out from the burning white ash, startling my sister from her nap.

It was just the two of us for the evening. My sister rocked slowly in a leatherwood chair, while I lay on my stomach near the mesmerizing fireplace. Happily rested, our bellies were stuffed with bread and warm soup, while we enjoyed the time together, until our father would eventually come home.

Out the far left window, I watched the circling moths and insects flutter around the outside torches. The entranced bugs danced and circled in a hypnotic gaze until the occasional bat swooped down; devouring them, before blending back into the darkness from which they came.

At the peak of my drowsy state, and no movement coming from Taela, our father jarred the front door open and came trotting inside, bringing some very unsettling guests behind him.

"Wake up you two, we're going to have some company tonight," he blathered very drunkenly. He tossed his thick overcoat towards the coat rack, not caring that it collided and fell to the ground with a sudden flop. Pointing with a few fingers, he introduced his cohorts. "This is Baril," he exclaimed, clasping the short hefty man upon the shoulder. "He loves to eat, so Taela get him some fresh ale from the cellar." The man called Baril laughed and nodded, as Taela got up from the chair, running out of the room, per Father's request.

After Baril slowly waddled in and took off his coat, another man, only much taller, came to the doorway. My father leading the man by the shoulder, announced, "And this is another truly remarkable man, who we like to call Lynx." The two of them chuckled together until my father closed the door behind them.

I was very surprised during this whole session because father never brought anyone to the house before. Occasionally he would mention people he'd worked with, and after seeing them before me, I grew increasingly curious, wanting to learn more.

When Taela came back with a large jug of Fiddlehorn Black Ale, I had hoped she could sit down and enjoy the new company with me. However before I could ask, our father yanked the ale from her grasp, "Ah, thanks so much for the drink," he crooned, looking over at Baril. "This here is the best stuff around.   I'm sure it will quench even your ferocious thirst." They both laughed loudly and even Lynx managed to add in a few chuckles as well. "Taela, did you ask our friend Lynx if he wanted anything?"

Taela looked spiteful but kindly asked Lynx for his order, in which he replied he wanted some dry fruit to nibble on. So, she immediately ran back out of the room, leaving me in the alone with the strangers again.

After a few awkward minutes of silence and sipping, I found myself unable to restrain my curiosity, so I asked, "Excuse me, Lynx, is it? Why do they call you that?"

The man named Baril finished the rest of his glass, rubbing the foam clean from his mouth, while my father gave me a weird stare. Lynx on the other hand, waved his hand and softly replied, "Oh, it's not a problem, Pernek. The boy is curious, and there is no harm in telling him."

My eyes were now focused on Lynx's slender head as he hunched over and looked at me with his deep brown sullen eyes. He had sullen cheeks and a stiff jaw. He looked to be about forty, but chances are, he might've been older.

"They call me Lynx because a few years ago I took a bet that I could catch at least fifteen mice in this old barn in the middle of the night." Hunching a little closer and putting his hand up to his mouth as if to whisper he added, "I caught seventeen."

"Wow!" was the only word my small mouth could muster.

"They also call me Lynx, cause I'm tall and liked to climb trees when I was young," he laughed, the rest soon joining in.

After some more small talk, my father saw it was getting late and sent my sister and me to bed. We both knew it was still rather early, but our father was keen, grumbling and shaking his glass in the air until we were in our rooms.

Lying perfectly still in bed, I stared upwards at the ceiling while listening to the conversations in the other room. Every once and awhile the loud echoing bellows of Baril broke the eerie silence. I could hear my father speak some muffled words, followed by Lynx, and then Baril would end with another laugh. This pattern continued well into the night, until my eyes grew very tired and I could feel my eyelids slowly falling, blanketing my world in further darkness. This is when I would have fallen asleep, if I had not heard a few words blurt out from across the hall.

"Pernek, do you think she's ready then?" asked one voice, whom I believe was Lynx.

Baril's voice was much clearer and low sounding, "You've taught her quite enough as it is. I think you should use her for this next heist."

"Trust me. I've put some thought into it." vouched my father. "She looks the part, but I'm not sure she will go through with it."

"You worry too much," responded Baril. His voice dipped in and out of pitch from what I could hear. "Tell her what you always do then, I'm sure it will be fine."

Lynx chimed in, "If all goes really well, we might not have to steal anymore for at least awhile."

"True, very true," our Father admitted to himself. "And in a few more years I'll get Shio to work for us too. If he's anything like his sister, then I'm sure we have nothing to worry about."

Laughter echoed softly as they all tried to keep their voices down, fearing one might disturb our slumbers. None of them realizing that I was now wide awake, contemplating what all of this added up to. One thing I knew was that my sister had to know what was going on. I don't think I would be comfortable sleeping through till morning.

Sneaking into the shadowy hallway, I tip-toed quickly across the hall, making sure I shut the door firmly behind me. When I turned around I saw that I didn't need to waste time waking her up; she was already as wide awake as I.

"Did you happen to hear anything from father or his two men outside?" I revealed, creeping closer to her side.

She sat up, leaning her head against one pillow confiding, "Yes, and it scares me."

"I heard them mention stealing and such. Is any of that true?" I waited for an answer.

"If it is then I want no part of it." My sister leaned over closer to me for comfort, believing I might need a hug.

I tried to resist, but I felt she probably needed it more than I did. During the brief embrace I breathed, "What are you going to do?"

Leaning back against the soft white pillow she continued, "We need to find out if it's true. Even if father claims it's not, we need to know. This is everything our mother hated in life, and I need to know if it's really true." Looking at me intensely she continued, "Maybe you heard wrong, maybe I heard wrong. We can't know for sure until tomorrow. Please go to bed now and in the morning we'll question him together."

We embraced one final time, then she shooed me out her room and back into my own cold bed. This is where I stayed, against my wishes, and against my worried emotions; but I did it for her.

The following day I awoke to some voices erupting from the hallway. I only had a brief chance to rub my eyes and stretch when my

153

sister opened the door to my room, followed by my father. The two of them exchanged looks of disappointment, neither one was willing to talk until I urged. "What's going on?"

My sister sat down on my bed as we both looked upwards at our father. I could see he was getting a little agitated over what must have transpired, but I could sense he was willing to talk calmly.

"Shio my son, your sister says she will not help our family anymore," he started.

Quickly breaking in Taela spoke, "That's not true, Shio. I asked him about what we heard from last night and..."

"What!" Father exclaimed. "Shio, you listened in on my private conversations as well?"

Looking back a little scared I uttered, "No, no, I never did it intentionally. You guys were just loud and I couldn't sleep."

"You don't have to make excuses Shio, "Taela expressed. "You did nothing wrong. It was Father who must tell us why he is stealing from people."

Together we looked at him, standing firm and committed to our demands. A part of me wished I had just fallen asleep like a good boy; maybe none of this would be happening right now, and we could go on to being a normal family again.

"Alright," he admitted. "I guess I should just tell you two." He paused to take a seat on the far chair in the corner. Once situated he continued, "I only did it help our family. If I hadn't done what I did, and still do, then we wouldn't be here today."

We both remained quiet, our attention always focused as he spoke.

"You see, back when we were at our old house, the jobs were scarce and few. I had no choice but to take a few crests here and there to make ends meet. After we moved here, I met Baril and Lynx, as well as some other men who are helping me...helping us, get through this rather difficult time. I know what I'm doing is wrong, but sometimes we adults must do what we need to do in order to survive. Your mother would agree with me on this, I know she would."

He got up from the chair and knelt down next to the bedside. Placing his rough hands upon ours he looked into our eyes and spoke,

"Please Taela, help me one last time. Do it for our family if not for me. After this, I won't have to steal for a long time, I promise."

She looked over at me for acceptance, even though I alone could not make this decision for her. When she saw I was unwilling to decide, she nodded. "Alright, I'll do it for our family."

"Great!" he stood up satisfied.

"But you must promise me that no one will get hurt," demanded my sister.

Holding onto her hand again he promised, "I can't promise you no one will get hurt, but I can promise you that your family will be safe."

- TWO YEARS LATER -

The next morning I awoke to another gloomy day. I made myself some breakfast then took part in the daily chores that my father insisted were always maintained. After which, I had nothing but free time. Free to play outside, free to lounge around the house, all these decisions and no one to help decide or share delight in.

When the sun shifted towards the horizon, the trees swayed with the warnings of an upcoming storm rising in the east. I felt a little cold and so I started the night fire early, hoping father would agree as well. The day disappeared, and with it the moon soon rose taking the sun's place. The house grew colder, and I longed for a feeling of someone to talk to; anybody. They still haven't arrived back yet, and growing weary, I turned to making dinner to help pass the time and create warmer emotions. As the food grew cold, I cleaned the dishes, then headed to bed, too sick to eat, and too hungry for my family.

Tomorrow soon arrived and I had still not heard anything from either Taela or our father. Deciding to ask around town, I headed out early with a determined mind and nowhere really to start. The first places I stopped were our few neighbors that were scattered along the countryside. Turning up nothing, I figured the next best thing would be to head in town.

After a quick detour home to pack a lunch and some water, I grabbed my pack and began to head down the road towards the closest town that I knew of; Pheto.

Arriving at the western entrance, I was immediately amazed at how different the town looked from the city where I was first born. I could remember only fragments, but with each step deeper inside and with each inhale of sweet smells from shops and merchants, long forgotten gaps in my mind were being filled with new emotions that I was beginning to connect with.

Before long, I had found myself distracted and lost. The day dragged on in my head, yet a few hours were all that had passed. People were beginning to close shops, and even the inn's activity was slowing down.

Refocusing, I immediately followed behind a middle-aged patrol guard making his way towards a small stone house. As the man fiddled with keys to the door lock, I ran up to him and tugged at his grey pants.

The unaware guard jerked around, almost falling over. Quickly regaining his balance, he looked down where I was standing nervously. "Yes, what is it?" he spoke in a rough, tired voice.

"Excuse me, sir," I managed to squeak out. "I'm looking for my father."

The man fiddled with his keys. He twisted and shifted his fingers around trying to find the right one, occasionally glancing down, only to see he was clasping the wrong one.

"Well, I would love to oblige, really I would, but I'll need more info than that." The man checked his hands again for the right key, but his guess was wrong once more. "How about, what he looks like or his name?"

Confused as to why I didn't mention my sister, I hesitated, but blurted out, "My father is named Savuur, Pernek Savuur, and I believe he was wearing a dark tunic and pants, with a long over coat maybe." My eyes tilted up to my brain, like I was trying to see the images projecting outwards. "Oh, and I'm missing my older sister too. I believe she was with him."

"One person at a time please," requested the guard, focusing all his attention on his hands. "You said Pernek right? That name was brought up some time ago. Ah, right!"

Just as he found the correct key, a thin rusty iron one with six teeth, he added, "A man named Pernek was captured and seized a few days ago."

My eyes lit up; partly from the mention of the guard providing info, but more so from what he had said. "Please, where is he? What happened to him? You must tell me!" I exasperated.

"Oh, I think he's being held in the Brunx Prison," he revealed, "I assume you aren't from here."

I nodded.

"The place is near the southern gates, below the garrison and electoral house."

"Thank you so much, for everything." bowing my head multiple times, watching to see the guards face turn a slight red tint after each gesture. "Oh, I forgot about my sister. Please, was there anything mentioned about a fourteen year old girl with him?"

The guard paused to think, holding tightly the elusive key so it may never escape again. "No, I don't think there was a girl brought in with him. Maybe she left before he was captured."

I wonder what might have happened to her. My nerves and feelings rushing like a wild beast being hunted.

"Oh, thank you so much again!" I graciously answered.

"Sure, no problem," the guard smiled. "Now if you don't mind, I got a lock to finally open," he recalled, turning around laughing.

Wasting no more time, I quickly ran down the road heading as fast as I could to the south garrison.

-THREE-
BRUNX PRISON

- THREE YEARS LATER -

As I now found myself taking on the role of sole provider for our family, my outlook on life was slowly changing and twisting into a less fantastic one and that of a grittier, dark way of life. What I had once seen as a playful, carefree, and unchallenging life as a child, was now a twisted reality where wealth, hunger, power, and entrapment beat the poor and unwise into submission. My youth was over now; erased and replaced with more concerning matters of life and death.

Everyday I walked the four hour journey into the small town of Pheto. It used to take me six of seven hours, but after years of continuing the pattern and daily habit, my muscles and stamina grew along with my body.

Always left home carrying a small sack of food and water for nourishment nestled in a tan satchel around my waist; determined to arrive.

The garrison itself always appeared much smaller from the outside than it really was. Knocking on the hard iron door, I was greeted by familiar faces, and then let on in to the Electoral House.

The soft cream building was almost always empty, aside from the half-dozen prisoners hollering occasional hollering below. The halls were decorated in plain white curtains, fur covered chairs, long tables of oak or maple, and the occasional oddly placed vase or painting.

Venturing away from the hallway and down the few flights of stone stairs, I was soon greeted by a stationed guard sitting relaxed next to the iron prison door that led into the Brunx Prison.

Granting courtesy back, the guard opened the door and I stepped into a place that almost felt alien from what the outside was like.

Walking faster, I never hesitated to speedily get by the first bunch of dark cells. It wasn't out of fear, but to avoid the awful stench that fermented from diseased people and rotting food.

Slowing back down, I faced the confined interior where my father sat in the shadow of the far back corner. His body had not aged like mine did. Each day as I grew taller and leaner; I saw that my father grew more grey, shaggy, and wearisome. I tried to remedy some of the problems by providing food and nourishment, but it never lasted. His suffering and the terrible confines of the prison drained all life and nourishment I was able to grant him.

"Hello father." I greeted him like I always did; cheerful and with sore legs from walking. Pulling over a small stool, I laid my sack down and sat slouched in the hard seat. "I don't suppose you have an appetite today?"

I watched meticulously for any movement. My face gently resting against the cold iron bars of the door, peering into the small cell. His frail body shifted ever so slightly; his way of letting me know, he was at least awake.

"I might not be back for a few days, perhaps even a week. A new job has come up and they will pay well. It's an opportunity I can't pass up." I waited for any more movement, before continuing. "I was talking to a banker recently, and he believes in a few more years maybe even one, I'll have enough money to release you. What do you think of that?"

His slumped boney corpse, shifted once more. I became silent as I watched him slowly roll to one side and gradually pick himself off the hard stained floor. His twisted frame and tethered clothes reminded me of a corpse or an undead creature making his way across the prison cell. A few mumbles and moans rose up as he eventually made it to the door, leaning up against the bars.

Taking in a deep breath my father spoke in a very rasp and dry manner, "Very good, my boy." He coughed and wheezed with each sentence. I sat back, pretending it didn't affect me, but sometimes I believe he enjoys watching me see how terrible of a state he's in. "Pretty soon we can finally leave here and become a family again," I finished.

Grasping the bars with one hand, I thought about how wonderful that would be. One thing was missing though, so I added, "Yes, once we get out of here and find Taela, we will finally become a family again."

Another rough cough echoed from the dark dungeon. Father's eyes lit up, while he leaned away from the heavy door. "No, forget your sister. She abandoned me, and she abandoned you when we needed her most. She's responsible for my imprisonment, and we will have no part of her anymore!"

His disturbing words shocked me. I was left completely speechless. What had been a typical day, had now been shattered and disrupted by that one sentence.

Rising up from the stool, I blurted, "What do you mean by that? You told me she ran off before the whole plan even went into action."

"Bah, you really think that's what happened? Then you are your mothers' son." he admitted chokingly.

A new emotion was beginning to rise up from the center of my heart. Feelings of betrayal and hatred filled my stomach and lined my chest, causing me to lash out once more. "Do you mean to say that Taela was a part of the heist?!"

"A part of the heist?" he chuckled in a raspy voice as best as a near dead man could. "Hardly. If she did anything it would be nothing. That's the problem. She abandoned her post and forced me to take the blame instead!"

"What are you saying?" I asked, now quizzically; trying very hard to imagine what must have went on that night.

"You idiot, she was supposed to be the one who got caught, not me! Because of her abandonment and betrayal to our family she got me stuck in here while she ran off and left us!" My father had to stop shouting to catch his breath. His lungs moving in and out rapidly, while his eyes shifted around uncontrollably. Moving backwards, he ducked back into the shadows of his cell. Even though I could not see him against the back wall, I could hear his decrepit wheezing.

Realizing now that the feeling of ever having a normal family was all based on lies and deceit; that I never even had a family, my life became nothing more than a discarded shattered mirror. All my memories of warm sunny afternoons and gentle breezes in the fields meant nothing to me anymore. Who was this man I was talking to? What have I been doing with my life for these past three years? All

160

feelings were now dead; dead and gone forever, with my mother.

"You piece of shit!" I hollered violently. "My sister knew the truth all along. She knew you were a corrupted, lying, good-for-nothing parasite that took advantage of your once precious family to satisfy your own greedy and desperate needs." I stepped close to the metal door. My mouth barking into the cell, so my voice could echo throughout, hoping to feel even more wrath-like. "You made me work and slave trying to earn crests for you so you could be released, when I should have been praying you die in your sleep, or trying to find my sister who actually believed in you at one point." I shook my head, "No, not anymore."

Slowly stepping back, I picked up my sack, tossing it over my shoulder. "Good-bye father, may you rot in this dark cell along with your dark heart!"

"Wait!" he shouted desperately. "Where are you going? I need you!" He hobbled his way up to the door. Sticking his boney arm past the cold steel bars he barked, "Shio!"

Looking over my shoulder, I stopped to give my final words, "I'm going to find my sister. She is my only family now."

The guard slammed the door behind me, leaving the prison to fill with the darkness once more. The only noise I could hear was the cries of a man who now realized that he would die alone.

-FOUR-
PURLIK

The plains of Demetria were not at all welcoming to children, lost, or adventurous.

A sea of golden grass was etched and painted along the paths and acres that wound and curved along the landscape. Traveling merchants and beggars wrapped up handfuls of the weeds, trying to sell them to ill-informed travelers unfamiliar with the land. Along with leatherwood, birch, spar, and fig trees; vast amounts of cattle, crops, and gnats helped fill in the farmlands, villages, and valleys. Log cabins were developed in a few areas, and ignoring the occasional caravan, merchant, or trader, the paths and scenery were a magnificent sight to behold.

A few miles up the road heading south, I sat propped up against a large boulder a couple yards off the beaten path. It was late afternoon and an elderly couple, pulling their exhausted looking mule cart, eventually strode past where I sit. Wanting to laugh or make some sort of comic gesture at their folly, I instead kept silent; my heart belittled my mind into feeling the cruelty of the idea. Instead, I gazed skyward, watching the drifting clouds live a carefree life.

After a few more uneventful days, the town of Purlik appeared over the distance, almost within a half-day walk. The glare from the sun over the eastern mountains blinded my vision, while the westerly breeze relaxed my sore muscles and made my stomach growl with hunger. Picking up my pace, I made sure I reached the town before mid-day.

The quiet town in the distance soon grew louder, as I marched up to the entrance and found myself staring at the outer wood walls and guard perches.

Houses of wood and stone stood firm and as varied as the families and denizens whom lived within them. Humans, orcs, and even a few young elves were walking around the village center, talking and mingling with one another, wearing an assortment of plain and pastel garbs, trousers, sacks, and facial expressions. Walking around the dirt roads and paths, I took note of where certain landmarks and houses were: a random pillar of stone, a couple of smashed vases, an orc pulling a pig through his backyard. Peeping in through some inn windows, I noticed they were quite roomy, and more than offered enough space if I had to spend the night.

Further along, I spotted some merchants selling various trinkets and armaments at stands, fruit and vegetable trades, pelt sellers, wine drinkers, and even a juggler. Over by the southern forest entrance, was a solitary guard tower, standing tall a keen. A lone guard with a tall pole arm was slouched over the rails, yawning.

When my hunger struck again, I immediately headed to the nearest tavern. Called Pale Paudry's, I then looking through the nearest window, smiling when I noticed there were few customers and drunks within.

Spotting an open stool near the front counter, I gently placed my bag under the seat, and made a notion for the only working man I could see to come over.

"What do you want then?" asked the grizzled man placed his rough hands on the counter top in front of me.

"Just a small leg of meat, whatever's the freshest, and a pint of ale," I said with pleasure.

The man nodded, went to the backroom, and then came out a few moments later. "While it's cooking, might I ask what a young fellow, like yourself, is looking to do here in Purlik?"

After adjusting my seat I stretched my sore back confessing, "Well, I'm looking for some jobs to help feed my sick wife."

The man rubbed his beard and chin, "You look fairly young to have a wife. But, I guess it's none of my business. Don't know why, you'd want to though." The man looked towards the back door, as if he was expecting it to open. Not seeing anyone, he turned back around and continued, "If you need work badly, which I hardly care if you do or not, then might I suggest you go east out of Purlik and down the road a little bit." My ears perked up and I listened carefully as he went on. "There's a nice family in need of some assistance. I know the father." He paused to go to the back and check on the food. After which, he returned looking a little less clean. "Apparently he was complaining about needing more helping hands."

"Wow, really? Thank you so much. I'll make sure to head out there tomorrow," my voice rose with excitement.

"Yep, no problem at all," he smiled faintly. "Oh, I think your foods almost ready."

A moment later, he walked through the back door and came out carrying one large plate with big steamy mutton joint and chilled ale in the other hand.

163

Later, I took a skinny gravel path that led out from the town, just as the tavern proprietor had described. Following the path for awhile, it eventually came to a small one-story wooden house. The place looked well maintained, and it seemed to be in pristine condition for a farm. Walking up the few steps of the porch and knocking firmly on the wooden door I was caught off guard by just who would answer.

Her light tan lips and cerulean eyes made me dumbstruck, causing my mouth to hang unintentionally open. A light warm sensation passed over me, reminding me of my childhood and the feelings I had during those simpler times.

Her body was thin and her hair was straight and light brown. She was standing tall and keen in the doorway, the gentle breeze ruffling her pure white dress. If not for a sudden voice bellowing from inside, I might have been petrified on her stoop all day.

A man hollered again; the beautiful girl blinked and spoke, "My father doesn't like it when the door is open for long. Please, let me know what it is I can help you with."

Her voice and gestures were causing my eyes to widen with each passing of her voice. For a moment, I was too afraid to respond back, fearing whatever it was I would reply couldn't even compare to the angelic tone she bore.

"Um, my name is Shio." I managed to stutter unevenly, raspy, and not at all well articulated. "Shio Savuur, my lady. I am looking for the owner of this fine house."

The girl, still standing firm replied justly, "That would be my father, Sir Shio. What might you be seeking him for?"

I gulped hard, almost feeling feint. The realization of admitting lies might doom all future prospects with this girl. "I heard from Purlik, that he is looking for some help. I don't know what that might incline, but after seeing you, I really don't care." I rattled, sweating after that last sentence, wishing I could run away.

Before she could respond again, the man who initially spoke from inside arrived at the doorway, placing one hand on the girl's head. "Father, this man here says he wants to talk to you about helping with some work."

"Ah, does he now?" The man smiled downward at the girl, who tipped her head to look back. He was wearing a tan shirt, with an animal hide vest and loose fitting pants. He also had short light brown hair and a small mustache matching his hairy arms. He shuffled the girl inside, before stepping his lean muscular body outside and closing the door behind. "If its work you want, I might be able to assist you; or rather, you assist me." He laughed as he gripped the side of the house with his large hands.

I could tell he had done his share of hard labor, when he shook my hand. His rough calluses and dirty fingernails told stories of long days in hot fields. His clothes were stained and speckled with the fragments of dirt.

Shy as I was with the exuberant girl, I was twice as afraid after meeting the girl's father. I didn't even know her name, and yet I wondered what kind of impression I was leading her father to believe.

"Great!" he bellowed. "You seem very competent and youthful. I can tell by your handshake that you are also very trustworthy. I'll tell you about the jobs and work that you'll be doing, but first introductions are in order."

Leading me inside his house, he gathered his family around the central room. We all took a seat around a small wooden table where the man spoke on behalf of everyone. "This here is Shio. Shio will be staying here for some time, if that's okay with him?"
I nodded nervously.

Starting from his left he stuck his hand out as he called each person's name. "Shio, this is my wife Illicia, my daughter Liliana, and I am called Graff."

At the mere mention of her name, my head and ears toned out everything else that night. I found myself staring at her hair, her face, and her lips. Her light blue dress was decorated with white trim and lace, as was the ribbon in her hair. Watching her glance at me, I could see that she also was eager to learn more.

Every afternoon, Graff would take me out into the fields. They belonged to various famers, friends, and tired old men. I learned the acres, the crops, the weather, and the soil. It was hard, grueling work, but we enjoyed our company. It was nearing the end of the 6th month, after the Fall of the Orchid, and we were out digging up elder roots, mulching the rows of dirt, and preparing for the Fire Harvest. The owner often came outside, sat on an old rooted bench, and talked about weather, local foods, and past grander times.

- Four Months Later -

This ritual went on for several months, till the dry season arrived, at the start of the 4th month. A drought had taken three-fourths of the plants and grains that we had worked tediously months before. The owner bartered and forfeited many crops to pay off his debts and sadly Graff was left with only a fraction of what he and I planned to have earned for much of our yearly work.

The shortage also took a toll on his wife and Liliana. A few more days passed and the house's food supply slowly dwindled. Later a rat infestation, and before any of us could find a new job, Graff and his family were now as poor as I had been during my childhood.

The coming weeks were filled with hardship and suffering. Graff was forced to head to Purlik everyday in search of small jobs, while his wife took to loans, begging, and other discrete acts. As for Liliana and I, we ventured out trying our luck with fishing, carving, planting, and other various ways to try and gain some tins.

Even though we were starving every day, and the house was slowly falling apart from lack of repairs, I enjoyed our little discussions we had. Every day for the past year, I got to know a little more about her, and she got to know a little about me. Interesting facts were brought up and discovered such as her fear of roaches, and her love of festivals. I never revealed as much as she did, but I slipped out a few minor details to wet her appetite and make us feel like we had more in common, even if that meant stretching the truth.

- FIVE MONTHS LATER -

During the cold season, Graff would normally venture into the nearby forest, cutting down and carrying back piles of lumber for burning. However, since he was busy with various jobs in town, I took on that duty in his stead.

The forest was decorated in coarse pines, prickly spars, and sweet smelling linden holly bushes. Sounds of twigs snapping and branches swaying gave off a simplistic peacefulness that helped past the time. Footprints of rabbits, squirrels, and deer looped around the path and nearby trunks, while the sun occasionally pierced through the clouds, warming the shady underbrush.

Discovering a three foot high stack of thirty-or-some wood logs, I sat the large tweed sack down, and began searching for the driest pieces filling the bag to the top. After which, I tied the top with sturdy rope and headed back on the trail towards home.

Everything was calm and relaxing. The anxiety and depression of our poorer lifestyle seemed to disappear along with the winds. Instead, my head was filled with visions of Liliana. Pictures of what she had prepared for lunch caused my stomach to growl softly, and my mouth to salivate. Warm ale, soft bread, dried fruit, and strips of juicy boar, danced around my head as I walked.

Slowly tilting my head back down from the clouds, I saw a small stream of grey smoke rising in the direction of Graff's house. Realizing the smoke was now a cause for alarm; I dropped the sack of wood and immediately sprinted as fast as I have ever ran before in my life.

Tall grass blurred and whipped ferociously while I ran; dirt and mud kicking up behind my feet. As the distance to the house grew shorter, I began to spot pieces of debris and furniture lying out in the surrounding grass near the front door.

Slowing to a jog, I stepped up to the door, before realizing that half of it was missing. Only a fragmented bottom still clung to the failing hinges and thin bolts, with large splinters of the frame jutting outward. Kicking the only portion of the door inward, I carefully squeezed past the wood spikes, and called loudly for Liliana.

The walls were singed, the floors were black and crumbling, and smoke was filling up enough to blind nearly all vision. Pausing to catch my breath, I heard a small cry along with shouts echoing from her parent's room.

Stepping lightly through more debris, I appeared in the doorway of Graff's bedroom. Standing in awestruck, I saw Liliana kneeling in pools of blood over the bodies of her two fallen parents. She turned to me slowly, eyes balling in tears, her blouse soaked with the red marks of death.

"They…" she managed to muster, as I kneeled down besides her, throwing my arms around her in comfort. "Bandits…"

Closing my eyes and holding her tightly I whispered, "Tell me, what happened?"

She let go of me and curled up over her mother's mutilated corpse. I could tell she was in more pain than ever, but I pestered her into hearing what happened. "A group followed them home. They attacked without mercy. I ran. Oh Shio, I was so afraid. So afraid, and I ran like a coward."

Trying to hug her again, I felt that she wanted desperately to feel their loving warmth again. "Liliana, there was nothing you could have done. Look at me."

"No!" she whimpered, "I was a coward, and I let them die!"

"Please tell me something, anything," I beseeched, trying to keep my emotions down, but the blood was beginning to affect me as well. Its stagnant odor was becoming rather prevalent.

"Shio, promise me, you'll stay with me forever. Promise to not seek revenge. I can't afford to lose you too."

Her eyes were now bloodshot and as red as her cheeks from sobbing. I tried my best to look away, but I kept feeling a weird tension or spark, building up deep inside. "Don't worry, I promise to look after you and no harm shall ever happen."

Somehow I imaged her expression would be different upon my promise, but all she expressed was a deep grimace as she clung to her father's hand, adding more tears to the puddles of crimson blood.

Standing up from the red soaked floor, I tried wiping my hands free of wet blood, but there was simply too much of it. I waited for Liliana to rise up with me, but her body was motionless; aside from some soft whimpers and breathing, she seemed even more distant.

I felt a surge of energy beginning to grow and swell up inside my chest. What feelings of sadness inside were hastily being replaced by something I had never felt since the betrayal of my father in Brunx Prison. At first I tried to suppress it, but eventually as each beat of my heart and each breath I took, I found myself wanting to release it. Somehow my mind was telling me to not fight it, and to let this new rage envelop me.

Liliana was still. I wanted to yell for her, but I figured she had enough to deal with as it is.

As the twisting and forceful energy built up, I found myself dumbstruck then writhing as I clasped my hands over my stomach and chest.

At one point during the ordeal, I pictured myself dead on the floor. Another corpse to add to Liliana's lost family. Somehow I could not imagine what Liliana would do if she discovered me on the ground, erupted heart, and all alone in this world. Becoming more afraid for her than my own well being, I quickly shunned away those images and went back to concentrating on this new, far less painful transformation.

A minute later the feeling was gone. It seemed to fade away back into the void of my heart. The stench of blood came back to me, my heartbeat no longer raced, the quiet sounds of a girl crying filled my ears again, and I was finally allowed to breathe.

Just as I unclenched my hands from my chest, the pain surged up again out of nowhere. I screamed loudly this time. Not from the pain, but from the sudden realization that whatever was going to happen, will happen.

My muscles tightened and convulsed as my back forcefully arced upright. At this time I could feel Liliana pulling at my waist, yelling for me. Her screams of sadness and shock couldn't save me. Nothing she did could help. I couldn't even help myself.

What happened next was almost too unimaginable.

Bright yellow and white mana collected in the air around my body, swirling upwards like a screw, flowing into my head and down my throat. A second later, a small electrical current erupted from my body, forcing Liliana to let go and stumble down to the ground. Blood splashed lightly as she fell, but she still concentrated on me.

As the electricity flowed around it singed and scoured the wooden floorboards, turning the wood and blood black. I tried to open my eyes, but all I could see was a bright white light, and I was forced to close them again for fear of going blind.

Pretty soon, all the mana dissipated into me and the rest of my body, causing the small electrical current to evaporate as well. Liliana rushed to my aid, as my body went numb and I collapsed to the floor. A few seconds later, my vision blackened and I began to lose consciousness. I could feel her warm embrace holding my pounding chest. My head close to hers. Her sweet calls fading till all was silent.

When I awoke, I found myself still cradled in her delicate arms. What felt like days, had really only been a few hours.

The blood soaked floor was moped up, though you could still see feint dried smears; reminders of the cruelty of this world. Looking out the window, all I could see was the cloudless night sky; a picture perfect view of the stars and tranquility that allowed a near half dead boy to embrace as his only means of escape.

Wiggling my fingers and stretching my back, I could feel my muscles pull and then all at once, seem to relax at the same time.

"I think you better go to your bed just in case," she encouraged. "I would have brought you there myself, but you were too heavy and I was afraid you might be hurt." She started to help me to my feet gently expressing, "I'll bring you something to eat shortly, but for now just please take it easy."

Propping myself on the wall, my body almost felt like brand new. In fact, I almost felt better than I have before. My joints no longer ached, my muscles were relaxed, yet strong, and for some reason I felt like I had more energy and strength. "Actually," Looking over at Liliana, I proclaimed, "I think I feel really good."

"Oh, do you know?" she asked tilting her head, "So, that big ordeal involving your body getting struck by lightning and you screaming was just nothing?"

I moved my arms and legs, viewing them over carefully for

wounds and burns. When I couldn't even find one smudge of a mark or bruise I replied, "Maybe being struck by lightning or something must have did something to me."

"Oh really, like what?" she sarcastically grumbled.

"Well, I feel really energetic for one thing. Like, my blood is getting hotter and my heart and lungs are getting faster."

"Sounds like you really need to see a healer," she commented, inspecting me over in greater detail.

"No forget going to a healer, this is something truly unique."

Feeling she had already done enough, and remembering that I probably should eat something, she quickly replied as she went out to the kitchen, "Call it what you want, but we have more important things right now."

- TWO MONTHS LATER -

Everyday since that incident, I have been training out in the fields behind the house. I discovered that my body ached and grew sore if I sat around too long, so getting fresh air and exercise felt only natural. Sometimes, I could feel my body getting very hot and I became sporadic and fidgety if I didn't do something active or strenuous.

After a week or so, my body was beginning to grow very hot again, it felt like I had too much energy built up inside. Deciding to blow off some steam like I usually do, I grabbed a few knives and headed out.

Once in the open fields, I began to throw them ferociously at various tree trunks. The trunks were already punctured and littered with holes from previous weeks, yet for some reason, it didn't help remove the tension. Realizing this wasn't going to be enough, I became agitated and stared down a lone spar.

Talking and shouting random insults I tried everything I could think of to release some of my energy and cool off. At the point where I couldn't take it anymore, I screamed and pointed my finger hard and fast at the center of the wooden trunk. Immediately, a huge jolt of bright white lightning flew out from my body, travelled down my arm and hand, where it flew out from my finger and straight into the tree. Sparks flew, wood singed, and pieces of debris splintered and fractured. I flinched, shielding my eyes from the raining splinters that followed.

After the blast, I checked my body for any wounds. While looking and feeling my chest I was stunned to discover that I no longer felt hot. My entire body seemed to feel more relaxed, and I didn't need to move around uncontrollably.

"What was that?!" cried Liliana running outside.

I turned around, "I…I don't know."

"What happened to the tree?" she questioned, running to my side, wrapping me in her arms.

Matching her eyes I smiled, "Whatever it was, I think I like it."

-FIVE-
POWER

- ONE YEAR LATER -

The seasons came and went as fast as the harvest winds blew in from the western coast. Days melded into one another, as I focused day-in and day-out training my body and honing my skills towards perfection.

Liliana sat out on the shabby, broken porch, relaxing and staring at me and the sky. Her feelings of her family often came and went, and though I attempted to soothe her with the promise of my new abilities, she became even more frightened that she would lose me as well.

This was the exact opposite for me however. As my abilities grew in strength, my rage and trust in myself grew with the courage to finally seek those responsible for the deaths of two innocent and caring people.

This is what I was training for.

Protecting our love could only come to fruition if there were to be no more evil in the world.

I grasped the steel handles of my knives; metal sparking and heating slightly as my rage intensified. I began another exercise. This time, recalling a trip to the town of Phento I had made with Graff. During some free time, I stumbled upon a travelling bookkeeper and cataloger. They showed me a series of books and sacred scrolls in their possession. At the time, I paid them no mind, quickly flipping through the pages and lists, like a scatterbrained child. It wasn't until after my transformation, that I came to recollect past memories again. The pages and scriptures suddenly came back to me; frozen in a state of animation. The images lifted off the page, as somehow I was able to read and interpret them: electricity, thunder, lightning, and mana. They were my guide. And I graciously accepted them.

Grasping the steel handles tightly, I stared down a straw dummy some twenty yards away standing crooked in the dry fields. Focusing the streams, I began pulling and shifting the pure mana in my own body. I could feel the steel growing hotter; their metallic blades turning a bright orange hue. Somehow, the heat never burned me, so long as I released it early enough. Once the buildup of energy felt sufficient for the simple spell, I extended both arms outward and flung both daggers simultaneously towards the mocking scarecrow.

The daggers stuck hard and deep, pieces of hay gently flew off from its back, with the dummy head jostling back and forth rhythmically. Within the next fraction of a second, a huge lightning bolt erupted from within both daggers. Bright light and energy extended like tendrils flailing around in all directions. The unprotected dummy shattered, exploded, and caught fire all at once. Debris scattered into the wind, as I walked over and picked up each dagger. Replacing to my sides, I noted they felt cool to the touch. Sliding them back into their separate sheaths, I smiled.

- ONE MONTH LATER -

Liliana erupted into fearful tears of sadness. Her eyes swelled up and she buried her face into her arms and my neck. Her warm embrace felt cold and barren. After my electrical transformation my body was naturally always hotter, so everything to me felt colder.

"Do not worry. I will finally get what we have always wanted," I promised. She held me tighter, squeezing my neck while balling into my soft white tunic. "With these new abilities it's like we have been given a chance. I'm doing this for you."

At this point she released her bear like grasp and adjusted the wrinkles in her dress while turning her attention to me. "Why can't we just live a normal life? Can't you see that I'm trying to fix things? Forget about the bandits or thieves, and listen to me. Please just stay here. Protect me and our home. We can be a family again."

My bright eyes grew dim as a sullen look cascaded down my face. I gazed towards the far entryway, trying not to look directly in her soft eyes.

When she finally stopped her sobbing, I looked deeply at her, not caring in the least that she was all red and her hair a mess. "I need to do this Liliana. If I ignore these gifts and forget about the chaos and evil those men had brought, then what's to stop them from doing it again?" I clasped her hands tightly, "What's to stop them from hurting other innocent people, slaying children, destroying families? No, my duty now is to enact justice upon them and by doing so I will create a better future for us; a better future for everyone."

Brushing her away, I got up from the bed and left the room to get packed. My mind had been made up years ago. No amount of discussion of persuasion would ever change that. She knew this was true, which is why she quietly stood outside waving to me as I walked north-west. A silent kiss goodbye carried on the wind.

I continued forward for several hours until finally my heart gave in and I looked back towards the direction of our house. Standing on top of a large hill, I peered into the shadowy horizon, pretending Liliana was standing on the top, calling for me.

I received a chain of info that eventually led me to a dark and dreary looking cave, hidden a few yards in the side of the northern Demetria Mountains.

Approaching from the eastern side, a light storm started. The rain above me splattered and bounced off my rugged hair and head. Beads trickled down my soaking wet face, as even more gloomy clouds joined their brethren in the evening dark-blue sky.

Walking up to the face of the cliff, I quietly listened for any voices echoing from high above. The rain made the effort rather useless, so I scaled the side of the rock face, slowly creeping ever closer to where my victims were rumored to be resting.

The steep rock wall was jagged and as slippery as ice, thanks to the rain. I pressed hard and deep into the sides with my coarse fingers. Belief in my cause was more than enough to fight through the cuts, bruises, and scrapes, as I slowly made my way up the steep cliff side. Face stuck in a pose of ferociousness, I tried to picture Liliana wrapping a warm cotton-knitted blanket around my shoulders and tiring back. I imagined her graceful smile, long beautiful hair, and eyes twinkling against the blackness around me. Shaking my head from all of the energy building up inside, the image sadly faded along with my heated vengeance.

Coercing myself to continue, I soon reached a large flat rock that acted as a floor to where the bandit cave's mouth gaped wide, inviting me in.

This was the moment.

The black entrance stood twice the size of an average man. A few wet barrels were decorated and scattered around the mouth, giving the presence that someone was indeed close by. Creeping low, I dashed forward, wits at the ready.

A soft torch light flickered and swayed as the first man I saw turned towards me. Drawing my blades without thinking, I violently threw one straight into the man's chest and sternum. A small electrical jolt drew forth, causing the man's body to convulse and his muscles to tighten. The body fell to the floor right as I ran up to his location. Grabbing the dagger from his blood soaked chest, I continued to head down into the tunnels; my rage ever building.

Dodging a fast moving bolt, I side stepped around a corner preparing another electrical attack. At this time I rolled out into the open and twisted my hands up and down releasing a large amount of mana into two melon sized balls of electricity. The perplexed bandit stared at the bizarre twin orbs while trying desperately to reload his crossbow. The two bright yellow and white balls of energy traveled simultaneously on the ceiling and floor of the cave until they located the helpless man. A large bolt of lightning passed over, connecting the balls and frying him in an instant. The twin spheres continued to chase after the next closest assailant, while the first one dropped to the ground; body and clothes black and crisp.

As the body count rose, my inner beast rapidly grew stronger and less merciful. I could feel the heat inside growing, then lowering as I fired off more spells and energy, before it would grow again as more of them died.

The next man I saw fumbled with trying to grab a lose spear on the ground as I ran up to him. I could tell he just woke up as he still in his undergarments.

Sprinting now, I leapt to the man's side just as he finally managed to grab hold of a spear. Blood spewed forth from his mouth as I punctured his kidney and throat. "No mercy," I whispered. The man's eyes rolled back. Sending out a few thousand jolts, I made sure he suffered even more.

Slaying the final man with a fast lightning bolt through his head, my fever and intensity began to calm back down. Blood was splattered like droplets of red paint on my shirt, pants, and face. My dual knives were also covered in thick ruby blood.

Looking around the rest of the cave, I soon saw a large heavy door. Kicking it inward, I stood gazing into a fancy room decorated with candles, torches, rugs, tables, and chests. One lone figure stood on the opposite side of the room, a weird rod shaped object firmly held in his right hand.

"Don't tell me a puny man like you is responsible for this ruckus?" he laughed casually. Stepping deeper inside, I began to see more of his body as my eyes adjusted to the brightness of the candles. "I don't know how you managed to do it," he continued, "but I have special means of dealing with people like you."

Wanting to slash his throat where he stood, I somehow felt a little curious as to what he might mean, so I remained silent.

"No comment I see," he jested, raising the mysterious rod upwards. Light illuminated from the object. It appeared to be a small staff made of gold, or a really shiny yellow metal. The ends had small engravings that were incomprehensible, and the top end that was pointing upwards bore a small yellow and white crystal. "Before you die, at least honor me by explaining who you are and why your killing all my men."

"I'll let you know once you're dead," I professed becoming more enraged as we waited. Energy began to rise up inside my chest and heart. I could see small mana particles inching their way from the air towards my fists like dust or little grains of sand.

"Well aren't you anxious," he smiled. "Very well, I guess there's nothing left to do." Raising his staff upwards he hollered, "I hope you like storms my boy, because you're about to feel my wrath!"

If only the bandit leader had looked down instead of upwards, he might have realized his mistake. It was too late.

The head of the bandit clan drew his arm downward fast and hard. The staff crystals hummed and sparked as a couple lightning bolts sizzled outwards and raced towards where I stood. Spreading my arms and legs apart, I embraced his generous offer.

The bolts stung like tiny needles all over my skin as they were absorbed. I felt a large flux in energy as each one joined the large quantity of raw power already boiling up inside. The man grinned at first, however upon noticing that his attack failed to even singe my skin, he quickly dropped his mouth and stared in befuddlement.

"My name is Shio Savuur," I began, walking forward. "And this is for the girl whose parents, hopes, and childhood, were taken by you and your men!"

"Wait, wait, I'm sure we can work something out!" he exclaimed nervously.

An aura of bright light and sparks circled and flew around me. I focused every ounce of energy and mana to come together, pulling and constricting them into one large ominous blast. The man cowered on the ground like a dog.

At the brink of what I thought was nearly all the energy I could muster, I released it. White electricity shot forth, raining hundreds of bolts down upon the helpless, kneeling man. His arms rising towards the ceiling; his screams extinguished by the sounds of rapture. His body was pulverized into the ground. Each bolt ran through him heavily and with the force of a hundred hammers. Blood boiled, muscles erupted, and eyes liquefied.

Falling to the floor just as the spectacle faded, I watched and stared at what little remained of the man – who now dead- would bring Liliana and I closure.

My journey was over.

On my way home, I no longer felt any kind of energy build up or heat from inside my chest. Breathing in deeply, I took in the comforts of things I had paid no mind to over the past years; the cool tranquil wind, the gently flowing tall grass. Birds flew by over head, and I could hear sounds I had only dreamt about when I was a child. Those days were long gone now. Even if I could go back and relive them, I wouldn' t want to. Liliana was where my heart was now. She was all I had left, and all I ever cared about.

Reaching the open field a few acres from our home, I saw the illustrious place next to the tall trees on the other side. The day was growing late, and perhaps dinner would already be placed on the table. A trivial thought, but a small ounce of hope was all I needed to tide me over until I arrived.

Opening the sturdy door, I was not greeted with open arms and soft kisses. Cobwebs lined the cracks and corners in many rooms, and after I took off my bag giving a look around, I soon saw that someone was home, but not the Liliana I remembered.

A rough couple of coughs barked in from her room. "I'm in here Shio; please tell me you're all right?"

The scene put a shock to my heart, the likes even I was not immune to. Blankets were stacked upon one another and all but her pale face and hair were showing. She coughed a few more times as I made my way in and pulled a chair over to her bedside.

"What's happening here?" I asked. "Are you sick, how come no one is here to look after you?"

"Don't worry about me. Tell me you're all right." Her voice fluctuated as she talked, crackling under raspy coughs.

Grabbing an ice cold hand from under the sheets I shuddered, "I'm fine, that doesn't matter. What matters is what happened to you."

"Oh this, I'm fine," she said seemingly half awake. "I had a friend stop by with a local medicine man who told me it was a simple cold. Feeling a little tired today I simply stayed in bed, that's all."

"You feel really cold, is there anything I can do? Have you eaten anything today? I'll go make you something." Leaving the room I started up a boil of potatoes and freshly brewed tea.

The rest of the evening we talked and enjoyed each other's company. Recalling tales of adventures we missed, until together we fell asleep.

- ONE MONTH LATER -

As the dry season came to an end, Liliana was buried out in the field where her parents laid rest. I worked hard a month prior to help rebuild the house while Liliana rested; her health slowly growing worse each day.

The grieving process was painful, and I had not slept peacefully since it happened. Images of blood, cries, and of my father, flashed violently whenever I closed my eyes. While rummaging through some of our old things, I came across an old hair pin with a smudge of grime on the handle. Rubbing the dirt off with my shirt, I reminisced about some fond memories of her using the pin to hold up her hair while she cleaned or did the laundry. Suddenly the image of her face evaporated and was replaced by another face of a girl I used to have memories of. A girl who also wore her hair pinned up to avoid getting into her face as she worked; Taela.

Her name jolted and awoke the demon inside me. Energy began

to fill dark voids where I was lost and lonely. My eyes were now bright and furious. Static clung and popped around my fingers, traveling into my arms. I had somehow forgotten about her. Forgotten about my father, and forgotten about my oath to stop all evil.

Grabbing a small pack filled with my closest possessions and a month supply of food, I left our small country home. Abandoning it forever and focusing the rest of my time and energy into mastering my abilities, hoping to find my sister.

There was nothing left for me here. Liliana shall always watch o ver me and I pray that she forgives me.

-SIX-
AVATAR

- FOUR YEARS LATER -

"As the saying goes," the old grey bookkeeper croaked, "A man can never be all powerful, until he can defeat his inner demons."

"Who says that?" I looked at him with a smirk.

"People of great importance do, but that's not important."

Rolling my eyes now, I took another sip of water from my tankard. After which I moaned, "Please get on with, I don't like to sit still for very long."

"Right, right," the man nodded. "Let me see if I can find it."

He reached below the counter, in which he stood over. Grasping and rooting for a few minutes, he arose again carrying a rather large, leather bound book. The lettering on the front was in elvish, human, and dwarven, which read, "Magic Compendium and all things spiritual"

The old bookkeeper heaved and yanked the thick book open to its contents section and thumbed down the large list of never ending small curvy text. "Ah, now let me see," he began. "Elements, Elemental Weapons, Elves, ah hear ya go, Essences."

My eyes and ears perked up when at long last, someone, somewhere, was divulging info on the elusive and much rumored Essences. People who've heard the word, very rarely knew what exactly they were. Old mages, catalogers, and bookkeepers were all questioned with little to no new info ever gained. That is, up until now.

The old man licked his wrinkled boney index finger and thumb, as he turned page after page until the word Essence was large and clear at the top. Squinting close to the page the keeper skimmed over the entry reading aloud and fumbling with words. "It's written here…the believed to be origins of the Essences, and also…a list of their names and what elements…they all are."

"Let me see," I calmly waved.

The man shifted the giant record compendium over the wooden counter, where I turned it around and began to skim the passage over.

Skipping over the useless info I already learned, I quickly followed the writing down to where a small list was written. "Yes," I said loudly.

"Did you need something?" the old man asked.

"No, that's okay. I can take it from here, you can leave."

When the man slowly trotted away, I began to memorize and study the list carefully. The listing made mention of eleven Essences. It also noted their respected elements and some info on what they looked like, and what abilities they were said to have.

Vortricus, what kind of stupid name is that? Says here he is the Essence of Lightning and Thunder. After copying some of the information down, I closed the book and called the bookkeeper back to take it away.

"Did you find what you wanted?" the old man whimpered.

"Almost," I beamed, "Where can one person find these Essences?"

The old man mumbled and thought for a moment, "Usually people don't go looking for their deaths, but since you're so keen on finding yours, I suggest you head towards the highest peaks and pray."

"I'm not familiar with the geography of Ahreidonia, can you at least give me more direction." I pursued.

"Go to the province of Ersive, the mountains there are said to be the highest and most dangerous in the entire world."

Sighing, I prodded further, "What good will that do?"

"Well," the man continued, closing the book. "If you'd read the passage, you'd know most sightings happened near the tall peaks."

"Thank you." I said while making my way out the door.

Leaving the small shop, I made my way out into the main streets of Trizdes. Determined now, more than ever, to track down an Essence, and hopefully find my sister.

The thin mountain air nearly winded me a few times while traveling up the last few hundred yards. The local guide claimed a terrible storm was approaching from the north, but I yelled at him and offered him more money if he stayed the course.

The final trek was the worst. For a man who almost had an endless supply of energy, this mountain felt like it would be my final resting place. My muscles and legs were cramping, my back was sore from carrying a large pack of supplies, and the mana in the air was feint and unfamiliar.

The top of the mountain soon leveled off, revealing various rock spires jutting out from its surface. Off in the distance, from all directions, stood even taller and staggering mountains than the one I had climbed. Farther in the distance, a large black and grey cloud was forming. It seemed to absorb and attract all other clouds near it as it slowly lurched its way straight towards us. The guide may have been correct, but I didn't come this far to be scared off by some small thunder clouds.

As the sun fell, evening began its course. The dark storm was now only a league or so away. The tension in the air grew still and quiet. A few hours ago, the guide had pitched a tent and was resting inside a few yards away from where I now sat. My attention was fleeting, and I could feel some static drawing in the air where there previously was none.

Watching the black cloud travel closer, I saw from its presence that this wasn't an ordinary storm. The mass seemed to engulf the entire mountain in which we were stationed, as well as, some of the other ones nearby. With the luminous storm now above my head, I began to hear thunder bellowing deep inside, like a war drum starting a tempo for an upcoming battle. Inch by inch, as the cloud grew larger; I grew more anxious to finding this so called Essence.

My chest began to heat up with intensity. Feeling I could no longer sit still, I got up and began pacing tediously back and forth around the mountain top, contemplating on what would happen if he never showed. Maybe it was all a dream. Maybe these Essences all died out ages ago.

Just then, a large lightning bolt struck the cliff side a few yards from my location. Hairs stood on end, and I even jumped a little. The sound was so loud it awoke the guide, who poked his head out from his small tent. Looking around, he immediately hid back inside, "I told you!" he shouted.

Turning back around, I gazed upwards, calling for more. My body was becoming charged, and I could feel energy filling the air around the whole palisade.

The dark surging storm cloud stood still. Small electric sparks went off inside the giant nebula, lighting it up a few dozen times. Waiting in silence, I assumed nothing would happen.

I assumed wrong.

Another, ever larger bolt of lightning struck down from the center, engulfing me whole in bright white energy and heat. My body felt numb, yet I was unharmed. Blinded temporarily, I stumbled to catch my footing, and then shouted upwards once more. "I seek the Essence Vortricus, not some pathetic lightning strike!"

Silence and patience were not my strong suits, but if waiting a few moments would grant me an Avatar's power, than I would take a vow of silence for one-hundred years.

The monstrous clouds rolled and shifted. Black clouds swirled and collided with other black clouds until a strange deep voice bellowed from the sky. "I answer to only those who are truly worthy of my supreme power. What makes me think that you would be he?"

Folding my arms together, I continued to stare upwards. Small bolts of lightning occasionally struck farther away, due to the ever increasing energy that was building up in the storm.

"I have travelled far, trained hard, and devoted my life to the powers granted to me," I bellowed. "I only seek to obtain the most powerful of abilities, and I know that being is you. Grant me my humble wish and allow me the honor of combat!" I opened my palms, releasing static and sparks from my fingers and hands.

The storm grew quiet, "Very well," the voice cautioned. "But know this, should you fail, you will perish."

I shouted in response, "I welcome death!"

The next thing I saw was perhaps something that could only be imagined in a dream. Running away from the center of the mountain top, I stopped a few feet away from the cliff's ledge.

The enormous cloud twisted and spiraled into a funnel. Like water in a drain, it swirled around forming a tip as energy, electricity, and bright yellow lights, gathered together into a huge ball that grew in size until the cloud had taken another shape.

Staring upwards, mouth open, I saw the enormous black and grey cloud turn into a large ball of pure energy and electricity. Forming in the center grew a large black eye. It glared back at me as random bolts of lightning extended off its surface and struck anything and everything.

The giant Essence, known as Vortricus hovered above the ground, before lunging at me. Over-estimating its speed, I dodged a little too late, and while rolling to the side my left leg penetrated the large ball of pure energy. My pants and boot ignited and burned away, revealing a reddened skin underneath. I was worried that it might hurt, but as long as I don't get too close I should be fine.

Not hesitating, Vortricus turned around and tried to ram at me again. Dashing away, I unsheathed my daggers and began to focus some quick spells.

A lucky side step caused me to get around to the back of him. Extending both hands and blades forward I punched into his mass with both hands; daggers penetrating deep, almost disappearing into the veil of yellow and white swirling energy.

All at once, I let lose a huge blast of lightning deep into his core, hoping it would hit something. I was not aware that Essences were not made of organic substances, but of only pure elements.

Vortricus' eye swiveled from his front and appeared onto his back, I sensed him laughing inside while my hands were still deep in his mass. The eye looked upwards, as did I, where a huge blast of energy struck down and covered my entire body twice fold.

The voltage and heat burned simultaneously, causing my body to collapse to the rocky ground. For the first time in years, I was bearing the pain that my own attacks must have caused my enemies. Though it wasn't the full force, my body and muscles were giving out. My teeth rattled, my hair singed, and the oxygen in my lungs gave out.

It was at this time, Vortricus raised skyward, levitating as if by mere thought, his sole eye never moving from me. I reached for my chest with both hands. Getting up on both feet again, I stood tall and firm, "You'll have to do better than that!" I exclaimed.

Gathering a large aura of mana, I focused it inside, and then down my arms into my blades. The metal glowed and turned bright yellow. Rage filled my eyes, and determination made me fuel the fires in my soul.

Taking a large leap upwards, I used some energy to gain speed and distance. As Vortricus began his own assault, I performed the impossible. I spearheaded forward, arms and legs extending the daggers' points, like a large arrow. Ramming head long into Vortricus' body, I passed into his giant mass. The blades stuck deep into his eye, as the rest of my body flew out from his backside, landing hard on the ground below.

Rolling over, I saw Vortricus flail and thrash in the air. Eventually the daggers dislodged and fell to the ground. Looking at me, I could see his anger and intensity was beginning to simmer. Eventually, he levitated back to the ground, just as I recovered and stood.

"It seems like you might be worthy after all," he grumbled deeply. "Though, a tie is hardly anything to gloat to your friends about."

Laughing till my sides hurt from the bruises I yelled back, "Then we have a pact then?"

Vortricus' form grew smaller and smaller, till it was half the size it started out as. "The pact shall commence," he hummed, drifting closer to me. "After which, we shall become one, and we shall gain much from each other."

Half-naked and weary, I nodded silently. I was glad it was over, but now I was even more excited as to what will come next.

Vortricus hovered; his massive cloud form gently balanced above my head. Slowly energy erupted between us, while he began to funnel down into my body. There was a slight discomfort at first, but once we were whole; I discovered I now had an almost limitless supply of new energy and power.

"You are now hence forth, Shio, the Lighting Avatar," exclaimed Vortricus, one final time before evaporating completely within me.

When the sky became clear again, and all lights faded, the mountain guide stuck his head out again and quickly ran out carrying my spare clothes, his face in complete disbelieve at how crazy I was.

Night arrived, and we still hadn't left the mountain. Starting a fire, we talked, sharing our experiences, while sipping tea. The stars shined brightly overhead, and for once, I felt as if all the stresses in life had been completely removed. Free to recall my past, I began to muster an image of simpler times; times when Liliana was resting on a grassy knoll, with me by her side. Images of my own family; my sister Taela, my mother, and even my father, before his depression and wickedness tainted his heart. All the way back, I pictured days when I had no cares in the world, and life was perfect.

Then, it all faded to black.

THE KING'S WAR

INTRODUCTION

Long before chivalry, order, and serenity, was but a whisper on the winds, the land of Ahreidonia was in a constant state of struggle, barbarianism, and power hungry men. The numerous wars, deaths, and violence spread among the lands, causing much upheaval and disarray. With no other options; leaders from the six great races came together to hold a meeting regarding the fate of the world. The delegations were long and tedious, but after many years they arrived at the same conclusion.

To help guide and balance their new world, Ahreidonia was divided into eight mighty provinces which eight kings would reign and govern. Xsivfer, the frozen mountain region was given to an orc king who led the mountain orcs through thirty-one battles and freed them during the battles of Orakel. Bev, the icy swamp and tundra land was to be reigned over by a prince, whose father owned and led their province through many dark times. The lush jungles and thick forests of Lorendia where given to the highest elven family who decided to open their borders to all other races after many years of seclusion. A passionate and strong human family was assigned king and queen of Ersive, a huge province with enormous mountains and expanding deserts. Lefiet, a fire and water plain region was awarded to a half-elf half-human who led a revolution over the goblins on Cromaro. The oldest son of a dwarven war chief who toppled eight towns and three cities was granted king of the desert and plain province of Zeben. Keifa, which was to be ruled by a strong and courageous human who led his kind from the western seas to escape orc pirates. The final province, Ranoia, was far too large to be ruled by merely one king, so it was judged that the enormous mass of land would be considered one province, but it will have two regions east and west.

As the meeting adjourned the races began squabbling and fighting over many of the decisions held, but one haunting remnant still lingered in each of their minds; will this new idea of Kings stand the test of time? Will it save and protect us all from extinction? Or will our savage hearts and untamed spirits tear this world into oblivion?

<u>PHASE I</u>
ONE WAY TO WIN

Enthralled over an upcoming meeting with the mighty reputable king of Demetria, Darren couldn't resist entertaining his fellow guild members with a handful of crests and the paths to several taverns and brothels while they stayed in Roncerse Castle. Each and every one of their flattered faces was enough for Darren to not have to worry as much over his future meeting and more towards what his men would be getting themselves into while he was disposed.

While waiting in the King's official waiting room, at the moment the sun began to graze just above the dark green horizon line, a royal guard exited the king's room, glancing towards his direction. Darren stood tall and firmly then walked quickly over to the lone regal guard, addressing him politely.

Dressed in shined silver and polished iron armor, the guard checked the slender door as Darren approached. "You may enter now, Darren of Treila." The mild-mannered, regal guard announced. "The king has taken it upon himself to grant you this rare meeting so don't keep him waiting."

Opening the bronze and silver ornamental door in front of him, Darren walked through the doorway proudly spotting the king far across the large open room starring out from an enormous window, while two other similarly dressed guards stood a couple yards away from either side of him. Darren hadn't received much of a welcome from the king, but one guard whispered to his lord and nodded across the room. The king, who wore thick black leather boots, matching black pants, and a pearl white and silver vest with a black dyed undershirt, glanced over his shoulder and exclaimed, "Darren, please come over here. I'm so glad we could have this meeting."

Darren stepped anxiously over to the foreboding window, which looked like a large gateway into the views of the surrounding kingdom. He momentarily halted, keeping his distance from the king when he saw fierce glares coming from both guards near the king's side.

"Oh, leave him alone," the king motioned for the two to leave. "I invited him here, now please be gone the both of you."

After the guards closed the door behind them, the king left his place near the enormous window and took a seat in his wide gold and black leather chair at the head of the bare long oak table which was positioned in the center of the room. "Join me Darren," the king gestured. Darren chose a seat next to his highness, trying not to be rude or impolite on his manner and stature.

Once situated, the king professed, "The reason I have invited you here Darrren is because the current state of my reign is crumbling from the ongoing war."

Darren started to open his mouth, but the king hushed him, holding up a finger.

"It is true we could very well be winning this civil war but at what cost; is what I'm afraid of. For years the bloodshed never ends, and even though we have tried to talk for peace, the Rachellian king still eagerly anticipates my head in his trophy hall."

Adjusting himself in his mighty chair the king continued, "Knowing all this, my advisers and I arrived at the conclusion that the only way to preserve Ranoia, and its entire people; is for a clear and precise victory once and for all. This is where you come in Darren," the king raised an eyebrow.

*   *   *

- Earlier At Roncerse Castle -

The city was lit by fires and torches that flickered among the curvy streets and otherwise dimly lit sidewalks inside the castle walls. In between the tall stone houses and fancy shops were folks conversing amongst one another as Treila stared at them enthralled over what their life must be like on a daily basis living inside this keep. She wondered if the children had decent pastimes, if old mothers got to settle down with their husbands, and whether the people still danced outside if it was raining. She didn't get to visit many castles, keeps, or even very large forts, but every time she did, she insisted to herself that she would try to experience as much as they had to offer during her time there.

Darren, on the other hand, sat at the small oak table across from her, forearms gently resting on the table, sipping his warm ale and never once looking outside the window next to them at the Rideknot Tavern. Treila momentarily stopped her daydreaming and turned to Darren whom she felt needed the beverage and relaxation most from their travels.

"When you're done with that," she started, "Can we please go visit some shops or other places outside the city?" She sipped some of her own ale, noting the light waft of spices and orange froth.

"Yeh," he mumbled by mere accident. He licked his lips and smiled, gazing at her fair complexion. The way her light brown bangs dangled in front of her eyes, forcing her to tuck the loose strands back behind one ear.

"What was that?" Treila lightly asked, not quite making out what her commanding officer said.

"Um...yes," he squeaked, not really correcting himself. "Why do you want to leave, we just got here? Besides, all the really great things are here near the castle."

Responding with a sign, she tilted her head, wondering if she chose the right person to relax herself with on this carefree evening.

Darren continued, unmoved by her expression, "I rather enjoy your company, but you can go if you want." He gazed one last time out the window, a young couple strolled by, cheerfully talking and holding hands. "I think I will stay here," returning his gaze. "This place has a nice atmosphere to it."

"Look," she begged, "I really appreciate the company you've given me, but please let me go and experience some of what this place has to offer, at least before we leave."

Darren guzzled down the remainder of his drink; light residue collecting at the bottom.

"Sure," he said, constantly switching attention between the outside and his present company. He watched the people walk down the cobblestone streets, trying to see for himself what she saw in all this busy life. "We won't be here for very long, so it probably is best for us to go take all look. I heard they have a really nice baker somewhere down south a few streets."

Treila's eyes lit up, and she quickly drank down the rest of her ale, laid two black iron crests down on the table, then grabbed his arm and together they headed out.

＊　＊　＊

"Darren," the king called out, noticing him in a slight daze. "The kingdom is asking you to secretly join the Rachellian army at whatever the cost. After upon doing so, you will slowly get close to the king, working for him and earning his trust." He paused, relaxed in his chair, folding his hands before adding, "Then you will assassinate him at your first opportunity."

"Sorry," Darren stated, recalling the evening prior, the drinks they shared, and the happiness that continued to elude him and his team. Shaking his mind clear, Darren started considering his options as the king continued, "I have prepared a route and inventory for you, as well as, your other six members' needs."

"Five." interrupted Darren.

"What was that?" the king asked.

Darren repeated while continuing to consider more options. "I have five active guild members now."

"Fine whatever," the king shrugged. "Inventory for the other five members. But, I must not be connected to this plan in any shape or form, is that clear?"

"Perfectly," Darren made the effort to sound reassuring.

"Excellent!" the king concluded. "You have two or three seasons at the most to get the job done, any longer and I will consider the plan failed and be forced to send in another team." The king bent over, adjusting his garbs and fiddling with his overzealous rings. "I need you to leave as soon as you can. Every day we are losing men and women to this fruitless battle, and right now this is our one and only chance to win."

PHASE II
PORT AUTHORITY

Darren and his fellow guild members travelled north from the castle, where they found themselves near the outskirts of the port town, Heraen. The king's naval royal advisor informed them that a struggle had been waging over the ingoing and outgoing ships. Apparently, the townsfolk were smuggling goods and provisions to aid the Rachellian king's soldiers along the northern coast.

This was four days ago, since Darren and his team left Trizdes, under the assumption that they were to spy on the townsfolk and report any treason, as well as, board or secure an enemy vessel and smuggle their way into the province of Rachelle.

"I don't know Darren, they seem a little too uncoordinated to be even considered a threat to the king," Gherrik spoke grumpily.

Darren sat motionless among the hillside, his vision and

expression never changing as Gherrik, the half-human half-dwarf continued to speak loudly. "I mean look at them." He sat up from his prone position along the grassy hillside where Darren and his team were keeping watch on the townsfolk some five hundred or so yards away. "In four days all we've got are goat farmers, dirty housewives, vegetable stands that couldn't feed a single pig, and fishermen who are so skin and bones they would fly away with the next large gust."

Feridan sat up from his position nearby after hearing the commotion. Gherrik looked around towards all of his fellow members determined to see if any took an interest in siding with him. Twisting his neck around he saw Taradiym, the very enigmatic genomorph, sitting motionless on top of a flat stone, eyes closed, seemingly in meditation. Turning his head the other way, Ufroum, the mage, surprised him by having his soft nose only inches from Gherrik's.

"Your eyes must be deceiving you Gherrik," the mage smiled, "because there are also merchants from Kelia, Driehn, and even many travelers from the Luspania Desert."

Gherrik rolled his eyes, shoving Ufroum to the side. "I know there are many other people, you over-thinking mage, I was trying to get Darren, or somebody, a clue as to why we are still here wasting precious time."

Feridan soon stood and approached Darren, "If we are to make the deadline, I suggest we commandeer a boat soon."

"I sent Treila down this morning to learn the next schedule for any Rachellian ships and to divulge information on any Rachellian supporters," Darren divulged. "She is due back three days from now. We can't move until a vessel of correct size and hull docks in order to not raise suspicions." Feridan gazed over towards Gherrik still conversing with Ufroum on the tall grassy hillside. Darren continued. "Anyone can just kill innocents and sail away, what we need to do is accomplish our mission without needless slaughter."

Feridan concluded, while staring at Gherrik and sighing, "I just hope we aren't given away before we even start."

A few more days had passed and now the governor and many Trizdes guards established a port blockade, further seizing the town.

They erected several wood and metal barricades over the docks and port houses, even going as far as halting or closing down ships and merchants from their regular sailing routes.

Darren and his team were constantly moving around the outskirts every so many hours to avoid detection, while they waited for more news from Treila who was still establishing contacts and information amongst the fishermen and port authorities.

It was night. Feridan, Taradiym, and Gherrik were sent to patrol and spy a mile or so east from their main camp, when Ufroum spotted Treila walking towards their position from the town. Ufroum waited until she got closer before he stood up and walked over to greet her. "I do hope you have something new for us today," he smirked.

Treila kept her pace as she ignored Ufroum's remarks and made her way up to the tent where Darren was waiting inside. The tent flap closed on Ufroum abruptly, as Treila's body disappeared.

Inside the warm tan cloth tent, Treila sat down along a bench, placing her small satchel down next to her feet. Darren stood over a tiny wood table with a map of the town spread over its surface. "I'm hoping for some good news Treila," requested Darren.

Taking a long drink of water from her calf bladder she replied, "It's not looking so good. Aside from the continued fights among the guards and the townsfolk, I found no one that would divulge or acknowledge a Rachellian presence or aid in this town.

You would think even some of the sleaziest of men I had to sleep with would give me something, but nope, it's all dry." She rose to her feet to stretch, as she kept talking, while Darren continued to look over the map quietly. Walking closer towards him she hinted, "I think we should try another town along the coast and maybe find a ship there."

Darren tilted his head down ever so slightly then turned to look into her hazel eyes. "We don't have much time to try another location. The king's advisors reported that Rachellian smugglers were here, and it doesn't make sense for them to not be."

Treila piped in, "We can still just steal a boat and sail there if we want. I'm sure the rest of the team will agree that waiting and doing nothing is getting us nowhere."

Darren replied, "No, what we need is..."

Just then, the tent flap flew open revealing Feridan who ran inside, halting before catching his breath. "Darren," he breathed in heavily, "the townsfolk are rioting!"

"How bad, and how many?" Darren demanded.

"Taradiym presumed nine fishermen and merchants, including a few women, against a handful or so guard squads. You know I never trust his calculations."

Darren interrupted, "I don't care if you don't trust him; I do."

They all exited the tent, where the rest of the team was standing, ready with their gear already in hand. "Feridan," blurted Darren, "Take Taradiym and Ufroum to the eastern side and watch for any Rachellian ships from all directions. If you see any, or one with a reasonable sized trade ship, procure it for us. Treila, you and Gherrik head to the western side and do the same. I will head directly to the southern side and decide on the appropriate measures if this riot doesn't end or if it gets worse."

The members began to spread out and leave, as Darren hollered one last time, "If the riot gets worse after twenty minutes, we will meet at the west trade dock and take a ship regardless!"

The team yelled and shouted together, after which they all disappeared into the dark nightly forest, hearts and blades eager for action.

* * *

- EARLIER AT RONCERSE CASTLE -

After Gherrik awoke from his small ruffled cot, he parted his coarse black hair out, put on brown trousers, straightened his dirty white undershirt and his jerkin, he then proceeded to head down the inn stairs and out into the morning streets. He hadn't walked but merely a few feet when he forgot his belongings, crests, and weapons, and ran back to his room.

The half-dwarf half-human got many odd stares and whispers as he walked down the castle streets, admiring the curved landscape, decorated pagoda, and servants making their rounds.

All taunts and rude gestures merely fell on deaf ears, as he continued to not even notice them anymore during his life.

Stopping in front of a small fry cook stand in between two residential homes, Gherrik's nose caught a whiff of something rather fancy. Grabbing the nearest coarse wooden stool, he plopped himself down before even realizing he had done so.

He often thought of himself as a half-breed who enjoyed eating and tasting much of what Ahreidonia had to offer. Part of the reason he even joined the Versparians and Darren's command, was because they travelled around allowing his stomach and taste buds to benefit the most from expeditions.

Licking his lips and swallowing the overflow of saliva, Gherrik stared intently at the chef who was in the middle of frying up some eggs and pig fat. The mouthwatering aroma and steam from the sizzling fat lit up Gherrik's face and senses, causing him to speak out enthusiastically, "I'll have two meals of your best dish!"

The short human chef casually glanced up at the stout half-breed, who gleefully leaned in closer to the searing pans, trying to inhale as much of the sweltering aroma as he could.

The chef finished serving the two well rounded humans sitting a few seats over, and then proceeded to wipe his hands clean, then wiping the sweat from his smoldering forehead. "You really want two?" the fry cook asked.

Gherrik bent forward over the counter, smiling uncontrollably, "Yes, of course. You think just cause I'm not a full blooded dwarf that I can't eat like one?"

The middle-aged chef only smiled and responded as he wiped more sweat from his brow, "No, I never question or judge my customer's stomachs. I only meant that preparing two would take twice as much time to make."

Sitting back even farther in the rickety stool, Gherrik folded his large coarse hands and said, "Oh I can wait, believe me."

＊　　＊　　＊

By the time Darren and his team secured a medium sized trade ship, they had noticed several guards seizing several merchants and fishermen both elderly and young in handcuffs, guiding them into a large dock house. By this time, Taradiym was above deck spying on any movement or suspicious guards that might wander too close.

The rest of the team was securing their belongings below deck as Darren and Feridan pulled out the coastal maps and began to set a course for the best coastal town in Rachelle. Gherrik happened across a few barrels and crates down in the hold. Stomach growling, he forced a lid open, revealing the tart aroma of cherry wine. Popping another barrel, he uncovered a spiced variation. Skipping the rest, he hurriedly moved to t he crates about to crack them open, when Ufroum called from the stairs, "You fat bastard, we have more important things to worry about."

"Piss off!" he shout in retaliation.

A few minutes into getting situated, the whole team heard several large cries and shouts coming from the docks. Darren sent Feridan and Treila to investigate and meet with Taradiym who was still on watch. After they left, the team heard even more cries ringing out, and then a large explosion bellowed, rocking the boat from the waves of the aftershock.

Suddenly, Treila appeared below deck announcing, "Darren, a large group of townsfolk are beginning to revolt against the guards! They are throwing and raising weapons in anger. The explosion was from a merchant ship that caught fire from the guards. Taradiym said they believed the merchants were smuggling Rachellian weapons and goods so they lit it up with torches!"

Darren came out from the shadows, map in hand and small lantern in the other. "We cannot give away our cover, even if these events are true. Send Feridan back down to help with the course." He

197

paused as another small explosion erupted. "You and Taradiym stay above deck and inform me of any more changes."

Treila hesitated, but then proceeded to head back above deck. Immediately she came back along with Feridan a few seconds later. Once again she called out, "They are arresting the entire merchant's family, even those who weren't aboard at the time!"

Darren nodded to Feridan who replied back for him. "Do you know if they are indeed Rachellian aiders?"

Looking frustrated she blurted, "I don't know. Taradiym told me they weren't which is why we must do something."

This time Darren stepped forward after handing Feridan the map to look over. "If the guards are merely abusing power, then what do you hope to achieve? We can't put the mission in jeopardy for one mishap. Just from these events you can see how this war is not just affecting the armies that fight it, but also the smallest of towns and the people who try to live their lives peacefully."

"We have the power to stop them!" she cried out.

"Yes we do," Darren replied calmly. "But as you will see, the farther we get into Rachellian territory, the more empathetic you will be when you see just what wars do to people."

Darren looked over to Ufroum who was fiddling with a few small books of his near some crates in the back. "Ufroum!" Darren called. "Start us some winds that blow north-west."

The fidgeting mage looked up, dropping some books to the floor. "Aye aye sir," he said as he fumbled his way above deck.

Darren headed back to the map table with Feridan, as Treila slowly walked to the back crates and sat down among them feeling depressed.

Taking his seat Darren insisted, "You must remember why we are here."

PHASE III
BATTLING FEAR

- EARLIER AT RONCERSE CASTLE -

This was the second weapon shop today, in which Feridan had left empty-handed. This wasn't due to his lack of crests lining his pockets, but merely a result of his stubbornness. Feridan had been without a decent weapon for quite awhile now.

Ever since the mission against the orc raiders of Jureil, he had been forced to pick weapons off his foes or borrow some from Gherrik, who hated sharing. In fact, his whole team hated to share anything with him, because it never made it back to them in one piece.

It was sometime later, that Feridan had walked into another weapon shop, nestled among the back streets in Roncerse Castle. This particular one was of medium size and had its own forge in the far back corner. Walking straight up to the corner, he felt confident that this was the day.

"I need to look at your strongest and most well crafted long swords," he said firmly to the small timid dwarf wiping the counters.

The young dwarf looked up at Feridan's tall build, large muscles, and sleek short hair, before answering nervously back, "I think you...you should speak to my uncle then. He...he works in the back crafting almost everything we...we sell here. If...if you wait here just a moment, I'll go fetch him for...for you."

Growing impatient, Feridan paced back and forth near some racks of long poles and brass pikes, before another dwarf called over to him. "You there!" the voice shouted, deep and clear. "My nephew tells me you are interested in purchasing some of my best works."

Feridan walked slowly over to the larger, more elderly dwarf who appeared from the back, "Just show me your long swords, or maybe even a bastard if you have one."

The older dwarf replied, "I assume you have some form of

currency then? I usually don't bother with window lookers."

"Oh don't worry about that," Feridan assured, "If you have what I need, you will be most compensated."

Leaving silently, the old white bearded dwarf appeared, carrying out a select number of long swords, cleavers, and even some bastard swords per request.

Feridan almost immediately began to inspect and test each one that was laid out on the counter space. He waived them in the air, tested their weights, and inspected the colors and hilts, moving from one to the next. When he came to the last two, he picked up the silvery long sword with a two-handed hilt, and bright shimmering silver cross guard.

"That one is one of my favorites," mentioned the dwarf smith. "Sadly though, because of its price it has been sitting in my shop for ages, never having the chance to feel the battles of a seasoned master."

Feridan glanced at the sword one final time then promised, "As long as it won't break, I'll be sure to show it many battles worthy of its crafting."

The dwarf smith nodded, heading back to his forge, "I wouldn't have it any other way."

*　　*　　*

The stolen trade vessel carrying all six members of the Versparians gently rocked and swayed as it grew closer to the land that lie in the distance. The far stretch of terrain belonged to the northern coast near the town Efeurlic. As the boat grew nearer, Ufroum began to gather in blue mana from the air and water around him, drawing it into his palms. Closing his eyes and concentrating, he twirled his wrists and extended his skinny arms in circles and wave like patterns as a pale white mist slowly began to roll away from his chest and forearms. Like a hunting whale stalking its prey, the mist flowed gently above the water, rolling and rising as it travelled out from the boat and towards the eerie coast. The team was all on standby. Feridan took a knee on the bow, gripping and massaging the handle of his new sword.

As the ship glided up the sandy shore, locking it into place among the lowering tide, the wave of mist sank beneath the ground and disappeared as fast as it had been conjured. Feridan ran ashore first, diving into the nearest brush, sword drawn, and eyes scanning the deep surrounding woods.

After a few minutes, he signaled for the rest of his team, and one by one they hoped off the boat, gear in arms, and weapons at their sides.

"Feridan," Darren whispered, after checking to make sure everyone was off the boat. "You and Treila scout ahead, report back when you reach a road. Everyone else, we are going to head southwest for awhile and make camp."

They journeyed for a day and a half till Treila reported a wide river up ahead past a crude forest clearing. When the whole team reached the river bank, Darren stopped the march, rubbing his chin as he scanned the landscape.

"Treila how far till Efeurlic?" he asked.

She rubbed the sweat from her brow, responding, "Well, if we keep this pace, it's only another day."

"We aren't going to Efeurlic," spoke Darren. "I just need to know how much distance we have from the town."

Ufroum took off his cloth sack, laying it on the soft ground next to his feet adding, "I can always make more mist or cloud cover if you are worried about the townsfolk."

"Yeah, I'm sure they won't be suspicious after seeing mist rise up from nowhere in a warm forest." Darren shook his head, "It's not the townspeople I'm worried about. This place has been getting frequent visitors and is commonly used for travel."

Looking out towards the winding muddy river Ufroum further inquired, "How can you tell?"

Feridan stepped forward grabbing Ufroum's boney shoulder, turning him so they could be face to face. "You've been walking all over their tracks," he grunted. "And you call yourself a mage."

"Yes," Ufroum declared, tossing Feridan's hand off him. "A mage that knows spells, not tracking."

"Alright you two," Darren barked. "We can try to cross now, or we can try going around. Treila; you and Feridan head upstream and try to find a more shallow area to cross. The rest of us will move back into the woods and wait." He continued to check the surrounding brush and river. "We don't want unexpected guests stumbling upon us."

Nightfall set in much sooner than the Versparians had expected. Not sooner than the sun hid below the tree line, had Treila and Feridan reported back to camp.

"Sorry it took so long," Treila explained. Feridan was busy laying down his pack and removing some of the contents inside, as she continued their report. "You were right about the travelers. We spotted several canoes, rafts, and even a small trade boat travelling eastward along the river."

"Any luck on that crossing?" Darren prodded.

"There's a few spots we can take, one is closer but involves slippery rocks and debris. The other is an old wooden bridge that connects to a path on the other side. Sometimes locals go there to fish, but they shouldn't be a problem."

They both sat down on the soft dirt, backs against their packs, weapons gently resting near their feet. "We will head for the bridge in an hour," Darren ordered. "Rest up until then and we'll see if we can avoid any nightly fishers."

During the quiet night, as the moon bounced and shimmered off the cold river water, Darren and his team slipped out from the confines of thick tree cover, jogging at an even pace along the embankment. Feridan travelled at the head of the group a few yards away so as to scout for any dangers or hazards. Treila was last along with Gherrik who preferred to keep towards the back because he loved to meet ambushers head on.

They had only travelled a half hour when suddenly Feridan was running back towards them waving his arm and whispering for them to retreat. Darren quickly shuffled everyone back into the closest foliage for cover.

Just after Gherrik leaped into the thicket, a small torch light came into view around the river bend. A few seconds later another torch could be seen, and then another shortly after.

Darren and his team remained perfectly quiet. Their breathing slowed, their feet and arms like a statue, and even the crickets around them seemed to hush as the eerie lights grew closer as they hovered just above the gently flowing water.

When the lights came more into view, Treila could tell that they were in fact belonging to something else. "I can see one is a small raft, while the other is a trade boat. Not very big, but it does have some people on it," she whispered to the group.

A moment later, the boats were now almost directly in front of where the Versparians were hiding. Without warning, a shout came from the other side of the river. The boats slowed to a crawl, and then another shout followed soon after. It sounded like some people from the other side were calling them over.

"By order of the forty-second militia under the Rachellian king, all vessels, no matter the size or class, are under direct obligation for soldiers to inspect and seize where in necessary!" shouted someone, whom the group now realized were patrol guards.

The two vessels slowed down even more, as one man that was on the trade boat hollered back, "We have nothing to hide, nor give. We use this river nightly for fishing and trade with the village west of here!"

"I will not ask politely again!" the guard bossed. "Dock your boats now for inspection or face confinement of you and your belongings!"

Darren and his team kept quiet, watching the spectacle unfold before them. They couldn't risk leaving now and creating noise, and they couldn't intervene without even more noise. So, they kept watching, hoping the event would resolve itself rather soon.

The few fishermen paddled their way towards the other side and docked as best they could against the reeds and tall grass. As the boats approached, the torches lit more of the embankment revealing several more guards all in Rachellian uniforms, standing along the riverside with spears, shields, and swords ready at their hips.

The people aboard remained on the boats as another fisherman called out, "You can see from there that we are but simple fishermen. If you want food or goods we have very little. This is only a night trip for catching. You stopped us before we could make it the fishing spot."

From far off, Treila was the only one who could spot some of the further guards whispering in each other's ears. She told the rest of the team that the guards were laughing and waiving their spears at the innocent elderly fisherman.

"By law you must assist us in our endeavors at protecting this region from the Demetrians!" one of the guards shouted walking closer to the vessels.

"There are no Demetrians here," another fisherman implored. "In fact we can assist you by telling you we haven't even seen any armies around here for nigh a few weeks."

Just then a spear impaled the middle-aged man through his chest, toppling him off the deck and into the murky water. "They are spies!" a guard shouted. "Honor the king by showing no mercy!"

All of a sudden the two boats were overwhelmed by guards and flashes of steel. The defenseless fishermen tried to jump overboard, but were grabbed, choked, or cleaved in all but a few moments. The butchery was so distasteful, so wretched and uncalled for, that Treila almost leaped out of the thicket with daggers drawn. Darren gave her a look, and Gherrik even clasped her forearm firmly with his hand.

"I can't permit you to reveal our location," Darren whispered sternly, face and eyes still staring at her disgusted expression.

Gherrik let go of her arm. Rubbing her arm gently she proclaimed, "Those bastards are just as cold and heartless as those men back in Heraen."

"That is true," Darren commented. "War is terrible, and creates terrible people. But we cannot lose sight of why we are here, and why our mission is so important."

Ufroum broke in, "We can wipe them all out; it shouldn't be too hard."

"No," Darren turned his head. "We wait ten more minutes after they leave, then we back out and continue our journey southward."

The guards across the river began to unload and pick through the fishermen's things. They scavenged the boat and raft, eating fruit, tearing apart crates, and pitching anything that was useless to them over the sides. When the guards were at last satisfied, they laughed and patted each other on the backs, as they walked off into the darkness.

PHASE IV
SOLDIERS & SERVANTS

Eight more days had passed, and still the Versparians hiked and traversed over soft grassy hills, dried creeks, scattered patches of forests, and whatever the lands of Rachelle laid before them. They would have arrived a whole day prior, but Treila and Feridan were constantly warning them of people coming close to their proximity. Multiple times they had to take the longer paths or found themselves on roads rarely travelled. Sometimes they took a short cut through some dense fields, while other times they trudged through swamps, or were forced to scale mountains at night; none of which any of them enjoyed.

On the tenth day, during the early hours, Treila reported back to the team that a small garrison of soldiers was departing from a fort a few miles eastward.

"How many are leaving?" Darren asked firmly, pondering other questions too himself.

"Feridan is still watching from a distance," she replied. "But, we counted at least ten maybe twelve."

Thinking harder, he inquired, "Can you tell what reagent or command?"

"No, but we had to keep quite a distance to avoid detection."

"Well, if we take them now, we will have to act fast in order to not raise suspicion." Darren looked up at her after swallowing some water from his canteen. "Twelve you say?"

"Maybe ten," she added.

"Alright," nodded Darren as he motioned for the others to pay attention. "Prepare your things for a fight. We are taking a detour east. Hopefully this will end rather fast." Looking towards Ufroum —who was busy flipping through some pages of a small book- he ordered, "Ufroum, I'll need you to stay back for support."

"I could kill them all if you want," the mage blurted, still thumbing through the tiny black leather book.

"No, we need them in one piece."

Gherrik let out a humble laugh as he made sure his boots were snug and wrestled his belt tighter; half a dried onion held between his teeth.

Not half a minute later, the team was making their way past the worn path and into the deeper woods eastward, drawing closer to the unsuspecting garrison.

＊　＊　＊

- EARLIER AT RONCERSE CASTLE -

It had felt like ages since Ufroum was able to stroll about a city or castle grounds. Waiving his skinny arms around, he breathed in deeply, ultimately opening his eyes slowly to see that he was not alone. Behind him, relaxing his stance, stood Taradiym; hired mercenary, assassin, and all too reputable, mute.

This tall mysterious man joined the Versparians right before Ufroum had, and to this day the thought of it grinds his inner mind, keeping him up at night.

It wasn't so much that they were enemies, but in Ufroum's mind, he knew Taradiym barely even noticed him. A mage such as him was always at the bottom of the list when it came to skilled assassins and heroic warriors.

However, on this particularly fine day, they were stuck with each other until Treila or Feridan came back from whatever it was they were sent to do -Ufroum had trouble remembering. It was Ufroum's idea to leave the confines of their room, heading outside for some fresh air and to stretch his cramped legs. After all, he had been re-reading his arcane book collection and notes from the arcane principle lesson hall in the capital of Trizdes -a task which would cramp up even the liveliest of druids.

The two of them walked along the side streets, neither speaking a word to each other. Instead, they admired views, smelled sizzling animal meat and fish, and wondered strange thoughts over who should speak first.

Since Ufroum rarely heard Taradiym talk, (if at all) he decided to break the tension first.

"So," Ufroum muttered, "any particular place you would like to see?"

He tilted his head to see if his mute friend made any motion or desire to respond. The silent assassin wore dark garbs, blackened leather boots, and a faded hood concealing most of his face. The sun blinded the mage from being able to ascertain much more, and instead guessed that he must not have heard him. Starting to ask again, Taradiym interrupted, "No place comes to mind."

Ufroum was awestruck. Neither of them spoke again until they turned down another stone street, bypassing some old lady hauling flowers into her home.

Recovering from the mysterious and low voice of Taradiym, Ufroum eventually played it off, "Well, I don't really have a place in mind either, so maybe you can tell me more about yourself while we let the roads guide us." Hiding his hands in his pockets he added, "We hardly get to talk, so I figured why not now. We have spare time."

"I don't like to talk about myself," Taradiym responded in monotone.

Ufroum shifted his eyes around trying to think of how to get Taradiym to open up more. "What if," the mage prodded once more, "I tell you something about me, and then you can tell me something about yourself? I'll go first then." He thought to himself, as the two of them passed a fry cook whose apron was coated in grease and sweat, along with the smell of sizzling pig fat. Ufroum nodded to the balding man, who smiled and waved, but Taradiym seemed to ignore their exchange altogether.

"Ok," Ufroum started, "on my free time, I like to read, clean my trinkets, and practice word concentration." He looked up at Taradiym who was still expressionless. "Now, you tell me what you like."

The assassin at first said nothing, giving the impression to Ufroum that he must have been thinking really hard, or maybe he was ignoring him, but suddenly he said, "On my free time, I like it when a scrawny mage isn't asking me which volume of arcane enchantment reports was the most influential."

"Wow," thought Ufroum to himself, "This is going to be a horrible day."

✣　✣　✣

The team had approached the garrison only an hour later. The sun was partially hidden by the forest canopy, and while the air was clean and refreshing, the tenseness building from the current mission was slowly unraveling itself. Feridan met with the team and informed Darren of any updates to the situation. As they talked, the rest continued to walk silently through the woods, far away and deep enough where they had an advantage as to the soldier's current course. The Versparians followed the garrison until they stopped for a break near a fork in the road further ahead. Some small boulders, which higher ranking soldiers sat upon, while the rest sharpened their blades, drank, and told stories amongst the group.

As the soldiers enjoyed their rest, Darren informed his team the plan he had been hatching since they began their pursuit.

"Feridan informed me that there are exactly ten Rachellian soldiers, and two royal servants, Darren started. "I don't know any of their ranks, but from what I can gather they must be important enough to be travelling with two servants of the king."

Before anyone could comment, Darren hastily continued, "I know this, because if you look down, the soldiers are giving the two servants water, fruit, and even letting them walk unchained."

Feridan mentioned, "Also, they did have on the royal colors and crests, before you got here."

"Yes, well," stammered Darren. "We can attack now, or wait until morning. However, if we wait, events could change, destinations reached, or our position discovered."

Gherrik squeezed in between Feridan and Ufroum, where he immediately sat down on the ground in the middle of the semi-circle. "I vote we take them down now," his rough voice protruded. "It's been too long since my hammer had last tasted blood."

"The less blood the better, I'm afraid," said Darren. "We are going to be borrowing their uniforms to make it into the capital and with luck, the castle."

Turning to the mage, Treila asked, "Ufroum, do you have anything that can do this?"

Ufroum stared into space for a moment, his mind raced through various spells and knowledge until at last he answered, "Nothing that can dispatch all twelve at once."

Darren continued, "No, you stay back and make sure no one escapes or is a mage themselves. The rest of us will aim for the head, neck, or internal injuries. Lay them softly or don't lay them at all."

Nodding, the team grabbed their weapons and then spread outwards among the thicket and surrounding tress, forming a large circle over the entire group. Once in position, Darren let out the call.

Treila was the first to kill. Throwing two of her knives -without any remorse- she impaled the two closest soldiers, right in the neck. Not soon afterwards, Gherrik, Feridan, Darren, and Taradiym were starting to dash down the short hill towards the rest of the unaware soldiers. Leaves, stones, and twigs flew and kicked up with their advancement.

One soldier along the perimeter shouted as he began to unsheathe his broadsword. It only made it halfway, because Taradiym halted it with his foot, slammed it back down into the sheath, breaking a few of the man's fingers in the process. Then, with a blur, he slit the man's throat with a small dagger.

Feridan met up with two guards who already picked up a spear and a sword, and were ready for his assault. The Rachellian soldier wielding a long iron spear thrust it towards Feridan's chest, determined to halt his progress. The other guard with the long sword was urging his fellow comrade on, as they both yelled and took consecutive swipes and jabs. Feridan busy dodging, didn't notice that Taradiym was leaping their way. The two ecstatic soldiers dropped one after the other, as Taradiym tucked away his hidden dagger and smiled before leaping away towards another group.

"You bastard," Feridan yelled, "Those were my kills!"

Treila dispatched another soldier who was notching an arrow from afar with another knife, as Darren was busy protecting Gherrik from a barrage of swords from three other men. As soon as they too were taken care of, Taradiym eliminated two more of the soldiers and one servant hiding in a tree.

Darren looked around, quickly counting the bodies. "Eight, nine," he behind, "ten," then upwards, "eleven."

Treila hollered out while pointing, "Twelve, he's heading far into the woods!"

Darren peered over his shoulder for Taradiym, but the shaded genomorph pointed towards Ufroum who was not at his post.

The frantic servant was stumbling on rocks, scraping himself on branches, and falling over two or three times as he desperately ran up the hill and deeper into the forest. His mind raced with thoughts of death or impending doom and tortures that might come to him. He was racing so fast and so half-hazard he failed to see the lanky form of Ufroum who was standing in front of him preparing a spell with his hands.

The servant gasped when his eyes met the stout mage, wearing dirty dark blue robes, and a large amount of pendants around his tiny neck. Green and black mana swirled in his hands and tangled around the mages wrists and forearms. The poor servant tried to turn around, but Ufroum had already ensnared him. Dark green mana worked its way like a snake up the poor servant's legs and around his torso and chest. It slithered and wrapped up to his throat, where it went inside of him, before finally choking his heart.

Ufroum walked over, inspecting his work. Satisfied, he nodded and straightened his robes and chains then proceeded to trot down where the others were beginning to search and scavenge the rest of the bodies.

As Ufroum made his way out into the clearing where his other team members were, Darren was the first to greet him. "Please tell me you didn't damage his clothes?"

"What do I look like," Ufroum started to say, before spotted Feridan, Taradiym, and Gherrik who were cleaning blood off their blades giving him a cold stare as if they all heard. Ufroum decided not to finish his sentence.

The rest of the team began hauling the bodies closer together so Darren could examine the clothes, as Feridan and Gherrik were quickly moving and rummaging through all the goods, bags, and sacks, the garrison was carrying.

"What's it look like?" asked Treila.

"Well," Darren said as he flipped over some of the bodies, inspecting some of the gear. "The clothes are fine, but the problem comes from those two servants."

Treila and Darren both walked over to the servants' limp bodies; their scrawny frames almost identical, and their clothes matched those of the Rachellian royal garbs.

"How many of us will need to be servants?" Treila asked almost cautiously so as to not volunteer herself.

"Well we can probably get away with one," Darren answered. "But, none of us really fit the part." He looked over at her, "Do you think you can wear your hair up?"

She didn't look pleased, but as Ufroum appeared, Darren waved for him.

As the mage approached Darren asked, "How many of us can you make like them?"

Ufroum stared at him blankly until he understood what he meant, "Oh, you mean how long or how many illusion spells can I cast?"

He took a moment to think in his head before responding, "At least two, maybe three, but I would have to be really close and concentrating for that to work."

"Let's go with two," Darren said. "Treila you will need to be disguised for sure as you are a female, and I'm sorry to say don't fit any of the body types. As for the other I guess you will have to suffice."

Ufroum stared at him quizzically, "Me. Why me?"

"Well you do want to keep all your knickknacks with you right?" said Darren, with a smile forming.

Ufroum sighed, while the rest smirked in silence.

After the bodies, remaining gear, and goods, were buried, the Versparians headed south for the capital and towards Ieburen Castle where the Rachellian king was known to take residence. Together they wore the garbs and armor of five soldiers, plus one royal servant boy who made it out alive. Along the way, Darren informed them that they needed to make it close enough to the king's court in order to assassinate him. They could inform stations along the way that they barely escaped a guerilla assault, in hopes it would lead to an audience with the king or at the very least his advisors.

Treila was not pleased towards her role in the plan, but kept silent regardless, and together they managed to make it all the way to an outpost several miles from the castle.

The crude outpost was made up of various small shacks, some stone houses, and a single tower, standing not three stories tall. The outer wall seemed to be constructed from rough stonework, and plenty of loose chickens, sheep, and goats came and went freely.

As the Versparians approached, a lookout on the tower informed someone below of the visitors. A few seconds later the large front gate began to rise up, as several men in royal uniforms took positions lining outside the gates. Darren informed his team that he was to do the talking, and if they asked Treila anything, she would act mute and traumatized.

They approached the outpost closer they could see a small squad of well armored men and one regal man dressed in royal garbs approached the team.

The man in the middle shouted, "We were beginning to think you fellows were all but lost."

Darren walked his way closer and approached the man in his best Rachellian royal manner. "A group of guerrillas ambushed us a few days back."

"Yes, yes, we will get to that later," hushed the man. "You say they were a guerrilla group?"

"Yes sir," Darren answered.

The man looked over Darren's shoulder and then back towards everyone behind him. "One servant was lost then?"

"Yes, I'm afraid they took him first," responded Darren lowering his head sympathetically.

The royal man stood firm, smirking back at Darren. "Well, these things happen I guess."

Darren sighed with relief over the man's casual response.

The man nodded to his armed guards behind him, "Fit the servant with appropriate quarters, and give these men some grub, they're probably starving. I will inform the king right away over this news."

Darren and his group then walked into the outpost, as the lines of guards followed closely behind. Treila was sweating from all the pressure to act her part, but when she looked at Ufroum, she was perplexed because the large grizzly man he was masquerading as was smiling with pure delight over his new persona.

PHASE V
TO SAVE A LAND

A day later, the Versparians were chaperoned to Ieburen Castle where they would meet with the king and a large number of other returning soldiers to report on news and various small victories.

The journey itself went unheeded, if not for a few instances where some guards asked Treila some questions, in which Darren informed them of her sudden muteness, and desperate need of rest; for which bought them some time.

During the day's travel, Darren rode closest to Treila, as the rest of the group rode behind in a semi-organized fashion. Before the large ensemble of soldiers and Rachellians converged upon the Castle borders, their numbers had already grown to the forties or more. Many were riding on horseback, while the rest took carriages, carts, or enjoyed the scenery as they walked in unison. Together they bottlenecked at the main gates, where they stood for some more time, before eventually they arrived under the enormous metal gates and into the heart of the Rachellian capital.

Darren whispered to Treila and even back at the others as they passed under the walkways and patrolling militia. "Depending on the condition of our royal meeting, we might need to wait until a more opportune time arrives." Feridan and Gherrik each made faces as Darren continued, "Nobody do anything unless I give the order is that clear?" He looked at each one of them, waiting till they all accepted, albeit some against their wishes.

Once into the surrounding busy streets, they were led over to the eastern inner wall, where they had their horses tied, before entering the castle courtyard.

While Feridan and Gherrik took their time dismounting and removing gear, the groom asked, "Are you the company who narrowly escaped the Demetrians?"

They all looked at each other, then at Darren who spoke on their behalf. "Yes, the guerillas. We were told the king was waiting to see us."

The young man lassoed and knotted the reins to the nearest posts, wiped his hands on his trousers, then continued, "He's going to be addressing all of you."

The Versparians again looked towards Darren in confusion.

"We really can't wait," Darren again spoke up. "What time is the event?"

The groom responded as he took the reins from a nearby hefty soldier who leapt down from his horse next to them. "I think some patrols said an hour or so. Gives you time to wash and clean yourselves up."

"Thank you," Darren expressed kindly, as his team began to walk back towards the streets.

"Oh, you don't have time to do that," the man chirped out. He pointed over to the inner castle gates and stairs that led into the palace. "All men of honor have rest and rooms in the guard quarters north of here. It's right over there."

Once again Darren and his team thanked the young lad, and then turned around and headed towards the castle entryway.

"And you," he pointed to Treila who almost forgot she was actually disguised as a royal servant. "The head servant asked for you to join him in the servant's quarters before the feast."

Treila stared at her commander with expressed embarrassment, who assured her with a simple nod, that she would be safe and should do whatever was asked in order to keep her cover.

After the team had time to wash and steal some nicer clothes, they headed out towards the main hallway which led to the grand hall and court of feasting. Along the way, the team almost forgot not all of them were under the mage's magic. And that Gherrik and Feridan alike were getting some second glances and raised brows from some royal guards patrolling the balconies, as well as, a few servants who tried to take his long coat off without permission.

The court was magnificently decorated and the lighting glimmered and waved as torches and chandeliers danced during their

215

entrance into the hall. The team was originally going to eat together, but Darren expressed his concern to give some space and wanted his men to blend in better with the crowd.

As they feasted, Darren kept a watch for Treila or any other servants that might walk into the grand court. He also kept an even closer eye for the king, whom he expected would soon make a grand entrance for everyone to witness. His other team members though, were already busy talking to attending soldiers and telling jokes amongst the staff. Feridan mostly drank dark ale and waived his arms around at others to see. Gherrik was arm wrestling at his table, and Taradiym had the unfortunate time of being next to Ufroum who was cracking up jokes at his expense.

The entire evening was saturated with laughter, full stomachs, and merriment among the ranks. It was clear to Darren that the soldiers had a pecking order when it came to eating, and the higher ranked members got their meals first and often had the best maids to wait on them.

Regardless of his opinions, Darren kept his mind clear on the mission at stake. The fate of Ranoia rested upon his decision and his determination to save his people; a thought that made it hard for him to swallow his meaty chicken thigh or guzzle down his sweet honey ale.

As the servants were gathering dishes and cleaning the tables, four regal guards walked into the room, and clearly made their presence known. The court settled down and two more guards walked in, followed by another two, then four beautiful maidens, then Treila and another servant boy, and then finally the king himself.

Behind the king came the queen or some obese woman who tried awfully hard to act like one, then two more guards who stood at the doors. Once the king sat upon the highest chair at the table in the front of the court, the guards at the doors closed them, and the room fell quiet.

A few servants immediately carried large amounts of food and wine to the king's table, as the queen motioned for Treila and the other servant boy to fix her plate for her.

After plates were stacked with juicy meat, bread, and vegetables, the servants all left the room as the men waited patiently for their king to speak.

"Are the food and spirits taming your insatiable appetites?" the king cried out.

The whole room responded in unison. Calls, yells, and hollers of gratitude and appreciativeness rang and echoed out into the surrounding halls.

"I know the war is hard on all of us," he again spoke loudly. "My future queen and I would like nothing more to see this war end, by either peace or the Demetrian King's head on a pike."

Men roared and raised their fists as their king stood up, looking around the room.

"You there!" the king pointed to a muscular soldier at a table of twelve others. The lone soldier stood up and bowed graciously. "Is this meal not filling?" the king asked.

The soldier raised his head and fist skyward replying, "Yes it is sire. A meal this great could have only come from you."

The honored soldier sat back down, as the king picked out another man in the room and asked him the same. "The finest in the land!" the man hollered.

Turning back towards his large chair and standing in front of it, hands grasping the table, the king encouraged, "As we continue to fight this war, and as you continue to fight for me, so shall you be fed from my largest feasts, and drink from my finest ale."

Men yelled out much louder than before, some even stood up and clapped. Darren found himself doing the same.

Finally taking a seat, the king spoke one last time, "I would like to personally hear from the lead captains for each patrol and garrison after the feasts end. Enjoy!"

After the feast was officially over, the soldiers and guards began to leave the room until only a few drunks and passed out guests remained. The servants were still hauling away dirty dishes and cleaning up tables, as Darren left with Feridan and headed back to the guard quarters.

On their way out they conversed. "If the king is not heavily guarded when the meeting takes place, I will dispatch him." Darren said to Feridan as they walked close to the wall of a dimly lit hallway.

Feridan might have been a little drunk himself, but managed to say, "I don't think he will be, but if it's a good enough place to do it, we couldn't be happier to have this thing over with."

What do you mean; the war or this mission?" Darren asked, before he had to catch Feridan from almost falling face first into the floor.

Feridan stumbled, but soon regained his posture and they continued to walk carefully. "Both, I guess," he said.

Darren only had to wait another half-hour before the king's advisors came out into the waiting room and called for all the lead soldiers.

There were seven men not including Darren who entered the room together. Stepping into the large room he saw right away that the king was sitting at another head chair at the front of a large oval marble table. The men, including Darren, formed a half circle around the table and bowed towards their lordship. The doors were then closed shutting them all in. Before the briefing began, Darren scanned the room one final time counting only the seven guard captains, and two royal guards standing behind the king. The captains he knew much about, since he had time conversing with a few of them before they were all called in, but the royal guards might cause some problems. They each wore full black iron armor decorated in the Rachellian colors and crests. They also had two swords around their waists and a spear in their right hands. If Darren were to assassinate the king now, he would need to first carefully consider his priorities and strategy. Luckily, he had some time to think, as the king made no mention or gestures that this meeting would be a short one.

"Before we begin, I need you all too quickly verify your rank, garrison, and your last mission or patrol," the king said as he prepared some papers and crossed his fingers into his lap.

One by one, from left to right, the captains gave the information the king asked.

"Second lieutenant; forty-third western garrison," the first one spoke. "Our last patrol was the eastern post near Ealin Peak."

Another captain followed, "Major of the third northern squad, our last mission was to assist the merchants near the crossing of Saralene."

Down the line they spoke, until the man before Darren was up.

"First Captain of the eighth northern garrison," spoke the man. "Our last mission was to patrol along the south coast of the Efeurlic River."

As soon as the man finished, Darren stared at him and started to remember his face and tone. The man next to him was the same man who was at the river when the Rachellian soldiers murdered the fishermen. Darren glared into the man's eyes and was thinking of all the ways he could kill him. However, the king was now watching, and so were the rest of the men in the room.

"What's your rank and garrison sir?" the king asked.

Darren regained his composure and excused himself of his daydreaming. "Second lieutenant of the fourteenth garrison, our last mission was escorting two of your royal servants from the north-western fort."

"Yes, I am very sorry it didn't go so smoothly," the king responded. "At any rate, the reason I have called for you all is to hear your info on your missions and status, as well as give new orders or judge your squad and garrison for further need." The king gathered some more of his papers, and spread them over the slick marble surface. "I will call for you all one at a time, please wait outside until then."

With that, the guards at the door opened for the men to step out.

One by one, the king called forth each man, until Darren and the murdering captain were all that was left.

Darren wanted to question the man for his past motives, or at the very least hear him beg for his mercy, with a dagger at his throat, but the king had called for Darren next and saving the pathetic man for at least a few more minutes.

Once the doors were closed behind him, Darren felt much better at the odds against him if the assassination were to happen at this time. Aside from the two stiff guards near the wall, the king was totally open and seemingly vulnerable. It was true Darren couldn't bring any weapons anywhere near the many rooms and halls he took to get here, but he was skilled enough to kill a man many ways with just his fists and rage.

"Please sit down for a moment lieutenant," the king waived as he continued to flip over some papers; bearing a troubled expression upon his face. Darren was afraid to speak before being asked, so he waited patiently.

The king stopped reading and looked up at him, "I don't recall your face being around the fourteenth garrison before." Darren tightened up. His brow growing heavy and he started to worry his plan might have to come early. "But," the king continued unaware, "we get so many recruits a week, and with my age, it's hard to keep track anymore. You must've done something right if you are a second lieutenant."

"Well, I believe I'm first now, as we no longer have a first," Darren chuckled, though trying to sound sincere.

"Ah," said the king, "Tragic I imagine. What is your name then?" he asked, "So, I may record the info you're about to tell me."

"Darren."

"Is this the correct spelling? He said showing the form.

"Yes, that is fine," Darren commented.

The king scribed some info then continued with his questions. "If I were to award you with ten or so more men to command, what would you do to rectify or salvage the guerilla attacks coming from the north?"

Darren looked down for a moment, imagining what a true Rachellian leader might say under these circumstances. However, his brain was not wired that way, and so he looked into the king's green eyes and gave the answer he himself would propose. "You could give me a hundred men, and the guerilla attacks will still continue."

The king looked a little surprised at the answer, but responded curiously, "Oh, why would that be?"

Darren collected his thoughts before proclaiming, "Guerillas -like all rebels and misguided subjects- are drawn towards violence and oppression." He watched as the king gained further interest. "They will keep fighting even at low odds. This war is like fuel to their rage. If you were to bind certain laws, remove excess soldiers, or even return some favor to them, I am almost certain they will respect you again, and will pledge loyalty to your sovereign."

"I don't know if I like you better as an advisor, or a poor fighter since your garrison suffered so badly at the peasants' hands," the king expressed.

Darren was shocked at how the king's emotions quickly turned.

"Those guerillas," the king broke in, "are becoming fewer and far less the closer to this capital. It is obvious the way they are being dealt with now is working. What isn't working, are soldiers like you who believe we can win this war through kindness and apologies." Darren sat motionless and let the king keep talking. As long as he talked, Darren had more time and more fuel of his own to finish what he had come all this way to accomplish.

"I used to think like you and many others," said the king. "The long arm of this war is grabbing hold of this once peaceful and joyous land, and is turning all of us into demons." Standing up the king now paced around the room; the armored guards still silent, never moving. "My advisors have told me that the Demetrian king is falling apart from the inside. They tell me that in a few more seasons maybe even a few more months that he will either give up or be eliminated by his own people."

The king motioned for Darren to stand with him, as he paced, "I am combining your garrison with the twelve, tenth, and sixth garrisons from your region. You will maintain your rank for now, but in five days time, your garrison, as well as, three others, shall move into the Demetrian province and begin an assault towards the capital." The king paused, looking over his shoulder to Darren. "If we are to end this pointless war, then let it be by our hand and not the weakness of the Demetrian king's own province. I really am sorry it had to be this way, but it is the only way, and I know you and many others will all rejoice when it is over."

If Darren was going to strike, now would be the best time to do so. The timing was right, the king was vulnerable, and above all the king was exactly what he thought he might be like. In fact, the king was strangely a lot like his own king. If someone had told him this, he wouldn't have believed it. But, after hearing both of them, attending long fruitless meetings, and understanding why they are the way they are, made Darren suddenly second guess his actions.

Before he knew it, the king led Darren towards the large doors across the room.

Darren wanted to slay this man. Everything inside his mind told him to turn around, twist his arm, bend him to the left, and snap his chubby neck, but somehow he couldn't.

The doors opened and Darren was greeted by the two guards who let the last captain inside. Darren walked out into the waiting room with a blank look in his face, as the captain nodded courteously.

The guards firmly shut the doors leaving Darren to stand perfectly still, pondering as to why he failed to act on his most basic instinct.

The quiet walk back to the guard quarters was a lonely one for Darren. The few patrols and soldiers along the way who nodded to him, found them ignored as Darren silently past; head down, and mind racing.

He thought about what both king's had said, and their reasons behind their actions. Why the war never seemed to end.

He could think about these matters for weeks, but he soon entered his bunk room where Feridan, Gherrik, Taradiym, and even Ufroum were waiting inside.

Ufroum was still passed out on his bed, while Taradiym quietly stepped out to give the rest of them some space.

Gherrik, looking slightly exhausted, sat down on the fur bed, as Feridan asked, "How did you get away so quietly? I didn't even here a single commotion or guard the wiser."

"The king is still alive Feridan," Darren replied. "I didn't get a chance to kill him."

Gherrik lifted his head up to talk, "So, what's the plan then?"

"Well, we wait for now I suppose," said Darren. "We have a few days to try and meet with him again, hopefully more than just me. After that we will have missed our opportunity."

Feridan shook his head, grunted under his breath, and then prodded Gherrik from his rest. "No sense staying around here then. Come on Gherrik, lower ranking soldiers like us have separate quarters."

Gherrik wrestled himself up, wiped his eyes and brow then followed Feridan out of Darren's bunk.

After they exited, Darren continued to think about the discussion he had with the king. The replays went on into the night, until finally Darren himself was satisfied that nothing would ever change, and went to bed.

❊   ❊   ❊

- Earlier At Roncerse Castle -

The night before Darren's meeting with the Demetrian king, Treila had found him down stairs and in the bar section of the inn in which his team was currently staying. She had walked down the few wooden steps that led from the main reception to the bar room, noticing the few patrons and common folk enjoying the evening.

The old-fashioned room wasn't very large, but it seemed accommodating to the few men or drunks that were asleep at the tables and counter.

Taking a seat next to Darren at the bar counter, she then looked around for a barkeep.

"I believe he went home for the night," said Darren groggily.

Treila scooted her stool closer and unfastened her soft green overcoat as she spoke, "You know, you don't have to drink alone tonight?"

Darren sat upright from his slouch and slid his half-full glass of a dark concoction over to her. "You're welcome to join, I was done anyway."

Treila made a gross expression then slid the glass back away from the two of them. "What do you think the king wants you for?" she asked.

Darren replied loosely, "I assume it is something highly important, if he pulled us away from our previous mission."

223

"Will he let us stay in the castle for a few more days," Treila asked, "There is still much more that I want to do? We hardly ever get time like this off, so maybe you can beg him for a little more time." She tried to smile and get him to notice, but after a few seconds, she assumed he was either to drunk or lost interest in her years ago.

"Well," Darren said, "if I can at least educate him over what has been going on in the east, then maybe we can work on fixing this war or maybe even helping some of the poverty stricken or ransacked towns along the coast."

Treila once again smiled, but this time it was purely out of appreciation that her commander was beginning to show his lighter side. "Come on let's go get you some rest. You have to get up early, and we need to think of some way to keep the other men busy while you're gone."

"Do you think there are any nice brothels here?" slurred Darren, as Treila helped him out of the stool and onto his feet.

On their way back upstairs Treila added, "Oh I'm sure if you give them anything, they will be out of your sight in a heartbeat."

They both laughed, continuing their way upstairs for the night.

*　　*　　*

A few weeks passed, and the Versparians were finally in the Demetrian province again. The bright sun over head welcomed them like a lost friend on this new and festive day.

Two days prior, they had entered Roncerse Castle where the people were busy celebrating a huge battle that was won over the Rachellian armies. Ignoring all of the commotion, celebration, and happiness, Darren was immediately called for by the king for a meeting of the highest degree. Leaving his fellow team behind, he encouraged them to attend the festivities and enjoy their much earned time off. Not one to argue with a plea like that, the Versparians all headed out into the streets and celebrated to their hearts content.

Darren finally made his way back to the waiting hall, where the same guard announced for him to enter. Darren didn't look up at the man this time, and kept his head down till he shut the large, thick royal doors behind him.

Inside the giant room, the king wasn't near the enormous window, but was in his chair messing with papers and conversing with an advisor who looked out the glass window for him.

"Ah, Darren," the king took a break from his busy work, looking up to greet him. "I'm sure you know Taohlin, my second noble advisor."

"No, I don't think I do," Darren spoke as he walked over to the large table.

The king motioned for the advisor to leave, and then even his two guards that Darren had never seen move until now.

Once they were alone, the king collected his papers and slid them aside as he began, "So, are you enjoying this wondrous day? You know, I heard from a source that the mission went off without the slightest bit of trouble. I knew I could count on you and your team. Perhaps tomorrow we will have to have an even bigger celebration." Before the king finished, Darren laid down a paper and slid it in front of him.

"What...what is this?" the king squinted his eyes at the small font and unusual handwriting.

"It's my permanent resignation and expulsion of servitude from your reign and duty." spoke Darren sincerely.

"Why are you handing me this, I thought your mission was a success?" he asked still confused.

Darren paced around the table and began to speak, "What I had believed was best for this province was what you had told us. I fought, slaved, and believed in the idea that a kingdom could be saved if the king was just and believed in his people."

The king still looked perplexed, but Darren paid him no mind and rattled on. "Oh, I succeeded in the mission. I awarded you the peace that Ranoia was long due, but not because you told me too."

Darren walked over to the giant window where he peered out

below and saw the hundreds of citizens celebrating on the streets and spending at least one day without bloodshed or violence.

"I'm actually glad you sent us on the mission," he admitted. "I got a chance to see what life was like on the other side of the battlefield. As it turns out, it was just like this side. An almost exact mirror image of what war and violence does to a nation when ruled by two kings who thought they were so different, but were almost like identical twins." As he spoke, Darren peered straight into the glass until his own mirrored image revealed itself.

"What are you getting at?" the king barked.

Darren walked back over to the king's large chair and looked him in his eyes. "I did it for us, not you. This is why I am resigning, and this is why I will no longer be a part of any more battles or wars that you or any other king decides to put this kingdom through. I did it for my people."

Heading out the door, Darren looked back concluding, "I did it for your people."

The mighty doors slammed shut, leaving the king all alone wondering to himself and gazing out from his overly large window.

OEDEPES

CHAPTER I
THE MALICIOUS TRAVAIL

The dreary weather -beginning a few hours prior- served as a warning to all the villagers and countrymen among the hills. Old widows barricaded themselves in dimly-lit rooms, chanting and grasping small trinkets and charms close to their heaving chests. Farmers, herders, and land hands, gathered in barns, cabins, and cellars, clasping dull tools and huddling near failing candles as the rains poured, swallowing the village in a gloomy veil.

Thick heavy fog soon rolled up the pebble coast, passing by the Kerles Sanctuary -a worn, barely stable seaside home- over the sandy hills, and into the small town of Lestrove. It was fairly common during this season to witness such saddening, dreary weather, yet somehow this evening was evolving into a stranger, and far more saddening state.

A noble of great stature from Tempurah, the capital city of Keifa, rode into the night upon receiving a letter a few days earlier. Raindrops splashed and ran across his cold, stiff visage. His horse, Kielfoot, galloped full speed; muscles hard, hooves muddy, and long black silky mane whipped in the air as they raced along the countryside. Seven of his closest men accompanied him during the week long travel. Constant worries raced through their minds on whether they would arrive before it was too late.

Screams from the soon to be mother, caused everyone in the room to shake and startle from her piercing cries. The old grey barn leaked from the roof and walls as the storm continued its endless assault; soaking the straw, walls, and floor, well after the rain had slowly began lightening up.

Another scream erupted from the shed.

It had already been four or so hours since the ordeal began and with each passing minute the pain and agony grew worse. While the labor dragged on, some elders stopped by, only peeking into the barn for a second, before slamming the door closed and blathering amongst each other, before retreating back to their warm cottages like sheep. Some close friends stayed near the woman's side and around the perimeter, deciding it best to endure the pain and weather together.

The steamy fog was beginning to dissipate as the riders arrived in front of the somber dimly lit town. A few bystanders near the stables helped guide them towards the rickety old barn nestled on the outskirts. Yeargoth was last to climb down from his horse. Patient yet aware of the urgency, he tied his fair mustang to the closest wooden post.

"Easy now, Kielfoot," the noble hushed. Covering his head with his cloak, then shuffled off behind the group determined to make haste.

The riders were led to the tall farm building that stood next to a rickety one-story house. Yeargoth told his men to wait outside, as he cracked the large dark-brown doors open and stepped into the musty damp interior.

Raindrops dripped from the ceiling as he walked past the threshold. A sudden gust of humid air rushed past him escaping out into the dreary brisk outside.

Removing his hood and silently folding his black and red lined overcoat on top of an empty stall gate, he began, "I'm going to have to ask everyone who is not a relative or close friend to please leave the barn immediately. The woman is in dire need of space and rest, and we all need to do what we can to help."

His tone was kind, but with emphasis that he was well educated. It was obvious he was around his late thirties, had smooth short black hair, and was semi-tall and lean. Most villagers have seen their share of soldiers before, but something about Yeargoth's presence and demeanor made them feel safer and far less tense.

After the remaining townsfolk left the premises, the local doctor took Yeargoth by the shoulder and walked him away, out of earshot of the exasperated couple.

"I'm very reassured that you've arrived, but I fear things aren't going that well," he spoke.

Yeargoth stared intently, nodding along as he listened, as the doctor continued, "I know you are a busy man Yeargoth, but please, if you have any advice or blessings we desperately need them."

The doctor's face grew still with anticipation. Small beads of sweat ran down his forehead and brow, a constant reminder of all the time he had spent in the humid barn. It was true that Yeargoth knew a lot about medicine and healing, but it had been a while since he was ever asked for advice, especially under these odd circumstances. He lightly twitched his nose and thought to himself before beginning, "I'm never too busy for helping my fellow townspeople." The doctor bore a quick smile of relief.

Yeargoth walked over to the woman laying on the blankets and damp hay. She was sweating profusely along with an exasperated red face and matted long blonde hair. Next to her kneeled a dark haired man -presumably her husband- looming close by her side with a sullen look upon his half lit face. "Alright now," Yeargoth took a knee by her other side, "I'm going to ask you a few simple questions before I'm able to help. Don't worry I'll try to go fast."

The woman winced with pain and her breathing became heavier as the minutes dragged on. The husband next to her tightened his grasp on her hand while he smiled and looked towards Yeargoth, thanking him for his aid and overwhelming kindness.

The birthing was hard and taxing on everyone that was in the barn that night. The woman cried tears of both pain and happiness when her new baby boy was cleaned and handed over to her gently. Wrapped in a cocoon of sheets and soft linens, the babe smiled. Yeargoth exited the barn immediately after, a look of satisfaction and relief shown upon his tired, yet proud face.

Taking in the cold fresh air, he conversed with a few of his men before the doctor came out and joined them. Yeargoth made a notion for his men to start heading back to their steeds, while the doctor began to speak. "Thank you, thank you so much for everything. You've saved the baby and possibly the mother tonight, we owe you so much."

"No you don't," Yeargoth responded, his voice quiet and calm. "I came here to help and pay respects to this town and after seeing that baby I believe I already received my reward."

The doctor smiled graciously in return, "You are too kind Sir Yeargoth, too kind."

"That's what I keep hearing," he added, laughing to himself. "Don't worry. I'll stop by every so often and check up on things. Plus, it would be nice to visit Lestrove more often."

"We would like that," bowed the doctor.

Swiftly breaking the silence from the conversation; sounds of people screaming, gasping, and calling out horrific cries of mercy, erupted from inside the barn. Yeargoth twisted around and ran to the doors revealing a very disturbing and tragic scene. The bodies of six mangled villagers were lying motionless on the floor along with the husband, while the newly appointed mother was writhing in pain, clasping her neck with both hands as if she was choking.

Yeargoth ran to her first. Supporting her back gently, he propped her head against his chest and began to inspect her as fast as possible. She was gasping for air like her lungs were clogged or being squeezed by an invisible vice. Yeargoth pulled her hands away as he looked over her neck and checked her throat for a lodged object. The mother's eyes were turning red, her face was turning blue, and no words could escape her lips but soft yelps of agony.

"Hang in there dammit!" Yeargoth yelled as if to penetrate into her body and mind.

It was no use.

The new mother heaved one final time, as her chest sank and she went limp.

Yeargoth gently placed her down upon the broken straw, folded her arms onto her chest, and then proceeded to inspect the child.

Much to his dismay, the small infant was wide awake and staring upwards at him with large emerald eyes. Yeargoth couldn't help but sigh with relief, yet still ponder why the babe wasn't crying or that he appeared unharmed. At this moment, the doctor came up next to him after inspecting the other bodies, and peered down at the small infant.

"Why is this baby so calm?" he asked Yeargoth.

"If what I think has happened than this child might have been responsible."

The doctor immediately turned to him. Gesturing towards the quietly nesting child, "You mean this baby killed all these people, how?"

Yeargoth bent over, securing the infant in his sturdy coarse hands. Following the motion, he enveloped the child in his soft overcoat and relaxing him onto his shoulder. "I'm afraid this child has been cursed."

"What?" the doctor remarked. "What kind of curse makes him kill innocent people in the manner that has occurred here?"

"The kind of curse that is very rare and uncontrollable at such a young age." Yeargoth took a few steps, swaying the child slowly as the boy began to close its eyes. "Have you ever heard of psychic users?"

"No, I have not," the doctor shook. "Are they dangerous?"

"Sadly, yes," Yeargoth cradled the babe even more, hushing him to sleep. "It seems this child has been born with the element and attributes of a psychic. From the moment he was conceived, I'm afraid he has become a huge threat to himself, as well as, everyone around him. I wish I would have known about this sooner, but what has happened now is in the past."

The doctor cut in, "If you believe he is so powerful, than what shall we do? Can we ignore the problem and hope it goes away? Or perhaps, dare I say, drown him?"

"No, that would be the last thing we should do."

Both Yeargoth and the doctor walked towards the opened barn doors where they both looked out into the clear fields and the surrounding dark blue country side. "It's true he will be trouble, but I think with proper guidance and training he could become less of an outcast and will hopefully not cause any more problems."

"He's not staying in our village is he?" the doctor questioned.

"Of course he is," Yeargoth responded. "This is his home. He was born here and this place is perfect."

"But..." the doctor tried to call, before the noble continued.

"My duties to the king make it hard for me to stay, but don't worry, I'll try to make it a habit to stop by every so often and check up on him."

"What shall I do then about all of this?" the doctor motioned towards the massacre scene behind them.

"I'll take care of that. The boy doesn't need this upon his shoulders. Place him in the best house or orphanage you can, and speak to no one about this."

Yeargoth handed the baby over to the doctor, and then began to head back towards his men. Stopping a little up ahead he called out, "The boy needs a name that can both suit him and what life he'll have ahead." And with that, he waved, "I leave that up to you, doctor."

He pondered a moment, before settling upon a name for this child. He wanted an uncommon name, yet one with meaning and purpose.

"I think," he said, gazing down at the sleeping babe, "Oedepes shall suit you fine"

❋ ❋ ❋

I awoke to a bright midmorning. Beams of sunlight escaped through the fluffy cloud cover, where it lightened the short green grass and chased away cool morning shadows.

After dressing my cot, I put on my tan trousers and loose fitting white shirt, feeling excited for the upcoming day. Combing my short brown hair between my fingers, I rushed down the stairs and straight into the mess hall.

The usual cast of children was already standing in line, each with bowls stretched outwards and mouths watering as hot porridge plopped down inside.

Jumping in line behind a younger boy I occasionally talked too, named Geff, I found myself immediately caught in an arduous one sided conversation with him.

"Hi Oedepes," the simplistic boy began, "You ready for some delicious energy rich breakfast?" Geff's mouth blabbered around as he spoke with a slight child-like slur.

Maybe a little tired or a tad annoyed, I didn't respond, fearing it would only provoke him into talking longer. So, not much to my surprise, Geff continued anyway. "I know it's not exactly grandmother cooking, but it gets the job done."

The line moved forward, as each child left with a small helping and ran to find a seat next to their friends or favorite table. Usually at this time, all the tables were filled to the shoulder, so I was usually stuck either sitting on the ground or leaning against one of the far windows where I preceded to gaze outside, pondering upon such questions that every orphan pondered.

"Want to sit next to me then?" Geff questioned.

"No that's okay, I'm pretty busy," mumbling back in response; my tone low and monotonous, possibly hinting at my boredom.

"Yeah right, pretty busy doing what?" he commented. "No one here does much outside of chores and picking on the girls."

Once again, I tried not to reply, but soon the line inched forward and I could smell the simmering oats and flaring burners enter my nose and I could only think about grabbing my food and running away like a fox with his evening meal. "Fine whatever," I finally gave in. "You can come eat next to me if you really want. Just don't talk that much."

The rest of the day was rather peaceful and quiet. After some simple chores, I retired to my cot, where I waited patiently for a few more hours.

Before I knew it, Lisra, an orphan girl around my age, ran upstairs and informed me that a very special guest had arrived to see me.

Getting up from the mere mention of a guest, I ran down the stairs knowing full well who I should be expecting.

At the front door I could see Yeargoth talking to Ulina, our caretaker. They were talking about weather and other boring adult conversations when I approached him from behind.

Leaping up, hoping to catch him off guard, I found myself

ensnared in his large clutches as he lifted me into the air whirling me around in circles by the arms. "You know me by now that foolish tricks like that won't work," he laughed, while still spinning me around, until I eventually gave in and joined in the laughter.

"Master Yeargoth, please you might hurt him," Ulina spoke in.

"Nonsense," Yeargoth replied still chuckling. "The boy is stronger than ever. Every child needs spun around every so often. I don't get to see him enough."

"Please, Yeargoth," I blurted. "I'm about to get sick."
Yeargoth's centrifugal dance ended and he placed me back down, where I felt dizzy and confused for a few moments.

"Will you be staying long?" Ulina asked politely.
Finally regaining my sense of balance I added, "Yes, please stay awhile."

Yeargoth bent down, granting me a large hug, "Now, you know my job demands much from me, but perhaps this once I can stay a little bit longer."

I smiled brightly and as large as I possibly could. My days without Yeargoth or the doctor felt cold and lonely. So having their company, no matter what kind of day or mood I was in, instantly made it one-thousand times better. I really wished one day I could leave this place, but for now they wanted me to stay and so I did.

CHAPTER II
PRETERNATURAL

Weary and tired from an afternoon of games and other outdoor activities, I retired to my bed while the other children continued their fun out on the grassy knolls of the orphanage. Occasionally, I peered out from the dusty glass window above my head, spying on the kids and finding myself wondering why some days I feel more exhausted than usual. It was as if a heavy weight was bearing down upon my shoulders, neck, and back. Some days it was my chest, some my energy, and on the few rare occasions, my very soul felt weary and distressed.

Growing a little older each day, I found that I often felt better during the times I was alone -almost like I only trusted myself and feared the company of others. Besides Yeargoth and the doctor (whom I enjoyed visiting very much), I wished to remain nothing more than a distant shadow; always present, but forever out of reach.

✳   ✳   ✳

The next few months I tried to set myself apart from the other groups of children. What happens with most forgotten children living in orphanages is that as we grow older, we tend to forget about trying to belong to a family and instead create our own. This is what the gangs and other groups were all about. And this is why many lone or shy individuals simply avoided them.

A small boy roughly my same age felt the need to follow me around, pretending to be my friend. For awhile I ignored him and his constant need for belonging. However, his pestering never ceased, until eventually I played along with his crazy hallucination and together I assume you could call us mutual acquaintances.

"You feeling down again, Oedepes?" Geff asked in his usual manner.

I didn't respond. I sat on my wrinkled cot, looking up pretending the ceiling was an open cloudless sky. Geff's eyes rolled as he kept talking, "Come on, don't you want to go outside? All the other kids are having a huge festival out there."

Once again I was quiet. Too caught up in my own imaginings, I couldn't even hear him speak anymore.

"Fine whatever," Geff blathered, "I'm going out there. You know sometimes I don't understand you."

The door to our bedrooms shut behind him, leaving me alone just the way I liked it.

After a few minutes later my headache went away and I felt like my body was regaining its energy. Moving over to the nearest window,

knight."

Just then something triggered deep inside.

I tried to see, but my eyes had gone black, soon nightmarish images filled the void. My head felt as if all my knowledge and all my thoughts erupted outward from my forehead. The world around me froze and felt lifeless. My limbs throbbed and tingled, while screams around me began to ring about. There was nothing I could do. I wanted the episode to be over, but with each new scream, and each new splattering sound, I smiled and wished it would never end.

When I awoke, it had felt like mere minutes passed. Reality soon kicked in, and it was night. The crescent moon was peering through the dark clouds, and all around me was silence. I was all alone.

After regaining my sense of balance and position, I spun around to take in my surroundings. The old birch tree was still standing firm and tall exactly how it always was, however, there were several large blood splatters painted over its once pristine trunk. Looking down I could now see that I had dried blood smears and splashes all over my front shirt and pants.

'What in all of Ahreidonia has happened?' I wondered.

Walking carefully around the red coated grass and field, images of death surrounded and shook me to my inner core. The mangled corpse of Deoril was face down with his fingers clenched into fists and a dried puddle coating the ground underneath. Vir's body also lie next to him; his head nowhere to be seen. Clasping my mouth, I ran away from the smell and the sight; tears and terror unfolding around me.

One by one, I walked around the orphanage's exterior. I kept track of the number of dead bodies and names of those who had mysteriously died. At first I believed some gang of thieves brutally slaughtered them all or some other beast attacked while I was unconscious. However, as with many scenarios and predictions that I mustered, one curious fact continued to stare me in the face. 'Why was I the only one left alive?'

This led me to believe that this incident, this horrific and disastrous episode was somehow linked to me. As the night dragged on, I slowly rounded up all the bodies and pieces of mutilated corpses;

dragging them into the house and piling them in the main living room.

Dawn soon arrived, and I was lying down on the front porch; exhausted and overwhelmed with guilt. The orphanage seemed to be the only thing affected, and yet I was the only one alive. If I tried to go into town and report this, people will wonder why I was the only one not hurt or killed.

'Perhaps they might think I did it. Maybe they would throw me in jail or hang me if anyone knew what went on here.'

As worried as I was, something inside made me feel happier, or at the very least, powerful.

So, before the golden orange sun rose up from the horizon, signaling the dawn of the new day, I had left the orphanage grounds, running off to wherever destiny might lead.

'Yeargoth, forgive me.'

CHAPTER III
CLOUDED CRUSADE

The beginning of my new life took me southward across the expansive grassy knolls, bright golden fields, and captivating dense forests through the province of Keifa. During afternoon naps and nightly dreams, I pictured and reminisced of the few conversations I had with Yeargoth whenever he was in town. He often told tales during his knighthood and other famous escapades he had while serving under the king of Tempurah.

Closing my eyes I often pictured him speaking to me as I sat upon his lap all those years ago. White horses, leather clad warriors, and riches even kings could not imagine, were only a fraction of the tales he spouted. I often wondered whether those stories were merely fables or perhaps there was some truth in them. Never-the-less, I was too afraid to show my face to him or the doctor ever again.

'What would they say?' I often pondered. 'Would we still be

friends? Would they turn me in, or help me hide?'

Too many thoughts and outcomes left me boggled and stupefied. That is the reason I am heading south.

✱   ✱   ✱

Walking alone made the time seem to flow faster. I spent a few months in and around the Seida Desert, only to later get sick of all the sand and raiding parties, forcing me to venture eastward towards the Stronguard Mountains.

I often journeyed along with caravans or small merchants that were heading around the same direction, cutting through farmlands, avoiding patrols, and evading the occasional highwayman. I never really talked to them, nor wished to become friends. I couldn't even remember their names; which was the way I preferred. If I had gotten anything out of spending time with them, it was that people were often desperate for food or anything to increase their own happiness. It became amusing. Watching the mothers and elderly sell their heirlooms and precious belongings, in return for some bread or tins.

Months flew by, seasons came and went, and before I knew it, I was working in a small town called Lestek, located in the southern tip of Keifa.

A couple of more years passed, when eventually I could afford to purchase a small shack near the outskirts.

Every so often I ventured away from the town's walls and boundaries, far off over some hills and into a dark forest where I practiced and tried to focus my psychic skills and abilities.

A year or so ago, I read a book from a travelling merchant that contained many long pages and descriptions of abilities and other attributes people could learn. The merchant informed me that whenever people are born they sometimes incur rare oddities or various things that prevent them from using regular magic. I had never heard of these things before, so I listened curiously, trying to ask all the questions I could without disclosing that which I hide. The old man, continued to talk, whispering such words as; mana, elements, and of course, the oddities like myself.

After I left, I had learned that my condition was a form of rare birthing in which, I was born under no signs. In fact, he described a few different versions people could have that were totally different than regular people.

"This is what made them so dangerous," he said. "It wasn't natural."

Psychic abilities were often very lethal and hard to control. People born with this unusual condition usually never make it past ten. I laughed at the mere thought of this notion.

The air was growing colder. Leaves shook and rattled as the winds picked up, blowing my hair and causing me to lose focus for just a second.

"Damn the wind!" I spat, closing my eyes and trying to clear my mind again.

Within minutes, I could feel my surroundings. Sense them. Understand them. Just as I was building up to something greater, I became enveloped in a vision.

I was transported inside a barn with strangers circling around something. Outside was a terrible storm. I could hear the screams of a woman, as if in great pain. The ghastly figures moved aside, opening a path as my body moved closer to what they were all staring at. It was a young woman, pregnant, and lying on her back. I tried to look away, but the screams were loud. Unable to return to reality, I was forced to stay, now hunching closer to her. I could feel warmth and pain emanating from her. She was clasping the hands of a man kneeling by her head. Then, the cries of a baby broke out. The scene shifted, and I was holding a child. He was tiny in my arms. No longer crying, and instead, was watching me with bright emerald eyes.

Noticing something strange, I began to look around the barn. Everyone was dead; mutilated, strangled, and bloody. Clenching the child tight, I was horrified and confused. A realization occurred to me. 'Was this me?'

As suddenly as the vision had started, it left. I was back in the

241

dark woods; alone, and clasping at nothing, as knelt on the cold ground.

Chapter IV
Psychic Engagement

After a few months, I decided to pack up what little belongings I had and move. From what I had been told, Denvek was very large, both economically and for seeking greater power. During the past couple of years, a new governor was elected, helping the city return towards a greater focus in its commoners and backhanded activities. My problem wasn't related to what I was going to do once I arrived, instead, focusing on how I was supposed to get there. Situated on the western coast of Bev, the city and surrounding landscape was littered with bandits, pirates, murderers, patrols, beasts, and the very wilderness itself. Scrounging around and working on small jobs whenever and wherever I could, I finally earned enough crests to afford the few ship fares and travel expenses I needed in order to arrive safely.

I spent weeks sailing on the Kiloos Sea. Cramped and sweating from long days in the hull. I felt tortured and uneasy as the waves hammered the sides, until at last the province of Bev was in sight. Towering black mountains pierced the gloomy sky that expanded over the treacherous snowy landscapes. Swamps of all sizes and smells encircled and swallowed neighboring settlements. It had a long history of violence and corruption; the land a feasting ground for the deadly and castrated.

The harbor bell rang out, signaling our arrival. Below deck gathering my things, I felt the floorboards shake and rattle, jostling my body as we rocked amongst the waves until finally coming to a stop. Breathing a sigh of relief, I shuffled past the other occupants, climbing outside.

The warm sun soothed and calmed me as its warmth touched upon my face. With luggage in tow, I walked off the docking platforms and onto the wonderfully crafted stone docks of the largest harbor I had ever seen.

Blue painted wooden houses showing much wear and chipped panels filled the surrounding docks. Shaggy bearded men, and weathered looking women shuffled about the seaside streets as fishermen in small rafts waved around their freshly caught hauls.

Smells of sea water, ale, and the occasional dead fish loomed in the air as I walked briskly.

Past the harbor, the pathways opened up to reveal an even larger brick and stone road that weaved around several large buildings and other streets of two-story houses and self-made peddler stands.

"For a city built on a marsh, they sure did a really good job."

Turning left at the first crossing, I tightly gripped my bags and began to peruse and gaze upon several merchants' tables and other strange oddities they were offering. Charms, swords, bracelets, trinkets, and scrolls of all kinds, littered the sides and windows of nearly every house and building along the busy streets. Reading the signs above my head and in windows, I noticed they were of various scripts and languages. Familiar with only the common tongue, I found myself pathetically trying to mouth out phrases such as Orenspoul, Chaer-li-gha, and Yor-breik.

Everywhere I looked, I found myself picking things up, trying stuff on, and asking questions to strangers with large smiles and open inquiries. In fact, the more I studied, the more things were catching my eye, and I soon lost track of what I came here for in the first place.

Night soon arrived. I watched as the crowd vanished along with the sounds and joyous atmosphere quieting to a mere whisper. I began to head off towards the eastern side of Denvek, hoping to catch an inn that was still yet vacant.

Candles and torches were slowly burning out becoming sparser as I walked farther and farther east down upheaval stone paths and dirt alleys. The houses were also becoming less tall and magnificent the further I ventured, and even the small shacks that had once littered the seaside avenues, were becoming farther apart and shady. Stopping dead in my tracks, I held my bags firmly as a group of men leapt out from the behind an alley. With partially shadowed faces, they slowly slid small knives and swords letting their blades glisten from the moonlight above.

With little time to think, a tall lanky man walked forward waving his silvery knife in the air, "I don't suppose you are all alone here huh?" His voice was deep, with a slight orcish accent.

With nerves still a little rattled, I responded, "Look, I'm just trying to head east. You don't want to rob a poor person like me."

Another man stepped forward. His long sword casting shimmers on his shallow face. A light smirk formed and I could see he also bore some elvish features. "We're not picky, as long as you're quiet about it," him and his band crept closer.

Glancing left and right, I tried to think my way out. Shutting my eyes, I wished I was back on the boat, or even back in Lestek. I could just hand over my things, and hopefully walk away with just the shameful experience. But, not after what I had to do to get here. Years of work, labor, courage, and mistakes, had brought me here. When I at last opened them I was still standing in the dark eerie path, about to get robbed on the first day in the city. So I ran.

Spinning around, I sprinted as fast as my legs could muster. I never once looked back. I could hear yells and clamor coming from various members of their pack behind me. They weren't catching up, but I also wasn't losing them.

Around and through streets, shacks, and back alleys, desperately holding onto my belongings. Either through lack of vision or from trekking through unfamiliar ground, I ended up in front of a large brick wall, halting all progress and trapping me like a mouse.

A second later, the bandits arrived. They were panting and breathing heavily. Building up the tension, they spread out, barricading the only exit. I was trapped.

Hugging my bags close to my chest, I watched as the group slowly walked forward yelling out various words and names, some in the human tongue, others in orcish. Soon, a creeping sense of strength and energy began to swell up from inside. I tried to warn them to stay back, but they never faltered and insistently kept advancing, weapons outstretched.

With each step they took, and each second that went by, my chest began to fill up with rage, anger, energy, and a feeling of ecstasy. So I let it take over.

Closing my eyes, I hollered as the energy burst out and began to act through my will. Severed arms and legs dropped to the ground as the first deadly psychic blade burst out from my extended arms. I closed my eyes tighter.

Stretching out again and again, I released three more razor-sharp energy blasts; slicing air, flesh, and bones all in an instant. Nothing was left alive.

Slowly opening my eyes, I smiled gleefully as nothing but flesh and crimson blood decorated the path and walls of the alley.

Not wanting to be seen, I hastily retreated back out into the main street, jogging eastward.

Stopping a few blocks away, I ducked into another side alley, and discovered a half broken board blocking an underground passageway underneath a building. Prying the semi-loose board open, I crawled through the two foot gap and shuffling my way into a larger area a few feet further in.

Dirt, weeds, splinters, and some rats were scattered around the open area. I walked the perimeter quickly and noticed the place only had that one entrance way, and for the most part, it was dry, warm, and safe.

Unpacking my cot, blankets, and some other small things, I laid down in a corner and went to sleep, wishing that I had killed the bandits sooner, and hoping that no one would find out what I had done.

CHAPTER V
THE UNKNOWN MAN

The dank, dew coated crawlspace, soon felt less like a hideout and more like a special place for me to stay. A new home, maybe, but something was always missing. An emptiness as some might call it. I often created and toyed with my new psychic abilities as a way to keep busy and help occupy my free time, and for the most part, it worked.

Whirling colors of violet and flat circles of dark blue weaved, pulsed, and zipped around the confines and corners of my tight entrapment. Leaves rustled, pebbles rolled, and the occasional wandering spider found itself with legs pulled, body squashed, and life drained. I could never be happier.

Over the next few days, I decided it was time to finally leave and get some more rations and other provisions. The nearest store was only a few blocks away, so I decided the best opportune time was to leave at dusk.

Crawling out from the small entrance, I quickly dusted off my pants and muddy shirt, where I then stood up and stretched my sore cramped legs. The fresh air felt cool and refreshing upon my face. As I looked around I took notice of the few people scattered among the streets, and it was still early enough that many torches weren't lit.

I had walked but ten feet, when a mysterious man in light brown robes began to walk straight towards me. Looking around, I quickly deduced that he was heading right for me. Hesitant upon whether force was needed or if I should carefully persuade the man, since some people were still close by, I ignored him and continued in a slightly different direction.

Walking a little further, I pretended not to notice the man, until finally he stopped a few feet from my side and gently spoke in a casual, yet direct manner. "I really liked what you did to those bandits a few days ago."

I ignored him and kept walking. The man continued to stay by my side, and spoke again. "I had thought you were going to die or get hurt and I would've stepped in, but you seemed to handle things just fine."

"Sir" I began, "I believe you have the wrong person. I don't even live in this city."

The man kept following me as my strides widened with the impatience I was beginning to develop.

The robed man spoke louder. "Alright, if you say so, but I think the guards will be curious when I inform them of a suspect I found on my way out of the city."

I stopped abruptly. Evil tensions flared in my eyes as feelings were starting to erupt uncontrollably from deep within. I managed to bring my rage down before quietly demanding, "Perhaps you might want to rethink that, unless you don't mind never leaving the city."

"Ah ha!" the man let out. We both looked around to see if anyone heard his sudden loud outburst. When no one did, he continued, "You are a killer after all."

"Leave me alone now, or I will be forced to kill you," I remarked while glaring at him intently.

He lifted his brown ragged hood off his head and smiled. The stranger had ebony tanned skin, and black short hair that waved with the wind, while his deep green eyes made me ever more curious as to where this man was from.

"I don't want any trouble, and death is certainly the last thing any of us wants," he waved his hands about. "I know what troubles you and what you seem to be capable of."

I stared coldly, watching and taking precautions.

"I also know that you are poor, hungry, and miserable," he acted sincere.

"What do you know of being miserable?" I asked, folding both arms firmly over my chest.

The man pondered a moment, but then placed his arm slowly upon my shoulder. I shrank back just before, preparing to act in a moment's notice. "We are all miserable," he said. "However, it's because of our miserable existence that we wish to rectify it by following dreams, aspirations, power, and knowledge."

247

Unfolding my arms, I relaxed a little, agreeing with maybe one or two things he had said. I was still cautious, but whatever this man was saying, he seemed to not be as bad as I first made him out to be, so I let him continue.

"What's your name boy?" the man pleasantly asked.

I wanted to lie, but I felt no harm in granting him this small favor. "Oedepes," I replied.

The man winced. "Really, that's what your parents gave you? Oh well, my name's no better I suppose."

"Oh really," I responded. "Were you watching me the last couple of days?"

He nodded in confidence, "Only during that scuffle with the bandits." He extended a finger, "I saw them chase you into the dead end, and then you killed them with something near invisible and fled. I was baffled. I didn't know what it was," he smiled, "but, you held firm and succeeded."

"I didn't mean to kill them, but they left me with no choice."

"Over and done with I say," the man exclaimed. "What do you plan to do now?"

"Well," I hesitated, "I need food and…some other things, and then I'll probably take off."

"What if I told you that I can help you with those abilities?" the man smiled softly, hovering closer as his voice got lower, transforming into a whisper. "What if we joined together for a few weeks and I helped you develop those skills, and you could help protect me from other bandits or people who wish us harm?"

"I don't think so," I contemplated. "I mean, it sounds good, but you don't want to be with me, really."

"You know what I think?" the man laughed a little. "I think you are scared to have friends. You don't want to leave your little secret home here and venture the world with a stranger. The unknown scares you just as it did for me once."

"Where would we even go?" I asked.

"Anywhere we want," he answered. "You name the place, and we'll be there. However, there is one stop I need to make before that, and once I pick up my things, we will be totally free."

"What do we do for money or food?" I inquired.

"I have plenty of both. That's why I need someone with your talents to protect me."

I took notice of some people passing by. Dressed in stitched garbs and hand-me-downs they peered through windows remarking over the smells of lunch being prepared. I licked my dry lips, "When are you planning to leave?"

The man responded as he covered his head with his hood. "In a few hours if that's okay with you?

I thought for a moment. What kind of life would I have here if I stayed? What kind of life could I have if I mastered these psychic abilities of mine? Could this unknown man promise such things? One thing I did know was that I would never find out for sure unless I did something. The urges and feelings inside pressed me into taking the man's offer. I didn't have to worry about him because of my powers, and the only downside would be that he couldn't teach me anything and I wasted a few weeks. The feelings of more power soon swelled up and took hold. I smiled and shook his hand almost over zealously.

CHAPTER VI
COMPANIONS

With Denvek behind us, we paid for a larger cruiser to take us to the small province of Xsivfer. It took around a fortnight, but we felt the effects of the island well before we even got within visual distance.

Xsivfer was a frozen island covered with pine forests, and sprinkled with swamps and deadly jagged mountains. It wasn't as big as the province of Bev, and definitely not as big as Keifa, but from what I was told both from people aboard and from my new friend, the place was highly dangerous and deadly towards all newcomers.

"We'll be landing shortly now," the unknown man announced.

"Have you been here before?" I asked, "What is it you need to get here?"

"I used to have a family here," he chuckled, "But after I left many years ago, they left too." We both stared intently out over the rails of the deck. Light snowflakes began drifting down from grey clouds overhead, just as the craggy brown and grey shore came into view.

Smiling, the man continued, "I know I don't look like it, but I used to work at the Shrine of Picarious on the eastern side."

I probed, "Did you like it there, or did something happen?"

"I don't really want to go into specifics," he leaned, clasping the rails with a hand and gazing further out. "But, we are here to pick up some related things from a similar part on the island."

"Since we're in this together now," I said. "Isn't it about time I learned your name."

The man smiled under his hood. The chilled winds filled the sails and caused all men on deck to shiver. Looking back out towards the surrounding landscape there appeared some small glaciers and snow capped spires poking and floating out among the ocean. I wrapped another layer of my robe around my head and shoulders, repelling the cold and trying my best to warm up.

"Well," the man started. "I abandoned my name long ago, but if you really feel the need to label me then whatever you come up with shall be fine."

I pondered for a moment at how relaxed and gracious he was to let me chose for him. I had never been given much freedom to choose before, but I welcomed the gift by trying to choose a name that fit.

"How about, Picarious?" I blurted nervously.

The man laughed, "The God of the Unwanted? Why would you choose that name?"

"I don't know," I shook. "You said you were from that shrine. I thought it would suit you."

"I'm fine with the name, but let me know when you think of a better one, he continued to chuckle.

"What was the shrine like?" I asked.

The man paused, breathing in the fresh chill air, and taking the time to remove his hood. "Well," he paused again, "it's been awhile, but from what I can recall it was rather complex."

I made a gesture with my head, urging him to keep going.

"Picarious is a strange god. He doesn't have any likes or dislikes, instead," he turned to face me smiling, "instead, he prefers to grant or take away luck, if you will."

Sensing my perplexing facial expression, the man stepped closer and continued to educate me. "Do you believe in luck?"

"I believe everything has a purpose," I responded surely.

"Yes, that's good," the man approached, "But, would you say people can incur bad luck?"

"I've never really thought about it before," I lied. Thinking back, I began to recall images of the pregnant woman, the pain I inflicted to various muggers, thieves, and highwaymen. My earlier days out on the fields, watching the poor wither, starve, and collapse. Days in the city, hurrying past the death alleys, beggar pits, and orphanages.
"I think luck is a rather odd thing to worship," I added, turning my attention back towards the distant coast.

"That's a real shame," the man retreated. "Anyway, that's also a reason I left the place."

The cruiser began to slow as a lone harbor came into view followed by the icy town of Rockek. Picarious and I went bellow deck to fetch our things as the ship bounced and jerked around until it eventually docked.

Once off the gangplank, we travelled up the docks, walking past fishermen hauling creates and barrels full of fish, clams, crabs, and chum. Once past the marina, we soon came to the cold center of town, until Picarious stopped outside of a busy supply store.

"I'm going in to get a few things, he turned to look at me. "You're welcome to come in and look around, but since we're a little low on money, you won't be able to get much."

"That's okay, I'll wait out here," I responded, placing my hands deep into my pockets to stay warm as a chilling breeze rolled by. "How much farther do we have to go?"

251

"I'll explain more when I come out, but we need to head west of here towards the mountains."

Leaving the town almost as fast as we had arrived made me feel a little sorry that I didn't get a chance to look around. Picarious was carrying a few sacks and bags piled on top one another, as he made sure we kept a brisk pace as we left through the gate and out past the boundaries of the town.

The weather, though a bit chilly and dry, wasn't so bad for my first visit to a snow covered province. Picarious purchased thick furred boots and gloves before we left the town, and we each had several layers of robes and cloth for blankets and to assist in shielding ourselves when the stronger winds and snow from the mountains would meet with us.

For most of the trip, the sun was hidden behind soft grey clouds. Sudden flurries broke out and disappeared in random intervals, and various wildlife stayed hidden as we crunched along the snowy path. Massive pine, golden grass sprinkled with white pure snow, and jagged hills and cliffs, decorated the landscape and created a sense of serenity.

During our first stop, Picarious brought out some precooked venison, dried plum slices, and water from our calfskins. Shedding off my layer of wool, I laid it down under a fir sapling and began to eat. The meat was a little salty, but it still held some flavor. I didn't much care for the dried plums, but the water felt cool and refreshing as it hydrated me from the tiring days walk.

Picarious finished first, where he then began to stand up and stretch his arms, legs, and back. "Alright, you ready for some teachings?" he blurted.

I stared at him blinkingly, "What, do you mean now?"

"Yes," he responded, stretching his arms and shoulders another time, "You think I don't keep my promises. I'll wait until your done, but afterwards come meet me up on that rock." He pointed behind him, where a large boulder was resting upwards at an angle along with several other smaller rocks that together resembled a crude throne.

Stuffing the last bits of meat into my mouth, and gargling some

252

water, I ran up the large boulder across the path and stood with Picarious on the top.

"Okay," he began. "Do you know about breathing exercises?"

"What does that have to do with anything?" I asked jokingly.

"Everything," Picarious exclaimed. "Look, follow what I do and practice this every time we're on a break."

Taking a seat on a flat stone, he crossed his legs, and closed his right hand into a fist, where he then enveloped it within the other. He closed his eyes and began to breathe soft and deep. "I want you to breathe in from your nose," he announced, still unmoving and with eyes shut. "And out from your mouth. While you do this, try to keep a clear head, and imagine that you have complete control over your body and its energies."

I followed his gestures and advice until we were both deeply entranced as if like two statues resting on a giant rocky throne.

CHAPTER VII
THE RUINS

The jagged base of the western mountains of Xsivfer seemed formidable as we walked the rest of the way towards them. The sky above was crystal blue, and aside from some lingering clouds and fog farther north, we had no trouble making it to the shadowy base.

Our journey was quiet and not a very thought provoking one. The few conversations we had were more-or-less about the weather, our supplies, the route, or various meditation techniques. Not one to probe into other people's affairs, I instead focused my own feelings and questions on myself, and future aspirations.

In the evening at the base of the mountains, we stopped to make camp, creating a small fire for the few snow hares we had caught earlier that day. Picarious was busy unfolding and propping up his tent and sheets, while I humbly brought over an arm load of broken branches, twigs, and leaves, from the nearby thicket.

"So, what's our ultimate goal here?" I asked, not really expecting an answer. "I know you tell me to wait and see, but I would like to know how much farther we have, and when are you going to teach me new techniques or control?"

Picarious sighed and finished nailing down the flapping sides of his tent to the firm half-frozen ground. Dusting his black slacks off as he got up, he turned to me. "Let's get those hares on the fire and then I'll fill you in on the specifics."

The flames danced and blazed high as the juices from the hares dripped and sizzled. They were each fastened to individual sticks and laid out over the flames just enough so they wouldn't catch on fire or blacken. We both watched as the smoke rose up into the dark blue and purple sky as the last bits of sun sank down below the misty horizon.

Licking my lips as Picarious tore off a leg and handed the hot morsel to me, I began to ask, "Is it time yet?"

"Very well," he too tore off a thick plump leg and began to gnaw into the meaty muscle parts. "I told you that I used to belong to the shrine here; well that shrine served under a king and magistrate a little west of here through the mountains."

I hungrily bit into the flesh of the hare and smiled as the warm food slid down into my empty gullet.

"That is where we are going," Picarious continued, "to the abandoned castle to reclaim some of my lost belongings."

Taking a sip from my water skin I said, "Why is it abandoned?"

"Well there was a war that went on many years ago, and ever since then the castle and tower have long been abandoned."

The fire snapped as sparks raced outwards, bouncing along the ground till they extinguished themselves in the snow.

"I was just a small boy then, so I was forced to leave with the rest of my family. That's why I need to return now. I need to go back there and get some of the things long forgotten."

"I can't help but wonder why you need me though," I further inquired. "Or why you couldn't just go yourself."

Picarious smiled and looked upwards as he licked the bone clean, tossed it into the fire, and then yanked off another leg from the meaty hare. "The place might have been abandoned, but what drove my people away might still be there."

"What sort of things might that be?" I wondered cautiously.

"Mountain orcs," he spoke. "That is why I need you. I can't really fend for myself, and knowing you have great power and skill, I figured I'd be much safer."

"Well I'm going to need to practice, if I'm going to be able to take these foes. I mean, I have never even seen an orc before, let alone a tribal one."

Picarious looked over across the fire and stared intently at me. I could tell he was serious, but hoped he could tell that I was as well.

"If you are that worried about a confrontation," he said, "then I might know of some back ways or secret tunnels we can try."

"That sounds like it might be worse than a frontal approach," I blurted.

He shrugged his shoulders, "Well it's up to you really. I'm not the one fighting, so which ever you choose is fine by me. We'll be heading into the mountain passageways tomorrow, so come up with something before then."

With that, he tore off another leg and happily munched on it while I was left pondering on the different scenarios and proper ways I would need to fight orcs.

The early warmth from the sun helped thaw some of the nightly frost, as well as, our bodies in preparation for our departure. Picarious led the way towards a ravine between two enormous mountains where he exclaimed was the start of the icy passage.

The first leg of the journey was mostly flat and remained less slippery. However, as the day dragged on, the mountains seemed to draw in closer casting deep shadows, and the path we travelled on soon became more steep and filled with boulders and sharp saw grass that poked and jabbed at our legs, even through our thick pants and fur-lined boots.

As the two of us ventured deeper into the pass, Picarious motioned for me to take the front and consistently pointed out various routes and other methods of travel we could take. I never really spoke up, so he often made it a habit of choosing the best path for us.

Hours passed by as we scaled over and through various small and large mountains alike. The weather remained mostly the same, though some small creeks and rivers were iced over and we took advantage of the many paths and game trails to capture for food.

After two days, Picarious took the lead again and headed up a steep cliff side where he claimed held a vast lookout point. I wanted to go up and see for myself, but he insisted I remain below as to cover our backs. When he came back down he said, "The keep is no more than three miles or so from here. We can keep heading along this trail 'till we arrive at the castle gates, or we can take the back way and it will cost us another two days. I don't care which, but you better decide fast and carefully."

"Well, if it's the back way, won't there be less of a chance that orcs or whomever might see us on our approach?" I questioned.

"Sure," Picarious answered, "But, that's why it's also more untimely to get through there."

"Let's just go the front way," I commanded. "If you're pressed for time, that's what we should do. I have faith in my abilities, and with your guidance we should be able to make our way to the keep without getting into too much trouble."

"Alright then," he agreed, "stay close."

We continued up the winding and jagged path until it slowly began to open up revealing a larger and more open path. Flora and fauna also could be seen growing along rocks and among small grassy patches. As we marched over the last hill and around a bend the castle ruins came into view.

Large pieces of grey worn stone were scattered every which way among the courtyard and surrounding gardens. The place looked very old and weathered, suffering from rusted iron, scattered debris, crumbling walls, and root damage. Ice stalactites were dangling off every edge and rooftop, and parts of the castle towers were either missing, destroyed, or had long since decayed and buried in the season snows.

Continuing slowly we walked forward, passing the central gates and up some misshaped granite stairs which Picarious said led to the inner halls. As we crept our way in, the bright sunlight from outside cut off from the darkness and frosted eerie interior. Old ragged flags and tethered banners with emblems on them dangled from the ceiling and walls. Pictures of murals and tapestries were faded and scared into incomprehensible images and colors.

"I'm sure this place would have been great in its prime," I whispered, "but now it seems nothing more than a grave of a once great people."

"They were great," Picarious chimed in, carefully walking past some disheveled stones and furniture. "They feared the god of luck, turning their back on him and his ways."

"Is this what led them to their doom?" I asked.

"In some ways, yes," he responded.

Picarious led the way further, till a giant archway led us back into another courtyard outside. Father up ahead he pointed out a tall tower that loomed in the distance, nestled between two ominous dark grey mountains.

"There's the keep where my belongings are," he said. "It's only a little bit farther then up some stairs." Looking back he proclaimed, "I believe if the orcs were still around, we would have seen them by now."

Up and up we climbed stairs carved from the very mountain. We trotted upwards until the dark stone tower was now right in front of us. Gazing skyward, it seemed to give rise to some thirty floors baring five enormous spikes protruding from the top that angled outwards like a spiked crown. Every few floors were also a window, but other than that, the place looked as barren and dead as the castle behind us.

"We need to go up to the twenty-ninth floor," Picarious stated.

"Let's hurry up and get this over with."

The giant steel doors that led inwards were half rusted and falling over. So, with a quick psychic push, the two panels flew back and rattled among the interior. The sound echoed and rang out through the mountain range. We both looked around and waited for the silence afterwards. Listening carefully, we waited until finally deciding to walk inside.

Just then, a large roar erupted from the nearby cliffs. Picarious and I gazed towards the hills and surrounding mountain slopes. Suddenly a dark grey figure rose up from the top and raised a long stick

257

high into the air. The figured howled and called out while other dark figures rose up from the hillside each carrying their own weapons and assorted combat arms.

"Get inside now!" I hollered.

Following behind him, we each raced inside the tower and began to run up the giant steep staircase. The stairs were black and chipped, but for the most part, easy to traverse. Picarious began to slow down and heave from exhaustion, but I kept prodding him to keep going. We were now halfway up when below us the orcs barged into the tower and yelled upwards at us with rage.

As Picarious continued to climb, I stopped to prepare a psychic attack. I knew that my abilities were often trigged through rage and emotions, but with the meditation I have learned to unleash my powers without the need to muster deeper feelings. Concentrating on the task at hand, I extended my arms and released two dark purple spheres downward at the advancing orcs. The two blasts smashed into the spiral staircase beneath some of the front orcs and demolished half of the platform. Three heavy set orcs were flung helplessly from the attack, toppling down to their deaths. The rest of the orcs never faltered for their brethren and only continued past the broken parts, sprinting maddeningly towards us.

Higher and higher we climbed. Every once and awhile I stopped to unleash another blast or slice of a deadly psychic attack. As deadly as the assault was, the orcs never stopped charging.

Very shortly I saw Picarious kick through a wooden door and barge into a dark room. I realized that must be the floor he talked about and so I made a mad dash up the rest of the stairs, diving past the doorway and onto the cold marble floor. Clasping both hands together, I concentrated on the damaged fragmented door. Using my psychic abilities to latch onto all the pieces and force the door back into place in the doorframe, creating a makeshift barrier to try and hold the orcs back. As I continued my hold on barricading the door shut, Picarious looked around the barren room curiously.

"What are you looking for?" I shouted, after heaving from some slight exhaustion from using the magic continuously.

Picarious kneeled down among the center of the room where a giant red round carpet was lying. "Just a moment, I think I found it," he said, flipping over the ragged dusty carpet. Dust and dirt kicked up into the air as he pulled the carpet over to a wall and out of the way. Bending back down Picarious used his fingers to feel among the rough stone ground until he pressed a seemingly hidden switch.

A few small stones shifted and turned as he stood up with a bright smile among his face. "Hold those orcs a minute longer," he blurted excitedly.

Just then, I heard as the heavy muscle-bound orcs climbed the last of the stairs and charged at the makeshift door I was holding. Beams rattled and wood chipped and fragmented as they began their assault on the psychic infused door. Every blow and hit they made, caused a pounding or blow to my energy and mind. I tried desperately to keep the door firm and tight, but slowly I felt fatigue and I was letting some pieces break off or escape. The orcs cried and hollered for blood, sensing they were gaining the upper hand.

Turning around again towards Picarious, I now noticed that he held a large leather black book in his hands and next to him stood a tall marble pedestal that wasn't there before. I watched as he quickly sized up the book, inspecting the bindings and cover. Trying to keep my attention on the orcs and him, I kept exchanging looks back and forth trying to understand what was going on next.

Suddenly, Picarious yelled out, "Ah ha, I found it!"

The books hinges and seals glowed bright-yellow and black. What looked like mana; erupted outwards and lit up the dim room with its bright colors and pulsing hues. Picarious' face was illuminated, with his eyes glowing to match. I called out as the magic intensified, "What is that?"

Picarious lifted the book high into the air and replied, "What we have been looking for Oedepes!"

The orcs pounded away, jostling me from staring at the book and my attention shifted back into holding the door tight. More pieces broke away and now I could see orcs extending their muscular grey arms through the shattered and torn openings. "Picarious, I don't think

I can hold it anymore!" I shouted.

From out of nowhere, I saw the yellow and black magic enter into me from behind, and then lighting my whole body like it did with Picarious. The glow and aura relaxed my muscles and helped recover my fleeting strength. I felt my energy being doubled, tripled, and then extending way past my wildest imaginations. Back to the days when I lost all control, this new energy felt better and now I could even control it.

"Quick," Picarious exclaimed, "Finish off the orcs before they kill us all!"

Gathering up some of my new strength, I summoned a large sphere of dark purple, yellow, and black energy. The colors mixed and circled around the ball of magic as it grew larger and larger in my hands. When it grew to the size of my arms, I shot it outwards, concentrating on where the orcs were and what I wanted it to do.

The ball smashed through the flimsy door and plowed through the orcs outside. Blood and screams were all that could be seen or heard. I pictured the ball rolling back down the stairs, smashing, slicing, and mutilating anything that got in its way.

After the sounds faded, I heaved a sigh of relief and collapsed to the floor. Picarious casually walked over to my side and looked down while holding the large text in his arms, "Very good," he smiled.

An hour or so had passed when I awoke and lifted my sore body back up from the floor. I looked around the room and spotted Picarious sitting on the ground paging through the mysterious book nestled in his lap. Walking over with sore legs, I sat down in front of him and smirked at what he was doing. "Is that what we came here for?" I asked, still rubbing my back and shoulders.

Picarious shut the book tight and looked up. "This book is something we all have been searching for our whole lives." He placed one hand on the top and softly rubbed its leather bound cover gently, smiling and speaking softly as if it were alive.

"Was all that energy and magic from this book?" I asked.

Picarious replied, "This book is a sacred tool from our shrine, and it has chosen you to receive the powers it holds."

"Why me though?"

"Like me, we are special, and the book recognized that fact." Picarious placed both hands in his lap then stared at me as if he was trying to pick my brain. "Have you ever heard of the Avatars?"

Looking back at him I shook my head, "I don't think I have, no."

"It is said that they are among the most powerful people in this world, and it is because of them that the gods have lost faith in humanity."

"How do you know what your saying is true?" I questioned, still rubbing my arms.

Picarious looked down into his lap. His hands folded into each other and a grim expression fell over him. "A long time ago, an Avatar came to our land and brought doom among my people. He had so much power and so much fire that we were forced to run away."

"I thought you said the orcs chased your people away?" I inquired.

"They did," Picarious exclaimed. "Together they attacked and destroyed our peaceful way of life." He switched his gaze back to me, then back down to the book. "This tome can help us reclaim what was taken in our lives. It can grant you the destiny you've always wanted."

"What kind of destiny would that be?" I responded.

Picarious opened the book up and thumbed to a page with huge illustrations of figures with magic whirling around them in all shades and colors. Images of a tall elf with trees and vines wrapping around its body; another image was that of a whirling scimitar man flying in the wind. Flipping the page over, I saw a women standing on water with an ice crown and grasping a sparkling trident of ice and jewels. Next to her was a dark man in red and black garbs, wielding an enormous axe of fire and with blazing red mana erupting behind him.

Pointing to the picture of the fire man, Picarious continued, "These Avatars hold vast powers because they have discovered a way to get close to what a god is capable of. If we can get close to these powers as well, then just think of the possibilities we could have. The destiny you've always wanted but were unable to get, my revenge for my people's destruction. The book has chosen you because it knows you have the abilities to make it happen."

Looking down at the mysterious book I pondered on the possibilities that it might actually lend itself to. I wondered what kind of mistakes I could fix or help prevent if I went down this path. All my life I had the feeling I was meant to be powerful and feared, but I shunned away from that life as Yeargoth and the doctor often spoke out against such ways. But, I have left that all behind. That wasn't who I am, and I know that with this power I could do, or be whomever I want.

"What do we have to do?" I asked confidently.

Picarious shut the book again and stood up. "This book details the past lives of some of these Avatars. It will be hard and long, but I need you to learn all you can about them for me."

I stood up as well, nodding as Picarious continued. "This place will serve as our new fortress. It needs some work, so I'll stay here and study the book while I fix the place up. I need you to go and start hunting them down. Get stronger, learn everything you can, and we'll stay in touch every so often. I'm not saying this will be easy, but if all goes according to plan, nothing will stop us."

"Because luck will be on our side," I added.

"We can create our own luck now," Picarious smiled.

Chapter VIII
Desertion Troubles

It had been three months since I began my mission. My destiny was now in my hands, and I felt a new sense of strength and guidance.

I sent word to Picarious that I was heading home. Back to icy province, back to the desolate ruins, and back to the looming tower, broken and deserted.

Off in the distance the giant dark tower emerged from behind a layer of fog, causing me to smile at the mere sight of it. *"It has been awhile."*

Making my way up the steep stairs carved into the mountain, I treaded carefully yet determined to arrive at the gates. Stopping suddenly, I saw how the once old and rusted metal gate was long gone, now replaced by a magnificent steel and iron door with gold hinges, knockers, and frame. Pushing against them, expecting nothing to happen, it immediately began to open inwards as if inviting me in.

The once dark inside from before had also changed. No longer was it in dire need of repair and service. Large unlit torches and candles were aligned along the newly erected walls and up the spiral staircase. A couple large white fur rugs were sprawled out before bookcases, urns, tables, and stands. In fact, if it wasn't for the sunlight coming in from the windows the whole place would have been pitch black.

Ignoring the lack of hospitality, I walked up the staircase growing a little impatient. Looking down, out of habit, I noted the stairs were remodeled as well. Built with dark blue and green marble and laced with silver decorations I admired the work done and even smiled noticing my reflection as I continued up. It was almost like the battle with the orcs, not three months prior had never happened.

Marching higher and higher I ascended the stairs, almost running now at full speed. Even though it was dark in many areas, and I was still expecting some fractures or loose stones lying about, I just didn't care.

Once at the top, I forced open another large steel door that I didn't remember being there before. Striking it four or five times with successive psychic blasts it finally bent inwards so much that the hinges snapped and the door skidded across the interior floor.

Running inside, the room was pitch-black, and it looked as if no one had been home in quite some time. Lighting a nearby torch that I grabbed off the wall, I walked over to a large wooden table situated in the rear of the room.

The large dark-brown table had pieces of parchment, old burnt and damaged books, and several odd trinkets and glass weights lying on the surface. Flipping through the books and papers, I then opened and perused the tables' cabinets and drawers for anything I could find. Figuring out that Picarious must be out or had vacated completely I walked out the room and sat down on top of the first stair gazing down wondering what to do.

I sat motionless for awhile as images, plans, and ideas ran around and created a jumbled mess in my mind. The first of which, was where Picarious might have gone. I guess I was expecting him to stay around the tower or its perimeter, but he is human after all, and it would be foolish of me to think he didn't want to get away once in awhile, or maybe he had business to attend to that didn't involve me.

Another idea that sprung to mind is that of which involved our master plan, where Picarious might have gotten wise and decided to leave me out of it. Even the thought of him excluding me from the deal caused me to become infuriated, slowly developing an emotional rage. I suddenly felt the need to let out some of my anger and rage into psychic blasts against the far wall and back towards the dark abandoned room, but decided at the last second against it.

Afterwards, my rage settled down and I grew still once more. The silent tower made no noise in its hollowed interior.

The afternoon came and went and I was starting to grow hungry. Rummaging through my sack for supplies, I picked out some dried fruit and bread and munched into them as I thought about plenty more scenarios.

After I quickly gobbled up my lunch, I had finally decided upon an action befitting of my nature. I had decided to pack up my things, leave the tower, and then set out to find Picarious and let him realize that he had made a huge mistake.

Storming out from the tower, my emotional rage rose up again and this time it would only be quelled by blood or apologies. Before heading back to Rockek, I stopped briefly near the old black mountains, smiling when an orc call echoed through the pass.

CHAPTER IX
THE COSMIC TOME

I followed a small lead that I discovered a few days ago while in the town of Nelba on the island of Alabous. I had travelled south-east along the islands asking around and following any information I could until I found the place. An older woman who owned a local pub in the town said she spotted a stranger a few weeks ago gathering some supplies and looking for a captain and vessel to sail further westward in the direction of open water.

After I offered the woman some crests, she even told me the exact dock he used and gave me some supplies as well. Using some persuasion on the docks, I eventually gained passage on a small sailboat, mainly used for offshore crabbing. We headed westward, until the captain and navigator informed me was nothing but ocean as far as the eyes could see. They had asked multiple times to turn around, but fearing my rage, they soon backed off, permitting me to fume instead with the ocean.

Another few days came and went, before a small island appeared out in the distance. Informing them to drop me off, I paid their remaining fees, plus a few coins extra for putting up with my temper, and watched as they sailed away back towards Alabous.

The island was partially covered in snow, while the rest was decorated in patches of pine forests, small hills, rivers, and fields. The wind was gentle, but with a slight nip as it blew in cold air from the north. I then trotted up the beach and into the nearest thick woods, determined to find my comrade, and determined to maybe not kill him before he could give an excuse.

Tall yearling pines were scattered along every six feet or so, and even some much larger oldspars grew upwards, poking out from the thicket and into the clear skies. Smells of their sap and fresh forest air often blew past, as I continued to travel westward, where I thought would lead towards the center of the island.

265

A few hours had passed when I suddenly walked into a clearing and saw a large tower almost identical to the one in Xsivfer. Walking closer I began to see that many parts resembled the structure. The same window formations, the same five protruding spikes resembling an iron crown. Yet, this one seemed much older and ever more sacred looking. The outer walls were black stone or marble, with slight chips and cracks running up the sides, and the tower rose up around thirteen flights from the look of it. At the top bore five large crystals incased in an odd chamber with a larger purple hued spherical crystal in the center.

My mouth was wide open, but my heart beat faster as I soon realized this must be the place. Running towards the front metal gate, I prepared a psychic blast that collided into the sturdy frame, bending it inwards and blowing it open with little effort. Racing into the small courtyard surrounding the tower, I ran continuously until I came to the main doors. Charging up another much larger attack, I sent it forward, creating a huge indent where it struck. Repeating this process, the door finally bent inwards, letting me squeeze through the opening and into the interior.

Once inside, I panned around, gathering as much of the place as I could. Spotting a spiral stair case, I shouted, "Where are you Picarious!"

Storming up the stairs, I was preparing several spinning discs of swirling purple and black psychic energy. All my thoughts were focused on finding him, as I yelled out once more, ascending faster and faster in the process, "Where are you hiding? Why are you so afraid to face me?"

The mighty staircase extended taller and higher with little to no end in sight. I climbed upwards expecting a room or pathway, but none ever showed. I almost decided to leave and give up, but eventually I spotted the top and ran until I at last came to the highest floor, where a doorframe and steel door barred the way. Flinging the razor sharp discs forward, they sliced and spun their way through the solid door. The discs continued into the room, as I kicked the fragmented door open, barring my teeth and preparing another assault.

The interior was surprisingly well lit and very decorative. Much like the last tower, this one was filled with shelves of books, tables with trinkets on them, and a single man standing forward with a weird unsurprised grin upon his face.

"Ah Oedepes!" he exclaimed. "I'm glad you found me. I expect you accomplished your task?"

Yelling headlong, I charged up several more spinning discs, after a second I released them headlong at the man I had once trusted. The purple and black energy zipped straight at his chest. At the moment before impact, the man waved his hand in front of him, extinguishing all the discs and seemingly absorbed them into his body.

Infuriated even more, I raised my hands forward and sent out several more attacks. A large sphere of energy, several spinning discs, and a few crescent moon shaped spells from every direction. Picarious waved his hands in front once more, blocking and dissolving every single one without ever flinching.

"Is this any way to treat a man who is about to give you everything you ever wanted," He questioned, folding his arms across his chest as he smiled sinisterly.

"What would you know?" I shouted, momentarily halting my attack. "When I arrived back at the tower, you had vacated."

"Ah yes," Picarious agreed. "I had to leave. You see while you were out, the book had shown me more of its secrets. It had guided me here," he motioned with both arms at the entire room we were standing in. "And it granted me a new awareness, as you might call it, about obtaining our new power."

Looking back at him still furious, I asked, "Why didn't you tell me? Why is it, the book never tells me anything? It gave me some of its power before. You said it…"

Picarious laughed and then gestured at with one hand, "That book gave you no such thing. It was me who granted you the temporary power. If it wasn't for me you wouldn't even be here right now. I guided you here specifically so we could continue are plans. Don't you want the destiny you were always meant to have?"

My mind raced and became lost in all the new words and insights Picarious was explaining. So many mixed feelings of betrayal, fear, and revenge, raced across my mind and clouded my vision. I didn't know who to trust anymore. Even my own self was slowly breaking down and betraying me. As much as I hated Picarious for what he had done, I needed someone or something to help me continue.

Glancing over I saw the glimmering book we both sold ourselves to. The book that apparently held all the answers yet provided only more questions. It was the book that had caused my life to come crashing down.

I had made up my mind.

Sprinting towards the nearest table, I reached out and tried to grab the tome. Only a few more inches and I would've grabbed it, but I was instantly smacked aside by an invisible force. Sliding along the floor, my side hurt and felt bruised and beaten. It felt like a staff or club had struck my ribs. Wheezing a little from the pain and shock I slowly got up and saw Picarious grasping the book with both hands, smiling once more.

"Fine," I exhaled. "You want to know what I had learned."

Gaping as I steadied myself upright, I explained the books and research I obtained during my travels. I told him about the Avatars and everything I knew from the months I had sacrificed for our master plan. While I did, Picarious took a seat by a small black marble table, where he silently smiled and nodded along, waiting for me to finish.

"It seems you have gained much foresight into how powerful these beings are," Picarious spoke out once I had stopped. "The reason we need to know everything about them is so we can capture them."

I stared at him quizzically and slightly worried. "But aren't they extremely powerful and deadly?"

"Yes, yes they are," Picarious shook. On his lap, he rubbed the precious book gently and continued. "This book is the Cosmic Tome. It describes a method or harnessing certain Avatars' powers so we may be granted unimaginable power of the gods."

He stared at me intently and began to speak more calmly and invitingly. "I know it had been rough for you, but I need you just as much as you need me."

I pondered a moment, looking down at my hands in my lap and thought about everything that had happened. I had abandoned my old life for the sake of starting this new one. I knew it would be tough and stressful, but he was right. It was too late to head back now.

"What must we do next?" I asked certainly.

"I need you to continue your investigation on any and all Avatars you can. Do research, ask elders, do whatever you can and however you can, so that we may start the next phase and be one step closer to our true destinies."

We both stood up and Picarious walked over to the shattered doors. As I walked over to follow, he handed me a small clear orb from his pocket, "This will act as a communication device that I'll use to talk to you and keep us connected. I quickly studied the device; noting its smooth translucent surface and tint of black ripples spiraling through the center.

"Only a little bit longer and it will all be yours," he spoke gently.

I placed the device in my own pouch then asked, "Why did you abandon the gods?"

He smiled softly then proceeded to head back to his table with trinkets and books. "The gods abandoned us first." Taking a seat he added, "A curse, you could say; for the reason we relied on luck, was also the reason they left."

"And, you now think their power can save us?" I raised a brow.

"Not unless we have all of it," he concluded.

Chapter X
The Age of Avatars

As the years passed, I had allowed my powers to cumulate and manifest, changing my features, emotions, and soul. I dedicated my life to our research and into obtaining enough information so we could continue our master plan. Picarious made it very clear that we need as much info as possible if we are to have any hope of catching or using the Avatars' powers. And so, every month I kept Picarious up to date with the goings on into what I had learned or discovered. Clasping the clouded orb in my hands, I concentrated and forced my thoughts into the device, where they faded away to my master.

I got to explore the different provinces and cities Ahreidonia had to offer: Ranoia's mighty capital, Trizdes, scaling the great mountains of Ersive, and even traversing the thick giant forests of Lorendia. I had gained much more knowledge than just about the Avatars. I had learned ancient Elven hunting techniques from the elves of Feisk, tribal practices from goblins in the northern mountains of Demetria, and I even discovered an old ancient mana artifact that later I discovered was the Uni Flute. It resembled as long silver rod, with five holes cut into the center. Mastering it was almost too easy.

My life became so much more fulfilled as I ventured and explored everything our world offered. Picarious mentioned that the more knowledge I had gained, the more knowledge he had gained as well. The Cosmic Tome fed off our experience and knowledge and in turn granted us energy and immunities from the curse of time. Skeptical at first, it only took me a few years to notice that what Picarious had said was true. The book was giving us what we had always wanted; power, strength, and immortality.

A few more years had passed, and I was about to signal our monthly discussion with Picarious. Locking myself in my room at a local inn in the city of Cianurah, I pulled out the orb from a small jewelry box and sat down on the bed.

Concentrating while grasping the orb between both hands, I pictured the tower and then myself flying towards the top window and into his room. Picarious was there as well, peering into the orb on top of a stand on his table.

"Whispering quietly I began, "I'm afraid I don't have much info to report to you for this month."

Picarious responded in his normal calm manner, "It's okay Oedepes. You have done so well with everything that it is now time to start our next phase."

"Please, I merely await your orders," I bowed.

The image of his face blurred slightly and twisted to correct itself in the clear glass orb. I concentrated harder and the orb's fog lifted. "There is a secret island long forgotten and feared throughout the ages. You will find it along the eastern side of Demetria, between the great plains and the island of Cromaro."

"What shall I do once there?" I asked graciously.

"Fishermen and sailors avoid those waters, so finding a passage might be hard."

"Oh, I'll find a way," I insisted pleasantly. "What is it I'm looking for?"

"It is not what you're looking for; it is what you must do," Picarious explained. "There is an old laboratory and forge, hidden on that island, and I would like you to re-establish it into working order."

"What do I know about laboratories and ancient experiments?"

Picarious' eyes slightly glowed yellow and black and then I nodded in silence. "The laboratory is where you will capture and contain these Avatars as you find and hunt them. Do what you think is best, but make sure they are kept alive."

The image was about to distort and fade away, but I quickly mentioned, "Is that all then?"

Picarious contorted back into view, "Very soon," he added. "Time is no longer an issue. The world has given us this opportunity, and we shall make them suffer for it."

I had one last image of Yeargoth and the doctor before the hunger and lust overwhelmed and replaced what I had once loved. Who where they? Why are their faces blurred? Promises, love, family; none of it made any sense to me.

GOBLIN TALES

PROLOGUE
GOBLINS

Situated between the dense Eraeno Forest and the putrid Zerni Swamp, a horde of Leerin Zebenese Goblins were eagerly traversing the lofty hills, dry-dirt roads, and rocky weathered landscape that made up the north-eastern province of Zeben. If you are not familiar with a Leerin Zebenese Goblin, then allow me to indulge you with some of their particularities and social behaviors.

Like many of Ahreidonia's goblins, Leerin Goblins are small in stature and girth. The shortest reported was around three human feet high, while the tallest, a little over five human feet high. They feature mostly lanky or bony body structures along with a pastel or earthly-tone hue to their skin. Most Zebenese Goblins are tan or light grey in color with stringy dark brown or black hair which they style or even braid depending on titles and class. At birth, their skin color is brighter, while nearing ones middle-age, their colors fade, blending them in with the rest of their tribe. Leerin Goblins are also a specific sub-sect of goblins that reside near the Zeben coastal regions, where they make their homes in caves or atop the ridged mountain cliffs. They have an acute ability to scale steep walls and rocky terrain, which is probably why their hands and feet have much stronger muscles and an overall increase in size than the other goblin breeds.

This particular horde of goblins was in a much intended rush, because three days prior, the three goblins -which all held income bearing trades- had just finished their week-long visit through some of the local towns and cities of Zeben, where they sold and traded their various goods and offerings. One goblin, Faradymios (a fat merchant belonging to the only rich family in the whole tribe) was joined by a farmer named Frik, who grew the best tasting radions (a half radish, half onion vegetable) that grows only along the windy mountain peaks near their resting caves, along with a metal worker called Teel, who could only make high quality boots (which many goblins preferred not to wear because it would hinder their climbing abilities). With the three skilled goblins requiring a trip outside their territory, it was also necessary for them to be guided and lead by two other more experienced goblins, both from the same tribe as their own, to guide them to and from their week-long destinations through the merciless province of Zeben. One was a young scout named Syzk, who could run as fast as he talked, and the other was Ota, a natural leader who often was the best and only selection for guiding any lesser-goblin through the dangerous foreign terrain.

The Leerin Goblin tribe, as well as, many other neighboring tribes took yearly trips to more populated towns to increase trade, negotiations, and curiosity. It is also true that many goblins, such as the Leerin tribe, hated most other races, which is why this particular horde of goblins was in such a hurry to reach their home in their secluded caves and precipices of north-eastern Zeben.

It was on the fourth day during their return home, in which the goblin leader, Ota, advised the rest of the horde to stop for the evening and make a campsite before the darkness ensnared them. Against some of the other goblin's protests, they soon began to unpack their things.

CHAPTER
ONE

A swarm of yellow-orange sulfur flies whisked out from the nearby tall reeds as the goblin troupe shuffled single file out from the swampy muck and into a nearby dry clearing. Dried mud coated their feet, like a makeshift mud shoe, along with splatter marks reaching almost as high as their boney shoulders. The first three lumbered up the small bank, heaving and sweating heavily from the long journey.

Their hefty luggage, cloth sacks, and cave-vine knitted baskets shuffled, banged, and swayed with each of their tiresome floppy steps. Though much lighter than from the start of their journey, they could still feel the heavy load and strain from having to carry all their goods across the many Zebenese territories. One by one they spread outwards, making sure to keep far enough away from their travelling neighbors' soon to be constructed tents and campsites, yet close enough to the central, soon to be fire, for warmth and safety. Leerinese Goblins preferred it that way.

Faradymios, the youngest of the three goblins of trade, rushed to a nearby large smooth rock where he immediately (and boldly) claimed the spot under his family name. The other two goblins merely shook their heads in silent, ignoring the young merchant's proclamations, and decided to establish their camps next to each other, on the farthest side from the insignificant rock with a loud goblin swinging his arms on top.

Bringing up the rear was Ota, and the overzealous guide, Syzk. The highly seasoned Ota preferred to stay at the end of the line when travelling, while he ordered Syzk to travel ahead of the group where he scouted for anything of interest or upcoming dangers that might befall them. Being the more youthful goblin that Syzk was, he often went out ahead regardless whether Ota had asked him to or not.

"It's my job," he often proclaimed. "I didn't pick this kind of work so I would be stuck next to wrinkly old elders."

The orange, hazy-setting sun soon dipped below the light shagwood tree line, casting long dark shadows among the nearby forest and pungent swamp. A chill slowly crept in over the goblin camp. Ota's long curved nose twitched, sensing the air temperatures dropping, motioned for Syzk to begin hauling in dry wood from the nearby thicket for a fire.

Feeling the cool breeze against his slender cheek, Frik looked over to Faradymios. "You going to get your Deverian triple-stitched cerulean shawl?" he joked, almost fumbling over the words himself.

The remaining goblins at the camp peered over at Faradymios; all assuming the question was aimed at him. Since goblins didn't particularly wear shawls, let alone ones that cost them several gold crests worth.

Faradymios (or Fara as the troupe called him) seemed to ignore the crude jest, as he often did. Instead, he continued to unpack many belongings from a large serpent skin trunk he had brought with him. Rummaging through linens, small boxes, and sack, this was the moment he felt proudest.

The lanky farmer, Frik, was about to call out another taunt, but Faradymios glared at him from across the camp, "I'd rather tear the garment to pieces, than let a dirt-digger like you so much as breathe next to it."

"Alright!" interrupted Ota, squatting over the beginning of what would soon be a fire pit. "You only have to get along for one more day. After which, we should be near enough to the coast, that I won't care what happens to you orc-brains."

Faradymios murmured under his breath then went back to pulling out various sheets, pillows, snacks, and even a tankard filled with what could only be assumed as a very thick and aged, red wine.

The sun finally dipped below the horizon, allowing critters and other nocturnal beasts to start their daily tasks. Every once and awhile, Syzk entered the camp only to throw his arm load of wood he had gathered near the large fire-pit that Ota had already begun digging out with a large hefty stick. The air was still growing colder, but the group could still feel the occasional warmth of the sun's last effort to stay above the sky, or maybe it was the anticipation of having a bonfire; the goblins could never come to a conclusion.

Frik was munching on some radions that he had dried and seasoned many weeks prior to their trip. Teel and even Ota licked their lips as the skinny, balding farmer, bit into the crisp pinkish morsels. A breeze around the campsite helped carry the smell, causing the rest to whiff and water their mouths. Frik, seeing Teel and Ota stare at the small vegetable pieces offered them each some to nibble on. Ota at first refused, but Frik insisted that these were from a stash that didn't sell, and it would have to be thrown out soon anyway. Teel's stomach just couldn't persuade his brain on the matter. The farmer then caught Faradymios looking over at him while he gnawed on the stem of a rather darker looking one. Frik grinned back, and Faradymios became agitated, storming into his tent.

"I have an idea," hinted Ota as he continued to dig out the soft soil for the fire pit, while finishing chewing. "This being our last night together, we should honor the time we've had by sharing any stories or tales that we've heard. I myself know a few from being a leader and guide all these years, but I would like to hear some from each of you if you know any."

Frik finished off the last of the dried radion pieces and thought for a moment in silence.

"At the very least it will help pass the time," Ota panned around. "Teel, why don't you go first eh?"

Being an experienced metal worker, Ota felt Teel would be a good start as story teller. His intuition must have been correct, because the middle-aged metal smith's eyes lit up as he began.

"Well, if you want to hear a tale about weapons, or something related to my field, I think I know one."

"As long as it's not the old goblin in the shoe, I'm good." Frik exclaimed.

Ota and him grinned, but kept quiet. Leaning closer to the fire and him, as he started pondering, slowly remembering how the tale went. "My father told my brothers and me this story quite a number of times, because it was always one of our favorites."

"Bah," spat Fara from the perimeter.

The Kyrikna-porin

In a region called Urinar, there exists a very prominent and most famous goblin weapon smith. The smith lived on the top of the highest mountain in Urinar, in a most luxurious house, which he built and paid for by crafting some of the greatest swords in all of Ahreidonia. The smith was so well known and so masterful, that goblins from everywhere came to visit him and ask for one of his finest swords. The smith worked and slaved under the hot fires and bellows of his forge for more than sixty goblin years, perfecting, designing, and hand-crafting each and every weapon for anyone who wished to own one.

During those long tireless years, the goblin smith had four male scurlings. Sadly, his wife died after the forth was born. So, the smith had to teach them everything he knew in between his constant work and demands of the people. Over the years, the four brothers grew older and since the smith had to keep working to pay for their care, his teachings were limited. In fact, he only got around to teaching one skill of sword making to each son.

To the eldest son, he taught how to make the sharpest and sturdiest of blades, able to slice and sever the strongest of defenses. The second oldest, he taught how to make the best grips and hilts to bear the greatest of strength and technique. The third son he taught how to make the best guards and pummels, to block and deflect the mightiest of attacks. And finally to the youngest, he taught how to create the best details and engravings, that of which held more beauty and majesty the likes even the most imaginable of goblins couldn't possibly wonder.

When he had just finished teaching them all he knew. His health took a turn for the worst, and the great legendary goblin smith had passed away, leaving a masterful legacy, as well as, the brothers all alone to take care of themselves.

After the tragic loss of their father, the four brothers declared that they shall create the greatest sword ever imagined (even by their father's standards) and offer it to their father as a memorial, symbolizing all he has done. The sword took the brothers five years of hard and tedious labor, but with each brother taking a turn creating a part of it, the sword was completed ahead of schedule.

Word soon spread to the neighboring tribes, and in a few short days, goblins from far around came to their house in order to gaze at the magnificent sword displayed over their father's grave and to pay their respects for all the great smith has done.

Not soon afterwards, the governor of Urinar arrived at the brothers' house and took a long hard look at the legendary sword displayed and presented over their father's grave.

Since the weapon was so glorious and so riveting, it was nearly impossible to describe to someone. You would have to view it with your own eyes to be able to take in all it has to offer.

The brothers all watched unmoving as the plump, short elder goblin studied it, until finally the governor turned towards them and explained how this was the most beautiful, magnificent, and splendid sword his old eyes had ever seen in all his lifetime. He then asked what the sword's name was so he may tell of its gloriousness to everyone when he returns to his mansion in the capital. All four bothers shook their heads. They were so busy with their work in creating the incredible weapon, that the thought of naming the sword slipped their minds completely. Each brother began to think really hard, but none could come up with a name that would do the mighty sword any justice. Eventually, they all decided that it shall remain nameless.

"Ah," the governor called out, "Kyrikna-porin, or the sword with no name, in the ancient goblin tongue."

In turn, the brothers all smiled, agreeing that it fit well.

The governor then turned towards the oldest brother and asked who had done the most work on the sword.

Being the older sibling that he was, the eldest brother quietly took the governor's arm and led him over to the side of the house where they could speak more privately. The governor agreed out of curiosity, and once the older brother was satisfied that his younger brothers were out of ear shot, he began.

"As you know, your highness," he whispered, peering over his shoulder one last time. "Since I was first born, my father has had more time to share and bond with me before my brothers' arrived, preoccupying all his precious time. During those initial years and many thereafter, my father taught me his most secret and special talents and techniques for crafting the sword which you see displayed today."

The governor's eyes lit up from the mere mention of the sword, he nodded allowing the brother to continue.

"It is true we all helped create the Kyrikna-porin, but they were merely my assistants, and it was I who crafted and labored that sword into existence."

The governor looked even more pleased. After nodding again to himself and ruffling his hands through his twisted, thinning white hair he asked, "That is very good to hear my boy, because, after seeing that most impressive work of skills, I would like you to create an even grander sword for me."

The eldest brother waited in silence before answering, making dead sure none of his brothers had heard, or was about to turn the corner and catch them both by surprise.

Finally the governor continued, "I assure you, when completed you will have the grandest knowledge that you created the greatest treasure for me and for all of Urinar. Plus, you can rest assure that your deed will be met with many more riches than you will ever have need for."

The brother agreed to the governor's offer, though he feared he really had little choice, after spouting such grandiose lies. So, the very next day the governor sent a patrol to guide and make sure the oldest brother made it to the governor's own private forge which he had created specifically for him and the long project ahead.

For the next several seasons the governor had been checking in on the eldest brother's progress. Each week, the brother would explain that he needed more time, or he needed more supplies, which the governor hastily responded to. Every time the governor grew impatient and asked to be updated with the news of completion, the oldest brother made up some excuse refusing to reveal the sword, claiming that to gaze upon it now would forever shame your eyes from the real beauty that you would have when it was finished.

More time had passed, and the governor soon lost all patience with the brother. Angrily he sent his guards to fetch the sword and the smith and bring them to him immediately.

After the brother was hauled in against his will, the governor asked to see the sword, whether finished or not. He said he already spent more money and resources thus far, and if the sword was not up to the sheer magnitude that the Kyrikna-porin was, he would face serious consequences.

Hesitantly, the brother handed over the sword and let everyone in the governor's court examine it.

The most beautiful part of the sword was the blade. Everyone's attention was immediately drawn to its elegant gentle curve, its pearl like edges and fine mirror-like shine. The blade was so beautiful that everyone didn't even see the rest of the sword for a few minutes. It wasn't until sometime later, that the governor yelled out when he saw the other parts of the sword.

Jeering and making faces of disgust, the entire crowd booed as the eldest brother hid his face deep in his rough dirty hands.

The remaining sword was a mockery of all his father had once stood for. The rusty, dented handle was brittle and flaking in several places. The cross guard was bent and bore an eyesore of a black ore embedded half-hazard in its center. And finally the pummel and details seemed to be made of burnt leather with crude childish drawings running up the sides.

The governor immediately issued his guards to seize the young smith and sentence him to life in prison for creating this horrid waste of time and resources, dishonoring him, and above all lying about his expert skills.

A few weeks had past, and once the governor calmed down over the recent fraud the eldest brother turned out to be, he began remembering the image of the blade the eldest brother had created. He decided that he still demanded a most impressive sword like no one has ever seen, and knew that one of the other brothers must have had a greater part.

So the very next day he left to go pay a visit to the brothers' house again. Climbing the steep mountain side, he eventually arrived.

The governor waddled up to the front door, rapped three times, and was about to leave due to his growing impatience, but suddenly the second oldest brother greeted him. After apologizing to the governor, the second brother welcomed him inside.

A few fast pleasantries later, and the governor finally asked the brother the same question he had asked the first. "I still desire a sword on the most grandiose of scales, and I would like to know which one of you or your brothers can create one for me. I can pay most handsomely of course."

The brother drank from his small mug of pale ale, before speaking, "This seems like something you should talk about in front of my other brothers, and well they are not home at the moment."

"If I wanted to talk to your brothers I would have," said the governor, leaning in closer.

The brother saw the pudgy elder's eyes slant, and after thinking about all the riches he could make for himself, he sputtered, "Well, being the second oldest I have had plenty of time to learn all there is to know from my father." Standing up and guiding the governor to the door he continued, "If you can provide the materials and costs, I will gladly forge the greatest sword for you. One that will top even my father's glorious memento, this I can assure you."

"Splendid!" the governor's eyes lit up. "As long as I am satisfied, you too shall be rewarded." And with that, the two parted ways.

A few days later, the second smith brother was already beginning the forging process deep inside the governor's custom built mega-forge.

After a single month, the governor asked to see how the sword was coming along. He seemed to be in a good enough mood, because after the brother made an excuse that he needed more supplies, the governor didn't reprimand him. No, instead, he simply asked to see a part of the sword. Just to make sure that some progress was at least being made. The brother accepted the proposal on the one condition that he show him only one part for now, until the sword was finally complete, for fear of ruining the greatness it would then have.

The governor remembered the oldest brother claiming the same, but his impatience was beginning to rear its ugly head, and so he quickly agreed, so he may get a sneak peak.

The brother came back from the back room with a blackened cloth that was wrapped over itself in a ball. The governor's eyes lit up as the brother began to slowly undo the cloth, opening it up to reveal a glistening pearl sword hilt. Immediately the governor felt blinded and dazed over the light being given off from the object. His mind couldn't decide whether to shield his eyes or keep staring at the most wondrous spectacle of beauty he had ever seen in such a small object. As precious as it was lying there in a black cloth nest, the brother quickly covered it back up, and took it back into the room it was stored in.

When he came back into the main forge area, the governor nodded with excitement and spouted, "Nothing in this world can compare to the gifts you and your brothers have. I look forward to seeing the rest of it."

On his way back to the outer hall he mentioned, "If it's anything like your older brother's blade, then you can expect great things to follow."

After the governor closed the large door behind him, the second brother pondered on why the governor mentioned his older brother's blade. In fact, after his eldest brother left their house up on the mountain, no one has seen or heard from him. He just assumed his brother went to a nearby city or town for awhile.

Some more months came and went, and the governor never received word of the swords completion. Obeying his word, he never asked to see it, but when time became more precious to him in his old age, the governor feared the sword would be finished well after he was.

These new thoughts ran through his aging mind until he became flustered and agitated. He was reminded of the first brother, who was still locked up in the prison below. Swearing the other brother would soon join him; he had his guards storm the forge, bringing the brother and whatever parts of the sword were created straight to him.

Pleading before his highness, the brother begged and urged him not to see the sword yet, and that he was under great stress. The governor ignored his pleads and had his guards unveil the sword for all to see.

The most noticeable part was the swords hilt. Just like he had seen before, the hilt was pure wonder and beauty. The governor could stare at just the hilt for hours upon end and not grow bored, but he was too angry to be mesmerized by it again. Instead, he used his hand to shield his eyes from the hilt and peered at the other parts. Through the shine and splendor that was the hilt; the governor saw a despicable and purely disgusting sight. Like the brother before him, the blade, guard, and overall design, were not even worthy for use as an orc feces scraper.

The governor rose up out of his large black leather and bone chair and ordered the pitiful brother sent straight to the prison.

It would be some time before the governor could calm down, but once he had the growing desire to own one of the famous smiths' swords was all he could think about. Demanding justice, he sent his guards to fetch the next youngest brother from their far mountain home, ordering him to make a sword at once.

A few days later the third son was dragged into the grand court room, where he was forced to his knees before the governor.

Shaking and scared over what may befall him, the young goblin smith was so nervous he couldn't even ask why he was seized and dragged into the court.

The plump old elder wedged himself free of his tall chair, hobbling down the few steps to the scared kneeling goblin before him. "I have no time for pleasantries," he blurted, "as time is of the essence, so I'll make this quick." The young smith could only keep quiet and pray. "I understand you are quite good at what you do," the governor continued. "So, I would like you to forge me a great sword like you did for your father all those years ago."

The small goblin wanted to speak up, but after seeing the guards next to him stare him down, weapons ready. He could only nod in silence.

"My court treasurer will offer you the necessary funds," waved the governor, forcing a smile. "Just talk to him before you go to your work station. I shall give you one full month, which I shall then check on the progress of the sword, and continue to do so until hastily completed. Is all this perfectly clear?"

The smith could only nod one last time, before the guards next to him picked him up off his little goblin feet and dragged him out the doors.

Satisfied that this time he shall finally get the sword he wanted, the governor plopped himself back into his tall chair, grabbed hold of a large red apple from the pewter bowl next to him and bit into its juicy center.

The first few months flew by and the governor was very pleased with the work the smith had done so far. However, upon his next visit the young smith had not been able to make anymore of the sword and instead begged the governor for his mercy. The governor raged a few times, and sent the screaming brother to the jail where he would soon meet his other brothers.

This time the governor was getting so old and sick, that by now he didn't want to wait anymore and immediately sent his guards to fetch the last brother.

Without delay, the last brother was thrown before the governor's feet. However, this time the youngest brother was not scared or begged for his release. Instead, he was glad he could meet with the governor, because he knew he might have had something to do with his missing brothers.

The governor leapt off his chair and began demanding him to make him a glorious sword.

"I'm sorry to tell you this, but what you ask for is impossible," the youngest goblin brother exclaimed quite calmly.

"What!?" the governor yelled. "Tell me why, before I have you thrown in my dungeon as well."

Once again the youngest brother spoke calmly, "Because the sword cannot be created by only one of us, no matter how hard he tries."

"Go on," spoke the governor, sitting back down impatiently.

The brother continued, "Many years ago after father died, my brothers and I used the knowledge he had taught us into making the Kyrikna-porin together. It took a long time, but because we all helped create a part of the sword it was able to have the best of everything."

The mighty governor sat motionless upon his tall chair with an angry expression on his old wrinkly face. The youngest brother sensed he was not going to ever be contempt, so he offered a solution.

"Is it true that my brothers are all locked up in the dungeon?" he asked.

"Yes, and you are on the verge of joining them," snapped the governor, "If you are not careful."

The young goblin smith spoke again, "How about we make an offer. I shall give you my father's sword, the Kyrikna-porin, in exchange for my brothers' freedom."

Sitting still for a moment, the governor thought perhaps this was some sort of trick, but alas, growing impatient he prodded, "Why should you grant me your father's blade when I have been nothing but cruel to your family?"

The small goblin smiled speaking calmly, "We can always make another sword, but I will never have other brothers. The point of us all making a sword was not for the finished project, but instead it was a way for us to all remember our father and everything he was able to do for us."

The old goblin governor managed to leak a single salty tear from his tired, wrinkly-old face. "Very well," he said happily. "Your brothers are free."

A couple of weeks later, the brothers opened a new weapon shop in the capital city. The magnificent building was partly built from the governor's own private funds. Together, the brothers created and forged new weapons for anyone that asked for one, as their father had done before them. It was true that the Kyrikna-porin was in the governor's care, hanging above a magnificent marble hearth in the court study, but much to the plight of the governor, visitors from all around continued to show up at his castle, demanding to see the greatest sword ever made.

CHAPTER
Two

As the sun's light all but disappeared beneath the land, the fire Ota had built was growing larger and more intense. Its orange flames cracked and danced as Syzk pestered Frik for some more snacks out of his pack.

Ota could see in the distance that Faradymios was sitting by himself, propped up near the rock he had claimed earlier this evening. Brushing off dirt from his boney knees, he walked over to Faradymios spouting, "Come join us by the fire Fara. We're going to be cooking once Teel gets back with the grub."

Faradymios continued to peruse through his belongings, but

responded anyway, "If you can promise that the dirt-digger won't be anywhere near me, than I shall join you momentarily."

Ota scratched the few long black hairs on his chin, "Eh, I can't promise you he won't be near you, but if he causes any trouble, you can bet he'll be given the crumbs."

Faradymios curled his lips into as best a smile as he could muster, than wrestled some things away in his pack before getting up.

Over by the fire, everyone was waiting for Teel to get back from foraging. He didn't necessarily offer, but no other goblin really volunteered (a habit many goblins seem to have).

As the night continued, so did the growling of their stomachs; a chorus that disrupted the melancholy of the crickets and gentle nightly winds. Stars began to shine brighter, and a few of them pointed out various constellations like; The Scepter, The Hand of Creos, Serrafe's Arrow.

"Well this is boring me to an early grave," Syzk blurted, poking the coals with a stick he'd found earlier.

"I agree," Ota sighed. "Perhaps we should hear another tale. Frik, you know of any you'd like to share?"

"I don't think dirt would be the best subject matter to occupy our time with," mumbled Faradymios. He took a seat on a fallen log that the team had rolled over before the night had befallen them.

"Yeh," Frik chimed in, "and I don't think pompous orc-for-brain merchants would be all that interesting either."

"Alright you two," Ota quickly exhumed, "Someone start a story, or I'm going to go find Teel and leave all of you to the hill beasts."

"Fine," Frik responded, "I got a really good one about a huge war, a beautiful princess, and a mystical lamp that grants wishes."

"Are there really hill beasts around here?" Fara started to bite his nails.

"No," Syzk replied. "Just tell us something involving what you do."

"Wait," Fara spun around hearing only the first part. "So, there aren't any hill beasts?"

"Yes I agree, "Ota commented, "We want to hear a tale from your family. That way we might learn something about you."

"I hate you all," grumbled Fara folding his arms.

"Alright," Frik pouted, "Here's a stupid tale about food. But I can't promise you it'll be as interesting as the one about wars, princesses, and lamps."

"Just get on with it!" shouted everyone.

The Magic Well

This story is all about a poor goblin farmer, his raggedy old companion, oh, and his wolf too. Together they lived out on a farm in the countryside. For many long years, they have lived very prosperous lives, however they eventually came under a long drought, which caused them to have to ration food and lose practically all their money.

One day, the farmer found out that his wife was pregnant, and very soon would have a little scurling running around. The farmer became very worried because he knew that his family was barely getting by as is, and once the scurling comes they might starve from a lack of food.

Now desperate, the farmer's wife asked him to take their wolf and try to find an underground lake or water source. Not optimistic, the farmer was willing to try anything for the sake of 5 family.

And so, after gathering some supplies, he began to wander the nearby lands with his wolf desperately trying to find water.

After wandering aimlessly for nearly half a day, his wolf started to howl, before running off. The farmer raced after him, until he eventually found his pet sitting near what looked like an old half-buried well. Brushing off some vines and branches that covered and grew along the outside, the farmer then peered down into its blackness.

Picking up a rock, the farmer dropped it down the well, listening closely for a splash; yet none came.

He tried another rock, this time leaning farther down, but still he hadn't heard any noise from below. Luckily for him, he found an old bucket and rope nearby, which he fastened to the well, and then slowly began lowering it down.

Suddenly, he heard a faint voice echoing from deep inside. "Please...water," it said.

Not quite making it out, the farmer peered below in case someone was trapped. It was far too dark to see, but the voice called forth again. "Please don't take my water," it asked.

Shocked at what he heard, he paused briefly. Licking his lips from the heat, he decided to continue lowering the bucket. Again, the voice cried out, "Please don't take my water."

This time, the farmer raised the bucket free, hollering in return, "Who's there? Is someone trapped?"

"If you take my water," the voice called, "I will die."

The farmer looked at his wolf, expecting some response. For a moment they both stared at each other curiously, until at last the farmer replied, "Can I just have some, my family and I are starving and we have a scurling on the way?"

He waited for a chance for the voice to respond. When none came, and all he could hear was the feint howl of wind, he decided to ask another question. "Who are you?"

"I am a magic well," said the voice. "My water is my life, and if you take it, so do you take my life."

The farmer hesitated at what the voice had brought to his attention. He had never heard of a magic well before, let alone one that could talk. He almost decided to just go away and look elsewhere, but he knew his family was counting on him, and didn't know where or when the next time he would find another water source might be. So, he asked politely, "What can I do? My family is starving and we need some water or else we will die."

"I shall grant you three wishes," the well responded, "on the condition that you do not take any of my water."

The farmer was very skeptical, questioning further, "You mean you will grant me anything I want if I don't take your water?"

"Yes," said the mysterious voice, "on the condition that they remain selfless."

The farmer thought long and hard about what kind of wish he

would even wish for. He was still unsure whether the well was telling the truth, but he knew that if the wish didn't come true, he could just take water from it anyway.

"Alright," the farmer began, "So I assume, I can't wish for more wishes right?"

The well commented, "They must be selfless, or they will not work."

"Selfless, huh," the farmer thought, as he scratched his bald head. "I fear my child will not survive under our current conditions. I think about him every day. Please magic well can you make sure my child is born safely?"

He waited again for the voice to respond. A moment passed and it finally rang out, "It is done."

Eventually, he stood up and tried to hear if the voice was still around. Not hearing anymore of the strange calming voice, he got up and started his journey back.

Together with his wolf, they returned home the next morning. The farmer didn't speak of the well to his wife for fear that she would think he was crazy, so he kept quiet about it. She was disappointed that he couldn't find any water, but together they continued their hardship.

A few months pass, and soon his wife finally gave birth. It was the cutest and most precious scurling they ever saw. Sobbing and praising the gods, they were happy. The farmer thanked the magic well for granting the wish true.

Because of how beautiful his baby looked, everything else the farmer saw became even uglier. As he preformed his daily duties, he began to see that the house was starting to fall apart and was in desperate need of repairs. They talked about fixing it up, and eventually, the farmer remembered that he could ask the well for help.

The next day, after making up an excuse to leave, the farmer travelled into the fields and neighboring wilderness to locate the magic well. It took him many long hours, but eventually he found the place. Still covered in bramble and dirt, the well was untouched just as he had left it.

Leaning over the side, he spoke down into the blackness, "Magic well, are you there?"

A soft voice echoed back, "What is your next wish?"

The farmer thought about how to word it so it seemed less selfish. "Please magic well," he mumbled, "can you grant a large and protective house for my wife and child?"

"It is done," said the voice.

Once again, the farmer waited until he was sure the voice was gone, and then hurried home as fast as he could.

As the farmer round the last bend towards his house, he immediately noticed that where his old rickety house used to be, now stood a huge three-story home made of pewter and chiseled marble. As he walked closer, his wife ran outside holding their child in her arms. She greeted him with an open embrace. They hugged for awhile, as she asked, "I don't know what happened, but all of a sudden this house appeared while I was outside picking flowers."

The farmer decided to tell his wife about the magic well. Offering it as the only explanation as to where this magnificent home came from. His wife was so happy and proud that they spent the rest of the day exploring the many rooms, redecorating, and relaxing in the sun.

The next day, his wife began asking many questions about the magic well. He told her that it grants wishes, and that he still has one wish left. The wife reiterated that they are still starving and that he should go ask the well for food. The farmer explained that he can't wish the food for himself, but can for his family. The wife then explained that they can just share the food with him after he comes home. The farmer agrees and the next day he leaves bright and early.

Eventually, he makes his way to the same spot, and before he even hears the voice call out, he shouts, "Magic Well, my wife and child are still starving every day. I would like to use my last wish to make them never go hungry again."

"It is done," said the well. "And, our deal is done as well."

The farmer had left before hearing the last part. His mouth was already watering, saliva drooling down his sides as he raced home.

As he came up to the house, he at first doesn't notice any change. He looked around for food or drink, but ultimately finds none. The cupboards were still empty, the pantries had cobwebs, and even the large underground wine cellar bore not even a mouse. Looking perplexed, his wife soon joined him on in the dining hall, asking about the food as well.

"Maybe the wish didn't work?' shrugged the farmer.

"Well one thing's for sure," said his wife. "Even if you find food, I don't think I could eat it. I just don't feel hungry at all."

The farmer stared at her for a while before asking, "You mean you feel full?"

"Yes," his wife nodded. "Our child hasn't cried for food either."

The farmer thought about what his exact word were to the well, and then remembered that perhaps the well interpreted his wish, and that it caused his family to never be hungry again.

Becoming mad that the well tricked him, he stormed off into the wilderness.

Because of his rush to get there, a sudden thirst soon came to him. Spotting the magic well, he quickly lunged for the bucket and rope. Forgetting all about his promise he had made, the farmer greedily lowered the bucket, pulled out as much water as it could hold, and began drinking the crystal blue contents.

After his fill, he then took another bucket full and began carrying it home.

When the farmer rounded the last bend, he noticed that his large house, the mansion with eleven rooms, beautiful stonework, and decorative glass, was now all gone. What was now standing in its place was his old home. Spotting him in the distant field, his wife charged outside, yelling at him, telling him that they are so hungry and that their child is sick with a fever. The farmer held up his bucket full of the crystal blue water, but when his wife attempted to drink it, it had turned to sludge and soot in her mouth. Throwing the bucket aside, the farmer cursed the sky, the gods, and the magic well.

CHAPTER
THREE

The roasting pine nuts and gyr berries popped and sizzled in the pan over the roaring fire. There smells floated and filled the campsite air, drawing the goblins closer to the fire, and closer as a group. Teel - now back from his trip to fetch tinder- took out a long wooden spoon, stirring the contents as steam lifted up and floated high above their heads.

Smiling, Ota pat Teel on the back, feeling contempt and togetherness for the group.

"Oh come on," squealed Faradymios. "That worthless boot shiner didn't even come back with anything living."

Craning his head Teel hollered, "At least I came back. Five-to-one says you would've gotten lost or eaten not a few yards away."

Ota and Frik laughed quietly, watching from their seats nearby.

"I know it's not much," spoke Teel, "but these berries become sweeter with heat, and the fungus helps remove stomach parasites." He gave the contents another stir. "We're low on food at the moment, so unless you want to share your own private stash, then I suggest you keep your flapping green gums shut."

Faradymios waved his hand and spat at the idea of eating like a common forest imp.

"While he cooks," Ota let out, "Anyone else want to share another story?"

Taking a seat on the log, Fara added, "If it'll take my mind off this crappy meal, I have a short one for you. I can't promise you you'll get anything out of it you didn't already know, but I wasn't expecting much from this group when I signed up."

Frik rolled his eyes.

"A bad story is sometimes better than no story at all," Ota reminded him.

Money For Nothin'

The tale begins with a middle-aged merchant, who has massive amounts of debts. He owns a small trinket shop in the city, but because of poor business decisions and gambling, he has made little money, and owes a lot to the cities goblin magistrate. Fearing his life may be in danger already, he decides to try and earn gold fast by entering the nearby dungeon.

Surrounding the city are actually numerous amounts of dungeons. So many in fact, that adventures from all parts of the world come and visit, creating wealth, jobs, and taxes. Because of the high amount of adventuring, the city has established an Adventurers Guild to maintain and provide services to clients looking to get rich, but not get killed in the process.

Merchants, nobles, and elders, all come to the guild asking to hire adventurers to journey with them into the caves and dungeons, guarding them from the dangers, while in turn getting rich. Based on the contract, the adventurer can receive bonuses, more work, or even deals from the hirer. It was a lucrative business model; and one that was luring our in-debt merchant to swallow his fears and attempt to get rich.

On the afternoon of his decision, the merchant mustered enough courage to waddle down the few blocks and stumble into the Adventures Guild. After waiting patiently behind a dwarf party of four, he approached the counter and asked for an adventurer to go into the hardest, most dangerous dungeon to fight for him. The guild happily took the merchants posting fee, left for a moment, then returned with a copy of the contract, message board posting, and receipt of the transaction.

"Please allow around five to twelve hours for comply," the woman at the counter smiled. "You may wait at the entrance in the meantime."

The merchant nodded, before slowly walking away,pondering if this'll all work out or if he'll just die before even seeing a single tin.

Waiting at the entrance to the dungeon, the merchant hummed and tried his best to keep busy. Sitting on a nearby bench, he gnawed through three apples and a keel of lawry bread, watching the clouds and travelers pass by. He waited and waited, but no one showed up.

Eventually, a scrawny man dressed in brown ragged garbs, baring a short sword walked up cheerfully. "Greetings sir," he introduced himself. He was a scrawny fellow. Probably late twenties for a human, and had curly short hair the color of coal. "I am your adventurer for this evening. My name is Tuk, but you can call me Adventurer Tuk."

The merchant looked appalled. He couldn't believe that this is the man the guild sent.

"You do know that this is the most dangerous dungeon in these lands correct?" the merchant explained.

"Oh yes," Tuk nodded, "quite."

"And yet, you don't look like you're prepared at all," he continued, his brow furled.

"Ah yes, well your guild had some trouble finding an applicant, so I offered my services." The adventure remarked as he tightened his faded belt and straightened his rough tunic. "I may not be strong, or even good in a fight, but if you'd still allow me to serve you, you can keep any and all treasure within. It's the least I can do."

The merchant pondered this a moment. He stuck his hands into his empty pockets, remembering how poor and in debt he was. "Very well," he sighed. "I shall allow you to accompany me."
Tuk the adventure's eyes lit up with excitement.

"You shall protect me from any and all dangers. Since, you appear to be such a young and inexperienced lad, any treasure we find shall be all mine." The merchant extended his hand, trying his best to hide his smirk. "Agreed?"

"Agreed!" said the adventurer shaking it ecstatically.

The two enter the deep dark caverns of the dungeon. The

merchant kept the adventure in front of him for safety as they walked slowly through the dark musty tunnels. When they came to the first bend, they heard a huge growl echoing from up ahead. The adventurer dropped his weapon and started to run. Fearing for his life, the merchant also ran back towards the entrance as fast as his legs would carry him.

Once outside, the merchant spotted Tuk gathering his belongings. "What happened?"

"I...I..." Tuk squeaked, his teeth rattling uncontrollably.

"You were supposed to guard me." The merchant fumed.

"Sorry..." and with that, Tuk the adventurer fled.

Back in the city, and after taking some time to recuperate, the merchant headed back towards the guild.

Once inside, he walked up to the counter where the same young woman stood, bright eyed and happy.

"The adventurer you assigned to me ran away!" the merchant exclaimed.

The clerk at the counter pointed to a sign on the wall behind.

After reading it the merchant said, "I don't care if its policy, I demand my money back!"

"Perhaps," the woman offered, "if you place a larger amount of money based on the difficulty of the task then you'd get a better adventurer."

The merchant's face turned bright red, but he soon went home to fetch even more money from his dwindling savings. Returning with a higher amount, he handed the clerk his crests, signed the contract, and was given a copy of the receipt.

Waiting again near the dungeon entrance, the merchant spotted an average built man dressed in leather armor holding a long spear of iron.

"Hey there," the man announced, "I'm here because of your post."

"Good, good," the merchant replied, looking a bit more confident this time around. "You do know how to fight right?"

"Yes, of course," replied the new adventurer. "You want my help or not?"

"Yes I want your help," the merchant grumbled. "Now let's get in there before the sun sets."

"Because of the task," the adventurer halted before venturing in. "I get to keep the first five treasures that we come across. After which you may have the rest."

The merchant felt reluctant with the idea, until he again worried over his debts. "Fine, fine," waved the merchant. "This place is huge. I'm sure the best stuff is near the end anyway."

Shaking hands, they began making their way through the dark tunnels. When they came to the first bend, the merchant heard the same growl erupting from just up ahead. This time, the adventurer dashed out and jabbed the monster with his spear. The merchant was so please, that he began to picture all of the money he'd soon have lining his pockets.

Eventually, the adventurer picked up the fifth treasure they came across, as was promised. As soon as they arrived at the next bend, an even larger sounding growl bellowed and rang in front of them.

"Well," the merchant positioned himself farther behind the adventurer for safety. "Go ahead a kill it."

The adventurer shook with fright, "I...I..." he managed to mutter, before tossing his spear to the ground and running back towards the entrance.

Left alone in the dark tunnels, the merchant fled immediately. Outside, the merchant followed the fleeing man back to the city; his pockets still empty.

Once recovered, the merchant stormed into the Adventurers Guild, demanding to speak to the clerk again.

"Yes, how can I help you?" the clerk calmly greeted him.

The merchant's face turned red as he pounded on the counter. "The adventurer you sent ran away as well! How am I supposed to get any kind of treasure, when everyone you send is incompetent?"

"Well," the clerk offered, "I'd suggest you post a much larger amount for the job." She leaned down from her high stool, "The larger the post, the larger the treasure, it's simple really."

The merchant was fuming. He put his hands into his pockets and remembered that he was running out of time. He had to risk the last bits of money he had saved if he was going to get the treasure and pay off his debts.

So, after paying the clerk the remainder of his savings, he waited near the dungeon entrance just like before.

This time, a huge muscular man, garbed in heavy plated armor, wielding a huge long sword approached.

"You come with me!" the adventurer spat hastily.

"Wait, are you the one the guild sent?" the merchant asked looking up as the man continued to walk towards the entrance.

Stopping for just a moment to stretch, the adventurer blurted, "I collect all treasure, except very last one. That my fee."

The merchant had little time to think about the offer. "Well," he placed a finger to his mouth, "I suppose since the dungeon is huge and difficult, I presume the last treasure would be the best, so sure, you have a deal."

Nodding, while securing his hefty sword, the hulking adventure led the way speedily into the depths of the dungeon.

The two of them made their way farther and deeper than the merchant had ever gone before. Anytime a monster would show up, the large adventure would simply dispatch it and collect any treasure they found along the way.

Eventually, they made it to a dead end. The adventurer now had sacks full of treasure, while the merchant waited patiently for his, hands and fingers always fiddling around in his empty pockets, humming to himself.

Pointing towards a pedestal in the middle of the room the adventure called out, "That's yours. Our deal over now."

The merchant ran over to the pedestal, while the adventure slowly turned around and began to head back without him.

Looking down at the pedestal, the merchant saw a small gold crest all by itself.

His eyes lit up as he smiled and grabbed hold of that single gold piece in the air, laughing as loud as he could muster.

"It's mine," he started to dance. "All mine."

Back in the city, the merchant had lost his small shop. Seized by the magistrate, he lost everything but the shirt on his back. Huddled in an ally way, the former merchant still clung to the shiny gold piece he found in the dungeon.

Walking up to the Adventures Guild, he entered, and then made his way over to the counter. Placing his single gold coin on the counter he said, "I'd like to join the Adventures Guild please."

The clerk smiled, happily taking his last coin.

CHAPTER
Four

The four goblins –and after grumbling at first- Faradymios gobbled down the roasted nuts and stewed berries Teel had cooked for them. Together they watched the stars slowly pass overhead as the hours of the night passed by. The sky became much clearer, and as the flames continued their dance, the chills of mid-night roused the troupe from their comfortableness.

"Pass the ground rock salt Fara," shouted Syzk. "These nuts are always good with some salt.

Faradymios passed him his tin capsule of ground salt from his lap. "You can keep it," he explained handing it over. "It just doesn't sell like it used too, when your competitor is offering free salt with every purchase.

"I would've added some," chimed in Teel, "but, I feared I'd be heavily taxed." The goblins expected Fara to have a quip of his own, but the dreary merchant has already forgotten about it, as he wrapped another wool blanket over his shaking frame.

Popping the last few pieces of crisped nuts into his mouth, Frik left momentarily to relieve himself.

"I'd ask for another story, but it seems even I am too busy enjoying this meal," laughed Ota, nearly choking on one particularly large morsel.

Syzk looked around, "You all go yet?"

The rest of them nodded.

"Why don't you go next, Syzk?" Ota Insisted. "I'm sure with all your travelling you'd have some good ones to share."

Syzk put down his bowl and spoon, stretching his back before proceeding.

"Geez, you're not going to war," kidded Teel, "just telling a story."

"I know, I know," said Syzk. "But every good tale deserves optimum conditions."

The group leaned in closer, taking in the warmth of the fire, and preparing for what might come.

"Alright," the youthful Syzk started, "so I'm sure you've all heard some sort of tale about the first goblin tribe? Most of those tales are just that; tales. This tale I heard from my great grand-goblin, who heard it from her great grand-goblin, who heard it from her great grand-goblin, all the way to the very beginning."

"Just get on with it," replied Fara, tightening the blankets further.

Syzk wet his lips, "Anyway, that's how I know it's real."

The Tale of Two Tribes

The first goblin tribe did not get along with the other races. As you already know, goblins don't like the other races, but back then, they really hated each other. They hated them so much, that they were forced to flee far away into a cavern where they could be alone forever. Shunned and outcast, they were forced to live by themselves, for themselves.

Eventually, due to decreasing space and increasing population, the tribe outgrew the cavern, thus causing them to split up again, forming two tribes.

Due to a lack of resources nearby, these two tribes were constantly at war with one another. One scrawny goblin from the first tribe decided to get stronger and develop better fighting abilities in order to beat their rivals. He soon learned the art of making weapons and fist fighting. Before long, the little goblin became very strong and muscular. So much so, that he could easily beat the other tribe's goblins and win many battles. Later on, that goblin began to teach his other tribe members the ways of weapons and fists.

However, back at the other tribe, another puny goblin soon began to learn the ways of magic, like how to manipulate it and control it. He practiced and practiced until he soon became very powerful and skilled in the art, thus making him win many battles against the other tribe. Soon, he began to teach his own tribe how to control and use magic as well.

Eventually, the two tribes became so confident in their own skills and abilities, that they called for an all out battle to decide the fate of their tribes. Only one would win; warriors versus mages, the winner would get everything.

During their epic day-long fight, the other races from nearby began to slowly move closer to their territory. The goblins were too busy fighting to notice the other races moving into their lands and stealing their crops, gold, and land.

After the fighting had stopped, and almost all of the goblins from both sides were either dead or collapsed from exhaustion, they finally took notice of what the other races were doing.

Infuriated, they decided to re-merge the two tribes, teach everyone how to become warriors and mages, and finally get revenge on the other races by using their skills together.

And that's why goblins hate the other races.

* * *

"That was the worst thing I ever heard," said Fara.

And for once, the rest of the troupe agreed with him.

CHAPTER
FIVE

The air soon grew quiet, as the last of the fire dwindled down from a raging blaze, to a simmering source of heat and relaxation. Teel and Fara were sent to gather more blankets and secure the cots and tent, while the others adjusted their seats and pretended like they were accomplishing something. Frik was chewing on some kaur root he had found under some bushes, while Syzk was poking the embers, causing flares of heat and redness to shine through as he prodded into the shimmering dark lumps of coal. Ota watched him for a moment, occasionally staring up into the clear night sky.

"You ever picture yourself in a different role?" asked Frik out loud, but mainly towards Ota.

"Well..." began Ota.

"If I were in another position," Syzk interrupted unknowingly, "I'd like to think I was king or maybe even a magistrate of some sort."

"That's nice Syzk, but I was really talking to Ota," Frik corrected him.

"Well," Ota started again, pausing to make sure no one else was going to interrupt him, "If you're not happy with your position in life, why don't you just find a new one?"

"Yeah, I'm sure it's that easy," laughed Frik.

Ota continued, "Frik, what do you think I did before I became our tribal guide?"

Syzk and Frik stared at each other then back at Ota, who was still gazing up at the bright stars and constellations.

"My father was a farmer like you," the guide shared. "He got up early, worked all day, then went to bed cold because he had no mate and lost his best shoes in a bad dice roll." Ota turned to face is companions. "You see, I knew that if I didn't find a new position in life, I'd probably end up like my father. A terrible life, but it was his to lead, I suppose."

Ota leaned forward, grabbed the stick Syzk was using to poke the fires, and started to prod them himself. He stuck the one end into a pair of burnt logs, twisting and giving a heave, as if trying to free the trapped dead coal beneath. Sparks, flames, and crackles, helped bring life back into the fire.

"You see Frik," smiled Ota, "just like this fire, life can come out of just about anywhere. What was once thought to be dying or fading away can erupt into something new and exciting again."
The farmer sat back against the log, pondering to himself.

"Eh, don't let that terrible metaphor bore you," chuckled Ota, breaking the stick in two then tossing it into the fire to burn. "I think we have time for one more tale tonight," he continued. "And I've got just the one."

King Rae

The story begins in a kingdom once ravaged by war and disease. With no king or queen to speak of, the land and people abandoned it, leaving the place to be overtaken by the wilds.

One-hundred years had passed, until eventually an explorer rediscovered the kingdom, buried and entombed inside a massive forest. The man spent weeks clearing the debris and vines, slowly making his way towards the castle and throne. Then, on a well-lit night, when the moon was high and lighted his way, at last he uncovered the throne of the king.

Smelt from gold and inlaid with rainbow jewels, it sat in the center of a grand throne room. Before the throne stood a white marble pedestal, with a dusty old tome lying closed on top. The man's eyes wept in amazement as he approached. Spending a few moments in wonderment, the man soon noticed the pedestal standing ominously in the center. He wiped the dust from the leather bound cover, and then gently pried it open to the first page. The writing seemed to be based in the goblin tongue, and as he continued to thumb through the pages, he began to grow irritated that he couldn't read any of it. Just as he lost interest and was about to toss it aside, he spotted a faded illustration detailing a treasure tucked away somewhere inside the castle walls. Excited and yet disappointed, the man placed the book into his sack and left the castle, heading directly towards the nearest town.

Arriving back at the castle, the man lured a young goblin slave with promises of riches and freedom, if only he'd help detail the book and show him the way to the treasure.

Uncertain at first, the goblin accepted the explorers offer, and together they stood inside the throne room, mysterious tome in hand.

The man handed the slave the book, opening it to the front and pointed asking him for the interpretation.

Mouthing the words to himself first, the goblin smiled when an idea came to him. The title read; "Last Salvation". And so, the goblin slave translated it as, "Castle Assessment Log"

The explorer winced, looking a little perplexed by the title. However, he had no other reason to no believe the goblin, so instead asked him to translate the next page.

Again, the goblin read the text, trying his best to hide his smile. As he pointed along with the words, he read aloud, "Second month of assessments listing herein are copied and transcribed by official regarding all personal property, servants, and treasury for the year."

As he spoke, the explorer's eyes lit up when he mentioned the word treasure. Taking the book from him, the explorer flipped to the page with the illustration he'd seen earlier, then handed it back to the goblin, begging him to translate.

"Ah," said the goblin. "There is treasure here. Follow me."

Together, the goblin led the explorer down twisting halls, cobweb rooms, and cold workstations. With tome in hand, the goblin stopped every once in awhile, reading some more text, and pointing as they went.

"Castle treasure inside crypt," he informed the man. "We need to go farther."

Down spiraling stairs of granite and black rock, they shuffled. Eventually, they halted in front of a small prison-like room with a strange burial coffin made of heavy slate.

"What does the book say?" the explorer tightly griped his torch, bending down with excited eyes at the goblin.

Pausing a second to read the text he then answered, "It mentions a lever nearby."

The explorer pushed the goblin back towards the entrance, allowing him to greedily scour the cell for a hidden lever or knob. The goblin slave smiled, watching the frantic man finger and prod around the walls and ground, until at last he found nothing.

"There are no levers," he began to grow agitated. "What does the book say? I brought you here to translate. You want some of the treasure right?"

The goblin could barely contain his own excitement, but not for the promise of wealth. "Perhaps," he spoke up, clearing his throat, "the treasure is inside the coffin."

The explorer started to push against the large stone lid, sweat and grim now visible on his brow. No matter how hard he pushed, the lid barely moved.

"Might I assist you with…" the goblin offered.

"No," the explorer shouted back. "It's my treasure."

He yanked a metal pole off from the nearby wall. Stabbing it firmly in the crevice of the coffin and lid, he started to heave and use it as a lever shouting, "I found the place. I brought us here. I did all the work."

Suddenly, the lid gave way. Dust and smoke spewed outwards as the lid fell to the floor with a hard thud. Coughing and waving for the smoke to clear, the explorer peered inside.

"What the…" was all he could muster, before a hand grabbed his neck and squeezed the life from him. Tossing his limp body aside, the boney skeletal hand grasped the edges and then all at once lifted the remains of a goblin up. The goblin slave held the book forward, taking a knee and bowing. The goblin corpse lifted itself out from the tomb, twisting its frame and bones until eventually stopping before the slave.

"My lord," the slave presented the book.

The skeleton clasped the tome, and then peered down at the slave with glowing red eyes.

Lifting his head to speak the slave continued, "That human was foolish enough to think there was treasure here. I led him to you, o' great one."

The eyes of the lord glowed brightly, illuminating the tomb and corpse of the explorer.

"After one-hundred years you may reign again," the slave commented. "Oh, mighty King Rae, what shall you do first?"

CHAPTER
SIX

The End

The fire had died out long ago. A gentle stream of smoke lifted into the air like a tiny stream of water gently flowing into the sky.

Ota was the last to retire to his bedroll. The rough straw pricked at his back, but he was too tired to care. He thought maybe it was the combination of nuts, fungus, and foreign berries that were causing the increase in tiredness. Whatever the reason, he felt happy. The troupe was almost home, and he couldn't wait to see his old pals again; the warm Blackroot Ale in one hand, the pretty barmaid, Celydre in his other.

Syzk was sent to keep watch, but after witnessing how much he ate, he would soon fall asleep as well.

Frik, Teel, and even Faradymios were all sound asleep. The trio of goblins that Ota and Syzk were assigned to watch over during their trip was soon coming to an end. Sure it was just like the previous trips and journeys he had been on, but he liked this group. He thought of them as more than just mere travelling companions. Maybe he would share a drink with them, he thought smiling. But, not Celydre, he frowned. She was all his.

This would be the last night for them. Tomorrow, they would pack up their belongings, trudge their way up the river bank, make their way over a few more hills and paths, and then by early evening they would be back in their village again.

A smile came over Ota's face as he nested down to sleep. Pulling the patched wool blankets over himself, he continued to look up at the stars even as his eyelids grew too heavy to keep open.

The cool night air brushed past his cheek.

Then he fell into a deep slumber.

...

"CHARGE!!!"

A roaring call woke the guide abruptly. By the time he rolled over, wiped his eyes, and grabbed for his spear, it was all over.

A band of men left the campsite in shambles. They cleaned their blades, picked through the valuables, and then left back towards the path almost as quickly as they had arrived.

It was an easy task.

Not much of a fight.

The loot was almost not even worth the trouble.

A pity really.

Maybe they were doing them a favor.

...Goblins

DAHJO'S BLADE

PROLOGUE

There is an old tale about a man who is said to have been the first known assassin. This man is also said to have been the meanest, most powerful, and most feared man to have ever walked the lands of Ahreidonia. He could slay men by the thousands, beasts with his breath, and babes by his eyes. No one alive dare speak his name for he may come to claim them. His blade thirsted for blood. His parent's rejected him, the world rejected him, and even the god's rejected him. Even today he haunts us; his shadow long and forever looming. Pray he is the last.

-Anonymous Scripture-

The torches in the chilly night burned a bright crimson red. The air was thick and putrid with their grey smoke as the roars of the masses echoed throughout the dark city.

"Kill the bastard!"

"Yes, punish him for his sins amongst the world!"

"The quicker he pays, the quicker we can be at peace!"

Off to the far right side of the crowd, a few men with faces cloaked in charcoal robes gathered, contemplating on how they should proceed. I was quickly pulled off the horse I rode over on. There was no need for them to be so rough. With my deep wounds and internal bleeding I wasn't planning on going anywhere. The sharp ropes that fastened my wrists together bore loose bristles that poked and itched across my scarred bare arms and back. Masked sneers and grumbles rose from the guards towards my back as I was being tugged and guided up the wooden cold plank steps.

"Destroy that abomination!"

"You do not deserve to live for what you have done!"

"I hope you die, like those you've killed!"

The few guards that held my bruised arms guided me towards the tall rickety shaft and rope in the center of the stage. I kept my head down, eyes averted as cabbage bits and old bread pelted my sore sides and chest. My concentration was fading away, and my vision blurred so much that the crowd's faces and blazing torches soon became blurry splotches of black and red.

"Shall my lord permit the accused to speak before his parting?"

"If the accused wishes, then so be it."

Two guards hoisted me up onto a rickety old barrel. My legs almost gave out two times before they finally could stand straight on their own. One large bellied guard came up behind me and slipped the noose around my neck, tightening it so I had barely enough room to breathe. As I coughed up some blood, all of the guards on the platform stepped back a few feet, like I was diseased animal. Not soon after, the captain of the guards gave a nod letting permitting me a final word.

Time seemed to stop. I tried to think of anything that I would like to say. When I thought about my sins and past life, everything seemed to remain clear and unclouded, and even though my death was inevitable I had no regrets. I knew peace was not waiting for me on the other side. That kind of life bored me. I had never once longed nor wanted something so mundane, so pathetic, and so uninspired. But, for some reason, in these final seconds before I die, I pretended that I did.

Closing my eyes I gave a silent nod back, followed by a large grin that I could no longer keep in.

"Even if you kill me, I shall not be the last!"

Snap!

DARKNESS

In the Dawn Age the world is raw and untamed.
There are no laws of man, and innocents die every day.
Order is diluted by chaos and destruction.
Seas run wild while fire burns the innocent.
And while the brink of all life rests on the edge of a blade,
A wanderer walks the path of none but his own.

-Tome of Mafagon-

I had always loved darkness. I fed off of it, gathered strength from it, and even killed with it. Perhaps this is what has shaped me into the man I am today, or at least what's left of one.

For nearly all my life I have wandered the world, travelling wherever the nights take me. I had no happy childhood to speak of, and if I knew who my parents were I probably would've killed them myself. So, I became a wanderer. Some people would call me a parasitic bastard. They are far too kind. I like to think of myself as a man searching for his lost soul. Perhaps that's my purpose.

A thunderstorm suddenly arrives from the south, and I am quickly caught in a heavy downpour. I had reached a fork in the road where a tall, wooden make-shift sign was left standing alone off the beaten path.

"Denvek", it read.

I have never heard of the place before. There were no other signs nearby and with the howling wind and stinging rain blowing in my face I decided to grace it with my presence. While travelling on the muddy path towards the city, I kept my head down, wrapped tightly within my dark black cloak, trying to keep as much of the pouring cold water out as I could. Lucky for me the city was now in full view as soon as my skin and clothes were completely soaked.

The dim flares of torches were all that I could make out from the distance. The rain made it so hard to see, that even when I was a few hundred yards away, I still couldn't make out any houses. Arriving closer I soon realized that the entire city was surrounded by a large stone wall nearly three times my height. Looking around I soon spotted a gate that was almost as large as the wall erected and built from grey stone. As I made my way up to the large metal gate, I tried to look for a smaller side door where a guard might be posted to let me in. A dark figure could be seen passing back and forth inside of a smaller gate to the side; his shadow swaying and bending with the torches as I crept closer. The young man was wearing a light beige shirt with a loose fitting chain mail. His pants were muddy and black, and he looked weary-eyed and irritable. When I approached the guard I could see that he was a fairly young man wearing some light white clothing and a chain mail shirt.

"Pardon me sir, but the gates are closed for the night." The guard staggered under the weight of his partisan.

"Are you sure you can't make an exception?" I kindly offered. "I am soaked to the bone, and I only wish to find shelter and some much needed sleep."

"Sorry sir," he shook, "but my orders are clear. I am not permitted to open the gates past nightfall."

Normal men would've probably gotten angry and threatened the skinny lad with a few words and rattling fists. Maybe they would try to lie or bribe the gatekeeper with money or goods. For me these methods were not only embarrassing and demeaning, but they were also something I would never do. No, I prefer a method that I excel at, something I have mastered and continue to live by till the day I die.

"Sir, there is a house a few miles north of here that can let you stay for the night." The guard leaned his partisan against the inner wall. He continued while pointing, "I'm sure they would be more than happy to let a wandering man such as you to stay."

I walked closer towards the gate, leaning the side of my body against its cold steel bars. My body and clothes were dripping. My breath was barely visible as I exhumed, tilting my face towards the ground.

"Actually can you come closer," I whispered, "so I may pay you for your trouble?"

The young guard rubbed his hands together before picking up his weapon again. "I'm not really supposed to accept money, what with me being employed by the governor and all."

"No really, I insist." Clearing my throat I smiled, "It's the least I could do."

Lightning crashed, and the fragile pale visage of the guard lit briefly in the stormy night. The rain was still pouring hard and fast while the lad held out his hands greedily in acceptance for what was coming to him. Another bolt struck over the mountains nearby as blood sprayed outward and into the air, mixing with the rain. The boy gurgled blood from his mouth before his eyes rolled back and he fell to the floor grabbing at his half attached neck. His body convulsed in the muck. Slowly he stopped twitching while his blood created puddles on the ground dissolving away with the rain.

Cleaning my knife off in the rain, my eyes were fixated on the cold steel blade. The perfect slight arc, the coloration of mist, letters still etched perfectly into the handle. After sliding it back into my sleeve, I reached over to the guard's body searching for keys. After finding a couple of large iron cast ones strapped to the lad's waist, I entered the city. Slipping into the shadows, I disappeared, leaving no trace. It was the least I could do.

The dark dreary alleys and city streets helped comfort me throughout the storm. After walking into the center of town I stumbled across a backdoor to an inn. It was as decent place as any to curl up for the night, away from lights and prying eyes. Some ruckus and loud thumping occasionally woke me. Leading me to almost sneaking my way inside, slaying the whole lot of them, then lying in the largest bed, while gorging myself upon their food and wine until daybreak. Perhaps, it was too much of a hassle. I'd rather just lay here. The darkness and cold are my blankets. The flashbacks of the gatekeeper's death: my dinner.

After some time, the rain began to lighten its assault, and a chilly breeze rushed by every so often. I squeezed out some of the water from my soaked cloak, while I stretched my legs, back, and neck. When I started to warm back up, I decided to walk around the city feeling that

313

I better get to know the place since I was probably going to stay awhile. Reaching the first open street, I couldn't believe how quiet and serene the city had become. When I first entered the city, creeping along the shadowy corners, I saw many shadows and heard many people coming and going. However, now that the rain has stopped and the moon rose high, not a soul could be seen anywhere. I didn't mind really. In fact, I was relieved to know that I could be out in the open and inspect the city freely. I can't even remember the last time I was out in a public area. It was almost better than being alone; almost.

As the warm morning sun raised high above the cobblestone streets, townsfolk began gathering in the square. The large numbers had caught my interest enough for me to sneak closer along the back alleys, positioning myself just far enough away as to be easily spotted. Their voices sad and angry all huddled near a large billboard where various postings and scribbles were hung for all to see. I quickly gathered some blue mana from the air, focusing it as I crafted a small sound enhancement spell. The blue particles twirled and collected over my ears, allowing me to hear the feint sounds birds and more importantly every conversation going on in the square.

"What's the word Dorfgar?" I leaned and cuffed my ear, the spell did it's best to funnel the sound and ignore the rest. "Someone from across my house told me there was a murder last night."

"Yeah, according to this post from the governor a guard was slain sometime in the night."

"Does it happen to say who it was or where it happened?"

"All it said was that it was a young guard, recently recruited. And, that they are looking into it."

"Damn, it figures. Anytime there's news of anything, we are always kept in the dark."

"Easy man, I'm sure it was nothing. Anyway, the governor said he was looking into it, so you might as well return to your home."

Funneling from one to the next, it was all the same. A guard was slain in the night. There's a murderer on the loose. Poor Fellow. Not necessarily in that order.

Dismissing the spell, I walked further back into the shadows, running my hand over the crude stone walls, spying inside the occasional patched up window. I knew when I arrived here that my stay would be short; I just didn't believe it would be this short. As soon as I was a few blocks away from center square, I picked up my pace and headed for the nearest gate to leave the city. It wasn't long until I reached the city walls. Their menacing height made even the tallest orc feel dwarfed. Staying against the wall I traced it around the city until I could see one of its large metal gates a few blocks ahead.

Reaching the ominous gate I halted, spotting a group of fully armored guards and a few others with lesser protection surrounding both sides. Walking casually closer I noticed they were inspecting people, pulling some aside to ask questions. I was never one to take chances, especially if the odds were against me, plus I don't exactly look like a regular citizen, what with my all black outfit and deathly presence.

Two options soon became clear to me. I could attempt to leave the city at night, or I could wait a week until the city eventually settles down and the guards lighten. I never liked the waiting game.

Night fell rapidly. The stars were mostly hidden under a cloudy sky, as I awoke from my sleep and hastily made my way to the roof of a small building. After a quick silence aura spell to prevent anyone from hearing my footsteps, I swiftly ran across a few rooftops from neighboring homes, inspecting the surrounding city walls for guards and exits. There were three guards per block and one guard for every lookout tower. I decided it would be best to create a distraction and then make my way to the eastern side of the city, which had the least amount of guards and the most gates.

The wind blew hard above the cityscape. Leaping across the roofs, I simultaneously scoured for the best spot, while avoiding the watchful eyes of patrolling guards and late night drinkers. Some were made of thatch wood, while the harder stone roofs I preferred more since they were easier to run on. Up ahead was an open window. I crept over to get a better look inside. A waited a minute. When no one appeared I snuck inside quietly making my way towards the door. I

315

pressed my ear up against the wooden frame, listening for any sign of life. After a few seconds of silence I heard a huge door slam from below me, and a large, deep voice of a man shouted at a woman. I opened the door, slowly leaning over the wood stair railings to get a closer look. The man was heavily drunk, yelling and flailing his burly hairy arms towards her tearful face.

I thought about whether I should find another house, or maybe even another kind of distraction. However, the more I pondered the less time I had to escape. Sometimes I'm just in the right place at the wrong time.

Jumping from the top floor, I rolled when I hit the ground, before standing merely an arm's length from the red-faced man. Without a gasp or scream from the woman, I quickly impaled my knife into the man's chest four times followed by a quick slice across his throat. The man spewed blood from his neck and chest wounds. His clothes were turning red matching his bright liquored face. I had already wiped the blade clean off on his wife's pure white dress, as her husband toppled to the wood floor. The frightened woman stood in silence like a statue. I started to walk away before I saw that she was still staring at me with her small hazel eyes instead of crying over her husband's lifeless corpse.

"If you ask me, I did you a favor," I said quietly as I ran back upstairs and swiftly out the very window I had invaded from.

While racing east on the rooftops I heard the woman shouting out in the streets for the guards. This was my only chance to escape. I had created the distraction and now I only needed to kill a little bit more until I would be free.

ASSASSIN

Upon the sapphire moon,
Two lovers shall unite.
While upon the ruby moon,
The blood of one runs bright.

-Anonymous Scripture-

Torches were being lit across the city. From my current vantage point they reminded me of my escape from Fyrdrin's Lair; a place of death and constant spewing mana; like a large red sea moving growing and chasing.

My time was short and I couldn't wait any longer. Leaping down from a single story building to the cobblestone streets below, I raced over to the nearest gate where four guards remained posted. Two of them held long pole axes while the others two bore long swords strapped to their waists. They all wore light metal armor with a painted seal of a bird melding with a tree sewn on the front. The nearest one didn't even see me coming. My blade pierced his neck, sliding between his chest plate and rounded helm. He screamed and fainted, collapsing in a heap of metal on the ground. The other three witnessed the end of the ordeal, drawing weapons and quickly racing over. Before the first stepped within range, I gathered some black mana from the dead guard and shot out a ball of black ooze, catching another unaware. The pitch black sphere splashed upon his chest, coating the confused man with the black substance. Shortly after, the man screamed horribly as the ooze began melting his armor and eating off his flesh. His compatriots could do nothing but watch as he was reduced to a black puddle of bubbling sludge and tainted steel.

Before the next guard could blink, I was already behind him. The frightened man gasped when the cold metal pressed gently up to his neck and rising towards his throat. Immediately I yanked the blade away, splashing blood outward, towards the last remaining guard. From the last man's body, I could tell he knew what would happen if he lunged at me. That is the difference between him and me; I have no

317

conscience. Instead he threw his heavy pole axe down and ran away calling for anyone to come to his aid. Not wanting to draw any more attention, I gathered a large ball of black mana together and released it towards the fleeing man. The sphere of mana folded into a single large arrow, impaling into the man's back. Pierced like a slab of meat, he flew forward like a ragdoll and straight into a stone wall. I paused, watching his blood trickle down from the debris. After losing interest (and realizing I was wasting precious time) I quickly ran over to the nearest gate determined to leave.

Melting the lock with a much smaller black ooze spell, I slipped out into the fields. When I was sure enough away from the noises of the city, I slowed my pace, taking my leisure as I hoped back onto the road. Just when I had reached a lone tall oak, I heard the thundering sounds of horses followed by people calling. I quickly took a knee behind the massive trunk; watching with still eyes. When the voices starting getting closer, I knew that they would find me. Extending my fingers, I concentrated, extending my mind for stray mana to draw upon. What little was around, would barely be enough to cast as simple camouflage or concealment spell. So, I was left with only one option.

I crawled along the ground, further inching my way to the tall grass, where I then stood in order to run. By then, three armored soldiers on horseback had crossbows aiming right at me. Shifting my eyes around I quickly tried to determine the best options for dealing with them, but before I could even blink one of the men shot a bolt down at the ground pinning my cloak to the dirt.

"I wouldn't try it if I were you," the one who fired shouted, "unless you wish to die where you stand."

The middle soldier took off his helmet and signaled the other two to lower their crossbows. I was a little skeptical at first, but I choose to at least hear what they have to say before I kill them.

Approaching cautiously, the brave soldier took a few steps, one hand ready on his fastened blade. "My master has a proposition for you," he started. "If you wish to meet him you better decide fast, because the whole city is looking for you and I could care less if you die by my hands or theirs."

Quietly staring at the man, I was somewhat curious as to what anyone would want from me. I was just a wanderer after all. I always thought of myself as one. True, I do kill people but since when has that made me feel resentful. Though for some reason I hadn't killed these men yet. Was there something holding me back?

"Of course," the soldier turned a cheek, almost like he was tempting my patience, "if you aren't interested, then we should probably just kill you now."

"No," I quickly extended a hand; one of the few times it was open baring not a single weapon nor spell. "I will meet with your master. Just how do you propose we do that?"

"Just put on this armor and we will guide you to him."

The armored man on his right climbed down off his similarly armored horse and uncovered a full suit of plate armor, chain mail, and some light clothes from a sack on the steed's back, which he laid down on the grass in front of me. After removing my cloak and rolling it up to put in the sack, I put on the clothes, chain, and armor, and then got on a spare horse that was provided. Placing the helmet on was almost too much. At last, we started to head back towards the city gates. We had no trouble getting back in, and once a few glances were exchanged, I found myself once again, unable to leave the city in which, I didn't really want to visit in the first place.

Our horse line travelled up the main road, when the lead soldier leaned over, "We're heading to the Governor District."

I pretended not to care, simply replying, "I assume it's not far?"

In reality, I was contemplated my current predicament, while quietly observing the locals. They mostly paid us no mind, shuffling off the road as we trotted along. My blade feeling hot and demanding blood as it rest against my thigh.

We rode on until at last we halted before a rather tall white building nestled between a few other similar mansions and large gated observatories.

Dismounting, the other soldiers stayed with the horses, while the leading soldier guided me up the stone steps to the front gate.

Once inside, I hastily removed the encumbering armor, did a quick mental check on my equipment, then allowed the man to further guide me deeper into the mansion. The walls of the first hall continued to the ceiling. It was an impressive display of chandeliers, paintings, vases, and elegant small tables with silk cloths and banners along giant windows. At last, we arrived before a large door, with four gold colored bird statues all pointing and merging towards a center tree engraved within the door itself.

"The master is waiting for you inside." The guard had his helm removed, tucked under one arm. His eyes felt cold and ever pressing, but I allowed him to live this long, I suppose I could wait and see what this meeting is about before I bury my thirsting blade into his jugular. "I don't trust you one bit," he continued, "but I'm under strict orders to stay outside."

Like a loyal servant, he opened one of the doors waiting for me to step inside. It was a grand room, with wood flooring shining and covered with furs. Candles were lit, decorated around the various chairs, tables, bookcases, and ledges. In the center stood a large dark brown table, along with several matching chairs and a single wine glass. I slowly walked towards the center table until I saw a man sitting at a desk along the far wall. He was wearing a clean white shirt and dark pants, and a dark satin robe with the same bird and tree emblem and crests on the front. The man had short dark hair and a black beard groomed into a point.

"You are one remarkable man," he let out.

I watched motionless as he stood up from his chair and began to meet me at the table.

"I have never seen a man take down four guards so quickly. And without much noise too."

His voice was low and calm, as if keeping many secrets about himself away from my deductive and intuitiveness. For now, I waited as he continued his speech. I could still feel the guard behind the door, perhaps still clenching to his sword's handle, also eager to slit my throat.

"Anyway, let me get to my point. I have not killed, nor turned you in because I am hoping you and I can come to an agreement." He looked down at the wine glass before picking it up and smiling as he took a gulp. "I would like for you to perform some small tasks for me which only you I am sure can perform."

"I'm not interested."

The man placed the glass back down. "Well please at least hear me out."

"Fine," I acted a tad impatient. "But, tell me who you are."

"All you need to know is that I am a noble, a very rich noble. And I would like for you to do what you do best; kill some people for me. You will be paid of course."

"If I do this, then I do it my way."

"Yes," he grinned. "I wouldn't have it any other way. You will meet me here, I will give you the person's information, and then you get rid of them. It's that easy. Of course no one can know you work for me, understand?"

My eyes shifted again to the door, "Yes."

"Good, I'm so glad we have worked this out."

Walking back to his desk, the noble grabbed a small pouch from a drawer, before returning. Tossing me the small bag, I untied the string, gazing at the large gold coins inside. I recognized them immediately as official crests, pressed with the head of a dragon and crown onto both sides.

"Consider that our contract," he grabbed for his wine again.

"From now on you have become my personal assassin. Come tomorrow night for your first assignment. And remember, we have never met."

Once outside the mansion and away from the guards still standing near the horses, I took the pouch out from my sleeve and began thumbing the coins. During my travels I've never once come across this much gold. It was like the city refused to let me leave. Have I been forever drawn here like the fat merchants and greedy nobles before? I could still leave. Who's to stop me? I should kill the lot of them right now. The guards, the noble, even the horses, if I should so desire. Assassin for hire; the words hummed and vibrated through my mind. I pinched the coins between my fingers. At what price does a man loose his soul? Have I already lost mine?

Damn this city.

DEATH

The worst thing in life is losing your own.
The best thing in life is taking somebody else's.

-Assassin's Requiem-

The city guards raced up the stairs. Their loud footsteps and heavy suits of armor echoed through the house. A few maids and surfs screamed from the foyer and kitchen below while the charging men banged and clanked their steel together as they reached the top. The doors burst apart, splinters flew across the study as the rest of door was hacked and sliced open by axes, maces, and swords. It was too late though, the fat bearded noble was already dead. As he hit the floor some crests rolled out from his hands and open shirt. Blood ran through the floor beams, dripping from my knife, and coating the coins with the man's tainted remains.

I turned around and shot a large blast of black mana at the guards in the doorway. The few ones in the front crippled in an instant, while the rest flew back, toppling down the stairs. I used this time to climb out the window and onto the rooftops. Using some siding, I slid down to the dark streets, summoning a dark concealment spell to aid me in my escape. The black aura enveloped my body, absorbing any light and causing me to become one with my surroundings.

A clean escape.

"You have done a remarkable job once again assassin," the noble applauded. He then tossed me a sack of crests, which I quickly weighed in my hand and placed inside my clean black cloak.

I looked up at him, "I was hoping that was the last one."

He opened his mouth as if to say something in reaction, but paused with a finger saying, "Actually you are in luck, I have only one more target for you and then you are free to go."

My pockets have been growing heavy these past days. It wasn't even about the money anymore. Why was I still here?

"All right," I sighed. "Who is it?"

Before he explained, he called over a servant offering fruit, nuts, and white wine. Rejecting his offer, I then folded my arms, acting impatient so as he'd stop and just concentrate on the orders. "This may be your hardest assignment yet," the noble drank from his own glass, shoeing the servant away. "But, it has to be done and I know you won't let me down."

"I'll be the judge of that. Just tell me who it is."

The noble leaned closer, almost spilling his wine on the bear skin rug. "I need you to kill the governor."

"But, why?" I asked, not really curious myself, but interested in the man's more devious plans, if any.

"That is something you do not need to know," he smiled, pacing back to the window.

I figured he wouldn't tell me. I was just hired help after all. Still, something in my mind kept prodding me to ask further, even though I already knew the answer.

The noble added, "Just do this last job and you won't have to do anymore."

My chance to leave this city has already left. "Fine," I almost spat. "I'll do it."

"Good," he turned around to seal the deal with a shake. He knew I was semi-furious; I made that fact almost too intentional. Swallowing my words and bile, I headed for the door as he finished by saying, "I know you won't let me down. Report back here when it is finished."

The coming night was almost too perfect. The air was warm, the city folk were scarce, and the moon was constantly being shunned by thick clouds, creating the best circumstances for me kind of work.

Slipping around the back of the house, I decided to try a spell I hadn't performed in quite a number of years. I waited around the side of the governor's mansion checking back and forth for any signs of patrols. When I was sure that no one was around, I gathered in the available black mana around me until I could press the mana particles inside my body. The black mana spread throughout my chest, head,

323

arms, and legs, creating a small humming aura. I could feel my appendages tingling as the spell weaved through my bones and muscles. When the spell was set I started to walk into the wall. I pressed my face through first, checking if anyone was coming. When the coast was clear, I brought the rest of my body through, right before the spell faded.

I slowly made my way up some large red oak stairs. I could see that there were people on the bottom floor walking around with torches, whispering amongst themselves. At the top, I took the first right and then followed the hallway down to the last room where the governor slept. Performing the same slipstream spell as before, I quietly walked through his door, appearing on the other side with knife drawn.

The bedroom was quite small for somebody who supposedly had more wealth than half the city. There were a few cabinets and dressers, but these were all dwarfed by the large embroidered master bed in the center, where the governor laid currently sleeping. Creeping closer, I studied his thick face and blissful expression. Politics were an unfavorable subject of mine. The city folk constantly bickered regarding the subject. Was he for the people or against them? I really couldn't care less. Staring at him made me realize that he was not much different from any other middle-aged man. In fact, if it weren't for his white beard, he reminded me of myself in some ways.

Shaking my head of such nonsense, I leaned over his plump body, running my fingers through along my blade. I could sense through his aura that he was a man with little to no power. He carried little energy, and that he was fearful. Whichever way you looked at it that man would soon be dead anyway, if not by me then by someone else seeking his position. That was the way things were. The reason I had become who I am was due to me believing in this one simple rule.

In one swift slice, the deed was done. The man never even woke up. His blood began to soak through his sheets, and all the while he still held that expression of bliss. After cleaning my blade, I headed back over to the door to make my escape. Casting another slipstream spell, I checked through the door, only to pull back immediately noticing guards preparing to beat it down. The door flew inward, as the impact forced me to the floor. I ran back towards the far wall, scanning for the nearest exit. For some reason, I never noticed the room had no windows. It would take too long to gather mana again for another slipstream, and so I had but one option.

My first victim was already upon me. Drawing my knife I quickly dispatched him as he fell hard to the ground with a bleeding kidney and punctured lung. The next few men had small hatchets that they threw at my head. I dodged them easily and pierced the men in their necks and sliced their sides open just underneath their armor plating. By now the room was filling with more guards, replacing the ones that were slain. I started to believe that maybe I wouldn't get a chance to escape.

After impaling another three guards, I began to wrestle with a larger man in chainmail. We knocked into the master bed, disrupting the permanent sleep of the governor. As my dagger cut into the man's cheek, something struck the back of my head. My arms went limp, as my knife slipped through my fingers –a first that as ever happened. My vision became blurry and something else kicked my legs from under me. As I fell to the ground, I looked up with my last strength to see a man appear in the doorway. He had a clean white shirt and dark pants with a long dark satin cloak with badges and crests decorating the front.   The man looked very familiar, and if I could have stayed awake longer I would have seen that if I believed I could be fearful, I was showing it now.

SINS

Pain is a word that people use to measure their emotions.
However if someone has no emotions,
Does that person also feel no pain?

-Anonymous Scripture-

"It's a shame really," a voice spoke. "I have grown rather fond of you."

325

My vision was clearing and I soon found myself face up on a small wooden table. My hands and feet were tied tightly with rope and it seemed as if I was in some sort of detention cell or prison. The air was stale and the floor was covered in chipped slabs of stone. I pulled and tested the strength of the ropes as I squinted up towards a small barred hole in the wall casting a glimmer of sun light.

"To be honest," the voice continued, "when I first saw you I was going to let you go. However, when I decided to get rid of the governor I needed to prove how effective my rule was and I needed to capture the man responsible. It was far too easy if you ask me."

I swiveled my now throbbing head around, attempting to catch a glimpse of the mysterious man. "What?"

"Please, you should have known this was coming." It sounded as if he was in the same room; pacing around in the shadows, tormenting me with his elusiveness.

I laid my head back, taking in a large breath of air. My lungs felt bruised and my head started to throb, yet somehow I felt more calm and relaxed than I have in years.

"Now that I am the new governor I need to set an example for my people. They want retribution and I want power. Beautiful isn't it?" I felt the air, trying to draw in mana. When satisfied that there was none, I smiled and lowered my head.

"Well," said the voice, this time from behind, "enjoy your few days of sunshine, you'll need it after we are done with you."

From the moment the steel door slammed shut, I knew that my life was coming to an end. Retracing my childhood up to my later days, I had believed that I held a good life. Not a wonderful life, not a horrible life, just a plain and simple good one.

Tied to a rack in town square, my life was no longer in my hands. The children threw rotten fruit and vegetables at me, while their parents and elders spit in my face, kicked dirt, and shouted insults. Even if my life was not what I had expected it to be, I still had fun doing it. Killing was who I was. I was good at it, and I led my life through its rules. Betrayal at its worst would drive even the most intelligent screaming off a cliff. That part was not what was bothering me. In fact, I felt nothing. People speak of sins and feelings of guilt, yet I have no idea what those must feel like. Long ago I had stopped caring about this world and what its people thought. I hid myself from sight and I learned to devote myself to the shadows, allowing it to nourish and turn me into who I am today. To put it simply, I have no regrets.

After spending what felt like a week strapped to the rack, the guards finally moved me back into the prison where I was welcomed with daily whips and beatings. Some days it was just one man, while other days there were three or four at one time. I had not seen the new governor since he talked with me the first day. I stopped caring about him, and turned my attention towards getting out of this place. It became a hassle since I was always in a state of internal bleeding or major pain. I couldn't concentrate on anything anymore. One thing spells required the most was concentration, something I'm currently struggling with.

After what seemed like another week or so of torture, guards came in and placed a sack over my head, leading me to an unknown location. Part of the journey was on horseback and part of it I was lead on foot by rope and chains. The entire way I was either blindfolded or with a sack over my head. When at last removed, I could see that I was standing in front of a large metal door. The guards unchained my hands and feet, and then pushed me through the thresh hold and into a pitch black room. There was no light to be seen and no way of knowing where I was. It was the perfect holding cell for someone who people wanted to forget.

I suppose my death will also have to wait.

ISOLATION

The silent waters always run deep.
The thoughts, they echo, as one sleeps.
The howling souls continue to weep.
As the slayer of minds, comes to reap.

-Forgotten Sage Passage-

The eerie dark stone walls of the damp cell wrap a layer of comfort around me, as I woke from another nightmare. They were all the same. The cracking and popping sounds of my bones as they were slowly pulled from my sockets, the smells and sounds that my skin made as I watched it melt off my fingertips. These images and emotions ran through me every few minutes. I would give anything if they were only nightmares.

Fear was something I excelled at. My life and job fed off of my nonexistent fear. I enjoyed seeing it fill my victim's eyes. Sometimes I would offer them a slow painful death, if they truly deserved it. Imagining my life again outside this putrid cell has kept my mind at ease, and granted my body some strength.

Time was unknown here. Ever since I was first dragged and dumped behind these iron bars, I had passed out, awakening with little to no sense of myself. It doesn't matter anyway. One doesn't need time if one isn't going anywhere.

When you are looking into a pitch black abyss long enough your eyes naturally become adjusted to it. It got to the point where I could now make out the bricks along the farthest wall while propped up on the opposite side. I decided to forget about finding a way out or making an escape. My body needed to heal. If I tried to push myself to much now, then I might end up worse than when I started.

When my bones stopped aching and throbbing for a bit, I decided to try my luck at locating some mana. Any kind would do, as long as I could gather enough of it to try and escape. Though my mind felt like it was on fire, I tried to muster up enough mental strength to determine that there was no mana in my vicinity. After a few failed attempts I decided to stop all together and let my body and mind heal some more. Why was there no mana? I found myself repeating. I don't mean in this cell, but when I was in the governor's mansion. I should have sensed something was wrong. Damn this city. If I'm even still in it, I wouldn't know.

I sat quietly in the farthest corner away from the door. Curled up in a ball with my head between my knees, I waited silently, listening for anything. A mouse, footsteps, crickets, I would even settle for the howling wind. It seemed like many hours had passed before I heard the feint patter of feet. The soft sounds of walking against stone began to grow louder and stronger. Soon, I sounded as if they had stopped right outside my cell. Just then, the floor hatch opened, and a bowl of my daily mush slid across the floor. I quickly tried to feel for the man's soul. Searching outward with my mind, I tried to grasp at any kind of magical aura. I grew frustrated and angry. I was losing my chance. If only I was back to my old self, I could have torn the man's soul away from him, absorbing it, granting me strength and feeding my starving spirit. The door had closed just as fast as it had opened. The darkness again swallowed all. I curled back into myself, letting the blackness consume me as well.

A few times through the power of dreams or just my mind losing its grip on reality, I have sworn somebody was sitting on the ground across from me. A mysterious black shape took the form of an old man. He often had a black thick beard, balding head, dried face, and brown gnarled teeth. His clothes were rags, fitting loosely over just skin and bones. His dark form seemed to reflect my height and stature as it sat, staring at me from across the cell. Sometimes it would go away if I looked somewhere else and then back over at it. Or, if I stared at it long enough, the black shape would grow and stretch through the entire room, encompassing me into the black solitude of which I call my new home.

Curled up in a ball on the coarse stone floor, trying to get some sort of sleep, I started to hear the sound of footsteps growing louder. It sounded like six or more soldiers were heading this way. I decided not to do anything about it. I didn't even stand up. I left my body as limp

329

and unconscious as I could in order to create more of a hassle. Call it, one final act of defiance, from a man no longer able to fight.

The door unlocked and opened, as bright lights from multiple torches flooded into the pitch black cell. The darkness was replaced by shadows of soldiers that danced on the walls of the small room. I now had the chance to see what my cell actually looked like. However, before I could actually concentrate on anything, the soldiers quickly threw a sack over my head and knocked me unconscious.

When I regained consciousness I found my body being carried on horseback. My hands were tied behind my back with rope, while my feet were tied to the stirrups on the horse's saddle. The sack was still on my head, and the constant bouncing on the horse made the back of my head feel like it was being pounded from the inside. Where ever they were taking me I knew that my death was sure to follow. I had accepted that fact long ago when I first was placed in the prison. With my body and mind as weak as it was now, I had little to no chance of escaping the cell or my departure. I couldn't even focus enough to sense any mana nearby, a task that even a young apprentice could easily perform.

The horse finally slowed to a stop and a soldier grabbed the sack off my head, before punching me hard in the face. My head rolled back followed by some blood running out from my nose. As I tried to look around I could barely make out a few of the soldiers on horseback that were next to me. I knew there were more from what I could hear, but my vision was fading in and out so much, and with my head throbbing in pain, I just didn't care. After the soldiers had their laugh, one of them grabbed my hair and made me look at him in his darkened eyes.

"Today's your lucky day," he smiled. The rest of the men laughed and jeered.

"Tell him why, Captain," spoke a soldier, laughing from the back of the group.

"Today is the day we have our revenge, and you get what's long been coming to you."

The captain threw my head back, kicking his horse back to the front of the pack. The rest of the men got back in line, while the soldier in front of me grabbed my horse's reigns pulling me forward.

330

Off in the distance I could hear a roar of people yelling and screaming. The horses began to slow, and I knew that in a few more moments the final torment was coming. Only this time in the form of hundreds of angry villagers and peasants who have been seeking revenge ever since I was first captured.

If my time in this world is truly over, then at least I hope I will be remembered. Not as a hero or as a savior, for those titles were held for men whom I have disassociated with long ago. I do not even wish to be known as someone who was well liked, but as someone who was feared. Fear and hatred is what keeps the world turning. Without evil in the world the good cannot exist. So even if I am dead, my existence shall not be over. My blade will remind them.

EPILOGUE

"Commander, I would hate to have to inform my superior of your incompetence."

"But sir, we have all the active guards in the city looking for…"

"I don't care what you have, I care that you do your job. I expect this to be taken care of before tomorrow, or you can hand me your resignation papers now."

"I am sorry sir; I shall find the assassin at once."

A scream in the night alerted the nearby guards to come rushing towards the nearest dark alley. As the guards surrounded all sides of the street and house, another scream suddenly shrilled out from one of the top floor windows. When the superior officer arrived, he signaled for a team to break through the front door and make their way inside. As the wooden door splintered open, the guards drew their blades and began to slowly fan out. A woman shouted for the guards to come up quickly. Making their way upstairs, the woman's voice was cut off by a gurgling sound and a loud thud to the floor. By now the guards had burst through bedroom door, standing in horror.

Two middle-aged women were lying on the wooden floor in a bloody mess, while the governor, an old man in his eighties was slain in a chair with several knife wounds in his chest. When the guards focused their attention to the center of the room, they saw an all black cloaked figure holding a small dwarven knife to another man's throat.

"Help me please, somebody help me! This mad man is going to kill me!" the victim pleaded, eyes filling with water.

"Lay down your weapons now!" shouted the cloaked assassin. "Or this man's blood will be on your hands!"

The guards hesitated, until the cloaked figure pressed the knife against the man's neck, causing some blood to drip down onto his shirt collar. The guards saw this and did as they were told.

"Now back down those stairs!"

The guards were about to take their first step back, when all of a sudden their captain smashed through the window behind the cloaked attacker. Caught off guard, the assassin stumbled as he tried to correct himself. The captain saw his chance, and he pierced his sword down on top of the man's hand, causing him to drop his knife. The desperate hostage fell to the floor, quickly crawled towards the guards, who now picked their weapons up and formed a circle around the assailant.

The captain thrust his sword into the man's shoulder, pinning him to floor. The man in black writhed in pain as his blood slowly mixed with the pools of his victims.

"Who are you?" demanded the captain.

The assassin craned his head, "Why shall I tell you? You're just going to kill me anyway."

"I just thought you would like a quick death," the captain pressed his blade further into the man's wound. "Now are you going to tell me why you killed our governor?"

Holding back the pain the man in black managed to reply, "It was just a job. He had it coming for a long time."

The guards stood motionless. They knew their captain didn't require their help; and so they watched, waiting for their next command. Rocking his sword back and forth, the captain twisted his blade along the man's open wound. The dark man now screamed and tried to grab his knife that was lying on the ground. Realizing it was out of his reach, he soon settled back down.

"Tell me who your employer is!" the captain shouted.

"You know I can't do that," the assassin laughed, spitting some blood. "But, I will tell you the name of our group, the name that will haunt you and this city forever. We shall be feared around the world for we are the darkness."

The man pushed his body upwards, causing the captain to take some steps back. While caught off guard, the man grabbed the captain's small knife that was sheathed around his belt. Smiling in defiance, the man stabbed himself in the neck. Blood gushed out onto the floor, spraying on the captains boots.

"No!" the captain cried.

With a final gurgle, the man whispered his last words, "We are Dahjo's Blade".

The team of men watched his body toppled over, blood continuing to flow outwards. The captain reclaimed his sword, cleaned it off, and sheathed it as his second in command approached.

"Have you've ever heard of them before?" the captain asked, still studying the scene.

"No, I was hoping you have sir."

The captain spotted the assassins knife on the ground. Its blade well crafted, reflecting the light that emanated from the room. Upon picking it up, he noticed something etched on the handle that simply read; "Dahjo".

GLOSSARY

Knights & Fish

Artrov	(Är-chrōv) (Are-trove)
Burhazen	(Bûr-hā-zĭn) (Burr-haze-in)
Crehak	(Krē-ăk) (Kree-ack)
Darnhor	(Därn-hōr) (Darn-hor)
Ersive	(Ûr-sĭv) (Ur-siv)
Ferilos	(Fâr-rĭl-lōs) (Fair-rill-low-s)
Fiderous Desert	(Fĭ-dû-rŭs) (Fid-dur-us)
Gorta	(Gōr-tä) (Gore-tah)
Grenwall	(Grĕn-wäl) (Gren-wall)
Huertsvor	(Hûrt-z-vōr) (Hurtz-vor)
Hurou Mountains	(Hyōr-rō) (Hee-your-row)
Iraph	(Ēr-rĕf) (Ear-riff)
Kerganon Castle	(Kûr-gä-nän) (Ker-gah-non)
Lein	(Lē-ĭn) (Lee-in)
Merncadous	(Mûrn-kāy-dŭs) (Mern-kay-dus)
Ordstril	(Ōrd-st-rĭl) (Ord-strill)
Petch	(Pĕch) (Petch)
Resak	(Rĕz-zăk) (Rez-zack)
Torrigon	(Tōr-rĭ-gän) (Tor-reh-gahn)

The Tale of Old Bersool

Almrich	(Älm-rĕch) (Alm-rich)
Atrinon	(Ä-trĭ-nän) (A-tre-non)
Bersool	(Bûr-sōōl) (Bur-sool)
Brannin	(Bră-nĭn) (Bran-in)

335

Dershire	(Dûr-shī-ûr) (Dur-shy-ur)
Farthen Brook	(Fär-thĭn) (Far-then)
Gaoton Point	(Gäw-tĭn) (Gow-tin)
Genneht	(Jĕn-nĭt) (Jen-nit)
Greykiin	(Grā-kĭn) (Gray-kin)
Grodin	(Grō-dĭn) (Grow-din)
Keerwit	(Kyr-wĭch) (Keer-wit)
Lara	(Lär-räh) (Lar-ah)
Tarrinfield	(Tär-rĭn-fēld) (Tar-in-field)
Thom	(Täm) (Tah-m)
Tiolt	(Tē-ōlt) (Tea-olt)

Trade Winds

Arien	(Är-ē-ĕn) (Are-ee-in)
Ardus	(Är-dĭs) (Are-dis)
Asdref	(Äz-j-rĕf) (As-dref)
Bajres, Captain	(Băj-rās) (Bah-dray-s)
Bolidos	(Bôl-lĭ-dōs) (Bowl-lid-dose)
Dod	(Dŏd) (Dahd)
Faseru	(Fä-sä-rōō) (Fah-say-roo)
Feerlor	(Fēr-lōr) (Fear-lore)
Gryton	(Grī-tĭn) (Gry-tin)
Hyleer	(Hī-lēr) (High-leer)
Jesni Arien	(Jĕz-nē) (Jez-knee)
Johen Arien	(Jō-ĕn) (Joe-in)
Leneal Sea, The	(Lə-nēl) (Leh-kneel)
Serdas	(Sûr-dĭs) (Sir-dis)
Soaban	(Sō-bän) (So-baa-n)
Tyris	(Tī-rĭs) (Tie-riss)
Weersker	(Wēr-skûr) (Weer-sker)

Zeetrok	(Zē-träk) (Zee-trok)

Dark Horizon

Alabous	(Ăl-ä-bŭs) (Al-a-bus)
Bev	(Běv) (Behv)
Braedor	(Brāy-dōr) (Bray-door)
Dyok	(Dē-ähk) (Dee-ah-ck)
Freilith	(Frā-lĭth) (Fray-lith)
Gragorith	(Grä-gōr-rĭth) (Grah-gor-rith)
Grotan	(Grō-tān) (Grow-tan)
Haerold	(Hăr-rōld) (Harold)
Hepsis	(Hĕp-sĭs) (Hep-sis)
Horvich	(Hōr-vĭch) (Hor-vitch)
Jurlicia	(Jûr-lĭ-sē-äh) (Jur-leh-sea-ah)
Jurra	(Jûr-räh) (Jur-rah)
Kehgan	(Kāy-gĭn) (Kay-gehn)
Krigren	(Krī-grĕn) (Cry-gren)
Lilycia	(Lĭl-ē-sē-äh) (Lily-sea-ah)
Lyronaech	(Lī-rĕn-nāk) (Lye-rin-nack)
Marigreen	(Mār-rĭ-grēēn) (Mare-eh-green)
Martaer	(Mär-tîr) (Mar-tear)
Mercia	(Mûr-sē-äh) (Mer-sea-ah)
Mirdorf	(Mēr-dōrf) (Mer-dorf)
Murchev	(Mûr-chĕv) (Mur-chev)
Odibur	(Ō-dĭ-bûr) (Oh-deh-burr)
Phalin	(Fāy-lĭn) (Fay-lin)
Ranoia	(Rä-nō-ē-äh) (Rah-no-e-ah)
Teinbal	(Tīn-bôl) (T-eye-n-ball)
Urlin	(Ûr-lĭn) (Er-lin)
Yerilov	(Yîr-rĭ-lôv) (Year-ill-lahv)
Yorvich	(Yōr-vĕch) (Yor-vitch)

Zarlom	(Zär-läm) (Zar-lom)
Zeydiin	(Zāy-dĭn) (Zey-din)
Zel'ahk	(Zĕl-ăk) (Zell-lack)

Storm of Savuur

Baril	(Bâr-rĭl) (Bear-ril)
Brunx Prison	(Brŭnks) (Brunks)
Daranth	(Dâr-rĭn-th) (Dare-inth)
Graff	(Grăf) (Graph)
Illicia	(Ĭl-lē-sē-ä) (Ill-lee-see-ah)
Liliana	(Lĭl-lē-ä-nä) (Lily-ah-nah)
Lynx	(Lēnks) (Links)
Pernek	(Pûr-nĕk) (Pur-neck)
Phento	(Fĕn-tō) (Fen-toe)
Pheto	(Fē-tō) (Fee-toe)
Purlik	(Pûr-lĭk) (Pur-lick)
Savuur	(Sä-vûr) (Suh-vor)
Shio	(Shē-ō) (She-oh)
Taela	(Tāy-lä) (Tay-lah)

The King's War

Darren	(Dār-rĭn) (Dare-in)
Driehn	(Jûr-ē-ĭn) (Jur-ee-in)
Ealin	(Ā-lĭn) (A-lin)
Efeurlic River	(Ē-fûr-lĭk) (E-fur-lick)
Feridan	(Fâr-rĭ-dĭn) (Fare-ah-din)
Gherrik	(Gâr-rĭk) (G-air-rick)
Heraen	(Hâr-ĭn) (Hair-in)
Kelia	(Kēl-lē-ä) (Keel-lee-ah)

Luspania	(Lōō-spä-nē-ä) (Lu-spa-knee-ah)
Saralene	(Sâr-ä-lēn) (Sara-lean)
Taradiym	(Târ-rä-dĭm) (Tare-ah-dim)
Treila	(Ch-rā-lä) (Tray-lah)
Ufroum	(Ōōf-frŭm) (Oof-from)
Versparian	(Vĕr-spär-rē-ĭn) (Ver-spar-ree-in)

Oedepes

Deoril	(Dē-ōr-rĭl) (Dee-or-ril)
Geff	(Jĕf) (Jeff)
Kielfoot	(Kēl-fŏŏt) (Keel-foot)
Lestrove	(Lĕs-ch-rōv) (Less-trove)
Lisra	(Lēs-rä) (Lease-rah)
Melgrive	(Mĕl-grĭv) (Mel-griv)
Oedepes	(Ō-dĕ-pĕz) (Oh-deh-pez)
Picarious	(Pĭ-cär-rē-ŭs) (Pick-car-ee-us)
Rockek	(Räk-kĕk) (Rock-keck)
Ulina	(Ōō-lē-nä) (Oo-lee-nah)
Vir	(Vēr) (Vear)
Yeargoth	(Yēr-gôth) (Year-gawth)

Goblin Tales

Celydre	(Sĕl-lē-jŭ-rāy) (Cell-lee-dray)
Eraeno Forest	(Ûr-rä-nō) (Ur-ray-no)
Faradymios	(Fâr-rä-dē-mē-ōs) (Fara-dee-me-os)
Frik	(Frĭk) (Frick)
King Rae	(Rāy) (Ray)
Kyrikna-porin	(Kûr-rĭk-nä-pōr-ĭn)
	(Kor-rick-no-pour-in)

Leerin	(Lēr-rĭn) (Lee-in)
Ota	(Ō-tä) (Oh-tah)
Teel	(Tēl) (Teal)
Tuk	(Tŭk) (Tuck)
Syzk	(Sĭz-zĭk) (Siz-zick)
Urinar	(Ûr-ĭ-när) (Ur-rin-nar)
Zerni Swamp	(Zûr-nē) (Zur-knee)
Zeben	(Zĕ-bĭn) (Zeb-in)

Dahjo's Blade

Dahjo	(Dä-hō) (Dah-hoe)
Denvek	(Dĕn-vĕk) (Den-veck)
Dorfgar	(Dōrf-gär) (Dorf-gar)
Fyrdrin's Lair	(Fēr-drĭn) (Fear-drin)
Tome of Mafagon	(Măf-ă-gŏn) (Mah-fah-gahn)

Other

| Ahreidonia | (Äh-rə-dō-nē-ä) (Ah-ray-do-knee-ah) |

ABOUT THE AUTHOR

Born in 1987 in Brunswick, Ohio, Justin is the middle child of three. His parents were both teachers and provided him with much encouragement to do what he wanted and assisted in expanding his future endevours. Deciding to become a media artist, he dabbled in 3D art, design, conceptualization, layouts, sketching, word print, illustrations, and various other software and digital applications. Graduating in 2008 from the Art Institute of Pittsburgh with a Bachelor of Science in Media Arts, Justin moved to Bluffton, South Carolina with his family where he takes in the sights and continues to create and expand projects and ideas.

On his time off, he can be found playing and discussing all manner of fantasy, films, or many other incredibly nerdy hobbies.

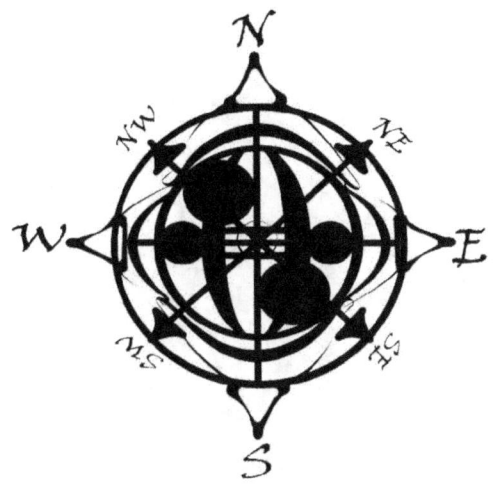

Want to learn more about the Mana Crypt Universe?
How about recieving special offers, daily news, updates, blogs,
and sneek peaks?

Please visit my sites at
www.lifeinaboxstudios.com
www.mana-crypt.com

-JC-